SILVER BUBBLES

by

Peter Fergus

Bloomington, IN   Milton Keynes, UK

authorHOUSE®

AuthorHouse™
1663 Liberty Drive, Suite 200
Bloomington, IN 47403
www.authorhouse.com
Phone: 1-800-839-8640

AuthorHouse™ UK Ltd.
500 Avebury Boulevard
Central Milton Keynes, MK9 2BE
www.authorhouse.co.uk
Phone: 08001974150

This book is a work of fiction. People, places, events, and situations are the product of the author's imagination. Any resemblance to actual persons, living or dead, or historical events, is purely coincidental.

© 2006 Peter Fergus. All rights reserved.

No part of this book may be reproduced, stored in a retrieval system, or transmitted by any means without the written permission of the author.

First published by AuthorHouse 11/28/2006

ISBN: 978-1-4259-6652-2 (sc)

Printed in the United States of America
Bloomington, Indiana

This book is printed on acid-free paper.

To my friend my dad and my mother
whose cup was always half full.

CHAPTER ONE

Light couldn't filter through the brown water. Below the dancing ripples, darkness enveloped him. *He* first made contact with the soft bottom with his feet then settled onto all fours on to the thin crust of firmer mud that sealed several metres of gelatinous silt that had built up over decades. He moved slowly, waving his hand nervously in front of him. He could almost feel the blackness; it was total and constricting. Then he felt something.

The tension above was high. Men wearing white safety helmets peered into the brown discoloured water. Suddenly the silence was broken by a crane's engine as it roared into life.

I looked at the driver and was acknowledged with a nod. I raised my hand into the air turning my finger in a clockwise motion.

'Take up the slack,' I shouted. The crane's steel wire became a tight bar, squeezing out all the water that shimmered in the light as it ran to back to freedom.

'Stop, stop!'

The crane's engine changed its tone. All heads turned staring, as two gloved hands appeared from the edge of the dock wall, slowly followed by a bright yellow alien-looking helmet.

'All secure,' the voice from the helmet echoed around. 'Pull it up.'

The crane revved loud and intimidating, bellowing out smoke from its exhaust like a big yellow dragon. Its jib shuddered and jerked under load as the wire was slowly retrieved. Oily circles painted the brown surface, each one expanding in multitudes of greens and blues as thousands of bubbles mingled and fizzed softly with the spectrum of colours.

Walking nearer to the dock edge, my inquisitive look turned to shock. The men wearing white safety helmets moved closer and their indifferent faces changed to looks of surprise, then disbelief.

I turned, staring at the diver with a look of total despair, then pointed assertively. 'What the hell's that?'

A bent steering wheel attached to its broken column swung from the twenty-ton crane's hook, resembling a head complete with vertebrae. Its ripped out wires were hanging like nerve ends. My look of total exasperation changed to anger. 'That's a five ton forklift down there and you just hooked it by the fucking steering wheel? I don't believe this!'

'Sorry,' the diver said, looking down, trying to hide his embarrassment.

'Sorry! Sorry! You've just made us the laughing stock of the century, and you're sorry? Have you any idea what those guys over there will be thinking now?' I turned, nodding at the group of dock officials that were now gathering together and staring across at us like a rival gang. 'They'll think we've all had fucking lobotomies for breakfast. Hell, I've been competing for work here for over ten years, and you've put me back to the start in ten bloody minutes!' I shouted, looking around in exasperation then I noticed the crane driver. He was laughing heartily. I gave him a mean stare then snapped, 'Shut it, Fatty!'

He pulled his newspaper up to hide his red contorted face. Annoyingly his bulging stomach continued to bounce up and down.

Sat having a pint in our local 'The Ship,' Billy grinned. 'The look on your face when the steering wheel broke the surface! I wish I had taken a photo,' he said, shaking his head while smiling to himself. 'It's your round,' he continued as he turned his glass on its side and rolled it around the table.

'It's his round.' I looked towards the bar. 'Where is he?'

'Probably done a runner,' Billy replied, without taking his eyes from his empty glass.

Phil appeared from the toilet.

'Don't sit down. It's your round.' I smiled smugly at him then turned my glass upside down.

'Yeah, yeah, halves, is it?' He returned moments later carrying three pints in both hands. 'I wish I'd taken a video. What a cock up,' he said with a grin, as he crouched to place the glasses down.

'Don't you bloody start,' I replied shaking my head. 'I take on a daft lad to give him a break, and he does that to us! Hell, he even struggled with his shoelaces.'

Ten minutes later Billy returned with another round and sat down. The old subject came up again.

'The idea is sound, but we have to get a decent boat if we want to do the job properly.' He passed the drinks around. We nodded approval. 'It's the changeable weather, a boat, say, fifty or sixty foot, would be perfect. We could go out further and stay out at sea if the weather turned nasty.'

'Well, we've talked about this for months and done nothing about it. There are literally hundreds of shipwrecks off this coast; it's an unexplored wilderness on our doorstep. All that non-ferrous metal, not to mention the cargoes the ships were carrying,' I replied, and received a familiar stare. 'What about all those collectibles waiting to be found, bells, portholes, telegraphs. Do you know what collectors pay for gear like that? Sneaky Barry sold a ship's whistle to a brewery for two hundred quid, and he found it while snorkelling.'

'I wouldn't go to that pub,' said Phil, while staring at his pint. 'Instead of ringing the bell at closing time, they'd blast you out the place.'

Phil had a habit of saying the wrong thing at the wrong time. Annoyed by his lack of enthusiasm I said firmly, 'When are you going to be serious?'

He sat upright and reached for his glass. 'You can't live on dreams you know, they won't pay your bills.'

Billy shook his head.

'What's up with you?' I stared at him.

'The kid's probably right, we're doing something wrong.'

'No! Any defeatist can say that. We're not in that luck stream, that's all, but that doesn't mean we can't create our own luck, does it? In our slot, the harder you work, the luckier you get. Anyway it's not dreams. It's fact. I've got information about shipwrecks that carried cargoes worth hundreds of thousands, probably more. Diamonds, gold, silver, tin, copper, just about everything of value has been lost to the sea. Off this coast alone there are over seven hundred located wrecks and only a small percent have been dived and identified. There are lots more that haven't even been found. This is a golden opportunity for us; we are the first generation that has the diving and location technology. It's pure adventure.'

Billy smiled, no doubt at my enthusiasm, while nodding approval. Then he said, 'But if we can't afford a boat, the only thing we'll have to find is our way home, pal. So what's the plan?'

'How old are you now Billy?' asked Phil.

'Forty-two,' replied the broad six-footer whose Popeye shaped arms added to his beam. 'Why?' He looked sternly back at Phil.

'Just wondered how much work you've got left in you.' Before Billy could reply he turned to me.

'How about you, Mike? You're thirty-nine, aren't you?'

'I'm thirty eight, you cheeky sod.'

'Wow! Ten years older than me. You old sods! I'm just an egg compared to you two.'

'Yeah,' Billy frowned. 'Eggs are fragile don't forget and break easy. And I've still plenty of work left in me. You bloody beanpole.'

'More drinking and less talking over there please,' Jonno the landlord shouted across from the bar.

'He ought to be a taxman with ears like that,' Billy said quietly while looking towards the bar.

I smiled, shaking my head. 'No, he was born in wedlock!'

A few moments later Jonno came over with something hidden behind his back. He grinned at me then produced the bent wheel from the forklift. 'What's this then, marine salvage, the ultimate treasure?'

'You rotten bastards, how did you get that?' I looked at Billy and Phil, who were avoiding my glare. 'It was nothing to do with me! It was that bloody idiot,' I said in defence.

Billy pretended to hold a fishing rod, as if reeling me in.

'You rotten sods,' I mumbled under my breath.

Jonno placed the wheel against the wall and turned to us with a devilish grin. 'What shall we call it?'

They had me fair and square this time, so I tried to make my reply dignified. 'How about 'The Wheel of Misfortune?' I replied with a roll of my eyes.

Jonno stood grinning as we sat in silence.

'What about the boat and the wreck salvage then?' Billy said in an agitated tone, which caught everyone's attention.

'Do you know?' Jonno placed his hands on his hips and shook his head, 'You three, with your accumulative experience, shouldn't be hesitating. Just get on with it before some one else does it. You're always on about how well you would do, so just get on with it!'

'Lend us the money then?' I asked with a wink.

'I wish,' he replied then returned to the bar.

'What do you reckon?' Billy said leaning towards us. 'We could go to a naval auction and bid for one of those loyal-helper class boats. You know, they call them fleet tenders.' His eyes turned to Phil. 'You were in the Navy.'

'Yeah, I've been away in them when I was in the cadets.'

Phil had joined the Navy Cadets. Later he became a Submariner, then a highly trained Navy clearance diver. After leaving he met Billy and me while we were on one of our diving contracts.

'Yeah they're good boats,' he said, still looking across at the barmaid.

'Is that it?' I stared at him.

'Is that what?' Phil replied. His eyes were glued on the girl.

'For God's sake, we're discussing something that could affect all our futures, and all you can do is drool and dribble over the barmaid.'

He took his gaze from her. 'What was that?'

'It's OK. If you're not interested we'll leave you out.'

He looked a little sheepish and said, 'Just kidding.' He looked back at the barmaid. 'Have you got a pen, gorgeous?' Then he split a beer mat and sketched a rough drawing of a boat.

'What can they carry?' I asked.

'About twenty or thirty tons.'

Billy looked at me and we smiled in mutual approval.

'But they haven't got much in the way of winches or lifting gear,' Phil added.

'We could always fit our own?' Billy looked at me for a response.

'Yeah I suppose so, but the last thing we want to do is spend loads of money, then spend even more converting and adding gear'

'Fair comment, but it's worth looking into,' Billy replied giving a hopeful smile while collecting the glasses for another round.

I started diving the day my father re-married. I was just fifteen. My new stepbrother, Graham, was a member of the local sub-aqua club. It was a really sunny and calm day, so he and his friends decided going diving was a far better choice than hanging around at a stuffy wedding reception with gronks. Luckily, they invited me. I had no idea that the experience would change my life. I accepted the invitation and hastily wedged myself into the back of a mini van. I can clearly remember the droning big bore exhaust and the smelly fumes, as the back door didn't close properly.

After the arduous task of carrying the gear down the long precarious cliff path, I was greeted by a calm blue sea, which embraced the rugged coastline. It smelt strangely alien, but exciting and inviting.

I was given an abrupt introduction into this new world, breathing through a demand-valve, how to use a snorkel and how to clear water from a dive mask. Everything had a strong, salty taste to it, but nothing was going to stop me now and before I knew it I was following the two older lads into the unknown.

The water felt really cold at first, but the excitement made the discomfort bearable. About fifty yards out from the beach we stopped. Graham asked me if I was OK. Not wanting to miss this opportunity I replied through shivering lips, 'Yeah, I'm fine.'

Fitting the rubber mouthpiece into my mouth reminded me of the dentist's, but this was worth any discomfort.

As I nervously dipped my head below the change in the sound was the first thing I noticed, it was so different from on the surface. The loud fizzing and bubbling was almost scary but soon became insignificant as the seabed started to appear below me. It was getting colder but bearable.

This was the most exciting thing I had ever done! I hadn't seen the sea more than half a dozen times, and now I was exploring beneath it, with big lads!

As the bottom rose to meet us, the feeling of hovering weightlessly above the unknown was better than any fairground ride. It was another world. Crabs and strange creatures scurried all around; small fish darted everywhere. Shapes in the murky distance summoned me as I floated in a dreamy trance, long strands of weed swayed back and forth in the current. There was nobody here to tell me what to do. I felt free in a world of adventure. It was like a fairy tale that I had escaped into.

We rounded a boulder and entered a gully to find a large piece of rusty steel, twisted and crumpled into the chalk wall. In one of its crevices two long blue things waved around. I looked with awe as a lobster edged into view, its big claws waving threateningly around, making several small crabs scramble away. Then before I knew it, I was being slowly pulled to the surface. Thousands of silver bubbles danced all around me. Shafts of sunlight darted and flashed like spears through the water.

The sun felt warm on my head. We were on the surface. Slowly swimming back to the shore I kept my mouthpiece in and my face below the water. When the bottom came into view more clearly, I felt like I was flying over the rocks and weed. Then a momentary glint from a patch of sand caught my eye, the sun was reflecting from something shiny. Ducking under I swam hard towards it. Hovering above the area, I saw what was causing the reflection; I quickly grabbed the object then returned to the surface gasping desperately.

Silver Bubbles

On the beach everyone praised my find and me. Not only had I experienced the most exciting thirty minutes of my life I was actually being acknowledged for achieving something.

'Did you enjoy that then?' asked Graham. Short of breath with excitement and shaking uncontrollably I replied, 'Yeah, it was fantastic...fantastic.'

Twenty-three years had passed since then and I had gained a lot of experience over the years. I felt strong and confident, but I've always yearned for that feeling of excitement, which had lodged, so strongly in my mind. I wanted to become involved in salvage, to get far away from the humdrum world. Alone and free with the sea searching for her hidden secrets.

Jonno returned. 'This looks technical,' he said with a smile looking at the beer mat.

'Wrecking,' I said, looking up at him.

'What? Getting wrecked isn't unusual for you lot!'

'No, you plonk. Shipwrecks! There are hundreds out there, two World Wars, natural disasters, all waiting to be found.'

'He's off again.' Phil grinned.

'Hey! I've been interested in shipwrecks since I was fifteen, and had my first dive. We got a lobster off a smashed up wreck, and I found a brass fleur-de-lis from some long lost galleon. You would have been five at the time, probably just starting school.'

Billy grinned at Phil. 'So that's that thing on the beam above your fireplace?'

'Yeah that's what got me interested in lost ships. Nobody knows what it came off. They reckon it could be French. There must be more of it in deeper water, perhaps some bronze cannon or an old bell with a forgotten name engraved on it. A treasure chest full of pieces of eight! You see that's another site we need to check out.'

Phil shook his head. 'Fuck me - I'm having a pint with Long John Silver.'

'Well, how are you going to find the wrecks then?' asked Jonno. We all looked at each other.

'The fishing boats use Decca,' I said. 'It's a radio-based navigation system. They use it when trawling so their nets can be steered around the rough ground and shipwrecks.'

'Well, if they know where the wrecks are, they've done most of the work for us already,' said Billy. 'We've worked on Terry's boat. That's got Decca onboard. We can ask him about it.'

'Yeah and there's a thing called global positioning coming out soon. In fact it could be out already, and it's dead accurate.'

'Yeah,' I said loudly. 'This feels right. There's nobody salvaging off our coast, not properly anyway. Jonno's spot on, we've got to get in there before someone else thinks of the idea. We've got enough diving gear. All we need is a boat!'

There was a long silence.

'How much money have you got, Billy?'

'Two and a half grand.' He paused and added, 'But our Sue wants to start up a hairdressing salon with it.' They have two children, a boy and girl, teenagers now. Billy continued, 'The idea is to have a steady wage.'

'That's the way, mate. Get the woman working,' Phil said, grinning.

'Well, she's free from the kids, more or less, now,' Billy replied.

'He's taking the piss,' I interrupted, looking Phil straight in the eyes.

'No I'm not,' he said, fidgeting in his seat. 'Anyway, how much have you got?'

'Not enough to buy one of those boats. How about you?'

'You must be kidding, man.'

'What! You haven't saved anything up, after all the work we've had?' Billy said surprised, his mouth partly open, waiting for Phil's reply.

Silver Bubbles

Phil shuffled more in his chair, looked a little embarrassed, and then went on the defensive. 'Well, I'm single.'

'What the hell has that got to do with it?'

'Well I'm younger than you two. I haven't had the time to accumulate as much as you.'

'Bollocks! In other words, you're skint,' Billy said, causing another silence.

Jonno broke the ice, arriving with four rum and cokes.

'Wow, what's the occasion? Is it out of date?' I said looking at my mate holding the tray of drinks.

'No you cheeky bugger, I want to come out on your boat,' he replied with his head to one side smiling. 'That's if you ever get one!'

I escaped into my bed, the secure warm place where my mind could wander free and safe from interruptions, but that night I tossed and turned. My body was itching and restless. Stupid thoughts occurred repeatedly. The responsibility of a large boat was a daunting thought. What type could we afford? We would need to make modifications. What about mooring charges and security? I had a modest property. I had bought a couple of acres of land, half of it woodland, from a farmer after the split from my wife Vicki. A barn at the edge of the wood was converted into a two-bedroom bungalow. It was a lovely place, all paid for, but without mains electricity.

We were comfortable now, but the small business was being affected by competition. Day rates hadn't gone up in years. New diving rules were complicating everything. Risk assessments, method statements, tax assessments were bogging everything down. Some of the Docks had formed their own diving teams. The lack of maintenance by water and rail companies had resulted in less work to go round. Hard times were on the horizon. In the dark vulnerable hours I felt a scary feeling of childlike insecurity. It was time for a change.

A few days later, we were together again. A job had come in. The task was to survey a sewer outfall pipe. This structure was almost one mile out from the beach. The pipe was one metre in diameter, mostly entrenched and buried. The last two hundred metres of the pipe were the diffuser section. Here the pipe sat half buried on the seabed, with two-metre vertical chimneys protruding every ten metres. These were the diffusers. They are supposed to diffuse the sewage evenly into the sea.

Our team was asked to video the diffusers in operation, and check inside an inspection box for any grit deposits washed from the roads. We had hired a local boat, loaded up and were on the site. The intention was to video the diffusers while the tide was still running, so the sewage would be drifting away from the diver. This operation went well and we had videoed the diffuser section without any problems.

We were having a break, before diving again to check out the inspection box.

'What a disgusting load of crap down there,' Billy said loudly in his thick West Riding accent. Billy had done the dive. I was in communication with him and monitoring the video. Phil was stand-by diver acting as a safety back up.

We also had a fourth diver with us. He was an unknown commodity, so to speak. He was a newly trained diver who was lucky to have his parents pay for his diver-training course.

'How much did your course cost then?' Billy asked.

'Three thousand, four hundred,' Andy replied.

'Holy shit,' Billy grumbled. 'We're in the wrong business.'

'What were you doing before the diving?' I asked him.

'Err,' he paused.

Billy interrupted, 'Probably a baker with those hands.'

Andy looked embarrassed then said, 'I was a van driver.'

'Ha, that's pissed on your bonfire,' shouted Phil. Billy ignored him.

Silver Bubbles

When I reached the inspection box the tide had eased. The effluent was suspended in the water, causing the visibility to decrease to a murky 'hand in front of the face.' At least we had the visibility for the video I thought and wouldn't have to come back tomorrow.

The inspection box seemed bigger than on the drawing. It was six feet long by three feet wide. Its lid was held in place by one-inch nuts and bolts.

'Twenty-four bloody nuts and every one's tight to its last thread,' I complained.

'Roger that,' was the unsympathetic reply.

'I've got the fucking short straw this time,' I gasped. This of course was heard on the surface as the diver is on an open circuit.

'Roger that,' was Billy's unconcerned reply.

Phil was grinning, 'I hope he doesn't break one of his finger nails.'

The lid was made of stainless steel. It was too heavy to be manually lifted, so I attached an air bag and shackled it to one of its lifting lugs. A rope was secured to the other lug and to the concrete weight coat that encased the box. I used an airline from the surface, and slowly inflated the bag. The lid started to lift. Suddenly it disappeared and something huge brushed me aside.

'What the hell was that?' I shouted. There was a pause.

'You don't want to know,'

'Take my slack.'

'Roger.'

'Leaving bottom.'

'Roger that.'

On the surface was a massive slick. In its centre was a block of something incredibly smelly. It was large, about the same size as the inspection box. The water was calm all around, and hundreds of gulls were swooping down to it. I climbed and was half-dragged into the boat. They released my diving mask and unclipped the umbilical line. Everyone was pulling faces at the disgusting smell.

'What the hell is it?' Andy asked.

'It's the biggest turd you're ever going to see!' I said chuckling, as the large smelly block slowly drifted towards the blue flag beach.

'I'll use the stand-by scuba set. Andy you use the surface supply,' I told him. 'You slowly let the air out of the bag using the bleed valve, and I'll pull the lid slowly back into position. Then you line up the holes and put the bolts back in.'

'OK.' Andy nodded.

'Are you OK with that?' I looked him straight in the eyes to make sure he understood what to do.

'Yeah, sure,' he replied almost casually.

When I made bottom, the visibility was still crap, virtually nil, so I banged the large podging spanner against the box and knelt with both my hands pulling on the rope. The rope quickly went slack. Suddenly a severe pain shot through my neck. In a second I saw a jagged flash of colour, which was followed by blinding cold in my eyes.

I was upside down without my mask. Swallowing water through my nose, I twisted round like a cat and grabbed for my mouthpiece, I found it, and stuffing in my mouth I slowly decreased my rapid breathing. Dazed and hurt, I tried lifting myself up, but couldn't. Feeling smooth walls I realised I was inside the inspection box. Total darkness, with no mask! I could feel the round bottom of the pipe. Keep calm, I told myself. Keep calm. I felt around the lid and finding a gap squeezed my hand through it. I kept trying to get to my knees but I couldn't. I was sliding on the smooth surface. It must have been coated with slippery body fats. Keep calm; slow your breathing, I kept telling myself. Then all of a sudden there was a loud scratching metallic sound, which seemed to be all around me, then excruciating pain stabbed down the right side of my body, it was like powerful electric shocks jolting through me.

Silver Bubbles

Apparently Andy had arrived on the box, and was trying to align the boltholes using a long spanner, which has a tapered spike at one end. Every time he levered the lid, it trapped my wrist. The pain was unbearable as it was compressing the nerves in my wrist. My instinct was to pull my arm out, I so much wanted to stop the pain, but realised if I did I could be entombed! Then I felt something brush passed my numb fingers. It must be Andy's fin, he doesn't know I'm here, that's when the fear really started. Thinking positive wasn't working any more. I knew from experience that my air was getting low. It started from my groin, like a wave rising slowly; getting stronger as it travelled through my body. I was struggling to keep control, but I couldn't hold it any longer. Sheer panic was taking hold. The urge to thrash about screaming was taking over. Again and again I suppressed the fear. Each time it got worse as the cruel reality of my predicament spurred on another panic attack, which ended in uncontrollable gasping.

'What the hell's keeping them?' moaned Phil as he looked at the watch taped onto the air panel. 'We could be in the pub now.'

'Andy, what's the problem?'

'I'm having trouble lining up the holes.'

'You're taking too much time. Send Mike up, his air will be low. I'll send Phil in to help you.'

'Negative. Mike's not with me.'

Phil started kitting up like a madman.

'What the hell's going on?' Billy, fully clothed, looked desperate as he suddenly noticed only one set of bubbles. He helped Phil over the side and he was on the box in seconds.

The surges of panic had now ceased. Sucking the mouthpiece was priority but each breath became harder and harder then impossible! I held the mouthpiece with my shaking hand as the air slowly and cruelly ran out. I held what breath I had, but the urge to breathe took over. The first gasping breath of water gave a strange relief, then detachment. Huddled alone in the cold blackness, I shivered and convulsed violently while making futile attempts to escape the inevitable. Then a strange feeling, like it wasn't really happening enveloped me; distant thoughts filled my mind, making me calm down. I could see faces and I could hear loved ones' voices comforting me as I drifted into what I had now accepted was my last and saddest dream.

The pain had gone. Detached from reality I felt warmer. I seemed to be weightless, spinning around and around. My body was bending. Noises - something on my mouth, something warm. Voices filled my head. I felt like I was at the dentist's after being given gas. I was spinning around in turmoil of bright lights and nausea then shapes appeared. I was gasping and coughing, choking on salty red bubbles.

I was in Billy's arms. 'We've got you bud! We've got you!'

The air was sweet, but my head was pounding violently and between fits of coughing, I tried talking, but could only gasp uncontrollably.

In hospital, the X-rays showed no sign of lung damage, although infection was a concern. Severe bruising to my wrist would heal. I was discharged a day later with a course of antibiotics. It was a golden rule not to tell loved ones about near misses, so we agreed to blame a burst hose for the cause of the problem and played the incident down. I was still annoyed with myself and would not be so trusting with outsiders again.

'Hey! You shouldn't be drinking on antibiotics,' shouted Jonno from across the bar.

'Bollocks.'

'Put a cork in it,' shouted Phil.

Alison, the young barmaid Phil was trying to impress, looked disgusted at him and shouted back, 'Are you a pervert or what?'

Silver Bubbles

'Why did she say that?'

Billy and I were in stitches. I was coughing like an old smoker while Billy spat a mouthful of beer back into his glass. Phil's face was a picture.

'What?' he repeated! 'What.'

After explaining to Phil that the barmaid must have misheard the word 'cork' there was an unusual silence.

Billy wiped his chin, gave a cold stare and asked, 'What the hell went wrong then?'

'I cocked up big style,' I said in a low voice.

'Wait a minute. He used the dump valve instead of the bleed valve,' said Phil. 'Instead of controlling the descent of the lid, he just dumped all the air out of the bag and fucked up the job and you!'

'Yeah, but it was still my fault.' I tapped my finger on the table, 'If we had reversed roles it wouldn't have happened.'

'He's a trained commercial diver, fresh from a course. For God's sake, he should know the physics of the job parrot fashion,' shouted Billy.

'That's the bloody problem,' Phil butted in. 'He'll know them, but won't understand them!'

Billy raised his voice, 'A baker one day, a diver the next!'

'No, he was a driver. He told us,' Phil said, looking confused.

'Yeah.' I joined in. 'I checked his CV, he was a driver true enough, on a bloody bread round!'

The next day we met at my place. Lucy, my girlfriend, had gone away. She worked as an airhostess, a 'flying flirt.' We had been together nearly three years in what you could call a casual relationship. I was often away. Lucy came and went. She sometimes stayed with work colleagues when she was on a short turn around. Even so we got on well together, neither one burdening the other with emotions or possessiveness. She was great with Kris, my eleven-year-old son.

We were sitting round the table waiting for a fax. Phil had contacted an old friend in the Navy and was promised details and dates of any future auctions that might include suitable vessels.

'God, I hope the prices are right.'

'There won't be any prices you nugget. It's an auction,' I said, shaking my head at Billy.

'Have you seen the paper?' said Phil, dropping it on the table. 'MYSTERY OBJECT WASHED UP ON POPULAR BEACH.'

'So they've found it,' Billy said indifferently.

'Yeah, just look what the lying bastards are saying.'

I picked up the paper and scanned it quickly. 'Yeah that's about right, they're copping out by blaming a passing ship for dumping it. How can they explain away what is basically a lump of body fats, soap and shit formed into an oblong block and what about the tooth-paste tubes and disposable razors compressed in it?'

It's those private companies. They just take the piss and charge us for it,' I grumbled. 'All that white stuff floating in the water around most bathing beaches is macerated toilet paper. You look closely on most beaches; there's always a well-hidden little pipe with water trickling down a worn path in the sand towards the sea. That's your local shit pipe. The big towns have long sea outfalls pumping raw sewage into the sea, like the ones we survey. It's supposed to be screened, but I've got video records that prove it's all lies. Hypodermic syringes, razors, as well as tampons drifting around like a plague of white mice on the seabed. They have the screening facilities when they're working but they don't use them all the time because it costs them money. I'm right, how else could all that stuff get there otherwise? It's the faceless bastards earning a fortune who are responsible. It's a 'public schoolboy' thing. Young kids playing in water contaminated by deadly viruses so the greedy twats can scoff over their share prices.'

'Whoa! Whoa!' Phil interrupted. 'Don't get so wound up.'

'It's bloody true! And the sad thing is, they play on the apathy of the public to get away with it. The Water Board started with local communities chipping in together to establish a safe water source. They appointed a member of their community to maintain and improve the supply. Years and years of public investment were creamed off in one calculated swoop. And the sad part is the people who owned it, bought it! They made the bastards rich. Clever maybe, they were all laughing up their sleeves and your local politicians just stood by and did sod all. Politicians are just elected dictators. They start off with good intentions but get manipulated then corrupted like all the others. I won't vote for any of the lying bastards. It just encourages them.'

There was applause from Billy and Phil.

'Well at least I could send the videos to Greenpeace. Yeah, I might just do that one day.'

'Trying to set the world to rights again,' Billy sighed. 'There's a fax coming through.'

As promised, Phil's old pal had done his best. Three pages listing gear from assault craft to fully operational frigates. There was one item that had a ring around it. The fleet tender *Loyal Sentinel*.

'That sounds brilliant!' I said looking for a response. We all agreed.

'I'll make a brew,' Phil said.

Billy and I nodded while reading the specs over and over again.

'Hey Phil, give your pal a ring. The number's here on the fax. Ask him what sort of money ex fleet tenders fetch, will you?'

We looked in silence as Phil talked on the phone.

'Yeah, yeah, I see. Yeah, obviously, yeah, yeah, course it will. That's great. OK mate, thanks. Oh, by the way, how's that lusty wife of yours?'

'Leave it out,' Billy protested.

'No, it's just my mate. He's a bit of a codger. Thanks again, give us a shout when you're on leave next and we'll organise a piss up. Cheers mate, bye.'

Phil came and sat down. 'Well, anything between fifteen to forty-five grand. It all depends on who is bidding on the day, apparently. Also, what condition the boat's in. You know, recent re-fit, new engine, last dry-docking. Things like that.'

'Well that's encouraging. If we could get one for fifteen grand we would be laughing,' Billy said looking around with enthusiasm. Phil suddenly winced with pain as Billy's big hand squeezed his knee under the table.

'Problem is, we haven't got fifteen grand between us, never mind forty five.'

'Yeah, but Billy and I have got some equity in our houses. Let's make an appointment with the bank. There's no harm in asking.'

Billy entered the small office where I was thumbing through a thick folder.

'What's that?'

'It's all my records, everything I've gathered over the years, cuttings, loss reports and scribbles of things I've heard people talk about.'

'What, wrecks?'

'Yeah I've got lots.' I pulled a piece of paper from the folder. 'Listen to this one. It's a story I heard about. A coaster breaking the trade embargo with Rhodesia in the sixties. It was said to be carrying copper, a full cargo of at least two hundred tons. Apparently it sank off here in a squall, so it must be on or around a sandbank. One of the crew lived local and he used to talk about it after a few drinks, but he wouldn't give out any clues unless you gave him a few grand. Eventually nobody took any notice of him, until one time he slipped up and told someone its name. I knew the bloke he told. He did some research and got encouraging results. They're both dead now, but I managed to get his records from his widow.'

'That's a bit morbid.' Phil said, from behind Billy.

'That's how you get on in this world, pal. Just imagine how many stories like that have been forgotten over the years. I know this will work. I've always said there is a lot to find out there. You just have to go out and search; it's still there. All of it.'

'Where do I come in then?' Phil asked with a look of concern. 'I haven't got any bloody equity like you two.'

There was a pause then Billy looked at him. 'Deck-hand,' he said.

'Galley slave,' I added and grinned.

Phil started to speak, but Billy interrupted.

'If you behave yourself, lad, we might even let you swab the decks.'

'Don't worry pal,' I said, patting Phil on the back. 'I owe you one.'

His face melted into a warm smile.

CHAPTER TWO

The lone poplar tree swept backwards and forwards in the gusting wind. Most of its leaves were replaced by a legion of shredded plastic supermarket bags. The tree had terraced houses as a backdrop. Sad eyed dogs moped around in small shit-filled yards. Anonymous faces appeared and disappeared through windows like silent prisoners.

Phil sat on the end of his bed, smartly dressed in his best and only suit. Still single, aged twenty-eight. Six feet two inches tall, good-looking with thick black hair and a complexion that showed a three o'clock shadow, even after shaving. He moved to the mirror, the lines of the suit clearly showing his lean body. He brushed the hair out of his eyes with his fingers.

'I could get into modelling,' he said to himself turning his head several times. 'Then again, I couldn't take all that shit. Shrieking Faggots dashing around with brush handles stuck up their buckets.'

He was staying at his mother's, a two up, two down terrace house in a place called "Newland Avenue," but there was nothing *new* about the place. It was good of her to let him stay, but the house was small. There wasn't any privacy and no way of entertaining friends.

Silver Bubbles

The room boasted a bed, an old chest of drawers and a wardrobe that the Adams family would have been proud of. He had stayed in the Navy town with mates after leaving. It was a good three months but an expensive affair. He had tried several jobs since leaving the Navy, but couldn't settle down. His almost too friendly attitude had been abused in the past. After being conned out of his savings on hopeless business ventures; he was low in spirit when he met us.

He had introduced himself while we were on a job in the docks. I was impressed by his apparent fitness and he had the necessary certificates. That was three years ago. Phil has been on every job with us since.

I blew the horn. We were in the van, dressed in our best suits.

'Where have you been?' Phil asked.

'We had to go back for Billy's comb,' I joked as I pushed forward the gear stick.

'God, you smell like a whore's knickers,' Phil shouted as the van's engine got louder.

'You should know the smell.' Billy gave him a condescending stare.

'Old Spice, mate,' I said grinning at Phil. 'He's had it for years, got it with that demob suit.'

Billy ignored our remarks.

Sat in the bank, the one place I hated, I wriggled on the chair.

'Do you know? I feel like a total prick sat here.'

'Yeah, you're supposed to.' Billy agreed, staring angrily around.

'Wow! She's chic. The ginger one at the third counter, I bet I could make her legs tremble.'

'Leave it out,' Billy snapped, 'or your head will be trembling. We're in a sodding bank, not a discothèque.'

'What's one of them? I shook my head at his cheek.

Peter Fergus

'It doesn't make any difference,' he continued. 'You can pull anywhere. Anyway you're not my dad and discos went out in the dark ages. It's called clubbing now.' Billy ignored him.

I looked at my watch. 'Why? Why do they always do this? They just love it, keeping us on public display like beggars. Everybody has to pass us to get to the cashiers. They all know we are grovelling for a loan. We're left sitting here like those three bloody monkeys and they're twelve minutes late.'

Phil leaned forward to see me. 'There were four in the monkeys,' he said with a nod. 'Davy Jones, Mike....'

Billy interrupted loudly, making several people turn their heads.

'Hear nowt, see nowt, and say nowt, those monkeys he means, you ignorant pleb.'

I got up and rang the inquiry bell. Billy and Phil looked around uncomfortably.

'Yes sir?' a young girl asked.

'We had an appointment fifteen minutes ago.'

'Did you leave something behind, sir?'

'No. No.' I took a deep breath, 'I mean we've been waiting fifteen minutes for our appointment.'

'Oh, just a minute sir.' She quickly disappeared.

A few minutes later Billy groaned. 'That did a fat lot of good.'

I was just about to start cursing but stopped as I saw the girl approach, out of the corner of my eye.

'Would you like to come through?' She spoke through the now unlocked door.

We were led through a dull corridor towards another door. The girl knocked and waited. She looked on edge and was wringing her hands.

'Yes?' someone shouted abruptly.

She opened the door and said nervously, 'Mr Morgan, sir.' After a wait of about one minute she turned to us with an anxious stare.

Silver Bubbles

'Show him in,' the voice said again bluntly.

We shared glances, which confirmed all our thoughts about this farcical bullshit.

In the stuffy room a fat man with glasses, adorned in a saggy pinstripe suit, stood up and offered his hand. He looked surprised as Phil and Billy followed behind me crowding his small office. I shook his hand. It felt clammy.

'Smyth, Bernard Smyth, assistant manager,' he said, holding his lapels. He was obviously finding it hard to do two things at once and his stomach bulged shamefully.

'Your friends?' he inquired, raising his eyebrows.

'They're work colleagues actually,' I said with a fixed stare.

'Quite, quite.'

Before he could continue I introduced them. 'Billy Wells. Phil Roper.'

'Yes,' he said, shaking their hands somewhat reluctantly.

'How can we be of service?' he asked in an unnecessarily loud voice as he sat down.

I stared at the dandruff on his shoulders then focused my eyes on his. 'Well, we've had an idea for ages now, and we feel it's time to act upon it.'

'Indeed, what sort of idea?'

'Well, as you know, I've been trading for about ten years.'

'Just a second,' he interrupted. 'You're trading as?'

I deliberately took a sharp breath through my nose. 'Coastal Diving and Marine Services.' He picked up his phone, mumbled into it, then looked up and gave a cheesy smile.

'What a tosser,' I said under my breath. Billy sat shaking his head while removing his tie, stuffing it rebelliously into his pocket

Phil was standing, squeezed into a corner. He was hunched up and looked misshapen like Basil Fawlty with his trousers up his legs, showing his pulled up socks. It made me smile.

There was a tap as the door opened and all eyes fell on a tall, extremely skinny man with a hooked nose, who appeared with some folders.

'Neil Eggland,' he announced while looking around with piercing, bird like eyes, which were set in deep dark sockets. The three of us looked at each other in bemusement.

'Financial adviser,' he blurted. Only I stood up. I was met this time with limp fingers, so I gave them a firm squeeze.

'Oh my word, you've nearly broken my hand,' he said with a disdainful look.

'Sorry mate,' I replied. Billy and Phil could hardly contain themselves. If one of them gave a little snort the meeting would have totally collapsed into sniggering sniffles. There was a laboured silence.

'Financial adviser,' I almost shouted, whilst glaring at my mates.

'Yes,' the thin one replied.

'Good advice is what we're here for.' I'll get shit for that, I thought.

The fat one coughed into his hand and continued, 'An idea, you say?'

'Yes. Marine salvage.' The bankers looked at each other.

'You know, shipwrecks, valuable cargo recovery. Non-ferrous metals, copper is making over two thousand pounds a ton and likely to go up. There are thousands of wrecks lying off here.'

'Excuse me,' interrupted the thin one. 'You mean ships that have sunk in the open sea?'

'Yeah…err, that's were it normally happens.' I replied, rolling my eyes at Billy.

'Oh.' He looked confused then composed himself. 'Well, how do you propose the recovery of these items exactly?'

'We're all experienced commercial divers. We've worked all over the world. Salvage, construction, engineering, explosives,' I said, enthused.

Silver Bubbles

'Yes, I don't doubt your experience Mr. Morgan, but surely companies with larger resources have had similar ideas in the past, and probably recovered most things of value by now? Surely this is a case of shutting the door after the horse has bolted?'

'No, not at all.' I was so annoyed and angry. What did this 'dick' know about salvage? 'They don't even know where the wrecks are!' I said with frustration. 'I've been researching them for years. I've got literally hundreds of targets to check out. Look at these.' I passed over my folder.

'Fat' and 'thin' pondered through my papers without reading a word then 'Thin' placed them back into the folder and passed them back. He opened the file laid on his desk and browsed through it. 'I see we hold your deeds.'

'Yes.'

'Your business hasn't shown good profits,' he looked over his glasses, 'for a number of years. It seems your overdraft peaks and then a payment is made which levels your account, only for the whole process to reoccur. You don't seem to maintain a healthy credit for more than a few days.'

'I haven't come here for a fucking bollocking,' I snapped, and they reeled back in shock. 'I'm buying this damn loan. I'm a customer. Have you forgotten where your fucking wages come from?'

There was a deathly silence. Billy looked at me with a raised brow while shaking his head.

'Look, I'm sorry.' I paused. 'It's because a job is financed with the overdraft and when it's completed the payment comes in. I can only run one job at a time.' I was annoyed at their cynical attitude and my poor answer.

'That's a problem,' said the fat one. 'Why don't you expand your operations?'

'The competition is getting worse. There are companies who take on unqualified and newly qualified staff, popping up all over. Bloody cowboys, just on an 'I'm a commercial diver - look at me,' trip. They can't even tie knots. They do substandard jobs and reduce day-rates to their level of wages. It's not even worth competing with them. That's why this idea will work. Those posers couldn't organise or plan a piss up err, I mean, a proper salvage operation, but we can.'

'So, how can we be of help?'

'We want finance or a loan to buy and fit out a salvage boat.'

The bankers looked at each other.

'What is the value of your property?'

'Well I've never had it valued, but I reckon about forty to fifty thousand, more when I get mains electricity.'

'Sorry?' queried 'Thin'.

'It doesn't have mains electricity yet.'

'Oh I see. Your colleagues, have they got any security?' He turned to them. Phil looked down nervously, flashing his eyes around.

'Mr. Roper has two thousand, and Mr. Wells four.'

'I see. How much would a suitable vessel cost, including the, err,' he looked at his notes.

'Twenty, forty, thousand depending on the condition of the boat and who's bidding against us.'

'Sounds a bit vague,' said "Thin".

'Yes, I can understand why it sounds vague to you.' I looked at Billy who'd just sighed loudly at me.

"Fat" stood up, knocking the folder into shape. 'I've got all your details, gentlemen. We will consider your proposals. We will of course have to consult Head Office and consider all the facts before we can make a decision. We will contact you in due course. Thank you.'

"Thin" opened the door, scanning all three of us as we filed out.

We stood on the pavement with our hands in our pockets, shuffling around.

'What do you reckon?'

Silver Bubbles

Billy looked down. 'I don't think they'll be inviting you out to lunch. You scared them shitless.'

'Bloody tossers! Shiny-arsed wankers! They never read a bloody word when they looked at my file, unadulterated tossers, wankers! Their whole approach is a farcical bloody game. Just look at the way they messed that poor girl around. They didn't even look at my folder properly; I've spent years compiling all that stuff. They didn't read a fucking word of it!'

'You're repeating yourself,' Billy said quietly.

'Well, what did you really think?'

'I honestly don't know. They seemed confused with us and a bit shocked,' he said, pulling an indifferent face.

'They seemed confused?' Phil blurted. 'Not as much as me. The two grand, where the fuck am I going to get that from, sell my arse?'

'I wouldn't hold your breath,' Billy quipped.

'Chill out, Phil. It was just bullshit. Those sad bastards in there need it. If you said you had no money, they would have seen you as an alien.'

Billy rasped his big hands together, 'Do you fancy 'pint, lads?'

What the hell! I couldn't believe it. There was a bloody parking ticket on the van. Phil peeled the machine ticket from the inside of the windscreen.

'Two-fifteen,' he said, then looked at his watch. 'Two-thirty, fifteen minutes over, what a bummer. The bank delay caused this.'

I put the wipers on to knock the bastard off but the ticket was taped to the windscreen; the wiper hit the ticket then snapped as if it was in pain. It gave a few jerks and dropped to the road. 'Bollocks,' I shouted, revved the engine and drove off aggressively out of the square.

There he was, round-shouldered, just like the snotty kid every one picked on at school, slinking along the pavement with a gait of an aged crop picker.

I stopped the van along side the traffic warden and wound down the window and shouted, 'Hey, you!' It was busy and everybody stopped in their tracks.

'Hey Adolph, did you put this ticket on here?'

He slinked on, deliberately ignoring us.

'I've seen you and your wife in that swingers' video, with the liquorice sticks and the oily python. You should be fucking ashamed of yourself.' A car blew its horn behind us so I stuck my finger in the air, revved up, slammed the van into gear and squealed off. Phil grinned.

Billy shook his head and sighed. 'That was just a waste of time, and you've broken the wiper.'

'No, everybody should do it. It makes you feel better. If everybody did it, there would be fewer of those sad creatures sliming around. Who could do that job anyway? Parking should be free, we all pay rates and road tax.'

The next few days were quiet. I helped Len to fit a solid fuel stove into his mobile home. He had retired from the Q.E.2 after a lifetime at sea. He had been brought up in an orphanage, which was hard in those days. His life got a damn sight harder when he was thirteen. He was sent to a sail training ship, moored in the infamous River Mersey. He bought a mobile home when he retired and sited it on a holiday camp overlooking the sea. When I separated from Vicki I walked out and left everything. I used our savings to purchase Wood End, which was just a barn then. I had signed my share of the house over to Vicki, so we came out even. I then moved my dad's mobile home onto a clearing in the wood and lived with him while we renovated the barn.

When the stove was in place Len shouted, 'Sundowners.'

'No, no thanks,' I shouted my reply. 'Oh, go on then.' This was a ritual. After our drink I left via the short path through the trees, to my small, unique home. I loved the place. No eyes, no noise, isolated from all the humdrum, just like being alone at sea on a calm night.

Silver Bubbles

The corned beef hash was great. I dropped the empty plate into the sink, poured a long rum and coke then moved to the window, looking out over the fields. It was early March and every living thing was preparing for the ensuing summer, a good time of year. I felt excited, we too were preparing for the summer. Glancing over towards the wood I had to smile on seeing a column of smoke rising through the leafless trees.

The following days were uneventful. Billy was looking over properties with Sue. Phil was round here at the workshop every day, helping to service the diving gear.

We were coiling a diving umbilical, when he stopped. 'Do you think the bank will lend us the money?' He looked at me.

'I doubt it.'

'Why's that then?'

'They only like dead certainties that they can exploit. We're wild cards, pirates to them. They still won't have a clue about what we were proposing.'

'Do you think Billy is keen about the idea, I mean really keen? He doesn't say a lot to me about anything.'

'Yeah, that's just Billy. He's only known you for a few years. He comes from a tight knit community. Did you know his dad was a bare-knuckle fighter?'

'Hell no. You're kidding?'

'No, all of them were Yorkshire miners, Billy his dad, his granddad, and so on.'

'Why did he pack it in then?'

'He, well they, didn't have a choice. They became surplus to requirements and the weasels turned on them.'

'Weasels? I don't understand.'

'The politicians shit on them. You know, the miners strike.'

'I was away in the mob when all that was going on.'

'Ask him about it sometime, when he's in a good mood.'

'He's never in a good mood.'

I smiled to myself. 'Don't be scared of him. Just relax and be yourself. He senses you're nervous and plays on it. He does it to everyone. It's the way they're brought up, a pecking order thing.'

'He doesn't do it to you.'

'Yeah, but we go back a long way. As I said, no, better still, buy him a large rum, then ask him what it was like in the mines, but don't ask him if he's pissed. He'd probably go off on one.'

'Why?'

'They just got shit on so badly. It's a sore point.'

'Was Billy a boxer then?'

'Why do you ask that?'

'Well, he looks like a boxer, with his broken nose and all that. He's got bloody arms as thick as my legs!'

'Yeah, but it wasn't by choice. Their elders forced them. It was a sort of sport I suppose, like cock fighting.'

'Bloody hell.' Phil leaned back against the wall.

'Yeah, that's a good way of describing it.'

'How could they do it?'

'A macho thing, they gambled on the fights. They didn't get seriously hurt, but it must have been terrifying for a young boy. That's why you will never see Billy scared of anyone or anything, come to that.'

'He looked scared when you were trapped.'

'That was different. And out of order.'

'Sorry, I didn't mean.'

'Forget it,' I said while walking towards the ringing phone.

The call was a welcome job inquiry. A pipeline company wanted a dive team to take trench levels and assist in placing an eighteen-inch steel pipe across a river. The job was down south and with a company we had worked for in the past so it should be routine. The main contractor was laying a gas pipe from the

East Coast to the South. Every river crossing had to ensure that the pipe was buried deep enough below the riverbed to avoid anchors or keels from pleasure boats damaging the pipe or its protective coating. Once the pipe was laid in the excavated trench, a diver using a long staff or marked stick would take levels from the top of the pipe. An engineer took the readings, and if the pipe wasn't deep enough it would have to be removed and repositioned, but this would incur large penalties for the contractor. This particular river was not navigational, but the rules still applied.

We were sat on the riverbank ready to dive. I had seen a kingfisher and was preoccupied in trying to point it out to Billy. Billy didn't hear me. He was betting Phil that he would encounter at least one bag of kittens and probably a dead and jellied dog while working in rivers and canals this year.

'OK lads, can you take some levels now?' the engineer requested.

'Get in then, lad,' Billy said to Phil.

'Roger that, Dad,' he replied.

'I'll snot him one of these days.'

'Chill out.' I looked at Billy.

Phil slid into the muddy water making the coms crackle loudly.

'On the bottom,'

'Roger.'

'I'm on the job.'

'Roger that.'

The site agent watched. The assistant engineer stood wobbling in an inflatable boat while holding a staff. When a reading was taken he would bang the staff up and down to ensure it was on the top of the pipe

'Take a reading where the pipe gooseneck starts,' the engineer shouted while nodding to us.

'Take a reading on the start of the gooseneck, over.' The staff with its bright red markings stood vertical. The engineer looked through the level and wrote down the readings. I walked towards the diving panel that indicates the air pressure to the diver and controls the air source, i.e. a compressor or large storage bottles. You can switch air source to either. I switched off the air.

Billy looked across, confused. I gave him a reassuring wink. Not much later Phil, although only twelve feet down gasped, 'Going to bailout. Pull me up.'

Phil surfaced and was pulled towards the bank. 'What's wrong?' he blurted, while pulling his band mask off. 'My main supply failed! I had to go on reserve.'

I replied loudly so the engineer could hear. 'That bloody van pulled up right next to the compressors' air intake. Carbon monoxide fumes straight into the breathing air. We can't have that.'

The engineer asked for all the vehicles to be moved away.

'I'll do the dive,' I said to Phil.

'No it's OK.'

I grabbed his arm assertively. 'I'll do the dive.'

Phil looked hurt; he was shrugging his shoulders and constantly staring disapproval.

I carried out the dive. The level readings were accepted and the job was passed. The company always celebrated the completion of a crossing with champagne and nibbles. We were guzzling the champagne like a pack of animals when the owner of the Pipeline Company came across to me.

'What were you doing? Why did you do the dive yourself?'

'You owe me one,' I replied.

'Was there a problem or something?'

'You're having a laugh aren't you? You know there was.'

'It wasn't deep enough was it?' He looked at me sheepishly.

'Your drag lines were working well until they hit rock then the buckets were just sliding across the rock and widening the trench. When Phil took the first reading it was ten inches too shallow. I know its all bullshit. It's not even a navigational river, but they would have failed the crossing.'

'Yeah, we had doubts but couldn't do anything. We tried different teeth on the excavation buckets, but we just ran out of time. We accepted that we would incur penalties. So how did you do it?'

'I took one of my lead weights from my weight vest and when the guy in the boat banged the staff up and down, I held the lead next to the pipe so it felt solid to him. I did it throughout the length of the pipe. The riverbed is like a bombsite - uneven with holes everywhere. Fortunately it was passed with inches to spare.'

'Thanks Mike. When you've finished tomorrow, come and see me. I'm in the office all day.' He cast a glance around the table so we made a hasty exit.

'Hell, where's all the champagne gone?'

The digs we returned to were rough to say the least. We had agreed to save as much money as possible towards the boat, but were having second thoughts. The place was called The Golden Fleece. It was a real fleece, a dump. We shared a room in the loft. Seven pounds a night was the cost for bed and breakfast. It stank of vomit and urine. The gutters ran inside the rooms and pigeons were making appearances.

I removed my pillowcase. The stains looked like a map of China. 'Holy shit, what the hell are we doing here? I gasped. 'That sod we've just saved thousands is probably in a five star hotel getting a blow job from a chamber maid while we're here sleeping in festering scrotum crumbs.'

'You really need to chill out,' said Billy. 'Wrap a towel round your pillow; go down to the bar, have a few beers and you'll sleep like a log.'

I grabbed a towel and unfolded it. 'Oh this is great.' I held it up. 'Look, it's got muddy dog prints on it.'

'This isn't as bad as hot bunking like we used to do on the subs. If you didn't like someone, you used to leave a smelly sock in the pillowcase,' Phil said proudly.

I had to grin. 'You navy pussies. If you didn't like someone in the Army, you used to shit in their pillowcase.'

'You were in the Army?'

'Yeah,'

'Really?'

'Yeah really, but that's for your ears only.'

Billy butted in, 'Get a shower, daft lad.'

Phil grabbed his towel. 'Pongos, street fighters, fucking Superman will drop in next!' The door slammed.

'What do you think of the kid? He's a bit worried about you, you know.'

'Why should he be?' Bill replied showing no emotion.

'Come on Billy, you've been giving him a hard time.'

'Yeah, I suppose you're right. He really came through when he pulled you out of that shit pipe though. When we went back to fix the lid we found the podging spanner. It was bent double. When he felt your hand he flipped the lid and dragged you out in seconds. That kid lifted near on four hundred pounds of steel in nil vis, got you topside and still had the sense to fill your lungs with air the second you both broke surface. No, don't worry on that score. I'll stand in his corner.'

Billy was right. He had saved my life. I owed him.

Phil burst through the door. 'Don't bother about the shower. It's cold as polar bear piss.'

'Shit, I smell like a bloody water vole,' Billy complained. 'I've got a crutch like a bag of cheese and onion crisps.'

'Yeah well don't pass them around.' I laughed while standing up. My towel fell down.

'Christ, you're hung like a donkey!' Phil shouted, while laughing.

Silver Bubbles

'Poor childhood. I had to play with myself to generate heat to keep warm.'

'Can you leave it out?' Billy said in his loud powerful voice, 'I'm getting bloody worried about you two arse slapping squaddies.'

We got dressed and after a cold wash and lots of spraying around with deodorant we headed downstairs to the bar. The menu was as good as the accommodation. After a meal at a Chinese down the road, we ended up back at the pub.

'Fancy a game of pool?' Phil asked.

'I'll get the round, you give him a game, Billy, and I'll play the winner.'

'Three dark rum and cokes doubles please.'

A girl sitting at the bar looked round at me. 'You're not from round here then?' she asked with a smile.

'No, we're just on a job. A couple of days, that's all.'

'What do you do then? No, let me guess. Err...'

'Lorry drivers,' I replied.

With that a second girl joined her. 'Who's this then?'

'I don't know.'

'Mike.' I replied, while walking back to the pool table clutching three glasses.

Phil had been watching me. 'Have we pulled then?' he asked with a deadly serious look.

'Don't be bloody daft. She only spoke out of politeness,' I snapped.

'You're joking pal,' he said, looking around. 'I reckon she's hot for it. I reckon they both are.'

'Your shot, lad,' grunted Billy.

Phil put the black ball down. He pretended to be annoyed then handed the cue to me. 'Your turn,' he said and then rushed to the bar.

Billy smiled. 'You've got to hand it to the lad. He's either had nowt for ages or he's just a knob hound.'

I racked up the pack and replied, 'I reckon a bit of both.'

We continued playing pool.

'Do you think they're on the game?'

'It's hard to tell. Probably.' I looked around at the shoddy decor.

About ten minutes later, a bang and the sound of breaking glass interrupted the game.

I looked up at Billy then took a look around the partition. 'Shit!' I gasped. With that Phil appeared, holding a bleeding nose.

'The twat hit me for nothing.'

Then three men walked up behind him. A big black guy about six feet tall pushed his lips out and shook his big bald head. 'Is this piece of freeloading shit with you?' His eyes were wide and glaring. He looked well pissed off.

Billy frowned. 'Phil,' he beckoned with his thumb for him to get out of the way then moved between the man and Phil.

'He's with me. What's your problem?'

'As I said, that shit was messing with one of my girls, I haven't finished with him yet, so get the fuck out of my way.'

Billy looked at him and shook his head. 'This is a hopeless case. I'm obviously talking to a cretin.'

The man rushed at Billy and swung a massive fist. Billy ducked and turned his shoulders whilst straightening his legs. He swung his right arm round and connected a punch into the side of the stomach of the big guy. There was a loud cracking sound and the man fell to his knees with his mouth and eyes wide open in a shocked stare. Billy grabbed his chin and pulled it upwards. He made a big fist and drew his arm back.

'Shall I break his jaw now and then yours?' He looked scary staring at the other two smaller men. They dropped their gaze and looked nervously at each other. Billy pulled the big man up. 'We only want a drink. The lad didn't know they were working girls.'

Silver Bubbles

The man said nothing as he was helped out grimacing, while holding his broken ribs. His eyes were still wide open and disbelieving as sweat dripped from his chin.

'Well that's it. It's time for bed,' I announced. 'Half the town will want a pop at us now.'

Phil looked at Billy. 'Hell, thanks mate.' Billy just shook his head.

After the pipe was covered over with sandbags filled with a dry mix of sand, gravel and cement, our job was over. I always felt contented when a job was completed. Every diving job had its risks and people could get killed on a site where heavy plant operated. It was even worse when men were underwater instructing cranes and diggers. After packing our gear away I went to the site office to see the client as requested.

'You've done a good job, Mike and saved us a lot of embarrassment, not to mention cost.' He opened a drawer and pulled out a brown envelope.

'There you go. A treat for you and your lads.'

I took the envelope and shook his hand. I thanked him then left.

Back in the van Billy was still giving Phil a bollocking for getting himself punched.

'Leave it out, girls,' I shouted. 'Check this out.' I threw the brown envelope at Billy.

Billy tore it open and pulled out a sizeable wad of notes. 'There's got to be at least two grand here!' Billy said, looking at us with a rare smile.

'Brill,' Phil said, 'Our first boat money.'

Billy put his arm round Phil and gave him a crushing squeeze. 'Well said, lad. You're not all that bad, despite that fat nose!'

After we cleaned the dive gear and stored it away, Len came across.

'The job went all right then?'

'Yeah, great. We prevented a problem and got paid a bonus.'

'Kris came round last night.' Len sighed. 'He stayed.'

'Did Vicki ring?'

'Yes, she rang before he arrived. Apparently he had a big row with Nigel, packed his rucksack and biked here. He stayed with me last night.'

'Hell! I feel so bad. That's my lad. That's me going through all that turmoil. I've got to do something. God, it's repeated a generation later. You split from Mum when I was eleven. The difference is Kris is with his mother and it's relatively amiable, them living close by. Not like I was, bloody housekeepers with boy friends, you always away at sea, and not seeing much of my mother due to the circumstances, and them moving away.'

'Whoa! He's fine. There's no problem. The kid's fine. He's just frustrated because he wants to live here and be one of the lads. That creep Vicki's with.... God, what can she see in that jerk?'

'Come on Dad, it's my fault, a bit like you I suppose. I was always away too. I missed too many Christmases and birthdays I was always at work. I neglected her. She was vulnerable and he slid in. It's so frustrating. I can solve difficult diving jobs, but can't even sort my own life out. Some father.'

'No, you just tried to provide and got caught in the tide. Kris is a good lad, and you have lots of happy years ahead of you, we all have. Come on lets be positive, this isn't you. Where's the 'faint heart never screwed a pig' attitude gone?'

'Cheers Dad, I'm turning in now. I'll see you in the morning.'

As I closed the door I looked on as he walked down the small path back to his caravan. 'Thanks mate.' I uttered to myself.

The noise encroached gradually as if in a dream. I tossed and turned but it persisted then became a phone ringing.

Silver Bubbles

'Hello, is that Michael?'

'Yeah,'

'This is Nigel. I need to talk to you about Kristopher.'

I sat up. 'Oh yeah?'

'Well there seems to be a problem, a problem with discipline.'

'In what way?'

'The other night for instance. He ran away. He just ignored my orders and left the house through his bedroom window.'

'Is Vicki there?'

'Yes she is, but I am dealing with this personally.'

I took a deep breath. 'Could I speak with Vicki, please?'

'I'm sorry, as I said I am dealing with this.'

I took the phone away from my ear and placed it on the bed. This guy, this arrogant prick is dictating to me. He stole my wife and now he's in my face because he can't handle things. 'What orders did Kris ignore?' I asked, restraining myself from melting the phone with verbal abuse.

'His bedroom, it's a complete mess.'

'Well what a bloody shame, that must be so depressing, my heart pumps piss for you. Put Vicki on now. Put her on now, you wet bastard.'

The phone made a loud noise and went dead. 'Oh boy, you're in for a spanking,' I thought. 'You've hung up on me for the first and last time and you had the bloody arrogance to slam down the phone!'

After running off my anger, I sat with a brew. If only Vicki hadn't met that creep. If only I hadn't always been away. Nigel was pushing Vicki to divorce me, but we had agreed not to, at least not until Kris was older. Anyway Lucy was on the scene now. Well, she was when she was home.

I looked down the track; the postman had stopped and was placing something into the box. Len had seen this and was already halfway there. The door opened and Spot raced into the house, panting and dashing around busily, sniffing everything. Spot, a long-legged Jack Russell, was Kris' dog, but Len looked after her.

Billy and Phil arrived. We sat round the table looking at the envelope from the bank marked 'Private'.

'Well open it,' Billy said. I tore it open. A long silence ensued.

'Mmm,' I couldn't hide my look of disappointment.

'Well?' Phil couldn't wait any longer. I threw the letter on the table and looked at Billy.

'It's a no.'

'Not exactly, but as good as piss off or give us your dosh.'

Phil read the letter out. 'They want to send a surveyor and will consider a loan of half the value of the property. Providing, and this is the rub, providing mains electricity is installed and the deeds are signed over to the bank. There would be an arrangement fee of two hundred pounds, plus the valuation charge. And if that's not enough, they've charged twenty-five quid for this letter. Oh, and you have to take out an insurance policy with them because of the manner of your work and that will cost six hundred and fifty quid. Just in case you get disabled, killed or can't work!'

Billy stood up and put the cups in the sink. 'They take a lot of risks don't they? Bankers, wankers - there's no difference. What a bloody waste of time! Business advisers, they're all bloody working for someone else! If they knew so much about business they would have their own.'

'What about the auction? Phil asked with concern. 'It's next week.'

'Yeah I know. There's not a lot we can do about it, we just haven't got enough money, but there again, we could - '

'Forget it pal,' interrupted Billy. 'Don't even consider such a greedy proposal. You're not risking this place. We'll get there in the end. The bank and its non-producing parasites can swivel on this.' He pushed his index finger into the air.

CHAPTER THREE

The next two weeks were spent surveying bridges for a rail company. The work was routine, but not profitable. We would rather win a tender with a low price and ensure ourselves a wage than go for big risk profits. Also there was always a possibility of finding a problem on a survey and getting the repair work. Unfortunately there weren't any jobs generated from our inspections. We suggested numerous repairs, but they were ignored or shelved to save costs. So after cleaning the diving gear we ended up in the Ship.

'They will suffer in the end, ignoring preventative maintenance in favour of share dividends,' I moaned.

'So, this file on wrecks. Where did it come from?' Billy asked, purposely changing the subject before I kicked off. He took a drink, making the froth cling to his thick moustache.

'Books, old charts, admiralty readouts,' I replied.

Phil interrupted, 'What's an Admiralty readout?'

'You a clearance diver and you don't know! You should be ashamed of yourself.'

'OK, I am. So what is it then?'

Billy was laughing to himself. 'Tell the lad, for God sake. They're told nowt in the mob.'

'It's a wreck report, well, obstructions report. The Admiralty survey and chart every foot of the seabed with sonar then file a report on every contact, height, length, breadth etc.'

'How did you get hold of them?'

'I was on a job in Dundee when I met an old salvage diver called Jim. He had worked after the war for a company called Risdon Beazley. They went round the coast dispersing wrecks that were shipping dangers, just blowing the shit out of them. But some of the wrecks were carrying copper tin and other valuable cargoes. They used big grabs to salvage it. This was OK when conditions were right, but as you know, nothing at sea is easy and lots of things were missed. I got the full list of wrecks and cargo manifests and all the positions, for a bottle of Scotch and an Indian takeaway. I'll never forget the dirty old sod. He brought a slapper back to the digs, his bunk was bellow mine, and I had to hang on for most of the night. He nearly wrecked the bed. It was like being at the fair, but instead of fairground music my shaky ride was accompanied by dirty talk in Glaswegian slang. He kept asking her if he could put his finger in a certain place but she was three sheets into the wind, so I said yes for him.

I've wanted to get at those wrecks for years. It's real adventure and it can have great rewards for those who dare! I also cleared a fouled propeller for a Danish fisherman. A wreck netter, he had positions even the Admiralty doesn't have. That's where I learned about the graveyard.'

'What's that?' Phil asked with genuine interest. Billy stared, stone-faced.

'During the two wars mines were laid in shipping lanes. Great losses were incurred. One particular minefield wasn't even known about until they started picking up survivors. The German subs laid mines in clusters. This particular patch of seabed, well, channel was heavily mined throughout both wars. Generally where there is one wreck there are more. And this area, the graveyard, is the biggest, with dozens of wrecks that have never been dived or surveyed.

Silver Bubbles

'The loss of life,' Billy said quietly. 'Those poor sods. Imagine a winter's night. You're asleep warm in your bunk then suddenly freezing water rushes in. God, it's inconceivable. It's bad enough when you're dry bag leaks, poor sods.'

'My dad was on the Murmansk convoys.'

'Who, Len?' Phil said surprised.

'No, my other dad, you knob!' Billy and I looked at each other.

'Yeah, yeah, all right,' Phil grovelled.

'When a ship was attacked, sometimes they couldn't even pick up the survivors. They left them to drown. Ask Len when you see him.'

'I will.'

'Yeah, the Merchant were treated badly during the war. When they were on trains for instance, because they didn't have a uniform all the squaddies thought they were war-dodging cowards and gave them unjustified shit!'

Two attractive girls walked through the door. Phil's eyes flicked from us to them at incredible speed, much to our amusement. Billy deliberately placed himself between Phil and the girls, which made him dip and sway his head like an animal stalking its prey. We carried on talking to him but he was totally preoccupied and fidgeting like a child. Knowing it was my round, I asked whose round it was and winked at Billy. Phil got up almost knocking over the table.

'It's my round. Same again?' He looked at us as if seeking approval, then rushed to the bar where the girls were.

There was a silence for a while. We didn't have to jabber on and on to appease each other. Useless conversation was always avoided.

'I think the lad's pulled this time,' said Billy with raised eyebrows.

I looked towards the bar. Phil was sitting between the two girls, pouring each a glass of wine.

'He's old enough to look after himself.'

'Just a lad,' Billy replied. 'Just a lad and he's forgotten the bloody round'.

As morning broke, rays of sunlight filtered into my room. I turned over to avoid the brightness. My mouth tasted like Gandhi's flip-flop. Despite a thick head, five minutes later I was running along the riverbank. The first mile is always the hardest. Come on, I spurred myself. Left right left right. I was going way back in time, but it always worked and I got into a rhythm.

About three miles into the run, I left the path to avoid a horse rider. She had a nice figure so I slowed down to get a good look. The girl looked me straight in the eyes and smiled sweetly. She threw me totally, causing me to partly trip in the grass. What a lovely smile she gave me - her figure was something else! A little further I looked back. The girl also looked back. That was the first time in ages that's happened to me, I thought, while grinning inside and out.

Spot came running past, panting loudly. Her paws lightly pounded the path like a small horse. A skylark sang high above. It sounded better than any stereo or sound effect. Daffodils were everywhere; some were gathered on the grassy bank, others lined the edge of the copse like small soldiers on guard. They all succumbed to the same invisible force as they swayed and danced in the indifferent breeze.

On the way back down the green lane, I noticed Spot had stopped and was wagging her tail. When I reached her, the girl with the horse surprised me, as she was behind the hedge. She had dismounted and was making a fuss of Spot.

'Come on Spot, don't jump up.'

'She's all right.' Bending over to Spot she said, 'She's gorgeous isn't she?'

She was younger than me. Her stunning figure was exaggerated in her tight riding pants. She looked up at me and gave a coy smile. Her bonny face was a picture, with her shiny black hair tied back with something red.

I smiled back at her, stuck for words then asked, 'Are you from around here?'

Pointing with her crop she said in a soft Irish accent, 'We're renting the cottage over there,'

'Oh yes, I know the place, "The Spinney."'

Spot suddenly ran off, following some hidden scent then promptly disappeared into a hedge bottom. Leading her horse past me, she smiled. I took full advantage, as she had her back to me I eyed her up and down. Then she turned around and looked at me, still smiling. She's caught me again I thought. So I started running. Knowing she might still be watching I increased my pace to almost a sprint. Approaching a bend I looked back, she was watching.

I pushed open the door to find Len sat at the table wiping Spot down.

'All right Dad?'

'Fine son,' he said looking at me. We locked our gaze for a second as only a father and son can.

'Here.' He gently pushed a brown envelope across the table.

'What's this?'

'It's for you son, and your team, well, all of us.'

I opened up the thin envelope and pulled out a cheque. 'Ten grand. Oh, come on Dad, you can't afford this. It's your life savings.'

'Look son, I'm happy here. Your quest for adventure is infectious. Your enthusiasm is a force. Live your dreams and I will share the adventure with you.'

I didn't know what to say. There was no way he would take it back. It was this gesture that really started the ball rolling.

'A bit slower this time, lad.'

'What do you mean?'

'You usually take about forty minutes, at least forty five today.'

He doesn't miss a trick I thought, smiling to myself.

Turning on the shower, I waited outside holding my hand in the stream of water waiting for it to heat up. My mind was full of thoughts, boats, wrecks and adventure. In the shower the water greeted me as it gushed into my face and through my hair. It ran down my body in little rivers, each one finding a sensitive place, making me tingle all over. Then a new thought flashed into my mind. A sudden excitement quite different now stole my thoughts; a wave of butterflies stirred in my stomach as the girl on the horse rode into my mind's eye.

We had a total of seventeen grand now. It was time to start looking for a boat. The auction date was getting closer, but there were two things that concerned us. Firstly, there wasn't enough money. And secondly, the Loyal class were good, but lacked lifting frames and winches.

'Let's go down the coast to all the ports,' I suggested. 'There are plenty of trawlers getting decommissioned, ex standby boats that have winches. Bloody big ones and their sea keeping qualities are great.'

Billy agreed. 'Let's go then,'

'Wait a minute,' Phil said. I've got a date. I pulled one of those birds last night.'

Billy dead-legged him with his knee. 'You'd only disappoint her,' he said, dragging him to the van. 'Even if we don't find a boat we can have a piss up somewhere different.'

'Yeah, but who's going to drive?' asked Phil.

'You!' was the joint reply.

The first port was Grimsby. There were a few boats there but they were all sidewinders. They worked trawls from the side of boat and had limits to what tonnage they could pull up; and they were all rust tubs.

Silver Bubbles

The next port after a lengthy drive was Great Yarmouth. To save time we asked at the wharf office if there were any boats for sale.

'Aye lad,' the old salt replied. 'There's a few, but only one I would call a boat and that's been seized by the customs for running wacky baccy. The *Sea Gem* she's called.'

'Is there a Customs Office here?'

'Aye, left down the road about a hundred yards.'

'Thanks mate. See ya.'

'Let's look at the boat, if it's been seized we could make them an offer, you never know.'

'Those bastards wouldn't give you the steam off their shit,' Billy replied.

'Well we can only try, can't we?'

We walked down to the harbour. In a corner was the *Sea Gem*.

We rushed closer like school kids. 'Wow! She's a stern dragger,' Phil shouted.

We were looking, intently scanning all around, we could see red tape draped all round the boat and a sheet of paper sealed in plastic tied to the small mast on top of the wheelhouse.

'She's bloody great. How long do you reckon?' Billy asked.

'Got to be at least sixty, maybe seventy foot,' I replied. 'She's in good nick too. Look at the winch. It's at least ten tonne. And look at the stern; it's got a ramp for pulling things up. The stern frame is perfect for pulling heavy stuff up. Christ, we've got to get this!'

'Let's have a look around,' Phil said as he cocked his leg over the rail.

'No, we best not raise false hopes until we've seen the Customs lot.'

After a forced march to the Customs Office we all crowded into a small room. There was a small service-hole. Phil rang the bell. After several seconds the glass door slid open.

'Yes, what can I do for you?'

'I don't believe it!' Phil burst out laughing. 'Snowy White. What the fuck are you doing here?'

A door opened and the man put his arm around Phil. 'Great to see you, pal. You look well.'

'It's these bastards working me too hard.'

Billy and I looked at each other and shrugged in confusion.

'Mike, Steve. Billy, Steve.' We all shook hands.

'Jesus, he's got hands like shovels!' Steve said looking at Billy, who smiled back.

'So, what are you doing here?' Phil asked while laughing.

'A cushy number, I got fed up with the mob. Twelve years and I still got treated like a sprog, so I fucked them off.'

'And I thought you were a twenty-two year Merchant.'

'So, what brings you round here mate?'

'The *Sea Gem*.' Phil looked more serious now.

'That's some little boat. Do you know we found nearly six ton of dope and fags in her fish room?'

'Is she coming up for sale?'

'We've only had one offer from a shipping company. They only want the engine. Apparently it's a Mirlees Blackstone, a big slow revving engine, perfect for one of their coasters. It's got no fishing licence so it's a bit of a white elephant.'

'How much have they offered?' Billy asked.

'I'm sorry. It's not professional to disclose such information.' I looked at Phil then at Billy. There was a long embarrassing silence.

'Ha, that got you all going. Just kidding,' Snowy grinned, 'Thirty-five grand.'

'You're serious!' I looked at him beaming with relief.

He grinned. 'As I said, a trawler with no licence is like a lorry with no trailer, it's bloody useless.'

'Not to us,' Phil said. 'What's the procedure then?'

'Would you chuckle mate.' He put his arm round him. 'It's my job to sell it!'

'Yes!' Phil punched the air. 'The biggest crook the Navy ever had is now a Customs Officer! Do you know this guy must have cost the mob hundreds of thousands?'

'OK, I did a few deals. Do you want to look her over first?'

Phil looked round the door. 'Who's the skirt?'

'That's Kelly, my secretary.'

Billy looked at me. 'I'm sure he bloody smells them.'

Phil grinned at Snowy. 'Have you then?'

'Do you mind? I'm a respected professional,' he said while opening the door. 'Course I have!'

We all laughed.

'I don't believe this.' I said to Billy.

'No I don't either, maybe our luck has changed.'

'Maybe it has, pal. Maybe it has.'

We stood on the deck. 'This is brilliant.' I couldn't contain my excitement 'Look at the winch,' I shouted like an eager kid.

'Where do you want to start lads?' Steve asked, as he unlocked the wheelhouse door.

The winch was central and behind the wheelhouse. There was a door at each side of it leading up into the bridge, which had a large, colour fish finder, sonar, two V.H.F radios, plus a big table for charts.

'What's this, Steve?' I pointed to a black box with a small display.

'That's one of those new GPS sets. It uses satellites to find a position. They're dead accurate, bloody druggies. They can afford the best of every thing.'

There was a master's cabin adjoining the bridge. Below and down several steps there was a mess room, galley and four cabins, two single and two doubles. Another door led to a passageway and the aft deck. Everywhere was fitted out in varnished wood. The bunks had portholes. There was a small washroom with two toilets, two showers and two basins. There was even a small room complete with washing machine and drier.

'This is it, Billy. It's all and more than we could dream of,' I said shaking my head. 'I've not felt this excited for years.'

Steve opened up one of the raised hatches. 'This is the engine room, I think. Yes, feast your eyes on this baby.'

One by one we climbed down the ladder. 'Bloody hell, it looks brand new.' The big engine was gleaming. In fact the whole engine room was immaculate. A workbench, spares in tin lockers and there was a sprinkler system.

'Look at this,' Billy shouted. 'The bloody generator is a six cylinder diesel.'

'Look at this.'

'What is it?' Phil was looking at another engine.

'It's got a sort of pump attached to it.'

'Hell, it's a vacuum pump for sucking up fish. Look, the pipe leads into the fish room.'

We rushed up the ladder like a gang of children.

'Open up this hatch mate,' Phil said with a look of anticipation.

'This is the fish room where we found the dope.' The place was a mess. In the search for drugs all the thermal cladding had been torn away and it was all over the place.

'Shit! Why have they done this?' Phil sighed.

'It doesn't matter, we're not carrying fish. Just look at the size of this. We can get tons of stuff in here.' Billy exclaimed.

'I didn't hear that,' Steve said.

'No, you knob,' Phil said. 'Salvaged gear, he means. You know, tat off the wrecks.'

'Oh, that sort of gear. Hell, upstairs wouldn't look kindly if I agreed a sale with another bunch of druggies. That's great. Do you like her then?'

Panting with excitement I said, 'If you were a girl, I would snog you!'

'Don't forget he was in the Navy,' Billy said with a rare chuckle. 'He might show you the golden rivet if you do that.' We all laughed.

Back in Steve's office Kelly was making a brew for us. Phil was acting as normal. It was as though his nose was attached to a piece of wire that was fixed to Kelly's bum, wherever she walked his stare followed. You could see her panty line. It was obvious she was wearing high-cut, sexy pants, and I must admit she did look nice.

'Well here's the other offer we had, oh dear!' Steve knocked his coffee over it. 'Well, that's a shame. Can't read this now the ink's run and it's the only one.' He screwed the letter up and binned it.

'Cheers mate.' Billy slapped Steve on the shoulder making him bend forward. 'It's good and rare to meet a real person under an official hat.'

Kelly came over to Steve. 'Another coffee, sir?' She smiled then walked to the tea room. She was enjoying all the attention.

'Were you a C.D., Steve?'

'Yeah,' Phil interrupted. 'When he wasn't in the stores pilfering dive gear. No seriously, Steve's a good diver.'

'Cheers mate.' Steve raised his cup. 'Coming from you, that's a real compliment.'

Billy and I looked at each other with surprised grins. 'We'll have to have a chat with Steve, won't we, and find out all about Phil's adventures in the Navy.'

'No fucking chance!' Phil murmured under his breath.

'You're lucky. She would have been sold this time next week. Upstairs asked me to hurry up the sale. They don't like the responsibility and harbour dues.'

'So what's the crack Steve?' I asked.

'Well, you make me an offer, say thirty-six, and she's yours.'

'Couldn't you make it less?' Phil said with a glint in his eye.

'I could mate, but if the other bidder finds out, I'll be in the shit, and you could lose the boat!'

'No he's right,' I said. 'It's still a hell of a bargain.'

I held my hand out to Steve. 'It's a deal.' We shook hands. 'Where's the bank round here?'

'I'll get the paper work sorted,' said Steve. 'If you give us a cheque, you can sail her away by Thursday or Friday next week'.

Billy came with me to the bank. He stopped and turned to me. 'So where the hell are we going to get twenty grand from?'

'Sod it mate. We can't lose this. We could earn twenty grand in one day. We're having it.'

After twenty minutes of grovelling and lying over the phone I came out of the room grinning and waving a bank cheque for thirty-six thousand pounds. 'It's destiny mate. Don't forget all those hours of shivering on muddy riverbanks, while groping among the hypodermic syringes and dead pets.'

'Yeah, good old Len, his money has made all this possible. This calls for a session.'

I withdrew seven hundred in cash - five hundred for Steve, the other two for a meal, piss-up and digs - nice ones this time.

'What have you done?' Billy asked. His voice had a serious ring to it.

'I've secured it with Wood End.'

'I'm not bloody wet behind the ears.' Billy stopped walking.

'OK, calm down. I said they would have the twenty back in two weeks.'

'How can we do that?'

'I don't give a shit. We've got the boat of our dreams. Leave the bank to me. They have security, so if they have to wait a few more weeks, they have to wait.'

'You're a bloody case and a half,' Billy grinned.

'A faint heart never fucked a pig. You must know that by now!'

Back in the office I handed the cheque over and signed some papers.

'Right then,' said Steve. 'I'll send this lot off, it will take a few days. They will sort it out with the Register of Shipping. Yes, that's fine, Coastal Diving. We should be able to release her next week. Oh, don't forget insurance, you can't sail without third party cover. Who's got a ticket?'

'I have.' I showed Steve my Certificate of Competence.

'That's it chaps, all done and dusted. It's Friday night, lets get pissed.'

'We're having a meal. Are you two coming?'

'Bloody right mate,' Steve answered. He looked at Kelly. 'Are you coming?'

'Where?'

'How about the Italian opposite here.'

'Yes, I would like to, but I need to get changed, I'll meet you in the restaurant bar at eight.'

'It's fixed,' said Steve.

'Mike!' Steve shouted. 'Catch.' He threw the boat keys. I caught them with a sideways catch and held them in my fist. I looked out the window at the water. 'Yes, at last we can search for your secrets.'

Billy and I were getting the round in.

'Do you know what that boat is worth, well what it would have cost?'

'I've no idea, a couple of hundred grand I reckon.'

'Yeah and the rest. That engine must be worth a few quid, it's nearly new. This is the luckiest day of my life. Cheers Billy, I've just got to make a call.'

Billy smiled, 'Give Len my best.'

After few minutes I returned.

'What did he say?'

'He's over the moon. He wanted to come down now, but I told him to wait and sail her back with us.'

'I bet he's having a "sundowners" right now. Here's to Len.' We chinked glasses.

'Steve, here mate take this.' I passed the wad to him.

'No way pal, no way.'

'Come on. You've saved us a mint, take it.'

'No. There's no way. I may have saved you money, but I owe my life to this kid,' he pointed with his glass to Phil.

'What happened?' Billy asked while settling into his chair.

'He pulled me out when I was trapped in a wreck. The tide had changed and was running at six knots. There were ten divers and one Rupert. Ignoring orders, Phil was the only one who had the balls to come looking for me. He freed me. When we surfaced it was getting dark and we got carried away from the barge. It was forty minutes before we were picked up. I had two broken ribs and a broken arm, apart from being trapped. Even if I had managed to free myself I wouldn't have survived forty minutes on the surface in the condition I was in. I definitely wouldn't be here if it wasn't for this skinny ugly git! Cheers mate.' He raised his glass to Phil then continued. 'He would have been awarded a medal, but because he upset the officer by making him look the useless prick he was, they hushed it up. The lads know the truth though, and that's what really matters.'

Billy looked strangely proud at Phil. 'Well done lad. So it wasn't the first time eh?' Phil looked embarrassed. Billy rarely gave compliments. I loved it. The team was getting stronger all the time. We were working and almost thinking as one, a successful formula for a good salvage team.

Kelly arrived with a friend. They looked chic in their short skirts and boots. Steve had arranged with Kelly to bring a friend for Phil. He had an idea what was going on and was like a dog with two dicks, making the girls laugh while watching their boobs bounce up and down. He was in his element.

The meal was good. Juicy garlic bread and large prawns for starters, followed by fillet steaks all round. We ordered champagne. It was the least we could do for our new pal, Steve. It's good to be generous with people that aren't greedy, and Steve had proved himself.

'We haven't got digs yet,' Billy pointed out to me.

Steve overheard, and nodded towards Phil, 'We're off back to my pad.' Phil was grinning as though he'd just been let out of Broadmoor.

'Why not stay on our new boat? Its got shore hook-up with mains, there's every thing you need, even a telly-video.' He swigged a full flute of the fizzy bubbly down in one, pulling a face as he struggled with the bubbles. 'Do you know,' Steve said looking hurt, 'I've nicked nothing from that bloody boat.'

Phil shaking his head said, 'I can't believe that.'

'No, straight up mate, I was going to nick it all this weekend. Sod it. Then you arrived out of the blue!'

Phil and Steve climbed into the taxi. As Tina, Phil's new friend climbed in, he pulled her skirt up revealing her bum, nicely complemented by suspenders and thong. Tina giggled and pulled her skirt down while slapping Phil playfully.

'See you in the morning chaps, and don't abuse your five fingered widows,' Phil shouted through a broad smile. The taxi drove off leaving a sudden silence.

'What did he mean?'

'Don't beat our meat too hard.'

'I'll have to slap the lad for that, the cheeky sod!' We stopped walking when we reached the boat and looked at each other. We grinned.

'Get the sleeping bags out the van, I'll open her up.'

The key turned with a neat click. Opening the door I felt for a switch. The small passage lit up. Billy arrived. 'Let's put all the lights on and have a good look round.'

'No, find yourself the best bunk down here and get your head down. There's all tomorrow.'

I awoke. For a second I didn't know where I was. Then a rush of excitement hit me. I jumped up and walked into the bridge. As is traditional, the skipper always has the cabin near the controls, close to the watch keeper. It was high up and had a good view all around. It was just like a small stand-by vessel. Billy came bounding up the steps.

'I've got the shower working. It's electric and works off the genny or the shore link up, so we can shower courtesy of the Customs. It will take a while for the water to get hot though. My cabin is great and it's roomy.' He looked around.

'Hell, it will take weeks to find our way round everything. Look at this gear.' I pointed to the electronics. 'This isn't toy stuff.'

'It will be fun learning. Anyway you're good with electronics.'

'I wonder how Phil got on last night,'

'Well, at least he'll have emptied his sack and won't be sniffing everything that hasn't a dick between its legs.'

'Yeah there is that. I bet the kids will like this.'

'Yeah we might get them working for their pocket money.'

'That would be a first.'

'I can't wait till my Dad sees this, he loves boats.'

'He's got shares in this one.'

I felt a need to reassure Billy that he was a part of all this. 'Hey Billy. Let's get one thing straight. Len gave us the money and I want two grand off you and Phil. It will help get my overdraft down and make you both joint owners of this little ship, all right?'

'OK mate, cheers.' His answer was short but the smile he radiated said it all.

The van pulled into the track. Len was walking Spot two fields away. He changed course and headed back home. We pulled the van under the lean-to, which adjoined the workshop and entered the kitchen.

'Put the kettle on, lad,' Billy said to Phil. I checked the answer-phone.

'Hi love, I'll be home tonight about seven. Put your apron on, we have a guest. Oh, and get some of that nice Chardonnay. Love you.'

Beep. 'Mike, it's Vicki. I need to talk to you about Kris, call me when you get in please.' She sounds a bit unhappy and then a sudden sadness hit me. We were so happy once. True lovers, my first love all those new experiences we shared together. A real pal, now this! I'm so excited, but she and Kris aren't with me to share it.

The drawing pad was on the table. Billy was sketching the deck layout; Phil was looking over Billy's shoulder taking the piss. I waved my head gesticulating to get Phil to stop before Billy saw him.

The door flew open. 'Now then shipmates. I haven't slept all night. What's she like then?' Len had a litre bottle of Captain Morgan in his hand, 'Time for celebrations, shipmates.'

'Wait a minute Dad, it's only early.'

Len looked around. Phil had the glasses out and Billy was rubbing his hands together.

'The ayes have it,' Len said. He unscrewed the lid, dropped it on to the floor then he squashed it with his foot!

'Bloody hell, I've got to prepare a meal tonight.' I made the fatal mistake and asked for a small one.

After unrepeatable verbal abuse, I got the biggest glass.

Peter Fergus

I managed to evict them two hours later. Further abuse followed until Len bailed me out by inviting them for more rum and a game of brag. I watched them staggering down the path, as they continued to shout abuse at me.

I had a cool shower, donned a tracksuit, grabbed my Bergen and headed for the shops on my mountain bike. It was a four-mile ride. I had just straightened myself up after chaining the bike to a fence, when I looked up and straight into the eyes of the girl on the horse. I know I had sweat running down my face and my hair was a mess. I brushed it back and gave her a long friendly smile.

'Hello again,' I said quietly. She blushed up.

'My, you take your fitness seriously.'

'Yeah, sorry, I didn't catch your name.'

'No you didn't,' she paused, 'did you, Mike?' She stared into my eyes for a few seconds, turning her head to one side as if in deep thought, which made me feel strangely vulnerable, then cutely she lowered her head and turned away.

She knows my name I mused as I walked towards the store. As I approached the entrance I caught her reflection in the glass doors. I saw her stop and look back, 'Caught you this time.' I smiled, but suddenly I felt a strange hollow feeling growing inside me, as if I'd just lost something.

Avocado prawns followed by fillet steak in a black pepper and mustard sauce, Chardonnay first, Merlot second. Best wine glasses out. Steak knives, wine in the decanters. I stood looking over the table feeling proud of myself. Hell, I hope they go soon. If I go into the wood to pick some daffs, they're bound to see me and take the piss.

A taxi drove into the track, stopped in the yard and pipped its horn. Phil and Billy staggered towards it and climbed in. As it drove past a naked butt pressed against the window. I had to laugh. It was good to have such mates.

I poured a glass of wine and put a Dire Straits CD on.

Silver Bubbles

I was awoken by a soft kiss. Perfume had filled the room.

'Sorry, I must have nodded off.' Lucy stood smiling with her arms open.

'Come and give me a hug.' I pulled her close. She felt good, small and compact. Looking up I stood back.

'Oh I'm sorry Mike, this is Kim.' A beautiful oriental-looking girl stood smiling.

'Hello Mike I've heard so much about you. It's great to meet you.' She kissed me on each cheek.

'It's nice to meet you,' I replied. 'I hope you're both hungry.'

'Yes,' they said together smiling.

There was a pause. 'Drinks ladies? Champagne?'

'That would be lovely. Yes please.'

I went into the kitchen and I could hear them laughing. Hell, I should have asked Phil round. Then again, he was rat-arsed and would be hard work in such a state, maybe some other time. The bottle gave a loud hiss as I restrained the cork from flying around the room.

'It's a nice place you have Mike,' Kim said as I passed the drinks round.

'Yeah, a bit small, but cosy.'

'I love it here. The privacy is a bonus, oh, what about the boat? How did the auction go?' Lucy asked.

'We didn't bother with the auction, but we have got a boat and it's fantastic. It's everything we wished for. A seventy-foot stern trawler and it's in really good condition. It's brilliant. We're going to do really well with it.' I continued telling Lucy all about the last few days then became aware of Kim's presence and apologised.

'Sorry Kim, I must be boring you.'

'No, no not at all Mike. Lucy has told me about your adventures. It's not every day I meet someone so exciting.'

'What! With all those pilots around and the VIPs you meet?'

'Plastic people most of them.'

There was a pause in the conversation. The CD I had put on caught the girls' attention, well Lucy's. 'What's he singing about, Mike?' she asked with mischief in her eyes.

'Err, it's, err, it's just about him and a friend, you've heard it before.'

'Yes I know, but I've never listened to the lyrics before, quite interesting.' She walked to the Hi Fi and restarted the track. She knew the lyrics. I felt like a naughty boy caught with a girlie magazine as the track played.

'Will you and your friend come around?
Are you and your friend gonna get on down?'

It was a song about a man trying to get his girl to bring her friend around for a ménage-à-trois. The excellent guitar solo completed the song. Lucy grinned while sipping her drink. Her eyes were bright and cheeky.

'Did you hear those words?' she looked over to Kim.

'I couldn't help hearing them. It's a great track don't you think, Mike?'

'I'll put the starters in, on, I mean get them out.' I rushed out the room. I could hear them laughing. The sods! They were winding me up big style.

'Your meal is served, ladies.'

'This looks nice.' Lucy kissed me on the cheek. 'Thanks darling.'

The meal went well. Everything went to plan like a military exercise. I insisted the girls relax while I cleaned up.

The fire was crackling away. The big pile of logs I gathered would last all night. The girls were sat together soaking up the heat.

'Come and sit here.' Lucy patted the gap between them.

'It's a bit tight' I replied.

'We don't mind, do we Kim?'

'Kim smiled, 'Not at all.'

I settled down and sat back, fumbling with my glass of red wine. I could feel the heat from them. Their tight dresses had ridden up revealing their thighs, which were pressing up against mine.

'This is cosy,' Lucy said as she sat back. Her small fingers started drawing imaginary lines on my leg.

'Relax, you're all on edge, my darling.'

'I'm fine, great.' I wasn't. I felt strangely anxious.

Kim turned to me. She was so close her face was just inches away from mine. I smiled. She smiled back, her interrogating eyes flashed around as they scanned my face, which made me a little nervous. Then she got up and walked behind the sofa.

'Relax, Mike,' she said, placing her hands on my shoulders.

'Kim gives really good massages, she was taught professionally,'

'Mike, when did you last have a full massage, a proper one?'

'I, I can't remember.'

'Your muscles need relaxing and soothing, like this. You're all tensed up.'

'I think any man would be sat with you two.'

Her touch was magic. Her small hands were so powerful, reaching every nerve and muscle in my shoulders. I was almost dozing off.

'Is that nice, my love? Kim and I often massage each other. It's so good for you.' I opened my eyes and gave a lazy smile

'You can have one now, if you want. Kim has all the oils.' I was turned on, inquisitive and a bit confused.

'What man could refuse such an offer,' I replied in a low voice.

'Stand up then?' I stood up. Kim moved to the fire with a small bag and placed several little bottles for warming. Then Lucy unbuttoned my shirt, undid my belt and slid my trousers down.

'You're still in shape I see.' She was kneeling and facing the growing bulge in my pants. I remained silent. Then Kim slowly stripped down to her bra and pants, as did Lucy.

'Err...' I was totally stuck for words and must have shown it. Their bodies were heavenly.

'It's so the oil doesn't spoil our dresses, silly.' Lucy giggled while putting a hand to her mouth.

'Lie down here on the towel,' Kim said softly. I quickly lay on my stomach, a little embarrassed. Then Kim poured warm oil over my back and gently rubbed it in.

'This is to relax your muscles, it will tingle slightly.' She stood up then sat astride me, massaging my back in long, strong waves, digging her thumbs deep into my muscles and along my spine. It was gorgeous, but just as nice was the feel of her moving against me. Stop it, I told myself, as I struggled with lusty thoughts, but as I turned my head and rested on my chin I was looking straight at Lucy. She had removed her bra and was rubbing oil over her perfect breasts.

'Is that nice?' she smiled.

'Yeah,' I replied. 'Brilliant.' She was so hot. I couldn't control the lusty tingling that was stirring in my groin and I felt slightly embarrassed. Kim wiped my back with a damp sponge then straddled across me again. Her legs must be wide apart. I could feel her; I was sure she was pressing herself on me, she felt soft and warm. They whispered something then chuckled.

'It's time to turn over now.' Kim breathed teasingly into my ear causing her long black hair to rest on my neck. It felt so soft and personal.

'It's a little bit awkward at the moment.'

'It's all right, we're big girls now,' Lucy opened her eyes wide ordering me

I turned over, my boxers weren't big enough!

'My, we seem to have a problem here.' Lucy grinned. 'We don't need these any more, do we?' she bent down and slowly pulled them down my legs, leaving me fully exposed. It felt so horny.

'My... you are excited.'

'Isn't he just,' Lucy replied, holding me vertical with her small hand. I was laid out like a dog's dinner with my head resting on my hands.

'You've planned this, haven't you?'

Lucy replied in a low husky voice, 'You're not complaining are you?'

'Hell no,' I smiled. I couldn't believe what was happening to me.

'Then shush,' she said putting her finger on my lips.

'As I promised, your turn first.' She looked at Kim, who was slowly removing her bra. Her pants were partly trapped between her legs. She was shaved and looked extremely provocative. Lucy released me.

'Don't you dare move!' She waved her finger at me. 'We're in charge. You move only when we tell you, not before!'

I smiled, nodding. Then Kim stood over me. I felt privileged and honoured as this beautiful woman lowered herself onto me without inhibition. She looked incredibly sexy and I couldn't stop myself from twitching.

'Ah, no twitching either,' Lucy said restraining her laughter.

Kim put her hands on my chest and settled on me causing us both to take a stuttering intake of air. Then she started sliding slowly back and forth.

'This... is a ...groin...massage,' she struggled to say between small gasps then leaned further over. Her expression turned lustfully serious as she quickened her rhythm. 'Oh yes, this is wonderful. Come on Lucy now!' She placed her hands on my hips and raised herself. Lucy held me vertical. Kim let out chorus of feminine whimpers as she found her target.

'Oh yes, this is... so good.' Her small bum began forcibly rising up and down with masterful precision while her beautiful face grimaced with delight.

'Can I move now? She really needs help.' I looked desperately at Lucy.

'No,' she snapped, 'but you can kiss me.' She gave a deep gratifying moan, as I obliged. I couldn't see a thing, but I assumed by the noise they were making that they were caressing each other between jerky attempts to reposition themselves. Then Kim let out a restrained scream. I could feel her throbs building then powerful waves gripped me, each lasting several seconds. I wanted to explode, it felt so good, but my concentration on Lucy held me back. Kim again upped the pace and I felt her whole body shudder repeatedly as she swam in multiple waves of ecstasy. Lucy started whimpering. I could feel her body go rigid as a violent spasm flooded through her; she moaned loudly then flopped onto the rug.

The two beauties lay panting and moaning. I mused over their small, shapely bodies, but I was still rampant. The drink had left me less sensitive downstairs. What a great time for this to happen, I chuckled to myself.

Lucy turned, exposing her secret places as she lay on her side.

'Oh Mike,' she cried as I took her. She was now kneeling with her bum pointing up almost vertical. 'Oh yes,' she screamed out. This time I was in charge. Don't move, eh. I bit my lip to dull the ecstasy while gripping her slim waist.

'The louder you scream the faster I'll go!' I almost laughed aloud hearing myself say that. I was working so fast and hard Lucy was rocking back and forth, jigging around out of control. She was moaning with pleasure. Kim watched intently, she was enjoying the show.

'Oh Mike stop, I can't take any more, oh God, slow down.'

Grinning triumphantly I slowly obeyed and her trembling body collapsed in a heap. I looked over at Kim. She gave me a provocative stare, which felt like a challenge. As I moved over to her she revealed her desire. She was so turned on.

'Oh yes, that's good, 'she sighed. After several minutes Lucy complained.

'Stop teasing, get on with it.'

'No, no. It's so good,' Kim said softly. I increased the pressure to good effect; she panted harder while her beautiful face burned eternally into my mind. I was in true heaven.

'Oh Mike,' she strained. 'Yes, yes.' Then gasped and screwed up her pretty face. So I obliged. Kim's knees were up against her shoulders and her back was arched. It was gorgeous. She felt so good, she was contracting and I could feel throb after throb gripping me. She was again swimming in waves of pleasure. She smiled; rolling her eyes with delight then gave out a long, 'Mmmmm.'

'Go on, Mike, finish it!' Lucy said as she ran her fingers down my spine then whispered into my ear, 'Come on, come on, she wants you to.' That was it. Intense erotic throbs ripped through me. Kim gave out a soft murmur as I exploded in seventh heaven. I was totally lost, pelvis jerking and thrusting uncontrollably between strength-sapping throbs of bliss. 'Bloody hell, I gasped and flopped over on to the towel. My whole body was shining with sweat.

'Was that good?' Lucy asked Kim.

She smiled, 'I'm not too sure, maybe we will have to try again later.'

They both grinned as they slinked to the shower like Greek goddesses.

I just lay amazed, looking at the embers of the fire, which were casting a warm red glow over me; I was smiling from ear to ear.

The sound of the water in the shower combined with the heat and the immense contentment was so relaxing and I fell asleep.

CHAPTER FOUR

I sneaked out and went for a run. It was Sunday and another day closer to boat day. Wow, what a session. It's got to be my best by far. I'll see if I can get Phil round and get the girls to do the massage trick on him. That could be interesting. I stopped at a small bridge where a boy about twelve was throwing a length of orange bailing string into the water. It had a brick tied to it.

'What are you up to?
"Have you lost something?" I enquired.
'Some men have thrown my bike in,' he replied.
'Aren't you from the farm, its Sam isn't it?'
He nodded 'I told them they were trespassing and one of them, a big man with ginger hair, threw my bike in. I think they were poachers, they had a dog with them.'
'The rotten sods! Was it a good bike?'
'Brand new. My mum and dad got me it for my birthday. It's a mountain bike with eighteen gears.'
'Where did they throw it exactly?'
'Around here, but it sort of went that way.' he pointed.
'Yeah, the tide is quite strong. It will have drifted as it sank. I tell you what, we'll get it back for you.'
'How?' he asked while screwing his face up with doubt.

'You come back here at high water. That will be about four hours, say dinnertime. Twelve o'clock, OK?' I smiled. 'We'll get it back, don't you worry. Oh, tell your dad we will be crossing his field in our blue van.'

He nodded, looked at the swirling brown water and then back at me. His expression was full of disbelief.

I called to Spot and continued my run. As I approached home, the smell of bacon drifted down the track. The wind must be from the south, I thought, while looking at the trees swaying in the gentle warm breeze.

After a good breakfast in the company of my gorgeous guests, I called the lads and explained about the bike. Phil had stayed at Billy's. They had gone from my place to the Ship last night and Phil had to be carried out almost unconscious.

'Yeah, they're coming about eleven,' I told Lucy.

'You'll see Phil,' Lucy said to Kim. She raised her eyebrow and smiled.

'What's all this then?'

'Kim saw the picture of you and Phil. You know - the one of you both in Portugal? She thinks he's dishy.'

'What about me? I asked, pushing my bottom lip out.

'I think that's pretty obvious after last night,' she said, grinning.

'Shall I invite him round tonight? Maybe Kim could give him a massage.'

'That would be fun,' Kim said. They grinned like schoolgirls. I felt another excited wave rush through my stomach.

Our van pulled alongside the bridge.

'Hell, the whole family's turned up,' Billy remarked laughing. The mum, dad and his dad were waiting for us. It was the farmer who I'd bought the barn from.

'How you doing, lad?' We all shook hands.

Young Sam was reading the lettering on the van. 'So you're divers are you?'

'Yes son, but this one's still a baby,' Billy said, clipping Phil across the head.

'Don't do that!' Phil shouted in protest.

'What? This?' He slapped poor Phil again.

'Come on, my head's dropping off. Leave it out.'

'Well mate, if you drink with the men you should know the consequences,' I said laughing. 'Do you know the best cure for a hangover?'

He shook his head sadly.

'Here!' Billy threw the band mask at him.

Twenty minutes later Phil left a long smear as he slid down through the mud and reeds, disappearing into the murky water.

'Coms check.'

'Loud and clear. How me?'

'Yeah, you're loud and clear.'

'Roger that.'

'Give me some guides, over.'

'Taking in your slack, stand by.'

'Roger that.'

The watching farmers looked well impressed - especially Sam.

'Face your hose and traverse to your right, over.'

'Understood.' The bubbles moved left in a straight line.

'Stop and move to your left, over.'

The sound of the diver talking and breathing and the noise of the bubbles had young Sam transfixed.

After five minutes Phil was now about thirty feet upstream. 'Yeah, I've got it. Take my slack.'

Billy responded.

'OK, pull me up.'

Billy's large shoulders dragged him effortlessly.

'Whoa! Stop, stop.' Phil shouted.

'Come back?' I asked him.

'OK, you can pull me up now.' Phil appeared, crawling up the muddy bank with the bike and something else.

'What's that?'

'It's a sack. There's something in it. Here, grab it.' He passed it to Billy.

'Probably bloody kittens,' Billy grunted as he took hold of it.

Sam looked at his bike with disappointment.

'Don't worry pal,' Billy said, rubbing his hair. 'It'll be as good as new after a clean-up and a spray with oil.'

Sam wheeled it away and laid it down.

'What have we here?' Billy said shaking the bag up and down. 'Doesn't sound like kittens.' He pulled out his knife and cut the string that tied the bag. 'Well, I'll be!' he said, staring around with a surprised look. He upturned the bag. 'Look at this lot!' Silverware, candlesticks, cutlery and several figurines spilled out amongst the ooze.

'Wow!' I looked at Sam, grinning. 'Sunken treasure.'

The farmer's wife picked up a figurine. 'These were stolen from the Hall months ago. They're worth a bob or two, I can tell you that now. There will be a reward for these, no doubt about it!'

'Well, the insurance company will be well pleased,' said the old farmer. ''Tis them we want to bargain with, tha knows.'

I nudged Billy and whispered, 'Yeah, he'll give them the run around all right. You should have heard him when I negotiated with them for Wood End. Tighter than a duck's arse, he is.'

'It's all fucking foreign to me,' Phil said. 'What are they saying?'

'I'll tell you later,' I replied, still grinning.

'You're in a good mood today,' Billy said as he was coiling the umbilical hose.

'Yeah, juicy Lucy's home isn't she?' Phil said with one leg half out of his dry suit.

I placed one finger on Phil's shoulder and pushed him. With his legs trapped half in his suit, he ended hopping along like a daft lad before falling over. I blew my finger like it was a gun. 'Piece of piss, 'S.A.S."

'Was he a diver in the S.A.S.?' Young Sam asked loudly.

'No lad,' Billy smiled, looking at Phil. 'He means he's as soft as shit!'

Sam grinned as if he was sharing a secret with us. Then his parents came round the van. 'What do we owe you, lad?'

'Nothing. Letting us run on your land is payment enough.'

'Well that's mighty decent of you. Thank you very much; it was a fair way down stream. Doubt we'd have found it with grapnel. If we can help you in any way, we will be glad to return the favour, lad.'

I acknowledged him. 'What will you do about those things we found?'

'I'll leave that to my father, he will deal with it. We will let you know how things go on. Thanks again, lads.'

Back in the yard Phil was helping me wash the mud from the gear. Billy had gone for his Sunday lunch.

'Phil, would you like to come round tonight for something to eat?'

'Wouldn't mind mate, but I don't like being a gooseberry.'

'You wouldn't be. Look.'

Phil looked up and stared without moving as a car pulled into the yard and the girls got out. 'I've died and gone to heaven, tell me I'm not dreaming,' he whispered.

'Hi,' Lucy said with her usual cheeky smile. 'This is Kim. Kim, Phil.'

Phil went to shake her hand. Kim by-passed it and gave him a proper kiss on either cheek, which made him blush profusely.

Not knowing quite what to say, he asked nervously, 'Where - where are you from?'

She smiled then replied, 'Hong Kong originally, but I have lived all over. My dad was in the Air Force.' She turned and walked with Lucy back to the cottage. She walked like a top model.

Phil turned to me. 'My pulse is racing. She's fucking beautiful.'

Kim stopped at the door, turned to Phil and smiled. 'See you later.'

Phil, not so daft, said, 'How does she know I'm coming later?'

'She asked me to invite you.'

'No shit? Right on!' he said with commitment, 'Yes!' then gave the air an uppercut.

'Not so fast, Casanova. They've got class. You better be on your best behaviour.'

'Yeah, of course. Can I use the van? I'll go and get some lobbies from Terry, get changed and be right back. What shall I wear?'

I was tempted to say 'clean pants' but restrained myself. 'Smart, clean and casual,' I replied.

Phil drove off, spinning the tyres on the gravel. While I went to tell Len all about the loot we had found.

A few hours later the van came into the track almost on two wheels. Phil leaped out, looking smart and well groomed. He darted into the back and brought out four cracking lobsters, then rushed them into the kitchen.

'Sorry I'm a bit late, mate. My mum didn't have a big pan. I had to boil them one at a time.'

'You silly sod, there's a stainless boiler in the workshop.'

'Yeah, I know but it knocks the shit out of the generator. We'll have to get a gas one. This should be a good lobster year for us.'

'Fair comment,' I replied, grinning at Phil who had a deadly serious look on his face.

A whiff of expensive perfume filtered into the room. 'Don't you love that?' He paused, sniffing the air. 'The smell of beauty.'

I'd started splitting the lobsters. 'All I can smell is fish, mate. Go through and make us a wet.'

Lucy came through. 'They look good.'

'Not as good as you.'

She kissed me, leaving lipstick on my cheek, and smiled. 'Will you ever get fed up with me?' She put on a sad face.

'Only if you get fed up of me first.'

'No, that was my question. What if Vicki wants you back?'

'She's too proud. Anyway, she wouldn't with you in my life.'

'That's sweet, me in your life.'

'Are you sure about tonight? You know, things might get a bit…err out of hand.'

'Perfectly sure. You know I like Phil, he's a dish. It's only a bit of fun. Do you mind?'

'Hell, no. We're like brothers.'

'Are you sure?'

'One hundred percent,' I replied, then raised my eyebrows. 'What about Kim?'

'After last night she's mad for it. "Uncomplicated sex with hunks," her words. Any way, we have a treat for you.' She placed my hand on her thigh.

'Suspenders,' I swallowed. 'Wow! I've got a twinge.'

'You will have,' she said, walking out. 'Oh yes, lots of them.' I felt like a boy on Christmas Eve.

Phil came in with two drinks. 'How many blokes pull an airhostess with the line, 'Somebody's a lucky bastard?' Do you remember? And you were pissed at the time. I tell everybody about that, no one believes me.'

'It was all in the cyc.'

'What do you mean?'

'The Japs eye,'

'You sod,' he smiled. 'Hey! What's this, a recipe for lobster thermidor, the times you've prepared that?'

'Get lost and put some music on, will you.'

Phil came back in. 'Listen.' He paused as David Bowie's, "My China Girl" burst into life. We listened for a while then he asked, 'Seriously, what do you think my chances are with Kim?'

'Just chill, and be yourself but remember, she is quite shy. Take things slowly. Kim's a great kid, but don't push it and she might get to like you.'

'Yeah, take things easy, that's what I thought. Cheers mate.'

I was biting my lip trying not to laugh. They're going to screw his balls off! I couldn't help myself and I burst out laughing.

'What's so funny?'

'Oh, nothing. I just thought of you hopping around earlier today and falling over.'

'Wasn't that funny,' he said pulling a face and shaking his head as he walked out.

'Hi.' Kim looked me up and down, making me feel slightly nervy. 'Nice bum,' she said, while leaning against the freezer.

'Go on, clear off. I'm involved in a masterpiece here. You're distracting me.' I looked her up and down. 'You could distract anybody.'

'I heard that, Morgan. Are you flirting again?' Lucy popped her head around the corner.

'Morgan as in the rum and that bad pirate?' Kim interrupted.

'Yes,' Lucy said picking up a large knife. 'He's a bad one all right. I'll cut your nuts off, you scallywag.'

'Oh! Sorry,' Len said peering round the door. 'I just popped in for a bit of lobster.' The girls ran through to the living room, giggling like kids.

'Sorry,' Len said again, 'I didn't...'

'Don't be daft. Anyway, how did you know we had lobster?'

'I saw Phil bring them out of the van.'

'Christ, you've got eyes like a bloody seagull.'

'You should close your curtains at night,' he added as he walked to the door with a bowl full of lobster. 'It's eyes like an owl,' he said, winking while turning his head to one side.

Hell, he could have seen everything last night if he was out walking the dog. I went and drew the curtains.

I felt proud that I had excelled myself with the meal and received lots of compliments, which made the effort worthwhile. The drink was flowing steadily, and all eyes flashed around in anticipation as the night matured. Funny tales were exchanged and Phil told joke after joke, but I knew I would have the last laugh.

During a pause in the conservation Kim moved and sat close to Phil. 'What turns you on then, Phil?' she asked. He nearly choked on his drink.

'Err,' he paused, looking at me for help, and then replied, 'What do you mean?' Kim loved the tease. Lucy did too. She was lying on the floor, with her face cupped in her hands like a teenager, swinging her leg up and down, grinning away while watching Phil intently.

'You know, Phil, what makes you really horny?' She looked into his eyes, then at his crotch. 'Down below,' she said softly.

He looked again at me, almost pleading with his eyes.

'Don't look at me pal,' I said, trying to keep a straight face.

Silver Bubbles

'You tell me what turns you on the most and I will tell you what gives me the hots.' Her eyes burned into his as she moved her face inches from his.

'Bloody hell! I thought you were shy.'

'I am, but not here among friends, especially sitting next to a man as nice as you.'

'Is this a wind up or what?' Phil said loudly, looking around while grinning.

'You still haven't answered her,' said Lucy. 'I thought divers were more forward than this.'

'Don't you start.'

'Start what, Phil?' She flashed her eyes.

Kim spoke again. 'If you saw Mike and Lucy having… sex and they didn't see you, would you walk away or watch? Be honest now.' She drew a cross on his chest. 'Cross your heart.'

'What?' He shot his head round to me. 'I…err, you said…'

'Answer her, then.' I'd never seen him so flustered.

'I suppose, yeah… I would watch.'

'You rudie,' Lucy said, pretending to be shocked.

'Well, wouldn't anybody?' Phil said looking desperately around for approval.

'I heard Mike screwing Lucy last night. I watched through a crack in the door. It was so…sexy.'

Phil took a deep breath and swallowed, then looked across at me again. I was getting turned on also. She was totally convincing and had me almost believing her. Lucy was in her element.

Kim continued, 'I had to play with myself, watching them made me so hot and tingly.'

'Come on. This is a bloody wind up isn't it? He's told you to say all this, hasn't he? I…?' Kim stood up and Phil shut up.

'Is this a wind up?' she said while putting her hands behind her. Her dress slid off her trim body into a small pile around her ankles. She too was wearing suspenders.

Phil's jaw dropped. 'Fuck me!' Kim raised her eyebrows and put her hands on her hips. 'I'm dreaming. Please don't wake me up, please. I'll become religious, the Samaritans, I'll go to church, anything! Just don't wake me.'

I shrugged my shoulders while looking at Phil and smiled, 'Some week, mate.' Phil didn't even look at me. His open-mouthed gaze was frozen.

'Yeah, not half,' was his delayed reply. He didn't even blink.

'You still haven't told us yet,' teased Lucy.

He thought for a while. 'Two chic women caressing each other, that's what turns me on.'

'Yes! The penny's dropped.'

'That's a bit naughty, but it's your lucky day today.'

Lucy stripped; leaving just her suspenders on and then removed Kim's bra and pants. They lay down and started caressing each other.

Phil looked at me. 'I'm on fire down below. Meltdown is imminent!'

'Yeah, me too mate! God they're beautiful.'

The girls didn't hear us talking; they were enjoying the show too much. Their moaning grew louder as they reached the pinnacle of pleasure. A few minutes later they both moved like stalking cats towards Phil, each placing one of his hands on their shapely bottoms. He swallowed loudly.

After a few minutes they slinked over to me and did the same. We were both at fever pitch. The girls glided in front of the fire and laid a towel down.

'Right, both of you, lie down here.' We did as we were told. The girls removed our clothes, revealing our interest.

'What a lovely sight, two horny men,' Lucy said. 'Now for a race. The one who wins gets the pussy, OK?'

Silver Bubbles

Kim grabbed Phil.

'And they're off!' Lucy was giving a running commentary. 'And the fat one is looking very shaky; now the long one is throbbing and twitching a lot more.'

Phil couldn't take any more and within seconds he grimaced and then moaned loudly.

I was in hysterics. 'Fucking hell, you nearly hit the ceiling!'

'Yeah, but I won,' he said, grinning from ear to ear.

'I bet you can't do this with yours.' I turned Lucy around and started to give her a portion.

'You sod,' he looked at his semi. 'Seen off again.'

Within less than a minute Phil was alongside me, grinning. Kim drew a sharp breath, as did Phil, and then she dropped her head on to her hands, pointing her bottom almost vertical at him. We continued for a while and the room was full of gasps and soft whimpers.

I rolled Lucy over. Phil copied then I grinned at him, 'Swap.' He looked surprised then smiled.

'Are you sure?'

'Come on mate, you two are always flirting, have a good shake down.'

'Hey, come here,' Lucy whispered to Phil. 'I've fancied you for ages.' She grabbed him, pulling him onto her. 'Come on, ravish me. Give me your best.' Her eyes burned with desire. Phil's face-splitting grin instantly changed into an admiring smile as he ran his hands over her.

I was engrossed with Kim, entangled in an erotic embrace, when I cast a glance over at Lucy. Her legs were spread. She gripped Phil's bottom tightly, pulling him into her with lustful body thrusts. Phil was lifting her; his hands cupped her buttocks while he drove into her incredibly hard and fast. Lucy's encouragement turned to loud gasps, shouts and moans as she succumbed to more intense pleasure.

The session lasted into the early hours, drinking, showering and becoming re-aroused. We were all so turned on; it was nearly light when we eventually fell asleep. In the morning it started all over again. The soapy shower got us at it. The whole weekend was spent drinking, making love and showering! It was an extraordinarily special and unique experience for all of us.

Monday came on the back of Concorde and before we knew it the girls had left for London. Lucy called from the airport to let us know they were safely there. They were on different flights, but Kim wanted to visit again, which was good to hear. Thankfully there were no moral regrets after such a wild weekend.

It seemed dead without them, dull outside and dull inside. Phil and I just sat around drinking water with large pieces of fresh lemon, a sort of detox.

Len walked in. 'Hell, this place is like a morgue. Ah, I know.' He paused shaking his head. 'You can have too much of a good thing and it leaves you empty.'

'Empty! Tell us about it,' Phil said, looking at the floor. 'I feel like I've just walked out from the best ever movie in the world, into a dark rainy street.'

'Go for a run, get some air through your lungs, get some exercise.'

'Exercise, fucking hell, I can't walk.'

'He's right, come on,' I said. 'Let's make an effort.'

'I don't think I've got the strength.'

Ten minutes later we were plodding along at a pathetic pace. The path was narrow and we ran one behind the other.

'Stop bloody farting,' Phil shouted between breaths.

'Hey, what's that?' We stopped. Phil pointed to a stretch of water that leads off the main river, about a hundred metres long. Its southern bank was lined with lush green willow trees.

'It's where the barges used to load grain years ago. There are some kingfishers around here and big pike.'

Phil looked around. 'Sod the kingfishers. I've got an idea. If we dredged this out we could moor *Sea Gem* here? No harbour dues or prying nosy bastards. We could unload here. You could get a truck down that lane, and there are only two bridges to negotiate down the river. You just call them on the phone and book them to lift when you want. The river is deep enough on high tide. She would sit in the mud at low tide and all that fresh water would do her good anyway.'

I stood looking. 'Do you know, you're right. It's a bloody great idea. You really surprise me sometimes!' Phil gave a proud smile.

'But I thought of it yesterday.'

We started running again.

'What a load of bollocks. You had one thing on your mind yesterday,' Phil shouted at me.

'You mean two.' I laughed.

'Who owns it then?'

'Our farmer friend owns it all.' I turned round grinning then tripped on a clump of grass, turning the fall into a forward roll.

'Race you back.' Phil left me scrambling out of the grass.

You cheat.' I cursed as Phil sprinted away.

When we got back, we rang Billy. He agreed with us one hundred percent. Ideas were becoming reality. We spent the remainder of the day resting and watching TV, in-between discussing ideas about the boat and what wrecks to look for first and of course the wild weekend.

The ringing made me slowly wake up. Five minutes later I joined Phil as he was pouring a cup of tea.

'Who was it?'

'It's a construction company working on the oil terminal. They wanted a price for burning out a damaged pile. Apparently a ship has hit and bent it. I feel bloody knackered.' After sipping the tea, I sat back and sighed. 'The last thing we need right now is a black water burning job.'

'Me too. My knob feels like it's been beaten with a rolling pin.' Phil shook his head, 'God, I still can't believe it. Thanks, pal. I never imagined it could be that good. They were so generous to us.' He paused. 'It all feels just like a dream now.'

'You think yours is sore. I've bonked so many times this weekend, my bell-end's bruised purple!'

'They're always that colour, you dick.'

'Yeah, it's great isn't it?' We broke out laughing.

'What did you tell them?'

'Who, the girls?'

'No, the burning job on the jetty.'

'I gave them a day-rate and a fixed price. They might get someone cheaper, but not locally.'

The phone rang. 'Talk of the devil!'

I came back and sat down. 'We've got it, tonight's tide, eleven o'clock, what a bummer. Still, it pays the bills. Start getting the gear loaded, I'll ring Billy Boy.'

After loading the dive and burning gear on to the jetty's work boat the boatman pulled alongside the damaged pile. It was one of hundreds that supported the pier-like jetty that massive tankers moored to. Each pile was welded to the top decking. We had to cut it at bed level, and leave it hanging, for the crane barge to remove. I spoke to the berthing master to confirm a burning permit had been authorised, while the gear was being set up.

'I'll do this one!' Phil shouted over the noise of the tide rushing through the piles. Billy looked at me. He didn't have to say anything.

'Let Billy do it.'

'Why? I can do it, no sweat.'

Silver Bubbles

'I know, but there's only twenty minutes of slack tide, and Billy is the fastest, more experienced burner.'

Billy was kitting up. He looked at Phil with a teasing grin, expecting him to say something, but he didn't bite.

Billy slid over the side, and the coms got louder with gasps of exertion and bubbling sounds as he worked hard to reach the pile. It was a deep-water jetty and the pile had to be cut at bed level, seventy feet! The gasps got more frequent as he tried to descend pulling his breathing hose along with the heavy cutting hose. (An oxygen hose taped to a thick copper cable.)

'This is impossible!' Billy gasped. 'Where's the slack!'

I checked my watch. 'Should be slack now,' I remarked, looking over the side of the boat.

'Bloody hell, pull him out. It's changed without easing at all. Damn it!'

Billy was helped out. He pulled off the band mask quickly; his head was steaming in the cold air like it was on fire.

'Im-fucking-possible,' he blurted, while wiping the sweat off his face. 'No way,'

The old boatman interrupted. 'It's all the fresh coming down the river. Sometimes it does this when it rains hard. No slack at all, like tonight.'

'That's just great and I put in a price for this. No cure no pay. Shit. We could lose out on this bastard, big time. Twelve hours before their bloody crane barge arrives and we're helpless.'

Billy sat exhausted while Phil looked on, lost in silence.

'Bollocks. I know.' I asked the boatman to pull alongside the pile.

'What?' Billy asked.

'Cut a hole in the bugger and I'll get at it from the inside.'

'Don't be bloody daft.' Billy stood up.

'I'll do it.' Phil joined in.

'You shut up,' Billy shouted at Phil.

Phil stepped back almost tripping over the littered deck. 'I -'

'Shut it!' Again Billy snapped.

I was clamping the earth to the pile. 'It's wide enough.' I drew an oval line with chalk and looked at Billy. 'No shit, just cut the bleeder now.'

Billy shook his head in protest to no avail. I got Phil to kit me up, whilst trying to make light of the situation.

The welding generator stopped labouring as the bright flashes abated. Billy levered with a crow bar and the oval patch fell down into the black torrent. It would have been funny in any other situation, as I hopped along the deck with the air hose taped to my ankles.

Billy was really agitated. 'Go in feet first, you daft bastard, or your mask will constantly flood!'

My reply through the coms was loud and clear and ended with an 'off!'

As I slid into the pile, Billy re-checked the air supplies with slow precision. Phil started putting on his standby cylinder.

'Don't bother lad,' Billy said. 'You wouldn't fit in with that on.'

Phil nodded, noticing my bailout bottle on the deck. He looked at Billy. 'Don't fucking ask!' he snapped.

I could just fit into the pile. Rounding my shoulders enabled me to descend, when I pulled them back I was able to wedge myself. Regularly, about twice a minute, I had to clear the constant inflow of water, which was the result of me being upside down. When it reached my nostrils I had to level my head as much as I could and blow the water out of the mask, using the free-flow valve.

On the surface it was Phil's job to carefully feed the hoses making sure they didn't catch the rough opening in the pile. I felt really uneasy as I reached the restriction in the pile. I squeezed myself through like a potholer in the total blackness while thinking this must be where the ship impacted.

'Give me-' I coughed and spluttered then a loud hiss interrupted as I cleared the water from my mask yet again, 'me a depth reading, over.'

'Fifty-five, over.'

I spluttered. 'Roger that.'

Several coughs and curses later, I made bottom. I adjusted myself the best I could then shouted, 'Make it hot.'

Seventy feet above me Billy replied through the comms. 'It's hot,' then disapprovingly threw the knife switch across, causing a blue electrical flash and the welder shuddered and changed its tone.

The welder revved and shook every time I changed the eighteen-inch thermic cutting rod and restarted the cut. Despite the discomfort and danger I got on with the job fine until my elbow felt something. I paused, totally confused, and then slowly felt around. 'Shit, it's twisting.' I pulled myself upward about a foot and cleared my mask. The power was still on, over two hundred amps DC. My fillings were fizzing as they were acting as small anodes and dissolving in the high current. I had to finish the job; I was so close, so I felt down again. I was two-thirds of the way round. What became apparent was that the pile was twisting under extreme load, the weight of the jetty or the impact of the ship. It didn't matter, but if I left it bridged like this they might not be able to pull it away. I carefully lowered the cutting rod until it stopped in the cut, repeating this until it slid past. This was where I had to continue. As I struck the ark I could just see a brownish ball of light. Suddenly there was a mighty bang. I was moving. A big jolt, then I felt something pushing me up the pile. On the surface the whole jetty shook violently. The surface crew, shocked and concerned, called me desperately.

'Mike, Mike, come back, come back.'

'Pull me up,' was my barely audible reply.

Phil pulled the hoses steadily, hand over hand, until they became tight.

'Stand by.' I gurgled. I was at the restriction and trying to approach it the way I had come through. Getting my legs past was easy, only to get stuck at my chest. I tried again and again, but either the lead blocks in my weight vest were wedging me or the pile had bent more. Memories came flashing back. Don't start that shit, I rebuked myself. I can't go down to get out. The pile had shot sideways into its scour wall and stuffed itself with clay. That's what had pushed me six foot up it.

'Pull me now.' I shouted.

Phil pulled as hard as he could. I felt so trapped now, and there was no way back. Billy was pulling with Phil. The tide had risen and the hole was underwater. Just the taught air hose vibrated in the black water.

Five frightening minutes had passed and I was in pain, trapped and wriggling frantically, like an eel to get free. Breathless and breathing heavy in between frantic straining gasps, I tried in vain. I lay panting, scared and angry with myself for being such a reckless dick-head.

'Sod broken ribs, I've got to get out,' I told myself, then shouted, 'Pull me up as hard as you can on three; count now.'

Billy looked at Phil and they nodded, then shouted, 'One, two.'

I was also counting, 'One, two,' I blew out every ounce of air in my lungs. Billy nodded at Phil with relief as the hose came in, the pain I anticipated didn't occur. I must have been stuck at the tightest spot.

The jetty lights looked welcoming as I hung like a bat, my eyes blinking as the water in the mask washed into them.

Sitting on the deck, Phil pulled off the mask. 'You're knackered, you crazy bastard.'

I tried to reply, but just took a deep shaky breath. Billy was coiling hoses and had a real shitty on. He snatched the bit I was stood on, and glared angrily at me.

'What's up with him?'

Before he could reply Billy stormed over. 'I'll tell you what's up. This thoughtless... bastard, this fucking walking liability....'

Phil stood up. 'Hey hold on a minute, he's OK.'

'Put your hands out. Go on, put your hands out.' I looked up at him. 'Go on.'

I held out my hands. They were shaking, out of control and I couldn't stop them. On a closer look Phil saw that I was shaking all over.

'You see.' Billy snapped. 'He's scared himself shitless again - and me! There's taking a risk and there's stupidity. If that pile had closed a fraction more he would still be in there...dead. Where the hell would that have left us?'

'Fucked. We don't know where he left the van keys.' Phil received a mean scowl from Billy.

'It's only because you're such a fat bastard and couldn't fit into the bloody pile.' I grinned, but my lips were trembling and making me look like a cheesy American chat show host. 'He's jealous, that's all. The job is done, we're in profit and we don't have to come back to this shit hole. Hello! Hello, Mr Grumpy? Isn't that right?'

In my heart of hearts I knew Billy was right.

After a shower, Phil poured two large rums. I told him he was welcome anytime. He was good company and our friendship was growing stronger.

Moving towards the flashing red light, hands still a little shaky, I pressed the button on the answer phone.

'Mike, Vicky. Will you please return my calls? I need to talk with you.'

Beep. 'Hi, sex machine, it's me. I'm in the Big Apple, but it's rotten without you. I loved the raunchy weekend. I will call again soon.' The sound of kisses went on until her money ran out. 'When is "soon" with Lucy? Vicki's call niggled me.

I'll have to ring her first thing. I sat down pondering. Then a sudden rush of butterflies stirred in my stomach as I thought about *Sea Gem*. We talked about her while finishing our sundowners. Phil started yawning, so we turned in.

As I snuggled into the pillow I could smell Lucy, which made me smile while drifting off to sleep.

I walked into the kitchen, drying my hair and pressed the ignition button on the gas cooker. Smelling a familiar perfume, I turned with surprise. Vicki was standing near the door.

She stared at my nakedness. 'I'm sorry, the door was open,'

I wrapped the towel around my waist.

'Still in shape, I see.'

'Yeah, you know the job requires it.'

After what seemed like a two-minute pause, Vicki spoke softly. 'I thought I'd pop around before work rather than phone. Kris is, well, he's like you. Nigel is a bit of a conformist and there's a personality clash.'

'The dick hung up on me. What sort of man does that? He's a tosser!' The bang made her jump as I slammed a mug down.

'Look, Mike. I don't want to go through all that again. I know what you think of him. Kris is always comparing him with you and your mates.'

'They're my work colleagues as well as mates. You're even talking like that knob!'

'Mike, you don't have to listen to the arguments. How many press-ups can you do? If you ran two miles you would drop dead with exhaustion. You couldn't hit a punch-bag like Billy. I'm sick of it. He compares everybody against you lot.'

'That's Nigel's problem now.'

'Yes but it's mine as well, Mike.'

'Is he bothering you? I mean, you know?'

'No, no. He's just, well a steady sort of person.'

'Yeah, a fucking anorak!'

She dropped back against the worktop, folding her arms lowering her head. 'We're going away to Nigel's sister for Easter. Will you have Kris? He breaks off school tonight. I did ring several times to ask you.'

'No problem. Is it a cross-stitch convention?'

She stood silent then looked up at me. She looked almost scared, which made me feel hollow inside. I paused in thought. 'Chill, you sod,' I told myself.

'Look, I'm sorry. I'm really sorry for everything.' There was no more sparkle in her eyes. I hated seeing her like this. 'Are you sure you're all right?' I moved closer.

'Of course I am.' Her manner was sad and distant.

I coiled a strand of her hair around my finger. We went back so far, all those nights of passion. She was my first love, a friend who I always trusted. Her smell, her movement was so familiar to me. Deep inside I felt she was still mine. I put my hand on her shoulder.

She turned away and stared at the floor. 'Mike please... don't do this.' She moved towards the door. 'We'll drop him off tonight.'

I noticed a tear in the corner of her eye. It broke free. She wiped it away nervously with the flat of her hand.

'Don't forget this.' I forced a smile and passed the handbag.

'Thanks.' She focussed on the bag, avoiding me as I opened the door. I stood silent, watching her walk to her car and without a glance back she left.

Billy and Phil were replacing the damaged tape on the air hose caused by the sharp edge of the pile. I was in the small office inside the workshop typing the invoice, when a dirty Land Rover pulled into the yard.

'Now then lad,' the old farmer said as he pushed his chest out and looked around. 'You've done us proud.'

Quickly his daughter-in-law pushed in front of him, holding a brown envelope in both hands, closely followed by his son.

'Err, we've had a reward given for that stolen stuff,' he stuttered. 'They have, well they have given us two thousand pounds, lad,' he said proudly. And we are here to give you your share.' He passed the envelope to me.

'Hell that was quick. Thanks. Thanks a lot. It's really good of you, considering the stuff was on your land.'

'You found it doing us a good turn,' the old man butted in. 'It's the right and proper thing to do. You better count it, lad.'

'No, I'm sure-' I was interrupted.

'Count it lad, I insist,'

'OK.' I pulled the wad of notes out and placed piles of one hundred pounds next to each other. 'You've given us too much.'

'Nay lad, two thousand, it's all there.'

'But you said the reward was two thousand.'

'Nay, nay, two thousand pounds apiece.'

'Brilliant.' I smiled at them. 'It's the easiest two grand we've ever made.'

'What goes around comes around, lad,' the old farmer said while holding his braces. He looked around. 'Aye, it's the done thing. The place is looking well, you've done it proud.'

'Thanks,' I replied. 'How did you get paid out so quickly?'

'I told them to double their offer, and pay out instantly or the things would disappear again.'

'Aye, he's had dealings with them before, tha knows,' said his son, grinning.

'Did you know there are badgers living in copse? Yonder copse over there.' He pointed with his stick.

'No, I didn't.'

Silver Bubbles

'Take your lad to see them if you want. Mind you keep low and down wind though. Dusk is best.'

'Thanks, I will. Oh, by the way, Mr Stubbins. You know that stretch of water,' I pointed. 'Where those trees are?'

'Aye lad, the barge cut.'

'Well, we're getting a workboat and wondered if we could moor it there. For a fair rent, of course.'

The son looked at his father. 'Fine by me, lad.'

'Isn't deep tha knows. It's fair silted up.' The old man rubbed his chin.

'We could dredge it out if you wouldn't mind? We would make it worth your while,' I said with a look of anticipation that I couldn't hide.

'Drain dredger's over there.' He waved his stick. In the distance a long-reach digger was working. 'That's my other lad. How deep do you want it?'

'Ten foot would do.'

'Ten foot on low tide, not a problem.'

I couldn't believe our luck. 'How much do you want for doing it?' I asked.

'The silt will do fine on field, let's say, two hundred. Would that suit you lad?'

Billy gave me a discreet nod so I hastily passed the money to him, then asked him about the rent.

'How big is your boat?'

'Sixty foot.'

'Three hundred.' The old man stood bolt upright, 'A year.'

I gave him the money without any consultation. The old man spat on his palm and shook my hand, whilst stuffing the money into his pocket, then he gave me five pounds back.

'What's this for?'

'Money back, lad. It's unlucky not to.'

I shook my head in disbelief.

He touched his cap. 'Oh, by the way, if you get any fish, say a bit of cod, we'd be mighty grateful.'

'No problem at all. Do you like shellfish?'

'Aye, we likes every thing that's natural, lad.'

'I'll drop you some in when we get working.'

'That will be a treat for mother. We'll get that job done lad, be seeing you.' They drove off and into the field towards the distant digger.

'Yes!' we all shouted. Len joined us. When he heard the news he rushed back to his pad for a bottle. He returned complete with glasses, ice and cokes.

'Cheers.' We chinked glasses.

'The biggest problem solved for five hundred smackers,' Phil shouted with a big grin.

Phil and I had been to get building materials. When the barn was converted I had two dormers built into the roof with a view for future expansion. Now was the time and my share of the reward money would pay for it. With Phil staying more regular, and Kris likely to be there a lot more, it was time. Len had offered to do the work. It was going to take the length of the building, and incorporate a shower, small sitting room and a bedroom. It was a sound solution to the lack of space for guests, as well as a permanent retreat for Kris if he needed one.

'Look at this knob doing thirty, holding everybody up. What a dick!' As we followed the car it pulled into the lane. 'Can't this bloke read? It says "PRIVATE" you moron,' I shouted.

The car stopped at the top of the track. The passenger door opened and Kris got out. 'Nigel must have a new car,' I muttered, 'the bastard.'

He got out to lift open the boot and on seeing the van, he froze.

'He looks like he's going to shit himself,' remarked Phil.

I got out of the van. Kris dropped his rucksack and gave me a high five.

'I, I don't want any trouble,' Nigel said, looking over the car like a sniffing hamster, keeping his distance.

I shook my head, and then fixed a gaze on him.

'Dad', Kris broke the ice, 'Come on, leave it, Dad.'

I returned his gaze. I was enjoying watching him squirm. 'I've never given you a good slapping yet, you wife-stealing creep, but there will be a time, and if you hang up on me again when I want to talk to *my* wife, I'll make you clean his room, then beat the crap out of you. Have you got that?'

'Is violence all you know?' he replied nervously.

'No it's not, but it's the only emotion I will ever afford you. So give me Kris's things, turn your boring little car around and fuck off. By the way, the accelerator is on the right. Our postman comes at about nine am, and this is a single track lane!' I brushed past him, putting hand to mouth and coughed. 'Tosser.'

Phil sat in the van bemused as Nigel did a ten-point turn, holding the wheel ten to two.

'How's it going, son?'

'Fine.'

'Is that it?'

'Fine now I'm here, Dad.'

'Granddad's fitting out the loft for us. You will have the best room in the house.'

'Great. Is Lucy coming home soon?'

'She went back on Monday, she'll be back in a couple of weeks, I hope. She's left you a present. It's in your room.'

'Cool.' He started running to the cottage. As he ran I felt proud. He looked good for his age, well built and destined to reach at least six foot. I'd planned to have a good chat with him this weekend.

When we entered the cottage I noticed the dreaded answer phone light was flashing.

'Hi it's Steve, bad news I'm afraid.' My heart sank. 'But not that bad. There's been a delay with paperwork,' there was a long pause... 'You can take her on Wednesday. Ha! I bet that got you going! Sorry for the delay, it's all that Easter crap. Give us a call back. Out.'

'The sod, he always does that.' Phil was standing behind me.

'God, I thought for a second that it was all going to turn into a cruel hoax. Hey that's seven days to prepare the mooring. I hope they can do it in time.'

'Look! The digger's gone.' Phil pointed. 'There it is, moving along the river bank.'

'It can only be going to one place, excellent we'll go for a run in morning and have a look.'

'Dad, Dad,' Kris came running in. 'Look at this, it's brill!' He was holding a flash-looking canvas bag with gold zips. He grinned at us while pulling out a small, hand-held computer game. 'Look at this, and there are ten games. 'It's brill!' he repeated. 'I bet it's the latest thing. Thanks Lucy! She's mega cool.'

He shot out of the door, 'Granddad look at this!' His shouts faded as he ran to show Len his present. I had to laugh. "She's mega cool!' What's he like?'

'She is cool,' Phil said with real meaning,

'Hey, mush. That's my bird you're drooling over.'

'I don't need to drool anymore,' he said with a wry smile.

'Don't get too cocky, pal. I might not invite you the next time they're here.'

'That would be the ultimate cruelty, but even If I was locked away for life, I would still have my memories of the weekend and be able to knock one out. I've been to the land

Silver Bubbles

of dreams.' He gazed upwards then said in a distant manner, 'Not many men visit those heights in an entire lifetime.'

'A bit of a closet romantic, eh?' I smiled. 'There's hope for you yet.'

All the next day Phil worked hard with Len. He never stopped, surprising everybody. He was turning out to be a real asset. Now that he felt part of the family, so to speak, he gave his all. Nothing was a problem and they had the floor laid in one day. Meanwhile, I had some quality time with Kris.

It was eight thirty. Phil was at Len's, chilling out. They had worked relentlessly. No doubt with numerous sundowners! I was getting restless watching crap on the telly. Friday night! What a load of rubbish. I jumped up. 'Fancy some badger stalking, Kris?'

'What, real badgers?'

'Yes, they live in that small strip of wood over there.' I pointed.

'Cool, let's go.'

On our hands and knees we crawled along a hedgerow. A song thrush was singing its heart out high up in an old gnarled oak tree. Panicking blackbirds were darting around. Kris was enjoying it all, looking regularly at me for approval. Entering the small cluster of trees we could hear strange noises.

'There!' Kris whispered loudly. 'Look! Look!' He pointed. Three small badgers were rolling around grunting and mock fighting. The mother was scenting the air, sniffing and blinking. 'The big one has a nose like Spot,' Kris whispered.

A grunt from her sent the small ones scurrying down the set.

'Come on, we don't want to upset them,' I whispered while nodding my head to one side. 'Let's go.' As I slid down the small bank, I looked down noticing a few cigarette stubs dropped on a flattened piece of grass.

Peter Fergus

We walked back to "Wood End" like two victorious white hunters. I stopped walking and caught Kris's attention. 'Smell that, Kris?' I asked.

'What?'

'Take a deep breath through your nose, and tell me what you can smell.'

Kris stood and sniffed in. 'Grass, soil, sweet sort of plant smells.'

'Good, that's good.' I dragged my boot through some wild fennel growing on the ditch edge. 'Smell that.'

'Wow! It smells like liquorice torpedoes!'

'Yes. There's so much in just one field. The sad thing is we're forgetting all this, sat watching telly like clones. Watching stupid soap operas, where drinking and arguing is the preferred way of life. No wonder kids are so bloody confused nowadays. All that shit.'

'Dad, chill out. You sound like Nigel!'

'Hey you, watch it.'

'Race you!' Kris sped off like a whippet.

I shadowed behind making growling noises, which made him giggle and run faster. When we charged into the kitchen, we found Phil. He was swaying from side to side, a pencil behind his ear trying to measure a piece of wood. Kris stood bemused as the tape kept shooting back into itself and Phil strained, pulling faces trying to read the vanished tape.

'Come on mate.' I led him to the bedroom. 'The old man, he's captained you and I bet it won't be the last time.'

In the morning Billy turned up with his son. 'Our young 'un,' as he called him. Kris and Ben disappeared into the woods, while we pondered over records and charts. Phil was still crashed out, but he had worked hard and was spared the indignity of being tipped out of his bed.

'The *Benmachdui*. It's got to be the first, just look at the manifest. Coils of copper wire, tons of them. It was mined fifteen miles offshore and no one really knows where it is, it's a

Silver Bubbles

position approximate. Listen to this.' I pulled out a crumpled page from an Admiralty printout, 'Sunk 1940, tonnage 6,747, length 420, chart symbol 15 meters, fifteen metres, sixty foot max. Fifty minutes bottom time. Three times fifty is nearly three hours. We can recover a lot of tat in that time, even on a big tide. Not every wreck carried valuable cargo, but they all have condensers made of brass and copper. Thick walled copper pipes running the entire length of the hull, to carry high-pressure steam to the deck winches. Gun metal condenser pumps and there's the collectibles. Port holes, bells, whistles, bloody all sorts lost and waiting to be found.'

The boys ran noisily into the room.

'Shoes,' Billy snapped at them while staring at their mud caked trainers.

'No Dad,' Ben shouted. 'There are some men at the badger wood.' I looked sternly at Kris.

'Honest Dad, I was only showing Ben. We got to the old oak tree and saw them digging. What do you think they're doing?'

'The bastards,' Billy jumped up, 'Baiters.'

I called the farmer to make sure it wasn't them. It wasn't, so I called the local police. After a few minutes of explaining the location, I came off the phone.

'Dad, look.' Kris was pointing at a tractor bouncing at speed and approaching the wood.

'Shit, he's by himself. Come on Billy, we have to help him. I turned to the boys. 'Stay with Len and don't follow us. We ran down the track and along the hedge, crawling close to the ground. We clearly heard arguing, and then someone cried out. Billy, being Billy, ran straight in, cursing loudly. I stayed where I was, watching. The farmer's son was on the ground in a ball. He had been beaten and kicked and was lying still. Billy walked up to them. There were three of them in sight. A big ginger haired man with a thick beard was digging furiously while two others stood over the farmer. Billy marched to the two and without a word laid into them. I stood up with intentions of getting the big guy, when suddenly a gunshot rang out.

'The next one's for you.' He jabbed the barrel of the shotgun into Billy's neck. A skinny weasel- featured man gritted his green teeth as he again thrust the barrels into Billy's neck, making round bleeding cuts.

'You think you're hard, do ya? Take this.' He repeated his cruel thrusts. Billy didn't respond. He kept eye contact with the creep. This was unnerving him. The big red-haired man looked across at the other two licking their wounds.

'Get digging, we're nearly there.'

Still hidden behind the grassy bank I was in turmoil, I had one move and it would have to count. Oh no! I cursed as he saw Len on his hands and knees right behind the badger set, holding a cricket bat in his hand.

'Oh shit, you silly old sod,' I said under my breath, I instinctively jumped up shouting, 'OK lads, close in we've got them.'

The weasel pointing the gun at Billy made a fatal mistake. As soon as he took his eyes off him he was on the floor, unconscious. The shotgun butt broke as it smashed the jaw of the one stood alongside the weasel. The other two stood fast holding their spades as weapons. Suddenly Len popped up, giving the man closest to him a crunching smash on the head. The big man swung his spade at Len knocking him over. I was there. I hit him hard on the side of his head then swung a left uppercut into his hairy face. The big man went down like a ton of spuds and then spun in circles in the loose soil, trying to get up. Billy walked over and grabbed his arm and pushed it up his back until there was a sickening crack. The man screamed out in agony. Billy repeated the painful move on his other arm. He then repeated the deed on all of them. Cool and firm like an executioner, ignoring their cries for clemency.

Silver Bubbles

He wiped the blood from his neck and shouted, 'You might get off with this, you scum, but you won't wipe your arses for a month.'

He was shaking with anger, a scary sight. He picked up the weasel-faced creep and stuffed his face into a nettle bed, then picked him off the ground with one hand and hung him on a broken branch like a tailor's dummy.

He shouted into his face, 'You asked me if I was hard.' The creep was sweating with pain. The side of his head had a deep gash where Billy's big fist had impacted. He, like all four of them, had at least one dislocated elbow joint! 'I'm talking to you.'

'I'm sorry,' he mumbled.

Billy walked over to big redhead. Grabbing his hair, he crouched down to him.

'You come here, throw a boy's bike into the river, kill defenceless animals, threaten to shoot me and hit a bloody pensioner. Oh yes, you're really hard.'

Billy went through his pockets. 'Now I know who you are, where you live. If I see you again my family and I will call on you. And you wouldn't like my family. This time you walk away. If there is a next time, you'll all be in wheelchairs. And don't complain, or your van over there, complete with dogs will be given to my travelling friends.'

He marched to the tractor and returned with a rope. Tying them all together he told the farmer to drag them to the side of the lane. He didn't need asking twice.

The local police were confused and couldn't understand why the farmer wouldn't press any charges, and how the poachers had ended up with broken and dislocated arms, when only the farmer's son had been involved. The local gossip heralded him a hero. Who could fend off four men at the same time and tie them up? No statements were taken. Billy's law had worked. The poachers got away, but they paid in a way they understood.

CHAPTER FIVE

The big engine purred as *Sea Gem* rose to meet another swell then gave a slight judder as she pushed powerfully through it. Bright sunlight streamed into the wheelhouse. I sat in the comfortable seat looking at the gauges; she was holding a perfectly straight course on the autopilot. Despite the tranquillity, all of us on board were nervous. This was the first trip and there was so much to learn. Billy had appointed himself chief engineer. He plonked a cook's hat on Phil's head and pushed him into the galley. Len was on deck familiarising himself with the ten-ton winch that stood like a powerful monster, waiting to pull anything attached to it. Kris was learning how to coil rope and tie knots. Everyone was so keen to claim a job, as if to secure a position on board. My thoughts were interrupted with a loud buzz from the intercom. The light marked "galley", was flashing.

'Hello, is that the bridge?'

'Yes,' I replied, not spoiling the game.

'Would the boss like wine or beer with his meal?'

'Wine please, dry white.'

The speakers all over the boat were blaring out, 'Grub up, grub up.' Phil had learned how to operate the intercom system.

Len appeared, smiling. 'Watch change, skipper,' he said tipping his cap.

'Do you know how to steer?' Before Len erupted I was gone, sitting in the cosy mess room. Billy and Kris sat down.

'This ship is so cool Dad. It's brill.'

Phil walked in with a large serving dish and placed it on the table. He lifted the lid. 'Gentlemen, today's dish is Pork a la crème.'

'In English,' groaned Billy.

'Pork in a white wine and cream sauce, Philistine.'

'Philistine, what's that mean?' Billy looked confused, then back at him.

'It means, eat your fill this time. It's Latin.'

'Bullshit more like,' Billy grunted.

Kris interrupted, 'No that's wrong, it means-'

'Kris, that's enough,' I elbowed him. 'Dish it out then!'

'But it doesn't mean that,' Kris tried again.

I changed the subject, saving Phil's arse but was laughing inside. What Phil couldn't do physically to Billy was made up by his intellect. And he was getting bolder the more he got away with it.

'Has this got garlic in it?' Billy grunted.

'Why?' Phil looked disappointed. 'You can't really make this dish without garlic.'

'I don't like garlic.'

'You scoffed all the bloody garlic bread at that Italian.'

Billy winked at Kris. The crack had started.

We had set off early Thursday morning. All of Wednesday was spent pushing buttons, pulling levers, cleaning the fish room out and familiarising ourselves with the running of such a vessel. Fortunately our combined experience was proving effective, even at such an early stage.

'Do you know this GPS is really good? Look, I've entered the latitude and longitude and it's given the course to steer.

Our speed, ten point two knots, and even our estimated time of arrival at the wreck are calculated. Beats all the chart work we did on the trawlers. It's brilliant.'

It was midday. I called a meeting. 'We've got two choices. We either go up the river to our mooring, or try a bit of wrecking. The van can stay with Steve; he will fetch it back when we ring him. There's no diving work on at the moment, so we could get into a bit of wrecking. The latest forecast is good. Force three to four south-westerly. Who says aye?'

Five ayes rang out loudly. It was unanimous.

'We start today.' I stood up, 'The SS *Benmachdui*. I'll punch in the numbers. Billy, you get the inflatable sorted. Phil, sort out the scuba gear. Len, you make up some rope, strops with shackles. You know, different lengths and some light lines for general use. Kris, you help your Granddad.'

The morale was high. I was on a high. After years of planning and researching, it was time to really prove myself.

It was approaching two p.m., one mile to go to the wreck site. A fifty-six pound shot weight, with one hundred foot of half-inch rope attached to it, was ready to mark the wreck. A large orange buoy was tied to the end of the rope. I slowed down to four knots. The colour echo sounder was mapping the seabed. The bottom of its screen showed a thick, dark blue undulating line. This was the seabed. We were looking for what would look like a red lump on the screen, a thick finger-like shape pointing out of the seabed. I watched as the GPS approach countdown decreased. Point four two. Point one two. Point six. Point two, beep, beep zero. 'Now,' I shouted through the intercom.

Billy hurled the weight into the water and it gave a big podush and the line snaked out. Then he threw the buoy after it.

'Right,' I rubbed my hands together. 'We can't be far away now.' Everyone arrived in the wheelhouse, waiting with anticipation. I circled the buoy, each pass getting larger.

Silver Bubbles

Ten minutes, thirty minutes, back and forth we went, still no contact. The pressure was intense. They all depended on me. It was my idea. It was so easy in the pub, now this was for real. I checked the position over and over again. What was I doing wrong? The keen watchers slipped away, not wanting to pressure me further. Only Kris remained.

'Come on Dad, you can find it.' I looked at him stood close to me. 'Can't you?' He moved closer it was the only support he could give.

It had been nearly three hours now. Kris was on the monkey island on top of the wheelhouse with binoculars as if the wreck could be seen. He was scanning the sea like an old salt. Billy was in and out of the engine room whistling merrily, which pissed me off, while Phil fussed around in the galley banging pots and pans for England.

I was gutted and losing confidence. I felt desperate. What am I doing wrong, I kept asking myself. It was after six now; we had been searching for hours. Some bloody maiden voyage this was.

Kris came rushing in. 'Dad, Dad, look over there. There,' he pointed.

I looked through the glasses. 'What have you seen, son?'

'Big white ducks, dad. Flying into the water and crashing. There's loads of them going bonkers.' I looked again. He was right. Gannets were plunging into the water like white darts. Instinctively I steered towards them.

As we got closer you could see flashes of silver boiling on the surface. The sounder screen went solid red. Gannets were diving; small terns were dipping down and snatching the small silver eels. They were sand eels, a massive shoal. We watched the spectacular feeding frenzy, then as quick as it had started, the sea repaired itself and the birds as if by magic disappeared into dots, then melted into the horizon.

'Dad, what's that?' Kris pointed at the sounder. A large finger-like shape was just disappearing from the scrolling screen.

'Get a buoy in, Billy, now!' I shouted, almost knocking Kris out of the way. I pressed the button marked 'Man Overboard' on the GPS, then swung the wheel to make another pass towards the buoy Billy had efficiently thrown in. I steered her up into the tide the same way we had drifted when watching the gannets.

I was looking at the GPS and compass when Kris shouted, 'There it is again, Dad.'

The contact on the sounder was at its peak. I shouted, 'Now!' and a third marker buoy was dispatched, this time right into the wreck. I looked at Kris, 'Well done, son.' Putting my arm around him, I added, 'Well done, first mate.'

We collected the other marker buoys with the sixteen-foot inflatable boat we had put aboard. Kris was driving while Phil pulled up the heavy weights. Billy was getting kitted up to dive. He had to establish a mooring for Sea Gem. The inflatable returned and off-loaded the gear.

Len passed a length of chain with a shackle and about one hundred and twenty feet of thick mooring rope. Billy kitted up with a small scuba set. Holding his fins, he stepped into the boat and shouted in his thick accent, 'OK bud, that way.' He pointed to the buoy.

Phil watched as the white cylinder slipped out of sight. Millions of silver bubbles streamed to the surface, making the sea hiss softly like a living thing. Billy's strong hands pulled him down the line. He focussed on it. It was all he could see. Deeper and deeper he pulled. His breathing became louder, sounding mechanical. The bubbles made alien noises as they escaped from the demand valve held in his mouth. The cold dark water closed all around him. As the light started to fade he reached the chain. Strange and weird shapes grew from the grey seabed. A large round object, the ship's boiler, could just

Silver Bubbles

be recognised. The visibility was poor, about ten feet, but it was good enough to work in. He pulled hard on the mooring rope, his fins pushing the coarse gravel bed into small piles. On the surface Phil threw the buoy into the water and it suddenly moved away as if it had its own propulsion. Billy, by now, had found a large engine. Bow, boilers, engine, he thought to himself as he pulled himself over the boiler which had a big shoal of striped pouting swimming around it. He dropped to the seabed then stopped, looking around.

'Strange' he said to himself. 'Where is the rest of it? He swam away from the boiler only to find sand waves. He returned to the boiler and swam out on a new bearing several times. Still no wreckage could be found - only sand. Looking at his contents gauge he cursed. It read thirty bars, time to surface. He hurriedly tied the chain around a hefty piece of steel, and then slowly surfaced up the line, keeping with the small bubbles to control his ascent. As it became lighter he could see the shape of the small boat and two heads peering down at him.

Sea Gem slid slowly towards the buoy. The tide was running quite strongly now as the eye of the rope was pulled quickly onboard and looped over the starboard aft bollard. She slowly spun in the tide and then settled like a sleeping monster, rising and falling on the gentle swell.

'I'll be buggered!' Billy said shaking his head. 'She must be in two parts, bow, boilers, engine, prop tunnel, stern. I didn't go to the stern. I wanted to fix the mooring to the bow.' The bow with its collision bulkheads is one of the strongest parts of a ship, one of the last to rot and collapse. 'She must be in two pieces.'

I delved into my files. Len stood looking into the radar. He was on watch.

'You sort it out. I'll do some grub,' Phil said. 'Kris, come on, there's work to be done.'

I was buried in papers while Billy went for a shower. It was peaceful almost silent, just the gentle hum of the generator could be heard.

'I've got it.' I made Len jump. 'Its right here, listen. *Benmachdui*. London for Hong Kong, with a general cargo including explosives. And listen to this. Mined 21.12.1941 and dispersed to a depth of thirty-one feet, lying in two parts. Bow and forward section in Decca red 10.63 purple 59.54 and the stern half plus engine & boilers, is some forty to fifty yards away to the west. Those positions aren't accurate. It must have been a Friday afternoon when they surveyed it. She's about half a mile from the position. That's it. Billy's confirmed it. It must be the Ben boat.'

Len smiled, while cleaning his glasses with his handkerchief. 'The sea doesn't give up things easy.' He paused, while looking out into the darkness. Shaking his head he said quietly, 'I still hear the screams and the splashing. Men choking in oil, then the hopeless silence as the cold gripped each man like an iron claw, slowly dragging them down... terrified helpless and alone.'

'Come on Dad.' I stood up.

'I'm OK,' he responded, 'but I owe it to my old shipmates never to forget. Never underestimate the sea.'

'It wasn't the sea to blame, Dad. It's the idiots who start wars.'

Billy sped up the steps. 'This is luxury. The shower is piping hot, just what you need after a dip.'

'I've solved it.'

'What, your infidelity problem?'

'No you dick, look, right here.' I passed him the printout.

'Yes that's it, bang on. The sand waves align with the shore, which is west. I'll get the bow tomorrow, no sweat.'

'Did you see anything shiny?' I asked.

'No I was too busy dashing around but there's loads of lobsters on it.'

Silver Bubbles

'Lobster for tea then eh?'

A crackling, "grub up," blared out from the speaker.

'All right,' Billy shouted down the steps. He looked back at Len. 'They're only down there. Turn that thing off, you plonkers.'

After another well-prepared meal, we quickly turned in. The tide was at six o'clock so a five a.m. start was planned. Len volunteered to do the watch. It would normally have been shared, but it was going to be a three-dive day, so a good sleep was needed.

The three of us were ready to dive, the tide was easing and although it was only six a.m., it was a bright clear day. Each of us had a length of thin 6mm rope and a small lifting bag. When filled with air this would pull the rope to the surface. The task was to spread out and survey as much of the wreck as possible. Wrist-worn dive computers backed by watches would give us the maximum bottom time. We were ready and excited. At seventy feet, at least one hour each was expected, with the dive computers monitoring our depth profiles. The lines would mark off any good bits and assist in a controlled ascent.

On making the bottom Phil went to the stern end. I followed.

Billy took a bearing and finned off into the green void. He was counting his kicks and stopping every ten to check the bearing. 'Where is it?' he said to himself. 'Sixty, seventy, I must have missed it.' He stopped and looked around. The visibility was about twelve feet. He pointed the wrist compass to the North and started finning again. Meanwhile, Phil had found a large hole in the hull and was investigating. I had reached the propeller shaft and was preparing to start searching from there.

Billy stopped at thirty kicks and looked around. He could see bits of debris strewn on the seabed. 'It's got to be close,' he thought. Then a dark shape just a shadow to his left, caught his eye. Swimming slowly towards it, it got darker. 'There's something there,' he thought. It was getting deeper as he entered a large scour. Suddenly out of the gloom appeared a black wall of steel. He took a deep breath as he looked up at this impressive eerie site. Swimming around it, he came upon a large anchor. 'It's the bow' he said to himself. From the small, side glass in his mask he saw movement. He looking around, then up at the wall of silver sand eels. They engulfed him, forming a small cocoon around him. Darting and changing direction like a flock of birds; the movement made him feel dizzy. Then they were gone.

The side of the ship had collapsed. It was lying flat and partly buried in the sand, exposing large voids, remnants of its deep tanks. Some were collapsing. Everything had a greyish brown layer of weed covering it. In places the steel showed distinctive orange patches of rust. Some parts were intact, others just a pile of twisted metal. Fish, large and small darted in and out on his arrival. The bow was pointing up at about forty-five degrees. Its large mooring bollards were still in place. Everything facing south was covered in sea anemones of different colours.

Swimming further, a massive winch came into view. Copper steam pipe was lying all over, some still with large gunmetal valves attached. 'All worth a bob or two' he thought, looking at his computer. Seven minutes left. He secured the rope to the winch and then, using the air gun connected to the breathing regulator's first stage, he inflated the yellow air bag. It didn't take much air before it was shooting up towards the surface. Four minutes left. He swam around the winch. He could see lobsters everywhere. A big one was hiding under a steel plate. He lunged for it, but the lobster shot further back into its lair. Looking around for something to poke at it, he picked up a length of wire and bent the end to make a crude hook. Slowly he pushed the hook behind the lobster's tail then touched it. The lobster hurriedly walked out and turned to see what was behind it, oblivious of Billy. With one minute left, he started his ascent holding the evening meal.

Phil had found me and almost dragged me to a small hole. He then disappeared into it, returning with a coil of fine copper wire about twelve inches round and weighing about forty-pound. He placed it amongst the twenty or so he had got earlier. I gave him a thumb up and made a squeal of approval through my mouthpiece. Then I started to inspect the area.

When everyone safely returned on board, it was difficult to get a word in edgeways.

'Did you see the boilers?'

'Did you see the prop?'

'Just call me Billy the bow!' Billy's voice drowned out everybody else's.

'You found it then?' I asked.

'Top diver, of course I did.'

'Well, what's it like? Any tat?'

'Enough to keep us going for a few days. I saw some gunmetal valves - heaps of copper and piping.'

'We've found some small coils of copper. There are loads of them, look.' Phil passed a coil to him.

'You know what this was used for?'

'What?'

'It's for electric motor windings. We'll get a good price for this, its pure copper.'

'You got the lobby then, Billy?' Kris asked.

'Yeah, it was a sod to get out! It went way back under a steel plate. I had to use a...' He looked around. 'I made this to get the bugger out.' He showed us the crude hook.

I looked with interest. 'Pass it here.'

'Make your own.' Billy put it by his side.

'No, pass it here, you silly sod. It's copper isn't it?'

Billy picked it up. 'So it is.'

I grabbed it. 'This is what we are looking for, copper coils. I don't mean small copper coils. These weigh about a quarter of a ton and are about four feet wide by eighteen inches deep. Did you see any?'

Billy paused. 'I bloody did, I thought they were coils of steel rope! Hell, they were everywhere. Christ, if that is copper down there, we're chuffing laughing.'

'Why didn't you tell us anyway?' Phil asked me.

'If I had told you, everything round you saw would have been copper coils.'

'Who do you think you are a blooming psychologist?'

'No, I just know what bullshitters divers are,' I replied smiling.

It was approaching midday. The weather was holding, a bonus in early May. Phil's marker was left along with Billy's. The mooring had to be moved. Phil carried this out, but he had used his dive time up, so he was changed and on deck duties. I was in first and on the bow in seconds. Phil had secured the mooring to one of the bollards nicely within sight of the coils. I scraped the nearest coil with my knife. It gleamed like gold, causing my breathing to increase with excitement. I returned to the line then surfaced.

'Chuck me some strops. Billy, bring down the winch wire, we're in business.'

With my arms full of strops, I struggled down the line. Billy dragging the inch- thick wire from the winch followed me.

The dive was physical, levering and digging at every coil to pass a strop through its centre. By the end of the dive eighteen coils were connected to the wire. It would the first real test for the deck winch.

'OK, nice and steady.' I signalled to Len, my finger in a winding motion. The big drum slowly turned until the wire running through the heavy block on the aft gantry became bar tight. The wire coiling on the winch started to crackle as it dragged the boat slowly against the tide, until it was straight

Silver Bubbles

up and down. Small waves slapped against the stern causing light salty spray to fill the air.

'Clear the deck everyone.' We all piled up the stairs to the wheelhouse winch controls. The stern dipped slightly as the whole boat shuddered and then she slowly drifted back again, straining on the mooring line.

'We've got something.' The wire was bar tight, but still coming in. 'Here they come,' I said looking at everyone. My face, I was told later, beamed with pure excitement. The coils, dripping and covered in silt, were swinging slowly. Billy passed a thick rope through the main shackle enabling the whole pile to be pulled on deck, using the whipping drum.

When all the strops were removed we saw there were seventeen coils in all.

'That's not bad eh? What a haul,' I shouted. We shook hands and congratulated each other.

There was five hours remaining to fill bottles and get the coils into the fish room. Using the steel boom and the winch, it was possible to lift the coils and lower them into the hold just like a small crane. Within two hours the deck was clear and washed as if the operation had never happened, except for a few scratches.

'Seventeen divided into four, is four and a quarter. Bloody hell! That's four thousand two hundred and fifty quid in one haul,' I shouted.

The next dive was even more rewarding. With three of us diving two lifts were possible and when the visibility returned after each haul, more coils were exposed. We were realizing a dream. But every dream ends, as did this one. This time it was the weather. The forecast was grim, with north-easterly gales imminent and estimated to reach force seven.

'The boat could take it,' I said quietly, 'but it would be too rough to dive and work the winch. Anyway, we've broken our duck and done well considering it's our first trip. And there's the mooring to sort out and we've got to find a buyer for the copper.'

Phil agreed. 'We'll have to say nothing to anybody, especially with all that copper lying exposed on the seabed.'

'It's a good problem though,' said Billy catching the end of our conversation.

Phil being the youngest had to remove the mooring rope, but before he did, I made several passes close to the marker, entering the position in the GPS for our return.

When Phil completed his task he was beaming. Apart from bringing up another two lobsters he claimed to have found a porthole and, in his words, 'I may have seen the ding dong.'

The sea was picking up all the time. No sooner had the inflatable been recovered than a thick bank of dark cumulus cloud moved towards us. The sea changed its mood. Larger white horses sprang from the wave crests, galloping in line as if chasing us back to land.

In the estuary all was calm. The lifting of the bridges down the river had been requested and the tide was flooding. It felt good to be going home even after such a short trip. The boat had performed beyond all expectation.

I pushed the bow into the soft mud, increased the revs, pushing the stern to face the cut, then going slowly astern. *Sea Gem* slipped into her new berth like she belonged there.

'I can see your house from here,' Phil said, grinning.

'It's all right for some,' Billy said.

'Listen to "Woe is me." Billy grabbed Phil's arm before he could finish.

'Kris. Here lad, slap this tart! He's bullied you in the galley throughout the trip. Now it's payback time.' Kris obliged.

'This is for the pots. This is for all that mud. This is for all those spuds.' When Phil was released he shot after Kris, who took a run and jumped on to the grassy bank, giggling out of control, as Phil refused the jump.

Silver Bubbles

The next day Phil got up early to cook the lobsters before we picked up Billy. We took them to the farmer and he was over the moon.

'We can see your boat from here. We'll keep a sharp eye on it for you lad, never fear. Good, lads, aye, fine, lads,' he mumbled looking at the lobsters as we drove off.

We visited lots of scrap yards, but to our disappointment most were taking batteries and rubbish from tramps and travellers. The mention of tons of copper confused them, and we received lots of suspicious stares.

Walking from another "no hope" establishment Billy asked a man who was loading up a lorry with scrap. 'The guy works with his family, they're from the West Riding. He's given me a number to ring.' Billy said on return to the van.

Jonno was pleased to see us again, and poured four large ones from a bottle beneath the bar. We sat in a corner telling him about the trip and what we had found.

'I'll get Sue to drop us back to your place. This calls for a celebration,' Jonno said.

'We can have a wet on the boat, even sleep on her,' Phil added.

'Great idea,' said Jonno. 'It will give me a break from here. I'll get some stuff together.' He hurried off.

Billy was on the phone talking seriously with the scrap dealer for the next five minutes.

'What did he say then?'

'He's dead keen. We couldn't say a lot on the phone though. He's coming here tomorrow, about two. He's got a ten-ton flat bed with a Hiab crane, and contacts with bigger trucks. Yeah, he's keen.'

Stood on the deck of *Sea Gem*, Jonno was unusually lost for words.

'I can't believe this! She's some boat - the winch is bloody massive!'

'Ten ton we've been told,' I said, arms folded, looking around with pride.

'Look at this then.' Billy removed the big, impressive stainless steel padlock from the newly christened scrap hold, and reached for the light switch. Jonno climbed down the steps.

'Bloody hell, all this in three days?'

'Two actually,' I said with a grin.

'Doesn't it smell of the sea?'

'Yeah, I suppose it does. We're used to it now.'

Back on deck and with the lock firmly in place, Jonno got a full-guided tour. He was well impressed.

Out of one of the cool boxes he had brought along, he removed a bottle of rum then a dispensing optic.

'Screw this somewhere out of the way and mark it, 'In case of emergency'.'

'Ideal, we'll put it here.' Billy held it in position. 'All agreed?' he asked.

'All agreed,' Phil said. 'But how long will it last with us lot?'

'Emergencies only,' Jonno repeated himself.

Len and Kris turned up. Kris was still on holiday. Billy's Sue and Ben arrived with lots of picnic food. Things were looking good. Three hours later, I was swaying around looking out of the window.

'This is great,' I slurred. 'That's my house over there and this is our boat.'

'This is like err... our house,' slurred Billy, 'And that's yours int it?'

Phil joined in. 'I can live over there, and (hick) over here. It's like two houses. Yeah, you're right mate.' He put his arm around Billy.

Sue and Jonno sat amused at the conversation.

Silver Bubbles

'Do you know I once stopped drinking for two weeks?'

'What for,' Billy asked, looking at the deck.

'I was getting a gut, so I thought it might get rid of it if I stopped drinking.'

Phil cut in, 'Did you lose any weight?'

'No, did I hell! I just lost fourteen days.'

Phil caught our attention, 'A black piece of tarmac walks into this pub and asks for a drink. He's drinking it when suddenly the door bursts open and a red piece of tarmac kicks over a table, grabs a drink from the bar then storms out. The black tarmac asks the barman what's up with him.'

'Oh, don't take any notice of him,' he replied, 'He's just a cycle-path.'

There was silence then a few sniggers.

'OK you miseries, I'm not going to tell you any more then.'

Sue, Billy's wife said, 'No, go on Phil.' So he started reeling them off, the crack was good.

'I thought you were going to smack that dickhead Nigel the next time you saw him,' Billy said to me.

'Yeah I know, but I talked with Vicki and.... well, she changed my mind.'

Sue looked at me and shook her head. 'You can't love two women at the same time. It doesn't work you know.'

'What do you mean, two women? I don't get you.'

'You still love Vicki.'

'That's enough,' Billy interrupted. 'Stop interfering.' He was getting annoyed at Sue.

Not really noticing Billy at all, I answered while rubbing the back of my neck and looking at the floor. 'I don't know. I was hurt, I still am.' I looked at her, she was a little uncomfortable making contact with my eyes and I broke her stare. 'I loved her for so long it's difficult to just turn off. I've been confused for quite a time now. It's not nice waking up alone when you've been used to having a partner even though it's been almost three years.'

I walked to the aft window and swayed heavily. 'Where did that bloody wave come from?'

Jonno stood up and looked out the window. 'The rivers not got rough has it?' He looked out of the window at the water then froze for a few seconds. Turning sheepishly he looked back at us.

We were in hysterics.

I woke up to the sound of a yellow hammer singing sweetly. 'Where the hell am I this time?' I asked myself. My head was pounding, making me regret drinking too much. 'Oh bollocks, not again,' I murmured quietly as I raised my head off the pillow.

The square observation window overlooking the deck was wide open, and a stiff breeze circled the small cabin. I just lay there, taking deep breaths. The air was thick with pollen from the numerous yellow fields of rape. It smelled sweet. I stretched then pulled the sheets under my chin; slowly drifting back to sleep feeling content as my thumping headache started slowly fading.

'Hands off yer cock and on with your socks.' The thunderous voice of Billy broke the tranquillity, making my head feel like my heart was beating inside it. 'This better be good,' I gasped.

'The scrap man's at the Ship. Jonno's here for us. Come on chop, chop.'

'Hair of the dog, chaps.' Jonno passed us a dodgy looking drink.

'What's this then?' asked Phil with his face screwed up.

'Shut up and drink it, you wuss,' complained Billy. 'Every landlord has his own cure.'

Billy drank it in one. We copied then looked at each other confused.

Silver Bubbles

'Its bloody rum, you sod,' Phil said looking surprised.

'Yeah, but I put an egg in it, you ungrateful tarts,' Jonno protested.

'Get another one in then, boy.' I said to Phil, as we sat down with the scrap men.

After introductions without handshakes, Billy said bluntly, 'We can supply good amounts of general non-ferrous. Will you collect it? Will you pay cash? And what price are you offering?'

'Ah, it all depends on the purity and the level of contamination,' the old man said.

'Bright copper wire and pipe, gunmetal and thick copper wire in quarter ton coils. No shit with it, just copper.'

'How much have you got?'

'At the moment, about four and a half tons of thick wire.'

'We'd have to take a sample, to check the quality, you understand.'

'Yeah, we know.' I said.

'Phil, go and get that wire from the van. You know - some of the thick and thin.'

'Of course if you want cash, you will have to take a drop of fifteen percent on the going rate.'

'Ten percent,' Billy said, looking at the old man, stern faced.

He held Billy's stare for a while then broke into a twitchy smile. 'Don't forget, that's in the hand. No questions asked.'

'Ten percent,' Billy repeated himself.

'Twelve.' The younger of the two replied.

'Forget it then,' Billy said looking at me. 'We'll give Bert a call.'

'OK, OK, ten percent then,' the man said with a sigh.

I looked at them again, 'How do we know that you won't tell every man and his dog what we're up to?'

'Look lad,' the old man said. 'If we offload ten tonne every trip, we make at least nine hundred each time. That's good money for us, a lot better than batteries and drink cans. It wouldn't be in our interest to kill the goose.'

'Point taken,' I said.

Phil returned with the samples. The scrap men left shortly after, promising to ring soon.

I looked at Billy, 'Who the fuck's Bert?'

He tapped his finger on the side of his nose. 'Our young un's teddy bear.'

I opened the door and stood looking around, then walked into the living room and was greeted by the smell of burnt logs. It felt safe and homely. As usual the red light on the phone was flashing. I pressed the button. There was a sound of music but no voice. The silence lasted for a while, then, beep.... 'Hello Mr Morgan. Alistair Smyth calling, Thursday ten a.m. thank you.' Beep... 'It's me. I've had a bad day and want to come home I miss you rotten. It's not fair I need your hugs. Sorry.' Beep... 'It's me again. Sorry for being sad, we had a real bad flight. I should be with you soon, I miss you.' Beep.... Again it was the call with no one talking, just background music so low it was almost indistinguishable. Another beep... 'Could you call the berthing manager from the coal jetty, regarding a diving job?' The machine stopped again. I listened carefully, but still couldn't make out anything from the anonymous recording. It was annoying.

'Could I speak with the berthing manager please?' Billy and Phil burst into the kitchen. 'Shush!' I snapped, while putting my hand over the phone. 'Yes, no problem. What time is the tide? Yes fine, we'll be there. Thank you.'

'Got to be done,' Billy sighed. 'Let's do it.'

The van moved along the long jetty, parallel with the rumbling conveyor that was off-loading the imported coal.

'It's a fucking disgrace. This is what knackered the mines. All this coal is mined using slave labour. Human rights and fair wages mean sweet knack all to the money-sucking bastards. This is the work of thieving killers in high places, who say their prayers out loud. The bastards.'

'So, you don't like them?' asked Phil. He was answered with a nasty stare.

I placed the van as near as I could to the stern of the massive bulk carrier.

'Shit, this coal dust is a foot deep. The gear's going to get blathered; I'll go aboard and make sure everything is shut down. Pass me those diver-warning boards.'

Phil and Billy were kitting up and rigging the gear when I returned.

'Here, take these.' I gave Billy two new serrated kitchen knives. 'I think you'll need them.'

'I guess I'm doing it, then.'

'Yeah, if you can't manage it I'll change you out with Phil.'

'Not a chance,' he grumbled.

After a hard climb down the long ladder, followed by a fifty-foot swim, he disappeared down the huge rudder.

'On the job, over.'

'Roger that Billy. Give us a sit-rep, (situation report) over.'

'Understood. Stand by.' Several minutes later a lot of grunting and cursing could be heard.

'It's like a big round bail of sodding straw. They must have pulled a full coil into the bastard.'

'Understood, mate. Do the best you can. I'll send the lad in if you can't do it.'

'Piss off. Over,' Billy replied bluntly. Phil was relishing the situation.

'Don't laugh now, mate. I can feel rain.' I said putting my hand out. A little later I cursed, 'Shit, it is.'

It fell slowly for a few minutes then the skies opened up. The deep, black dust turned into a clinging paste. The air hose became black, slippery and hard to grip. The goo clung to our boots like mud and painted anything we touched. I started laughing at Phil who was looking more and more like a black and white minstrel. Repeatedly wiping his dripping nose with his sleeve was ensuring good coverage and within five minutes, apart from his mouth and eyes, he was as black as the coal.

'This is sodding useless!' I said, while wiping my face with the now black cloth.

Phil burst out laughing. 'You look like bloody Al Jolson.'

'I wouldn't chuckle mate,' I replied. 'I can't see any taps around here.'

Billy's voice on the coms interrupted us. 'Got ya, you rope faced bastard! That's nearly all of it. Pull it up, over.'

'Roger, stand by.' I jumped out of the van and slid in the goo, falling face first into it.

'Oh shit. Look at the state of me,' I cursed. Phil couldn't talk. He was bouncing up and down like he had been knifed in his stomach.

'It's not funny,' I looked while shouting, creasing Phil even more as I waddled to the mooring rope.

'All done, pull me out of this shit hole.'

My finger slipped repeatedly off the switch on the coms box. 'Say again, over.'

'I've sorted it, pull me up.'

'Roger that I'm taking in your slack now.'

Phil was still laughing and shouted across. 'He thinks that's a shit hole. Wait till he gets up here!'

Billy was helped out of the water and then sat down on a large bollard. Taking his Kirby band mask off he did what every diver does, and wiped his face with his hand. Phil squealed like a girl, trying not to laugh. Billy was looking around like Rocky Racoon; he had smeared a thick, black line across his face. He looked at his hands, looked up and around

Silver Bubbles

then shouted in his heavy Yorkshire accent, 'Hell! I've surfaced in fucking Bradford!'

Helpless laughter followed for a while and then the harsh reality that we were in one hell of a mess took over.

'It'll take weeks to clean this gear.'

'And us,' Billy added.

Back in the yard with the help of Len, Ben and Kris, the dive gear was looking as it should look. But even after several good scrubbings, all three of us still looked strangely off-colour, almost grey in appearance.

'I hope you charge them for all this inconvenience,' Billy said, after removing his finger out of his ear and checking it for coal dust.

'I thought you would be used to all this shit,' I said.

'It's a lot finer than our stuff. Fucking cheap imports!' he cursed.

CHAPTER SIX

'Mike, Jonno's on the phone.'

When I returned it was obvious I was concerned.

'Is it bad news?' Phil asked.

'Someone in the pub said there's a dive boat in the dock from up North, and there are rumours about divers and salvage.'

'Hell, not now.' Phil looked at us both. 'We, we've just got started. Shit!' He cursed loudly and threw the rag he was holding onto the floor.

'Don't lose your rag, cock!' Billy squeezed his arm looking down at the rag.

'This isn't the time for jokes,' I said with a worried look. 'We've left all that copper exposed. Any idiot could find it.'

In the Ship we asked Jonno over and over again what was said then headed for the dock. Parking the van out of sight, we walked along the dockside, passing several large standby vessels that were awaiting orders.

'There it is.' Phil pointed to a grey fishing boat that was about sixty-five foot long. 'That must be it!'

'Yeah, the bastards,' Billy whispered.

'Why are you whispering?' Phil looked at Billy.

'We need to infiltrate,' I interrupted. 'I'm going to suss them out. You stay out of the way. I won't be long.'

Silver Bubbles

Leaving them arguing about what was and wasn't a whisper, I walked nonchalantly towards the grey intruder. *Stormdrift* was carved into the bow.

'Hello, anyone aboard? Hello?' I shouted louder.

A young man climbed out of the hold and rested his arms on the combing. 'What can I do for you?' he answered in a light Scottish accent.

'I wondered if you had any jobs, deck work or diving. I've got tickets and I'm all in date.'

He climbed out and stood on the deck. 'Come aboard,' he said, offering his hand. 'Jamie Ferguson.'

'Mike Morgan. How do you do.' We shook hands.

'I may have a bit of work,' he said. He was about twenty something and quite well spoken. 'My dad sailed her down with me, but he's not too well and had to go back home. I could do with a hand. I've got a charter, some divers from Liverpool. I met them at Scapa Flow. That's where we're from.'

Christ! I thought. They must be wreck divers.

'They gave me good money to come here and take them somewhere offshore, but I don't know where yet.'

He seemed honest enough. 'Do you do charters then?'

'Yes, as well as scallop diving.'

'Wow. Scallops, I love them.' I stared into the water then looked up, partly squinting in the sun. 'Is there any chance of a bit of work then?'

'Well, to be honest I could do with a hand. You said you've got a ticket?'

'Yeah, I used to fish out of here.'

He thought for a while then looked at me. 'I can't pay a lot.'

I shrugged. 'I'm just kicking my heels at the moment. Anything is better than nothing, and I don't want to go back fishing,'

'Thirty pounds a day, that's all I could pay.'

'Yeah, that's OK. As I said, anything is better than nothing.'

'You're on,' Jamie said, holding out his hand.

'Thanks a lot. When are you thinking of sailing? And how long will it be for?'

'I'm sorry, they're coming in the morning. It should be about two or three, possibly four days. Could you still make it at such short notice?'

'Is eight o'clock OK?'

'Yes fine, I'll see you at eight then.'

I hurried back to the van and told them everything.

'Bloody Scousers, anybody but Scousers,' Billy moaned. 'They'll have to chain everything down round here.'

I had an early night but couldn't sleep well. I was almost watching every hour tick slowly by. My mind was active and thoughts were running away with themselves. Eight o'clock on the dot the next morning, I threw my kit bag onto the boat, and then followed it.

A voice from the galley shouted, 'Would you like a bacon roll?'

'Yeah great, thanks.'

We chatted about diving and fishing while I was shown around the boat. It was quite old; its worn wooden frames were testimony to that. It had an old, eight-cylinder Gardener engine and a small deck-winch, hardly a salvage boat. Maybe the Scousers were just using it for reconnaissance. That would mean they knew of something already. Still, I would soon find out. Later into the morning Jamie asked me to look after things, while he went to get some last minute stores.

I stood in the wheelhouse looking around. There was a St. Christopher taped to a photo of a pretty, auburn-haired woman holding a little girl. 'Love you, my darling Jamie. Take good care. Love Katrina.' was written on the back. A pad with bearings and buoy names jotted on it was positioned next to the wheel. I smiled. The kid's got balls. He's come all this way to what must feel like a different country, to try and make some money. I instantly liked him but also felt sorry for him in a way. People from where he came from still had decent values and were trusting. God knows how he's got mixed up with a gang of Scousers.

It was dusk when a black transit van pulled up. Jamie had gone to phone his wife. A tall, burly figure got out of the van and slid open the side door. Two more men got out and stood discussing something. The driver walked over to me.

'Are you Jamie?' he asked, in a rough Scouse accent.

'No he's...'

'Who the fuck are you then?' he interrupted rudely.

'I work for him. I'm the deckhand.' Without a word he turned and walked back to the van.

What an ignorant prick, I thought.

The other two men stepped onto the boat without asking, carrying two large bags. 'Where can we put these?'

'Down there in the hold,' I pointed.

They brushed past me. The driver brought two more bags.

'Have you got any dive bottles?' I asked.

They didn't answer me, so I retreated into the wheelhouse. 'Sod you too,' I said aloud to myself.

When Jamie returned, they were putting the last of their bags down the hold. Jamie spoke to the driver then came into the wheelhouse.

'I don't understand it. They're not the divers I had on board.' His face showed confusion. 'Apparently Paul couldn't make it, but the trip's still on.'

'Paul was the kid you met at Scapa?'

'Yeah, but he hasn't come with them.'

'Where are we going?'

'He didn't say but there are more of them coming later.'

I looked out through the glass, then at Jamie. 'How many more?'

'He didn't say.'

'Doesn't say much, does he?'

They boarded and disappeared down the hold. 'I'll ask them if they want a drink.' I walked over and looked down at them.

The driver turned surprised and shouted. 'What?'

'I just thought you might want a brew.'

'No!' was his abrupt reply. I noticed them sliding one of the bags from my view.

'Please yourself,' I replied and returned to the wheelhouse.

About two hours later a big Merc. pulled up and one man got out. Looking all around he signalled to the car's occupants, then two men carrying smaller bags dashed to the boat and joined the rest.

'How many is that now?'

'Five,' I said. 'Wait, there's another.'

A sixth man entered the hold. 'They must be having a party down there,' I smiled at Jamie. He stood staring for a while and then turned to me. His youthful face bore a helpless look.

A few minutes later, two of them left and the vehicles drove off. The one we had nicknamed 'the driver' came to the wheelhouse. The poor light emphasised several scars on his face.

'When can we piss off out of here?'

Jamie looked at me. 'In about one hour for the first pen out of the dock,' I said.

'I didn't ask you,' he said, staring at me aggressively. He's provoking me for a response I thought carefully. 'Sorry mate, I thought you were asking me.'

'Yes, about an hour,' Jamie repeated nervously. 'Where are we bound?'

'To sea for now,' he said, while looking all around the wheelhouse and then he walked back to the hold.

'They… they were really nice on the phone. Talking about diving and you know… just normal. I wonder why they're behaving like they are now?'

I looked at him. 'Don't worry mate. When we're at sea and the sun is shining they'll chill out, I'm sure.'

'Do you think so?'

'Yeah I'm sure. You had better call the dock master and tell him we're leaving.'

I walked into the galley, which was at the rear of the wheelhouse, clenching my fists with anxiety. Sailing with those thugs was the last thing I wanted to do, but I had to find out what they were up to. It was obviously something dodgy the way they were behaving.

Leaving the Estuary and past the headland I last saw on a much happier occasion, one of the passengers, or 'the gang' as we now called them, came out of the hatch and walked towards the us.

'Have you got any food?' he asked smiling, while looking around anxiously. A cold chill ran down my spine on hearing his strong Irish accent.

'I'll sort some out,' Jamie replied, still trying to please. The man turned saying nothing. Walking back to the hold he looked back at me, smiling and nodding to himself.

'Mike, are you OK?'

'Sorry, yeah, I'm fine.' I had been thinking back to the early seventies. Falls Road, Ballymurphy, Andy Town, Crossmaglen. It was hard in the Paras in the early seventies, and that accent had brought it chillingly back.

'Irish and Scousers, it's not a good mix you know.'

'Why don't they like you? They don't even know you.' I looked at Jamie who was holding a partly peeled spud, which was dripping with water.

'I'm not in their plan, they distrust me.' I smiled at him and raised my voice, 'Let's hope I'm wrong, mate.' I turned my attention to the compass. Out of the corner of my eye I saw the picture of Jamie's family. This could be a rough one, I thought as the bow cut into a big swell, and I doubt it will be because of the weather.

We had been steaming at seven knots for one hour. The sun was up and the weather looked fair. The driver and the small Irish guy came over to the wheelhouse. I looked at the compass avoiding any eye contact. The driver put a piece of paper on the chart space.

'Here, steer on this bearing.' The paper had written on it, one hundred and twenty degrees.

I played dumb and said, 'Aye, aye' then he changed course.

'Are you diving today?' Jamie asked enthusiastically.

'No.'

'Why not? It's going to be a nice day.'

'Listen Jock, get this in your daft head, you've been paid half up front. You're ours now. If you want the rest, shut the fuck up and stop sticking your nose in our business.'

'Sorry, I...'

'You will be if you don't shut the fuck up right now. Just do the cooking or whatever you do.'

His manner, like his accent, was intimidating. The Irish man was burning a hole in my back, waiting for a response. He was wearing an off-white woollen jersey, which reflected in the window. I could smell whiskey on his breath as he said to the driver, 'Watch this one, I don't trust him.' He remained staring at me. He and his reflection had me trapped. I could see him smiling sadistically while shuffling nervously. Then after what felt like an eternity he walked back to the hold, and as he crouched to climb down the ladder, the wind rippled and lifted his ill-fitting garment revealing a Browning pistol tucked into his belt. He looked at the pistol, then at me. Smiling he pointed his finger, mimicking a gun being shot. I felt scared, like I was a schoolboy again and being forced to fight a big bully at home time.

Silver Bubbles

'I'll take them the food.' Jamie looked at me for approval.

'No! Just shout to them. Don't go near that hatch. We're in deep shit, Jamie and I mean deep. Just say nothing and do as they ask.' I looked at the compass and turned the wheel a little. 'Please, just trust me.'

Jamie looked scared. He was anxiously looking around.

'Just chill out, kid and stay calm. They'll probably be gone soon.'

'How can I stay calm with a boat full of thugs?' Terrorists would be more apt, I thought.

Later into the morning all four of our now unwanted guests climbed out of the hold and walked about the deck. They looked on edge, constantly smoking and passing a bottle around. The Irish man with the pistol was talking to a large, bearded man who I thought looked like Pavarotti. The conversation was getting heated. Suddenly the big man grabbed his jumper near his throat and swung him violently sideways, making him fall into the hold with a loud thud, which reverberated throughout the boat. I lowered my head pretending not to have seen anything.

'Did you see that?' Jamie almost shouted.

'Keep it down, for Christ's sake! Remember, just ignore everything!'

The big man was now shouting at the driver. He looked scared and was holding his hands up, trying to console the enraged hulk. As things calmed down the big man moved uncomfortably towards us, grabbing and holding any support he could reach.

'Stay in the galley and look occupied,' I snapped at Jamie.

'Skipper, have you got radar?'

'Yeah, sure it's here.' I tapped it.

He squeezed passed me. He was breathing heavily as fat men do and perspiring. 'How far can you see with this?'

'About ten miles. That's with a fairly large target.'

'Are there any boats within ten miles?'

'Not at the moment.'

'Thank you.'

He stared at the screen, then at the boat's instruments, squinting as he thought. 'Can you give me our position?'

I looked at the Decca set. 'Yeah, give me a few minutes?' Only the sound of the sea washing past the boat and the big man's breathing broke the uncanny silence.

'There.' I pointed to the cross on the chart. 'Two miles south-east of that gas rig.' I looked at the radar and pointed. 'That's it, there.'

The man looked at the chart, fumbled in his pocket and then produced a piece of crumpled paper, which was limp from his body heat. He struggled to unfold it.

'The Race Bank Buoy, where is that in relation to us?' he asked frowning.

I looked at the chart and pointed it out.

'How far is that?'

'About seven miles, one and half hours away, we're pushing a big tide.'

'Good man. Take us there.' He put his hand on my shoulder. 'And thank you.' He squeezed past and went back into the hold. I stared at the radar. There it was again, the small occasional blip that was maintaining the same distance abeam of us.

'He's all right,' Jamie said with a look of hope. 'He's got manners.'

'Manners make a man, eh? Well I don't think so in this case, mate.'

Just over one hour later a new blip appeared on the radar screen. I had been thinking hard, wondering if it was to do with drugs. Scousers maybe, but where did the Irish tie in? It wasn't rocket science. A Mick with a pistol teamed up with

Silver Bubbles

Scousers and Liverpool the gateway to Ireland. But the East Coast, what did they want here?

Billy, Len and Phil were sitting in the kitchen.

'We shouldn't have let him go,' Len said quietly. 'One of us should have gone with him.'

Phil added, 'The bloody weather's settled down, we could have been at sea ourselves'.

'Phil! If we had gone out to sea and those Scousers had gone too, we could have been sussed out "just like that". It would have put everything at risk. You know what Mike says. If there's one percent of the job in doubt, find it and eliminate it. He's probably having a laugh watching those idiots fighting over colour-matching snorkels. And he'll be having a good rest. Anyway, at least we'll find out what they're up to and if I know Mike, he'll discreetly dishearten and discourage them quite efficiently.'

'What time is the lorry coming?'

'Three thirty.'

'We better get going then.'

A little later the scrap man arrived with a large sided tipper, and parked alongside *Sea Gem*. It was easy to load the coils using the boat's derrick. Len's years of experience in the Merchant Navy was proving invaluable and teaching them a thing or two. With all the coils loaded, the lorry left, followed by Billy and Phil in the van. Len stayed on board washing down the deck and tidying things up. When everything was shipshape he went into the wheelhouse and stood proudly with his hands on his hips like a sea captain. Looking to the north-west he could see the wood and to its edge, Wood End. He smiled feeling proud of what they had achieved. Then the bottle of rum caught his eye, with its enduring label depicting a dashing pirate, standing bravely as if guiding the bottle's dark contents. 'In case of emergency only. Fiddle-faddle,' he said to himself as he pressed a glass under the optic.

'There you are!'

Len startled, leaned forward. 'I...I must have nodded off. This chair's so comfy.'

Billy looked at the bottle of rum, its level was now even with the pirate's waist. He smiled. 'You couldn't wait could you, you old salt. Feast your eyes on this!' He pulled a large, brown envelope out of his jacket and emptied its contents onto the chart table.

'How much is there?' Len asked while lowering himself out off the chair.

Phil shouted excitedly, 'Over five-and-a-half sodding grand!'

Len grinned then said, 'I wish Mike was here.'

Billy picked up a glass and replied, 'I don't suppose he would object to us celebrating.'

Len shook his head 'No, we shouldn't. No, no... oh, go on then!'

'RACE BANK', could just be made out on the lone red warning buoy, despite its heavy covering of white bird droppings.

I walked towards the hold. The fat guy was sitting talking to the thin tall man dressed in a once expensive suit. The Mick with the gun was lying on a pile of rope asleep, with a near empty whiskey bottle by his side. The driver turned his head and looked up at me. His eyes showed no hint of feeling.

'We're at the buoy,' I shouted and then returned to the wheelhouse.

Jamie was in the doorway. His hands were clenched together. 'What do you think they're going to do?' He had accepted me, and appeared relieved that I was taking charge of things.

'Well, I don't think they've come all this way to paint the fucking buoy!' I replied sarcastically, instantly regretting my cruel answer. Jamie didn't reply.

The big man squeezed into the wheelhouse again. 'We're meeting some colleagues,' he looked at his watch, 'several hours ago!' he snapped. Then he stood silent holding onto the chart space as the boat wallowed in the swell.

'Are they from Holland?'

He turned looking at me through squinted eyes. 'Why do you ask?'

'Don't forget we're BST here. That would make us an hour or so earlier.'

'Of course, how stupid' He looked embarrassed then left. I had mixed feelings about him. He spoke well and had a sort of authoritative manner. He dealt with the Mick in no uncertain terms, and didn't really seem to fit in but I know from experience that the old saying 'never judge a book by its cover' is true. I needed some space so went out on deck and climbed the ladder at the rear of the wheelhouse.

Sitting on a buoyancy aid I asked myself, 'What the hell I am doing here?' I rested my chin in my hands. If Jonno had forgotten to mention this bloody boat I would be at home now, it was no threat to us at all. A seagull flew past and turned its head. I'm sure it glanced at me. I wish I could fly out of here, I pondered as I gazed at the shimmering horizon. Then my thoughts turned to Jamie, his wife and daughter. If I wasn't here things might go bad for him. What am I thinking? Things still could.

Through the galley vent came the smell of food. Poor Jamie was cooking meals like a top chef. It's strange how men react differently in scary circumstances. Then my thoughts drifted to the time I was serving time in the Military Corrective Training Centre at Colchester. 'A' wing was a corrugated iron Nissan hut with forty or so Army, Navy and Air Force reprobates, each trying to be at the top of the pecking order. It was like a big school, only they hit harder and didn't know or care when to stop. After being marched, marking time like an Irish jig, to my bed, complete with tin locker, I stood sensing the seventy-eight desperate eyes looking at me. A stocky youth in a camouflage suit walked up to me.

'Hey super duper paratrooper, bull these boots for me.' He threw his boots on my bed then walked swanking back to his. I noticed a look of disappointment all around. This jerk was a bully and the arrival of a member of the notorious 'Two Para' would surely sort him out.

I could sense, almost feel the disappointment, as I picked up the boots and started bulling them, making small circles with a duster, until they shone like ebony. When the boots were finished I walked down the aisle with them. You could have heard a pin drop as I said 'I've done them.' The bully who was lying on his bed sat up smiling. Before he could get a word out I swung the boots into his face so hard that he was knocked to the floor. I dragged the creep up and into the aisle and shouted. 'Does anyone want a bit of payback?

After five days in hospital he never bullied anyone again in the MCTC.

I had to do something then and I had a gut feeling that I might have to reluctantly do something here if these crazy buggers kicked off.

'What the fuck are you doing up there? You're supposed to be steering the boat.'

The small Irish guy, now with a big lump on the side of his face, stood staring at me.

'There's the buoy,' I pointed. 'Or do you want to go somewhere else?'

'The radar isn't working properly and your man's seasick!' he replied spitefully.

As I entered the wheelhouse the fat man was wildly pressing the radar controls.

'Sort this out,' he shouted. 'Does anyone on this abysmal vessel know how to operate the equipment?'

I was right. Never judge a book by its cover. The man was obviously a schizophrenic. He was bright red and panting like a fat dog trapped in a car. I glanced into the galley. Jamie was holding a piece of kitchen roll to his nose; it was stained blood red. Above his eye was a deep cut. It's started, I thought. As long as they need us, we're safe. I went to the radar and reset it.

'There's a boat coming towards us,' I almost shouted, pointing out of the window.

'There, look over there.' They rushed out. I went to Jamie.

'Are you OK, mate?'

'My dad always does the radar.' I bent down to him. His lips were swollen. They must have hit him with a pistol or something. He had a blue bruise surrounding the gash on his head.

'I pressed the wrong button and it went off. The man, you know the driving man, just hit me and the big fat man went mad and kicked me. I didn't do anything wrong.'

'Just stay there and say nothing, OK?' He nodded, causing tears to break and mix with blood as they ran down his cheeks.

I returned to the wheel. I need payback, I muttered to myself through gritted teeth; my body was tensed up with anger and pumped with adrenalin.

A coaster with the name *ALEX* painted over its original raised letters, of about eight hundred tons, slowed, and then drifted with the tide. The fat man, now composed, filled the doorway.

'Can you go alongside, please?'

I stared coldly at him for a second, gesturing my disapproval, then swung the boat round, slowly approaching the coaster upwind. The big orange fenders squeaked objections as the rusty beige hull squashed them. I stood at the wheel, scared but curious.

A man in a blue boiler suit greeted the fat man and then they disappeared out of sight. Then the Irish man with the gun suddenly appeared at the door, staring at me.

'Do you fancy a go then?' I said nothing, my mind spun, but no answers came to me.

'Do you fancy a go then?' he said again with more aggression in his tone.

I turned looking at him. He was beckoning me, both his hands out. I had to do something. It was against all that I stood for. So I quickly grabbed him by the throat pinning him to the doorframe, my hand was choking him. He struggled to get my hand off, while reaching for his gun at the same time.

'Do I fancy a go at what? That gun you've got nestled between your tiny balls?' I spoke loudly, unavoidably spitting into his face.

The driver suddenly appeared and snatched him away. He pointed a gun at my head. 'You're mine,' he cursed with genuine hate. 'You'll get yours soon enough.'

'You fuck,' the small Irishman cursed, holding his throat. His eyes disturbingly transformed to thin slits of hate.

The fat man returned and defused the stand off, which left me shaking with anxiety.

The bags aboard *Stormdrift* were passed on to the coaster. About thirty minutes later several men appeared with wooden crates of different sizes and lowered them into *Stormdrift's* hold.

'Let's go,' the driver said to me.

'Where?' I asked.

'Back,' was his blunt reply.

As we pulled away I noticed the fat man had stayed on the coaster. Although he was unpredictable now he was gone I felt all alone and in deep shit. I was so pissed off for getting in such a hopeless situation. Drowning was a crap way to die, but

Silver Bubbles

getting shot by a moron was a personal insult. The small Irish idiot again stood behind me. I felt so helpless and scared.

I turned to face him. 'What's your problem, pal? We're just trying to make a living. When you're gone we will never see each other again. We're doing as you ask, so what's the problem?'

'You're the problem. I don't like you.'

'Yeah well, I don't like you either. So fucking what! Do you want to take over? Here - take the wheel.'

I stood back and the boat lurched off course. The driver looked round at me and not seeing the approaching wave, he got soaked as a green one burst onto the deck.

'What the fuck's going on?' he shouted, as he ran into the wheelhouse.

'If you want to get back safely you had better keep this sad bastard out of here.' I looked him in the eyes and shouted aggressively, 'and my face!'

'Get out,' he screamed, half dragging him out of the door. Pointing at me he said, 'You just get us back into the estuary or you'll get some real hassle.' I stood at the wheel swallowing deep breaths. Jamie looked on behind. Nothing was said.

It was dark and we were about six miles from the estuary. 'Jamie, keep her on this bearing, I won't be long.' I dragged a small rug aside and pulled open the engine room hatch. I passed the old gardener engine that was revving methodically. Lighting the way with a small torch I reached the wooden bulkhead that separated the hold from the engine room. Turning off the torch, the lights from the hold shone through every hole in the old bulkhead like rays of sunlight. Eventually finding one that gave the best view, I saw the man in the suit with no tie, holding a rifle. He pulled it to his shoulder and turned it sideways. He cocked it, and then pulled the trigger. It was clear what was going on. I recognised the shape. It was an M16 assault rifle: a high velocity weapon. There were at least three boxes I could see. Twisting my chin and straining like a pervert in a toilet cubicle, I could just make out the words M72 x 4 stencilled on another smaller crate. They were 66mm L.A.W.'s (Light Anti-tank Weapons, or rockets) and there was more I couldn't see.

'Shit' I cursed under my breath. I had seen enough to realise we were in the front line with international terrorists running arms and, albeit reluctantly, helping them.

'Did you see anything?' Jamie asked with a sad stare.

'Enough.' I looked at the flashing buoy then at the radar to check our position. The familiar blip was still there. Something was following for sure; it was on our beam about four miles away. Jamie's neck had turned to rubber; his head was dropping and lifting.

'Go and lie down. I'll keep an eye on things.'

'Thanks,' he said and went to lie down on the long bench seat in the galley.

Throwing the anchor over caused a head to appear out of the hold. It looked around like a meercat.

'What's going on?' the driver snapped. He looked rough and unshaven.

'The tide is ebbing. We have to wait for the flood before we can go any further.'

'Where are we?'

'In the mouth of the estuary. We're at a safe anchorage.'

He looked at his watch. 'We will talk in the morning.' He scanned suspiciously all around then disappeared below.

I sat in the chair. Although tired, I could not sleep with my mind full and frantically thinking of an escape from this bizarre situation. As dawn sneaked up on me I felt shattered, cold, dirty and forlorn. Relieving myself over the stern, the lonely feeling returned, as a curlew's mournful call echoed across the water. I estimated the headland to be about half a mile away. With the tide flooding I could make it to shore and get help. I almost jumped on impulse. Then Jamie appeared, rubbing his eyes to life like a little boy.

Silver Bubbles

I whispered close, ironically noticing I had bad breath. 'Are you a good swimmer?'

'No not really.'

'Shhh! Keep it down,' I whispered.

'I can dive, but swimming... No I'm not good.'

'Could you make it to the shore?'

'Hell no, not all that way.'

Out of the corner of my eye I saw movement.

'What's this then, an escape plan?'

'You wouldn't last three minutes in there,' I said. 'Anyway, why should we escape from our own boat?'

Irish pulled out his pistol. 'I wonder.' He pointed it at my face.

I pushed past, looking down at him. I was bigger and stronger.

'This isn't Northern Ireland,' I said.

'And what would you know about that?' He looked me up and down.

'I watch the news.'

'Oh. Is that so?' He moved closer to me. The gun was now an inch from my face. 'I waste British filth like you.' He spat at the deck and then cocked the pistol. 'You're too sneaky. I reckon you're trouble, so I do.'

I looked away then swung my right fist into his face so hard that he flew backwards, landing hard on his back. I quickly bent down and grabbed the gun he'd dropped.

'I wouldn't, if I were you.' The cold unemotional voice made me look up and to my left. The suit was holding a pistol with both hands, pointing it at my head. I turned slowly while holding the gun in the air. There was a pause, our eyes locked. The wind blew in short gusts, blowing his long black hair into different styles.

'Make your move, English,' he said softly, his black eyes showed no fear.

'I was only disarming him. You shouldn't let him loose with a gun; he's a fucking psycho! What the fuck's wrong with you? Do you feel big pointing guns at people?' I was pushing my luck but it was working.

The driver arrived and put his hand on the gun pushing it down. 'That's enough, there's no need.' Thump! All went black.

'Mike, Mike. Are you OK?' Jamie was shaking me.

Dazed, I regained consciousness. Holding my thumping head in my hands I stammered, 'Wha...what the hell happened?'

'He hit you with the deck brush. I thought he'd killed you.'

I felt the large bump on the side of my head. Congealed blood matted my hair.

'Not a fucking brush!' I paused, taking a deep breath, then looked round the bulkhead. 'What are they doing now?'

'They've been on the radio, boat-to-shore. They called but there was no answer. They're back in the hold. What shall we do?'

I sat up. I was concussed and finding it hard to think straight.

The driver and the suit came in holding a chart. 'Take the boat to this jetty.' He pointed to a place that I knew.

'What time is it?' I asked.

'Nine fifteen. Why?'

'It's tidal, but we should have enough water now.' I stood up and pretended to lose my balance. 'I can't see properly.' I held my head.

They looked at me. 'He's fucked. Get him out of the way and take us to the jetty.'

Jamie wound the brass wheel that engaged the gearbox and we were under way. The driver came back and told Jamie to go to channel six and listen for call sign 'Shore'.

Silver Bubbles

The boat bumped heavily alongside the jetty and the mooring ropes were secured. A small timber company periodically used the old jetty for mooring vessels, while awaiting suitable tides

Suddenly the radio came to life. 'Shore-to-boat over.' We looked at each other.

'You'd better tell them.'

As Jamie went to tell them I looked over to the seaward side. A mast from a grey customs cutter was holding position behind the headland.

They rushed in. Irish grabbed the handset. 'Boat-to-shore, come back.'

'Shore-to-boat over.'

'Shaun, is that you, where have you been… over.'

'Can you come for the van… over.'

'Bring the van here now, you idiot.'

'B' Jesus, what's going on?'

'Give me the mike.' The suit spoke. 'What's wrong, where's the van?'

'I'm alone. The van is delayed. It should be here later.'

'I don't like this,' the suit snapped. 'How the fuck could he get here without a van, what's going on? The van should be here now.'

'But he just said, come for the fucking van!' Irish grabbed the mike.

'Shaun, how many sisters have I got?' He looked at the others.

'Sorry, you're breaking up. I can't hear you.'

'The bastards, something's wrong. He's been got at. He's going out with my only sister, we're fucking compromised.' He stood silent, and then dashed out shouting, 'They're onto us!' He rushed back in. 'Get us out of here now!'

I was thinking for my life now. How could I tell them that they were almost aground as the tide was going out, and we would be here for five hours at least! If there were a hole anywhere I would have crawled into it.

I suddenly jumped up and shouted to Jamie, 'Start the engine.' Then I ran to undo the mooring line. Putting my hand to my head I fell over landing hard on the deck and then lay still.

'You see, you nutter,' the Scouser shouted at small Irish. 'The only one who knows this shit hole and you've rendered him fucking useless.' Looking at Jamie he shouted while waving a pistol around. 'You get us out of here!'

Jamie revved the engine, but she didn't move an inch. The Scouser was having a tantrum. The two Irish were banging around in the hold.

I crawled, fumbling around till I bumped into the wheelhouse.

'Get that pathetic pile of shit out of the way!' the Scouser bawled. Jamie helped me inside the galley and out of sight.

'Mike, can I help?'

'Keep quiet,' I whispered, and winked at him.

'But I thought you were...'

'I'm fine. We have to stop these loonies. If we could only get to the radio.'

'Here under the seat.' Jamie pulled out a hand-held set. 'We have to have carry a spare.'

'Look, I'm going to lie like this. You press my foot with yours if they look like they're coming in here OK?' I lay with a coat over me looking helpless. Inside I selected Channel sixteen.

'Station monitoring this channel, this is one of two hostages on *Stormdrift*. Do not, I repeat, do not answer this call. To acknowledge, key your pressel twice. Then wait out, over.'

After about twenty seconds the small speaker in the hand held gave two distinct crackles.

Silver Bubbles

'Yes, they're listening.' I felt Jamie's foot press mine. Small Irish grabbed the mike on the main radio and looked round the bulkhead to check us. As planned, we looked pathetic. He continued.

'Talk to me then,' he snapped.

'Rob, it's a...' The radio clicked into silence then a new voice spoke.

'This is the Police. You cannot escape. We urge you to give up peacefully. You have no means of escape. Your position is hopeless. Put down your weapons and walk onto the jetty with your hands in the air. Acknowledge, over.'

Charts, cups, everything on the shelves went flying as he exploded in a fit of rage. 'The bastards, the bastards, they'll not get me this time. Listen you bastards, we hold hostages. One smell of you and they're wasted. Got it?' He threw the mike down strutted around swearing loudly, and then he picked it up again. 'Get us a helicopter, you have got one hour.' He looked around panting. 'This is to convince you we mean what we say.' He looked at the suit, who was holding a small rocket launcher on his shoulder and nodded; he nodded back, aimed and then fired.

A loud whoosh and then a trail of smoke drew a line that finished with a mighty explosion taking away two walls and collapsing the ceiling of a brick pump house on the bank side. Small Irish laughed like a demented child as he kicked the empty launcher overboard.

'A hostage next, you bastards,' he screamed into the mike, 'You only have fifty-five minutes left.'

Two clicks emitted from the small radio. I talked into it. 'I know this is an open channel. Anybody listening please maintain silence, the situation is desperate.' I continued, 'There are three of them, two Irish and one Scouser. They are well armed and desperate. Stand-by...out!'

In the mobile incident room, the anti-terrorist commander sat twisting a pencil.

'Get me the list of escapees from Long Kesh. He talks like he's been in the Service, give me the mike.' He clicked it twice.

I said in a whisper, 'Receiving, over.'

'Can you give me a sit rep on weapons… over.'

'At least three more M72 throwaway launchers, M16 rifle's, and I saw a box of HEAT rounds (high explosive anti tank). There may be other stuff, but I can't be sure, oh and small arms…. out.'

'He's ex forces for sure.' He clicked twice.

'Receiving… over.'

'State your service number… over.'

'24226754, over.'

'Roger… out. I knew it!' He jumped up. 'Get me all you can on him and get me London.' He sat back down. 'This could get nasty.'

'Why sir, isn't it policy to make them wait?' his assistant asked.

'Look at the chart. Tell me what you would do in their hopeless situation?'

'I'm sorry sir, the hostages or the terrorists?'

'Come on man,' he stood up and pointed at the chart. 'The bloody hostages are no threat!' He stabbed a finger onto the chart where the refinery stood.

'No, surely they wouldn't, sir?'

'My God man, of course they would and probably will if we don't stop them soon.'

His assistant, realising the severity of the situation, stood up. 'But sir, a missile fired at the refinery would cause massive casualties.' He looked again at the map. His finger remained on the populated area next to the large storage tanks. A girl's voice broke the silence. 'It's London, sir.'

Silver Bubbles

The commander grabbed the phone from her. 'Yes, you received the sit rep, sir. Yes sir, we do have two scrambled. Not yet, but we expect them to. I understand, sir.' His voice lowered, 'We have no choice.' He placed the handset down and grimaced.

'Sir, we have details on one of the hostages.' He passed the facsimile.

'I thought he must be ex forces. Mike Morgan ex two Para, he served five tours in Ireland 'A' Company and Support Company. He's thirty-eight now. A long time ago but elite soldiers never forget. We have thirty minutes left.' He lowered his head, looked at his clenched hands as he banged them on the table then looked up. 'Then we call in the air strike.'

'Look across the river Jamie? Can you see the tankers?' I continued. 'That's a petroleum refinery. Even a badly aimed round from an anti-tank weapon would flatten a highly populated area. They will soon take us all out. They have no choice. We must get away.'

The Scouser was shouting and pointing at the suit. The bubble had burst. The idea of returning to Ireland as heroes with a handsome collection of weapons had turned into a hopeless nightmare.

'All that bloody work,' the Scouser shouted. 'The bank robberies all those risks and now this. I shouldn't have trusted the bloody Irish.'

'It's your plan that's fucked up, so it is,' the suit shouted back while picking up another rocket launcher. 'We're like fucking rats in a trap, but rats don't have these.' He held up another anti-tank launcher.

Through the powerful lens, the anti-terrorist branch could see the figures moving around the deck and the weapons they were wielding.

So too could the press and television companies. It was big news and the conversation on the open VHF channel had the media in fever pitch. Everybody had heard Mike talking. Billy, Len and Phil had been turned down with their offer of assistance, and were helplessly watching it all on a live TV broadcast. Len was sitting alone with Spot, his eyes heavy with sorrow.

'Where's the fucking helicopter?' The wild-eyed Irish man screamed down the mike.

'Its en-route, it had to refuel. We're doing as you asked. You will have to give us more time.'

'Bullshit!' He threw the mike down. 'What do we do now?' he screamed at the Scouser. 'It was your fucking plan!' He looked around desperately, his chest heaving from his gasping breaths. Then his stone face turned to a sneer. 'Oh yes,' he looked at the others and then turned, pointing to the tankers. 'That would piss them off; for sure so it would.'

'Oh god, the tankers are next.' Jamie whispered.

'Morgan…over.' Two clicks followed. 'The tankers on the South bank, they're next, over.'

'Get out if you can! Get out, you have two minutes maximum.' There was a pause. 'And good luck… out.'

I looked at Jamie. The word 'out' sounded final. 'We were all alone now. We would just get stuck in the mud if we jump. We can't reach the jetty to run, there's only one way or we're as good as dead.'

I edged my way to the door on my knees giving Jamie's arm a squeeze as I passed. He looked so scared. 'If you're religious, start praying now, pal.' We made eye contact. I tried smiling but couldn't.

Small Irish was extending another rocket launcher. As its sights flicked up he started adjusting them, trying to gauge the range.

'This is it!' I said to myself.

The Scouser walked to the port side, just forward of the wheelhouse door, and unzipped his fly.

Silver Bubbles

He looked nervously around then across at the big tankers painted against the rows of large, light blue storage tanks.

My heart was beating so hard I could feel my whole body pulsing as I positioned my feet and then rushed him. Turning with a look of surprise, his hands still occupied below, I snatched the pistol from his belt. At the same time I turned my shoulder and knocked him over the low rail. I fumbled frantically with the safety catch while turning to face them. They both turned. Irish pointed the launcher at me. Then Suit's pistol gave out a sharp crack. I felt a severe burning sensation run down my face and right side. I was knocked to the floor. A roaring sound, then a massive explosion filled the air, as the missile shot past me, exploding in the shallow water behind us.

Way above and fast approaching, the American fighter pilot's voice interrupted the tension.

'We have them locked on, await your command… over.'

The commander grabbed the handset; his other hand held a pair of powerful binoculars. 'Hold, await my order…over.'

'Copy that, just you say the word and they're toast…out.'

Behind the winch, gasping for breath and huddled in a ball, I looked desperately through a gap. Small Irish was on his knees, having dropped the spent launcher for a pistol, which he held with both hands waving it from side to side. I pointed the gun. Bang! The shot rang through the winch like a bell, forcing red dust into the air, obscuring my view. I moved to look from the side. The Suit was holding a pistol in the same manner. Crack! A bullet ricocheted inches from my head, then another and another. My eyes squinted and I flinched as bullets ricocheted around me. Expecting the worst, I held the gun then emptied the magazine in their direction without aiming. The click of the firing pin in the empty chamber echoed like my life was being switched off. I lay terrified, covered in blood, waiting for the burning bullets to rip into my cowering body. But nothing happened. Crouched, not daring to breathe, I heard Jamie.

'Mike, Mike,' he shouted while staring down at me. I lay shocked for a while not knowing what to do. Bleeding heavily from my face and my top stained black and sodden with blood, I slowly and painfully pulled myself up and looked over the winch. Small Irish was lying there staring, eyes wide-open with a neat hole above his left eye. The back of his head was missing as if it had been scooped out. His jersey was now two-tone and deep red at the back, where it had soaked up his gushing blood.

The Suit was lying like a Guy Fawkes dummy on the fore-deck with one leg bent almost double behind him, one of his shoes was off and lying by itself, which made it strangely personal. Their joint blood trails stained the larch decking as it ran out of the scupper holes, like a tin of deep red paint had been tipped over. Jamie rushed to the side and started vomiting, all over the Scouser, who was standing almost waist deep, trapped in the clinging mud, screaming for help as the tide slowly advanced.

I picked up the radio. My wet sticky hand squeezed the button. 'Call off whatever you have planned, it's over.' I drew a deep shaky breath. 'We need an ambulance please… out.'

I walked on the deck and took another big gulp of air, carefully touching the long gash in my cheek. The crackling roar of afterburners from the two jet fighters filled the sky as they circled the boat then sped away as quickly as they had arrived. I looked at Jamie who was leaning against the wheelhouse crying and picked up a picture from the deck. It was the one of Katrina. I pressed it into his hand. We stared at each other, but said nothing. I pulled a bottle from a holdall and took a big swig, looking at the bodies while wiping my mouth with my sleeve as the spirit burned into me.

Leaning against the winch I moved one of their bags with my foot exposing several bank notes. I crouched down and opened the bag, which revealed a handsome amount of twenty and fifty pound wads. I quickly emptied a carrier bag containing some clothing and stuffed all the notes into it, then moved into the wheelhouse where I pushed the bag up behind the small sink. Back outside I reached for the bottle and swigged another mouthful.

My arm and face started throbbing with severe pain as my adrenalin rush abated, while cars sped towards us the whiskey kicked in warm and heady, easing the pain slightly.

I passed the bottle to Jamie. 'Here, take a big one. You deserve it,' I said through the left side of my mouth. My cheek felt numb and I noticed I was dribbling uncontrollably. We sat and finished the bottle while the frantic officials closed in on us with guns pointed.

'Put your hands on your heads and kneel on the floor,' One officer shouted.

'Piss off!' I shouted back, 'We're finishing this first'. I held up the bottle. Looking down I saw a pool of blood. I didn't even realise it was mine.

Then the Commander pushed through them screaming; 'Get the ambulance here.' Stepping on the deck with his hands out stretched; I trapped the bottle between my knees and offered my good, but bloody hand.

Clasping it with both his he looked at me with genuine concern. 'You did well, son'. He looked around at the mayhem. 'We saw everything'. He took a deep breath and shook his head. 'So did the entire world'.

A medic placed a dressing on to my cheek and started cutting my sleeve away. A few minutes later the Scouser was dragged past hopelessly struggling. I looked up as he cast a hateful glance at me.

'Who belongs to you now, dickhead?' I slurred out, the best I could.

As the ambulance turned off the jetty, hundreds of reporters with big lenses lined the road that ran parallel to the river. They were pushing cameras above their heads. Flashes lit up the interior like a disco.

'You're celebrities now, top news all over the world, they broadcast your shootout live. The viewing access was too large to contain, everybody in the country has been watching events, the radio conversation was open, everything. You will be debriefed of course. There are security risks, we have kept as much back as possible, but you did say your name on the air.'

I looked at him. 'And my number,' I said wearily.

Nodding he continued. 'You were live on television, their zooms are powerful. Fortunately only people who know you will have recognised you. Discretion will be needed from everyone who knows it was you'.

'I thought all that stuff was in the past.'

'Your ID and past must remain out of this'.

'I know'. I looked at Jamie who was asleep, his many bumps and bruises showing different shades of purple. The Commander was buzzing. Thankfully the medic intervened.

'This will take away the pain,' he said smiling. The jab warmed through me, all the discomfort faded as I laid my head down and succumbed to the misty blanket that gently engulfed me.

> *He was pointing a gun at Vicki. She was holding Kris behind her, crying and pleading. Shots echoed loudly. 'No! No!'*

I sat up, confused then winced as pain throbbed in my arm and face. A hand on my arm made me turn my head, eyes wide open. I must have looked like a scared child.

'It's all right, it's all right, just a bad dream,' the pretty girl said with a look of concern. 'It's all right, I'm here to watch over you.' She smiled warmly.

After a moment or two I was calmer. I looked back at her. 'Am I in heaven?'

She pulled a chair up and gave me a sympathetic smile.

I looked around then asked. 'Where am I?'

'You're in a hospital room.'

'I thought it looked a bit posh.'

'It's private. You're hot news at the moment. We're sort of hidden.'

'Oh yeah,' I sat back, staring emptily. 'It's all coming back to me now. Where's Jamie?'

'He's here too.'

'What have they done to me? I feel like I've been mummified.'

'The doctor will see you soon.'

'What's your name?'

'Jessica.'

'Do people call you Jess?'

'Some do.'

'No I think Jessica is best, it sounds nicer.'

She stared at me and shook her head. 'I saw what happened, I'm sorry I shouldn't...'

'No, no It's OK I, err, I don't mind. What did it look like?'

'It's not professional.'

'Give us a break,' I said softly.

She smiled and then stared, looking down. 'When you knocked that man over the side of the boat we all thought you would get killed. I remember feeling so sad for you and wanting to help. The smoke left the gun and you could see the blood spray into the air as you fell to the deck. It looked like they both shot you. Head shots. Everybody gasped with horror and disgust - convinced that you were dead or dying behind the winch. We all were going through it with you.

Everyone was speechless and then you popped up against all odds and dropped them like James Bond. Everyone cheered, even the boss. It was like England scoring a winning goal. They were shouting and jumping up and down. That was in the station. The pubs and everywhere else were probably worse.'

'It wasn't like that... I was terrified... I didn't want to die. I thought... I thought I was going to for sure.' I must have been staring into nowhere for a while. Then I thought, but said out loud, 'Every day's a bonus from now.'

Jessica looked at me not knowing what to say. 'The problem now is keeping your identification quiet. The sad thing is they would pay a big amount to interview you and will do any thing to get a lead story, an exclusive.'

'What a bummer. I could be famous and then dead. I'll go along with you, especially if all the good guys are as nice as you.' She smiled affectionately.

I tried smiling back. 'Ouch! What have they done to my face? It feels sore as hell!'

The man in a white coat gesticulated with his hands. 'The bullet entered here from this angle.' He pointed to his own arm, explaining what had happened. 'It ploughed along your bone and then was deflected out of your arm due to the angle you had your arm at the time of impact. Unluckily for you it then entered into your cheek. On hitting the cheekbone it did a similar job there before exiting. Unfortunately the bullet was spinning and has made quite a mess. We removed numerous pieces of bone from your arm and several from your cheek. We have tidied it up with some grafts the best we can, but you will be left with quite a scar. Your ribs are heavily bruised. The head wounds are mending. You are a lucky man, Mr Morgan. By the way, well done! You were extremely brave.'

'Thanks.' Looking at Jessica I painfully raised my eyebrows, making her smile discreetly.

A familiar sound boomed outside then in they came: Len, Billy, Phil and Kris. Kris burst into tears while burying his head in my chest, which caused a moment of silence, during which each one made contact with squeezes and pats. After a few sniffles and eye wiping the flowers taped to a rum bottle were removed and cokes and glasses appeared. The bottle top was dropped to the floor and squashed. I was home.

After all the emotions had been aired and the moans about the tight security, they started talking about *Sea Gem*, knowing my enthusiasm would burst out as it always does. After two hours they left, leaving me feeling comfortably numb.

I opened the card Kris had given me.

> *'My Dear Mike, the thought of losing you forever scared me so much. You are so brave. Thank you for coming back for Kris and for me, love Vicki.'*

Jessica returned after seeing them to reception. 'Mike, are you all right?'

'Yeah I'm fine,' I said looking at the card. 'Fine.' I sniffed.

Jessica, sensing my mood, smiled. 'Now I know where you get that sense of humour from. They're a crazy bunch.'

'Yeah, the wild bunch, we're like a family.'

'Who's Vicki?'

'Why... why do you ask?'

'You kept saying the name when you came out of the theatre.'

'She's my ex, but still my wife. You know I didn't, we didn't want to hurt Kris, so we agreed to just leave things for a while. She left me for someone more attentive, for someone who's always there, to go shopping with, cleaning windows and stuff like that.' Shaking my head I continued, 'I was only building our future. I suppose I neglected her but I was gutted when she left, especially for such a snivelling creep. It's like she picked him just to annoy me. I was born with adventure in my blood. She knew that when we met.'

'I'm sorry. It's none of my business.'

'It's all right, anyway its nice having someone here to talk to. My pals, well you saw what they're like. I'm glad you're here, it could have been a king sized mama with a moustache.'

'Who's Lucy?' she asked, with an intriguing smile.

'Hell, I must have done a lot of blabbering. She's a good friend, yeah a real good one. Who's relieving you then?'

She smiled as a large policewoman almost waddled in.

'Good night ladies.' I pulled the sheet over my head.

Morning came and with it more questions.

'You will have to stay in your home and answer no calls. The press are good detectives. They'll probably have bets running on who's going to find you first. They will eliminate all the Morgans in the phone book. It's a matter of time before they call on you. Your father, Len, has been briefed and will tell anyone that you are working in the Gulf and are two months into a six-month contract. We have a company name your father will innocently tell them, to try and eliminate you from their list. It is imperative you are not seen by anyone who is not one hundred percent trustworthy. Better still you could disappear for a while.'

'It's the diving season. My partners need to earn now to get by.'

'Go to sea then. They won't find you there. After your wounds have healed and you have been counselled, that is.'

'Counselling, that's bullshit. No one gave me counselling when I was just eighteen, involved in bomb blasts and all the violence during service in Northern Ireland.'

'It's policy. What you went through could affect you psychologically'.

'I doubt it. My emotions were clipped a long time ago. Things have changed since then. A policeman gets leave and the shrink treatments if he sees a cat get run over nowadays!'

Jessica laughed then covered her mouth, looking at her superior.

Silver Bubbles

He leaned closer to me. 'You are in grave danger. If they find where you are, they will shoot you through the head, along with anyone with you. This is no laughing matter,' he said sternly then sat back without disconnecting his stare. 'We are putting rumours around that the whole thing was under observation and you were a Special Forces infiltrator.'

'Like an agent.'

'Yes exactly. The press will like that and should back off when it leaks out especially hearing that the name and number was the agent's code.'

'That's a good idea. By the way, we were being shadowed, weren't we?'

'Why do you assume that?'

'The Customs cutter that covered our exit was following us all the way back from the race buoy.'

'Very good, but you cannot have seen much on radar.'

'I saw enough to know.'

'Someone may discuss this with you at a later date.'

'Did they get the fat guy?'

'Yes,' he said with contentment. 'We have been after him for years.'

'So it was all planned?'

'No, not the way events developed.'

'So you knew we would be in danger then?' He looked away and remained silent.

'How close was it? At least be honest with me.'

He recomposed himself. 'They had you locked on, seconds that's all. It's not the normal way we operate but it was your lives against hundreds, possibly thousands. They had us in a corner. Our intelligence somehow missed the M72's, which changed the whole scenario, small arms only, we were assured,' he said with an annoyed stare at the floor. He gathered his coat then stood up and passed me an envelope. 'This contains information and some do's and don'ts, and a number to ring if you are compromised. I will be in touch. The nation is in your debt Mr Morgan. The refinery would have been flattened and with it a large, populated area. The results would have been devastating. Your act has not gone unnoticed.'

'Self survival, that's all it was.'

'No, not quite, you informed us of their capabilities. They would have acted before we could stop them. No, do not be so humble, you are a rare breed: a genuine hero.' He shook my good hand while nodding. 'Good day,' then he walked straight-backed through the door.

'A ticket to the policeman's ball, no doubt,' I looked at Jessica. 'I could go with you.' She smiled; her perfect teeth and moist lips made her look truly attractive. 'Ah, but you work for John Steed, don't you?' She shook her head, still smiling. 'At least Special Branch. I bet you're my minder aren't you? Are you carrying a piece then?'

'You should have been a policeman, you think like one.'

'I don't know whether that is a compliment or a piss take.'

'The first one, I can assure you.'

'Would you go to the policeman's ball with me then? Or are you spoken for?'

'What about Lucy and Vicki?' She grinned and then cheekily uplifted her eyes. And Kim, haven't you got enough women?'

I paused, 'Err… I did a lot of talking then?' I readjusted on to my side, facing her.

'She widened her eyes while nodding, 'Enough.'

'You have a point, but Vicki left me and Lucy rides on the wind. Anyway I might need someone to help me through the door and you know, bed baths, that sort of thing.'

'Sounds more like a nurse's job.'

'There would be some perks.'

'I'm sure there would be.'

'You never answered my earlier question.'

'My job kills relationships. A bit like yours I suppose.'

Silver Bubbles

'Yeah,' I paused. 'I understand.' I looked at her. 'Don't rush through life then regret it. A job like yours gobbles you up then spits you out.' She held my hand leaned over and kissed my good cheek.

'You're so right. You do understand.' I nodded as a nurse walked in.

'Time for your wash,'

'Are you staying to help?'

Jessica waved her fingers and smiled, 'Be seeing you.'

Two days later I was at home, sitting near the window, gazing at the boat and chilling out. No one was hounding me and I felt relaxed. Despite the wounds, the dream was recurring and the thought of my subconscious being affected worried me but it was my problem and I wasn't going to share it. Lucy had missed it all. Leaving several messages and not expecting a reply, she was none the wiser. Phil had been taking messages as well as taking care of the things with Len. The whole affair had put a big damper on the previous trip and its rewards, which annoyed me.

After a few more boring days spent mostly alone, I stood in front of the mirror and carefully removed the dressing on my face. The scar was big, red and ugly I sat and sighed, then murmured, 'Fucking great! I look like Al Capone.' I poked my cheek and it felt numb. I hoped it would go down before Lucy came home. The other side of my head had been partly shaved. The stitched scar looked black and ugly. Making circles with my arm I was pleased that it felt a lot stronger.

I walked over to the phone and played the last message from Lucy.

'Hi babe, where are you? I can't catch you lately. You must be at sea. It's one of the crew's birthdays and we are having a bash. See you, lover. Bye.' I replayed the message, hearing men's voices and laughter, music and the familiar sounds of a party. What was she wearing? Something short, revealing her sexy thighs maybe something tight, showing off her curvy bottom. The hollow grip of jealousy ran through me. I tried to change my thoughts, but only saw Lucy smooching with some debonair airline pilot, maybe feeling his hard on when their groins met. This wasn't me. I banged my fist on the wooden beam but I couldn't escape. The thoughts were like an annoying tune that sticks in your head, but this was worse than any tune. It was getting stupid. I imagined her making love, her legs gripping someone whilst she shouted, 'Don't stop, harder, harder'. It was like someone had got control of my thoughts and was hurting me deliberately.

Everything was going so well, but now it all seemed irrelevant. Nothing appealed to me. Negative thoughts flooded my head. 'I can't go out' Phil and Billy are avoiding me. I feel crap. I look crap. I grabbed a bottle of rum and took a swig. It burned deep inside me, but my thoughts were burning deeper. I walked to the window. The words that "John Steed" said echoed through my head. "If they find you they will put a bullet through your head, you should relocate."

How can I leave, I love this place.

I saw Lucy again, this time on her hands and knees biting her lip and rocking back and forth; his hands were fondling her breasts. 'Stop it,' I shouted. 'Get a fucking grip.'

I got changed and ran out into the field and didn't hear Len shouting. The wind was fresh and cool and blew me off balance at every break in the hedge. Up on the riverbank I leaned into it, the dressing slipped down my arm. One flick and it was gone. 'No pain, no gain,' ran through my mind as I upped the pace to a sprint, while I gasped for breath. How long I had run for I didn't know. As I ran through a patch of deep grass my foot found a hole and twisted, causing a severe pain in my ankle. I fell heavily on to the ground, opening the long wound in my arm.

I lay for a while panting and sweating. The pain in my ankle and arm made me curse loudly through my teeth. Then a gentle voice shut me up, I looked up.

'Mike, is that you?' I snatched my head sideways, turning away. The girl with the horse knelt beside me. 'My God, what's happened...are you all right?' I turned my head. She looked at me sympathetically. 'It *was* you then.'

'It was me what?'

'I thought it was you on the television. I recognised you.' She put her small coat around me. 'God, I'm so pleased you are all right, come on you can't stay like this. Let me clean you up.'

I sat quietly, annoyed at myself, focussing on one point, in a daze.

'Here, don't move.' She dabbed wet cotton wool on the dry blood slowly and patiently.

Looking round the tidy farmhouse kitchen I noticed several photos: a horse jumping, children with a dog. In the middle of the hearth was a heart-shaped frame. Its photo showed an older man with his arm round her, smiling.

'Is that your husband?'

She looked at the photo, her pupils moving to the corner of her eyes. 'Yes, he is a land surveyor, he covers the North, but works in London mainly.' Her eyes returned to me. 'What were you doing? You should be in bed with these injuries.' She carefully pulled my stained shirt off; the black bruises were still large and looked painful. 'My God,' she gasped to herself. 'For sure, it was some ordeal, Mike.' She sounded so Irish. Her sweet face looked for a response.

'Yeah, yeah it was,' I said quietly. 'Haven't you any kids, then?'

'No we ca ... haven't any.' She walked out the room and came back with a clean shirt. 'It is an extra large. Gerald likes them baggy.' What she meant is he was probably on the fat side.

'He's away a lot, is he?'

'Yes' she paused. 'Are you all right? You seemed to be in shock earlier. It was…' for a while her dark eyes fluttered around. 'It was truly awful watching it happen.' She smiled and squeezed tears from her glistening eyes, she stared for a few seconds dropped her head and then turned away.

'My mind was in shock… I don't know - I was feeling sorry for myself, it all got on top of me, everything seemed hopeless and stupid negative thoughts crowded my mind. I feel I'm going full steam ahead in the wrong direction.'

She brushed the shiny black hair off her face then put my hand between hers and smiled. The corners of her mouth curved up, making her look even prettier. 'You're still in shock, Mike. In Belfast I trained as a nurse. I can see it in your eyes. You cannot ignore it. Even if you think you are fine, there's a part of your brain that you don't control. In such a scary situation things get mixed up and take time to fall back into place, causing anxiety, short temper, forgetfulness, even jealousy.'

'Jealousy,' I muttered looking at her. 'I'm jealous of your husband,' I thought.

'Yes, it's caused by insecurity. You need mental rest as well as physical rest.'

'My friends are avoiding me.'

'Are you avoiding them?'

I thought for a while. 'Well yes, I suppose I am in a way.'

'Talk to them. Tell them everything that happened. Share it with them so they can feel what you felt and understand and feel the same as you, then you all will be in the same boat so to speak and then you will be back in control again.'

I looked at her. Her eyes were glistening again. She was truly concerned about me.

'You have an old head on young shoulders. Thank you.'

'I'm from a large family, three brothers and two sisters.'

'Wow, some family.'

Silver Bubbles

'A typical Irish family, it was hard, but fun.'

'You're going to have lots of kids as well?'

She stood up and turned away. 'Sorry,' I stood up. 'I didn't mean to...'

'No, it's all right. We just can't have any. Gerald has a problem, something hereditary. He has had all the tests. It's very rare. I... We were thinking of adopting.' She perked up. 'Anyway Mr Hero, you look a bit better than when I found you cussing in the grass.' Our stare lasted a while, and then melted into smiles.

'You said, 'were' thinking of adopting.'

She looked at me, my eyes interrogated hers and I could sense sadness behind her smile.

'Hey, I'm sorry, it's none of my business, sorry.' There was silence. 'Thanks, thanks again for helping me, you're very kind. Hell, I don't even know your name.'

'Andrea.'

I stared at her for a while and almost under my breath said. 'Irish Andrea.' Opening the door I looked back, 'Your husband...Gerald is a lucky man Andrea.'

Her head lowered as she gave a coy smile and I saw it again, that nervy sadness in her dark eyes.

CHAPTER SEVEN

There was silence as *Sea Gem* passed the jetty. I stared at it.

'The first two days were the worst,' I sighed.

They looked at each other. Billy cleared his throat. 'Why was that, mate?' he asked sympathetically.

'I didn't have a wet!' I replied, laughing.

'You twat,' Billy shouted, then, out of character, put his arm around my shoulder. 'You are famous, mate but only we know it.'

I smiled. 'A few do, I thought while visualising Andrea's bonny face.

The sun shimmered on the calm water. This was it. The quest for adventure was like a drug. Far stronger than the memories of the terrorist business and it was building inside us the more we talked.

'There is only two miles to go.' I shouted. Billy gave me the thumbs up, confirming he was ready with the marker buoy. I pressed the horn as the finger shape on the sounder peaked. Seconds later the weight dragged the white rope deeper and we could see it well below the surface.

'Vis looks good,' Phil shouted with excitement. In the background the sound of the seagulls and the great featureless expanse around us gave a feeling of freedom. I signalled with a thumb up as Phil climbed into his dry suit. Then I spun the wheel round altering course back to the orange buoy, which rested like a big tomato on a sea of shimmering ripples.

'OK'. Billy tapped him on the head. Phil held his mask and jumped, disappearing into the splash. As the bubbles cleared he could be seen pulling arm over arm for quite a while, the heavy mooring rope following behind him like a black snake.

The visibility was so good that at first white stones came into view and then the wreck appeared to rise out of the grey seabed to meet him. The shadow of the bow was clear to see. 'Yes' he grinned to himself as he swam hard while pulling towards it, dragging the thick rope.

He could make out circular shapes everywhere. *'Coils, bloody lots of them, all that dosh.'*

Several turns around the old bollard, followed by three half hitches and *Sea Gem* was secure. Holding his wrist, he looked at the computer. 'Seven minutes left' He pulled himself along with his hands flying from one launch point to another, head turning from side to side, scanning the unfamiliar terrain. He was looking for the bell he thought he had seen on the last dive. Dropping to the seabed he grabbed the edge of a large porthole, pulling it out of the coarse sand. He left it standing on its edge to collect later. Turning and finning in the direction of the bow he caught sight of the rope curving up towards *Sea Gem*. A quick fin to it then he was riding the elevator of dancing bubbles to the surface.

'Diver on surface and well,' Billy shouted as he secured the mooring rope and then rushed to assist Phil on the dive ladder.

'The Vis is shit hot.' He pulled off his hood. 'There's a lot of stuff down there.' He took a breath then spat to the side.

'Here, stop farting around and get this on site.' I passed Billy the eye of the winch wire, which was snaked on the deck in long loops, ready to be pulled below. Billy free fell down the line, the weight of the wire quickly pulling him down. Landing on the bottom he knelt, adjusted his mask, cleared his ears and looked around.

I landed next to him, making squealing noises through my mouthpiece, drawing circles and pointing to a pile of coils.

Forty minutes later, after a flurry of activity, a shoal of pouting moved in, snatching small creatures from the suspended cloud of silt, which the large bundle of rising coils had left behind.

Billy was riding the bundle up. I waited for the tide to carry the silt away and as the visibility returned I surveyed the now deepening crater. Box ends were appearing like coffins in a horror movie.

The newly uncovered coils were free from marine growth and coated in a sooty black film. When brushed by hand the distinctive shine, almost like gold, could be clearly seen. I pulled at one of the box ends, but it was solid, almost as good as the day the ship sank all those years ago.

Four minutes left. Lobsters for tea I thought. As I passed Phil's porthole I glanced at two purple black antennae waving from under a piece of rusty steel plate that had lines of old rivet holes drawn across it. Then I looked with disbelief as the biggest lobster I had ever seen made its way towards me with its claws at the ready. I put my hand in front of it, getting its attention and then shot my other hand behind it, firmly grabbing its back. It was so big I could only pin it down. It took both hands to hold it. As I swam back towards the line a round shape caught my eye. It looked like the top of a bell. Must be what Phil had seen, I thought. My computer was flashing zero bottom time, so I looked around for some recognisable pieces of wreckage then returned to the line for a slow ascent, while holding the double figure prize.

Silver Bubbles

'Get hold of this!'

'Bollocks!' Phil shouted. 'I'm not touching that!'

Billy brushed past him and grabbed it with one hand. 'Bloody good un, got to be a ten pounder. Fire up the boiling tub, we are in for a feast.'

I counted the coils. 'Sixteen, not bad for a first dip, eh?'

Billy pulled off his hood and agreed with a nod.

It was almost dark when we finished on deck. Phil was busy in the galley.

'It's a shame Len couldn't make this one. He's a good grafter,' Billy said, as he finished brushing the crud off the deck.

'Yeah... he won't miss the next trip, press or no press,' I replied.

The speaker crackled and knowing what was coming next we headed for the galley. This time Billy got there to catch Phil playing with the tannoy. 'Leave it!' he bellowed, making Phil jump like a surprised child. I set the approach alarm on the radar, then sat with them round the well-found table and poured the chilled Chardonnay.

The attention turned from eating to the weather forecast being announced on the VHF Radio. Westerly force two to three with bright spells.

'Excellent forecast,' I said, 'Cheers.' We chinked glasses as I turned my attention to the lobster. I saw Billy and Phil smile at each other, obviously pleased that I was getting on with things again after such a scary ordeal.

The sun spread over the sea as it rose. Little white terns danced above the small ripples, their harsh calls were comforting. It was the start of a perfect day. It was four am, Billy's turn on watch. I stretched and then walked to the stern for a leak.

'Is the water warm?' Billy shouted.

'About ten or twelve degrees I reckon. Couldn't be sure though. I had to cut short, a big jellyfish nearly wrapped around it.'

'That would make your eyes water,' Phil said, standing next to me, fiddling with his fly.

'So it's an early start then?'

'How can anyone sleep away a morning like this,' Billy commented as he flicked a towel over his shoulder then headed for the shower.

I looked around to Phil. 'Days like this live forever in your memory mate. Savour it. Soak it up. It will make you smile when you're old.' He turned and grinned.

'I've saved some crackers recently.'

Tea and toast was hurried down. We had an informal briefing. 'Billy, you go on surface supply. I'll do the coms. Phil you work the winch-whipping drum on my command. The coils are pretty silted up. Rather than use an airlift we're going to use a hook to pull them clear. Take the big gate block and fix it on the mooring line in a position-'

Billy interrupted. 'I know where to put the bloody thing.'

'OK, sorry. When we have enough clear we can lift them, but don't unravel any of them or we will have a right bloody mess to sort out and it will just waste bottom time and what does time mean?'

They looked at each other then back at me. 'Piss off!' they said in harmony.

Billy left to kit up followed by Phil.

The coms box crackled. 'Diver on the bottom.'

'Roger that.' Five minutes later, after lots of straining grunts, Billy was ready.

'Stand by. Phil,' I called to him. He put his thumb up.

Billy's voice gasped from the coms again, 'OK, pull now, nice and steady.'

Silver Bubbles

Phil coiled the rope three times round the drum and pulled it tight causing the drum to retrieve the rope.

'OK, slacken off.' After a short pause he continued. 'Pull again.' This continued for fifty minutes. Then Billy appeared on the surface, breathing heavily with every step up the ladder.

I hit bottom. The heavy wire eye threw silt up as I dropped it. Billy had done a good job. The hole was now larger and was flanked by a big pile of coils. The boxes and crates were further uncovered now and tantalisingly inviting. As planned, Phil arrived next to me with a bundle of strops.

It was great working with good visibility. The tides were in their neap phase and just a steady flow like a summer breeze, but without the warmth, although sometimes the tide caused a flood of slightly warmer water from the surface layers, increasing the temperature a few degrees before being replaced by colder deeper water.

We worked like astronauts, springing up and floating around, grabbing a waving strop then launching ourselves effortlessly towards a selected coil with fish-like precision, at one with our weightless environment. Twenty coils were stropped, approximately five tons. The mandatory computer checks gave me five minutes remaining dive time and Phil eight. I went to look at the wooden boxes while Phil faded into the green distance towards his porthole. The crowbar could just be forced into the neat joint. With a rock I drove it further then prized the gap open about an inch, working along, levering as I went. When the gap got larger I felt inside.

There were bottles, lots of them. I pulled at one, wiggling it through the gap while levering the springy wood further, easing it out. 'Got you.' The wood sprang back leaving a gap of about one inch. Holding the bottle, which still had its label, I read the words Scotch Whiskey. A sudden shock made me jump as something gripped my leg; I turned then shouted a babble of abuse through my mouthpiece as Phil slowly made his way up the line with his back to me.

I had dropped the bottle, and it was now in the centre of several coils and temporarily out of reach. My computer read three minutes decompression so I started the slow ascent. As I looked up through the millions of ascending bubbles I could just make Phil out. He must have that porthole with him, I thought. I could see him struggling with something then he was gone, having climbed through the shimmering silver barrier, which was the surface.

Several minutes later I climbed the ladder and was greeted with a noisy reception. Phil was running around the deck holding a large bell above his head like a footballer with a cup.

I blew the snot from my nose then shouted, 'I saw that ages ago.'

'Bollocks!' Phil shouted back, 'Its mine all mine, the bell to end all bells.'

'Bell end eh? Let's have a look then!' I held the shapely trophy and rubbed the name, it was easy to read, having been partly covered in sand. *Benmachdui* 1941. 'You cheating bastard, treasure hunting while Billy and I do all the graft.'

'Yeah,' Billy grabbed the bell. 'This will go away until you earn it.'

'Hey, come on!' Phil looked at us then at the bell.

'You're excused this time.' Billy passed it back. 'You can make the breakfast in return.'

As Phil and the bell went for a shower we winched the coils on deck. The small tide, combined with the clement weather, was making life at sea easy for a change.

After breakfast all the bottles were filled, and the wire and strops were made ready.

Eleven a.m. After a six-hour interval Billy again made bottom with the drag hook and released twenty-four coils from their silt filled tomb. As he climbed up the ladder accompanied with the familiar grunts he passed a bottle to me. 'It's called Buchanan's.'

I looked at them. 'There's a full crate of…shit no, alloy tops.' I unscrewed the lid, which made a gritty sound and smelt the contents. 'Still smells like whiskey.' I lifted the bottle to the light. 'A bit cloudy though. Well, there's only one real test.' I took a tentative sip. 'Bollocks, it's bloody awful.' We all had a disappointing taste and agreed it was ruined

'What a bloody shame. If they were good they could have been auctioned. They're getting on for fifty years old and with a history. Collectors would have paid a mint.

Billy interrupted. 'There might be some good ones left. God knows what's in the other crates, but for now, girls.' He looked at us and shouted. 'Get those bloody coils!'

It was becoming a routine, fixing strops to the coils and we completed the task in record time. Phil went off to find the evening meal while I closed in on the crates, which were even more exposed now. I struggled with what appeared to be a large rope fender wedged between two crates but couldn't move it. About six crate ends were exposed now, but still mostly buried and the silt was building up all the time.

Phil had bagged three good lobsters and three nice cock crabs. He also noticed some large cod lurking under parts of the wreckage. They would make a nice meal another time. Arriving at the mooring line together, we made our ascent.

Twenty-four coils were safely retrieved and stored away. 'Fifty coils altogether, that's great.'

'The bank will be pleased,' Billy sighed. 'At least we will own her, lock stock and barrel.'

'Yes, but just think of the potential! There are lots more beside this. We're not even scratching the surface yet. I know of wrecks with gold, silver and one with diamonds. There are loads to go at.'

Phil smiled at me ranting on and then shouted. 'That's twelve-and-a-half ton at one thousand five hundred.'

'Sixteen thousand eight hundred at least,' I interrupted him. 'That's with the five at home. Where could you earn that sort of money ashore? We can get Alistair bloody Smyth off our backs.' I stopped and stood silent.

I had caught the reflection of myself through the glass in the door putting my hand to the scar. I just stared. Billy, seeing this, put his hand on my shoulder and asked quietly.

'Are you OK, mate?'

'Yeah, yeah I'm fine. I haven't had any dreams since I've been on board. That must be a good sign, but this shitty scar pisses me right off, the bastard even makes my mask leak.'

'It's gone down a lot,' Billy reassured me. 'Grow a bit more stubble and you won't see the bugger. Anyway it looks, well, it gives you character.'

Phil butted in. 'Yeah, all you need is a fucking wooden leg and a parrot.'

Billy turned, staring at him. I started laughing. Billy looked back at me. 'I was going to give him a slap for saying that.'

Still laughing I said, 'He would be good to take to a funeral. At least it would be entertaining.'

'Get the food started, you cretin.' Billy slapped him on the head. Phil sneered at him then escaped into the galley.

Billy put his hand out to me. 'Thanks mate, for all this. We have a future and we're only dependent on the weather. Nothing or no one else.'

'Cheers,' I replied, feeling proud.

After six hours the tide was slack again.

'Get some of the crates free…over.'

'Roger that… standby. OK, pull now. Got ya, you wooden sod. Give me slack. OK, pull again. Bloody hell. There's a bag of lead or something. Stand by.' After a lot of straining and gasping Billy continued his commentary, 'Yeah, it's lead in strips about sixteen inches long. There's loads of it in hessian sacks. Shit, the silt is filling the hole. We might need an airlift.'

Silver Bubbles

'Understood, get some samples,' I replied. The excitement in my voice was obvious even to me.

'Roger that. I'll start somewhere else… Stand by.'

Billy returned after thirty-five minutes with a handful of the small lead sticks. He threw them on the deck then pulled the band mask off, then gobbed into the water. 'About fifteen this time, I'm knackered.' He sat against the rail breathing heavily.

'Well done mate,' I praised then he pulled on my hood. 'It's our turn now,' I shouted at Phil. 'Come on, what are you messing around at? See you on the bottom.' The water hissed with bubbles as I disappeared - quickly followed by Phil. This was the last dive of the day and we were tired, so to avoid decompression sickness the bottom time had to be limited. So as soon as the coils were connected to the wire we surfaced.

The weather was on the telly. We sat and watched with interest. T-shirts, shorts and flip-flops made us look like holidaymakers. A pretty weather girl came on. 'Look at the top bollocks on that. I'd crawl miles over broken bottles just to stick matchstick in her shi…'

'Shut it,' Billy snapped and looked at me. 'What do you reckon? Northerly four to five occasionally six at times.'

I sat on the edge of the seat. 'It will be dodgy working and northerly winds are the worst. We could continue but we have enough to pay the bank and the loan is well overdue. They will hit us with interest. And we could do with an airlift. The pump should work well but we would need a bloody long suction hose. An airlift would be easier for now.'

'Shall we go in then?' Billy suggested.

I stood up and picked up the tide table and took a look at the clock. 'If we have a slow ride in we could get into the river for about nine p.m. We can get some sleep in the anchorage then catch the flood up in the morning, what do you reckon?'

'Agreed,' said Billy. Phil nodded his agreement.

In the sheltered anchorage the black anchor ball displayed on the bow was dancing in the freshening wind and white crests were building at the estuary entrance. Tucked behind the headland safe and calm, the beers came out.

'Have you ever been so pissed that you cannot recollect anything that happened the night before?' Phil asked.

'You're not drunk if you can lie on the floor without holding on,' I replied.

Billy added, 'I was once on a job and we had to live for days on nothing but food and water.'

Phil smiled, shaking his head at the floor.

Billy continued, 'Our Girt is a light eater, as soon as it's light she starts eating.'

'Ha!' I joined in. 'It only takes one drink to get me pissed. Trouble is I can't remember if it's the thirteenth or fourteenth.'

'Nutters,' Phil said, 'Bloody sad old gits.'

'I always wake up at the crack of ice,' Billy said laughing. 'After seven rums our Girt turns into a hideous animal, after the eight, I pass out altogether.'

I butted in. 'Bed time. You two look shagged and I'm well tired. I'll set the alarm on the GPS so if we drift off station it will wake me up. Go and get your heads down, we're safe here.'

The seagulls woke me before the alarm. The brisk northerly wind brought a chill with it. I looked out of the window. The water was getting restless and the sun was hidden behind low grey clouds, which raced across the sky.

I turned on the VHF for the weather forecast. Bloody hell, six to seven north-easterly. It's a good job we decided to come in, the boat could take it easy but we couldn't work the deck or dive safely in those conditions. I felt good about our decision.

Clearing away the empty cans into a bin liner I went down into the galley. The kettle was already on. Billy appeared with a towel round him.

'Showers are free. I'll do the brew.' As I showered I thought of Lucy, then Andrea. Looking down below I said, 'Well fella, you're getting a bit hungry aren't you?'

'Who the hell are you talking to?' Phil banged on the door.

'Just thinking out loud mate.' I grabbed a towel and opened the door.

Phil looked into the shower. 'Where is it then?'

'Where's what!'

'The randy Rachel inflatable doll you were serenading.'

I flicked a towel making it slap painfully on Phil's back as he rushed into the shower to escape. 'If I had a doll in there I wouldn't have been talking to it, you knob.'

The bridge was raised to let us through. It was the rush hour. All the commuters were trapped in long queues. 'Look at all those poor bastards.'

'Yeah, just look at their faces,' Billy said. 'They look so pissed off, so unhappy.'

'Yeah, imagine having to do that every day for less than two hundred quid a week.' I blew the horn. The loud deep tone echoed all around as we waved at the sad faces. A few feeble toots were returned from the few who were still breathing. The rest sat stone-faced like zombies. 'Sad bastards, it's a sad world.' I sighed then turned my attention to *Sea Gem* and to keeping her in the middle of the narrow river. It was the same at the second bridge. All the sad depressed faces watched our smiling faces.

Phil got a bunch of schoolgirls going by shouting. 'Bring your mothers for a cruise.'

Billy quipped, 'Its not just their mothers at risk.'

'What? They're only kids,' Phil said in defence but then a six-former in a short skirt waved to him. 'Well, err... Christ, look at the size of her tits.'

As *Sea Gem* slipped further inland the buildings dwindled and lush green fields surrounded us, giving off sweet earthy smells.

Rounding the last bend a white flash shot through the deep grass on the bank. Spot stood on her back legs, jumping excitedly up and down. Len was waiting for us. He tipped his cap as I put her astern and moored her in the berth. Billy swung out the walkway. It had barely touched the grassy bank before Len was on it with both hands pulling himself onboard.

'How the devil are you?' He shook Billy's hand and whispered into his ear.

They spoke for a while then both looked at me nodding. 'What's this, a hen meeting?' I shouted while closing the door.

Len slapped me on the back. 'How are you, son?'

'You just asked Mrs Wells. Didn't she tell you? I'm fine Dad, seriously, I am fine.' Len had obviously asked Billy to keep an eye on me and he was getting the report when I caught them. I looked at Billy and raised my eyebrows. Billy just shrugged his broad shoulders. Spot jumped up at me for a stroke. I picked her up and walked to the stern, looking towards Wood End. 'Home again, eh, Spot.'

The red light was flashing. Next to the machine was a pile of letters and a notepad with messages, time of calls and all that.

Len walked in. 'The phone's been busy. The bank has called relentlessly.'

'Yeah, I thought they would.' I pressed the button. Beep.... 'Mike, it's Andrea. I thought I would call to ask how you were... Bye then.' I gave a broad smile.

Len tutted, 'I didn't hear that.'

I listened to the next message.... 'Hi Mike, it's Jamie. Give me a call, we have moved away for a while.' He left his number.

Beep... 'Bernard Smyth, Mr Morgan. Will you please contact me as soon as possible? You are way overdue with your bridging loan. We will have to introduce penalties. We need a meeting urgently.'

'Urgently, that fat bastard doesn't know the meaning of urgent.' I grumbled. 'Anyway, I expected that.' I looked at Len. 'It doesn't matter, Dad. We have the money. He can swivel on his shiny pinstriped arse.'

'You have it all?'

'And a bit to share out. I'll tell you later, I want to sort out this lot. Phil's already on the boat. Will you go and count the coils for me? Then we can ring the scrap man and get the stuff sold.'

Len called Spot and left humming a tune.

Beep.... 'Hi, Lucy here. We're coming up to see you in two days, Kim as well. We have to be back for Sunday night though. I will call to make sure you're home.' Great, Phil will be chuffed. I grinned at the thought of feeling her close to me.

Beep... 'Commander Lewis, nine forty. Mike, call me on the number I gave you.' 'What the hell does he want?' I thought. 'What day is it?' I looked at my watch, Wednesday. I called the bank and made an appointment. Then I called Vicki. 'Hi, it's Mike.'

'Mike, how are you? I've been worried about you. Kris said you were pretty bad. I wanted to see you, but Len advised me not to.'

'I'm fine. It was a bad experience, but I've had a few of those. By the way, thanks for the nice card.' There was a silence... 'Hello.'

'I'm still here... '

I heard a sniffle. 'Are you all right?'

'Just blowing my nose, it's so good to hear you I... I missed you.'

'Yeah, I missed you too; look you will have to come round some time with Kris. The work on his new room is nearly finished. We can go through the decor, all of us together.'

'That would be nice.'

Then I thought what if Lucy is home? 'I'll give you a ring first. As I said, I've lots to do at the moment, you know, things to sort out.'

'OK Mike, thanks for ringing.' There was a pause.... 'Bye then.'

'Bye, bye.' I put the phone down gently.

Phil and Len burst in. 'Seventy-five of the smelly beautiful bastards that's...'

'About twenty-five thousand three hundred, give or take a grand,' I said, with a thin smile.

'What's up with you?' Phil asked.

'Ah, it's nothing, the bank, bloody John Steed wants me to call him. Vicki isn't happy and, well, Lucy is due home tomorrow.' Phil looked thrilled in anticipation.

'Yes, yes... Kim's coming as well.'

'Yes, yes, yes.' He jumped up and down. Len looked at him.

'Settle down you idiot, she's only a woman.'

'Not this one! She's a goddess. How long is she coming for?' Every muscle in his face was stretched like a clown.

'It's only for a few nights. They have to be back for Sunday.'

'Three night's brilliant, I need some vitamin tablets.'

'It will only take you three bloody minutes so don't waste your money.' He just grinned.

Len shook his head. 'Don't get too attached. You know it's better to have an average looking woman for oneself than a beautiful woman to share with others, and that goes for both of you. Anyway are you coming for a wet on the boat? Jonno's donated a replacement for the bottle on the optic that unaccountably evaporated at sea.'

'Yeah, just give me some time to sort this lot out. I'll join you in a while.'

I dialled Jamie's number. The call was intercepted. After giving my name I got through.

'Mike, Mike! Dad, Mum, it's Mike.' Jamie sounded excited, which made me smile.

'How are you getting along mate?'

'Fine now my ribs are better and all the bruises are fading. How are you?'

'I'm getting there. The wounds are getting better.'

'How is your face and arm and the scar?'

'To be honest still crap, but they say it will go down. I look like a gangster.'

'Hang on, my mum wants to talk to you.'

'Hello.' The strong Scottish accent made me smile again. 'Michael I must thank you from the bottom our hearts for saving our son, thank...'

'Hello, hello.' After a pause Jamie returned.

'Sorry Mike, my mum's... she is a bit emotional at the moment.'

'That's OK pal. Have you got the boat back yet?'

'Yes, we got it over here this morning. It's a good job too. We need it to earn some money scalloping.'

'Are things a bit hard at the moment?'

'Yeah, you could say that. We were depending on that charter money to get some pots and increase our earnings this summer, but it looks like we'll miss the season.'

'Jamie, your phone, is it monitored?'

'I don't know. Every call is intercepted. They tell us who's calling and ask if we know them.'

'Say no more mate, Oh, by the way I left my dive undersuit onboard. I don't need it now I've got a new one. You can have it Jamie.' There was a pause.

'It's OK Mike, we'll send it on to you.'

'No, Jamie take it as a gift I wanted to surprise you, but I'd better tell you. It's got a divers watch in the pocket. I want you to have it, counting bottles to judge your dive time is too dodgy. You will be able to time yourself properly. It's in a carry bag wedged behind the base of the sink.'

'Mike... thanks matey. Thank you for everything.'

'Jamie, we will come and visit you when things cool down, I promise. In the mean time get the watch and use it, it will help you more than you think and remember, it didn't cost me anything, it was a gift, OK? Take care mate, see you soon. Bye then.'

At least someone would come out of that mess happy.

The silence was welcoming so I poured myself a Captain, dropped two ice cubes in then filled it to the top with cold coke. The red light was still flashing so I pressed the button.

Beep... 'Hi babe, you can't be home yet so we won't drive all that way if you're not there for us. Will call you soon, kiss, kiss, Bye.'

'Shit.' I walked in circles. 'Bloody hell,' I shouted loudly then I saw myself in the mirror. The scar looked crap. Maybe it was a good thing they weren't coming. There again, I haven't seen her for ages and I was looking forward to it. She never leaves any numbers... she's always away. Bollocks, Phil will be gutted. The little voice in my head started again.

If she's not here where will she be? Such a good looker in London with the gorgeous Kim, they could pull anyone any time they wanted. 'So what,' I shouted out loud. 'So fucking what, it's her life, but I want her now. Sod her. She could leave her bloody number. Or is it just an excuse to stay with someone else, maybe a slimy... posh-spoken pilot. Pilots, I hate the smug bastards. This is your pilot speaking. Why don't you

Silver Bubbles

just fuck off and wipe that daft smile of your face before I snot you one, bastards all of them.' I sat rubbing my knees, staring around. I was losing it again and it was making me furious. The phone rang.

'What?' I shouted. There was silence.

'Mike, is that you?'

'Who's that?' I snapped.

'It's Andrea. I'm sorry if it's a bad time.'

'Oh no, no, I'm sorry. I, err, was just throwing a wobbler. No I didn't mean that, I was just angry at something. Thanks for calling. How are you doing?'

'I saw your boat and thought I would call to see how you were getting on. Have you talked to your friends like I suggested?'

'Yeah I have sort of, in a way.'

'I'm going for a walk. Would you like to join me? You could bring Spot.'

I've loads to do, I thought... Lucy let me down, sod it. 'Yes that would be nice. About fifteen minutes.'

Spot's ears pricked up as I whistled her. All on board were starting a session so they didn't notice me slinking off.

'Hi.' She was standing rubbing her hands together nervously, then Spot jumped up at her, breaking the ice. She bent down and stroked her and then looked up. Her dark sleepy eyes mesmerised me leaving me speechless for a while.

She looked better than I remembered her.

'You look well.' She stood up. 'Your scar has gone down a lot. You will hardly see it in a few weeks.' She touched it. Her fingers were warm.

'Do you think so?' I replied feeling it. Again our eyes met and we smiled. I started walking slowly. She stayed close, putting both hands into her pockets. She was grinning as if she was going somewhere exciting.

'You said you were throwing a wobbler or something, what did you mean?'

'Yeah, I don't know. When I'm at home, things seem to agitate me. Lucy and her friend were coming home then the next message she said she wasn't. If I had been home a day earlier she would be here tonight.' She turned and smiled.

'I'm sorry. Lucy is my girlfriend. That's when she's here. At the moment it's not that often, I'm getting bad vibes.'

'I know the feeling. Gerald is coming home this afternoon. I haven't seen him for weeks. He's only staying for a short time.'

'Lucy doesn't leave numbers. She, she seems so full of the high-life. I feel forgotten.'

'I know, Mike.'

'How do you know?'

'Sorry, Mike, your son Kris told me.'

'The little toe rag.'

'No, don't think, I mean we just got chatting one day. He was on his bike. He had made a jump in the middle of the track and I couldn't get my car past. He wasn't going to move.'

'The little sod. I'll have a word.'

'No, no, there's no need. We're friends now.'

'What happened then?'

'I moved the car forward until the bumper was touching his tyre then revved the engine. He stood his ground, looking scared, then I put it in reverse and did a wheel spin backwards. We both started laughing. He moved the jump and we got chatting.'

'How long ago was that?'

'A few weeks ago I suppose.'

'I stopped walking and turned to her. 'So that's how you got my name.'

The wind blew her jet-black hair across her face causing her to brush it aside. I couldn't help myself and said, 'You're beautiful Andrea.'

A stronger gust blew. Holding her hair with both hands she stared at me with her head to one side. Time seemed

Silver Bubbles

to stand still and we remained locked in our gaze. Sod it, I thought and I moved closer.

Her lips were so soft and her smell made me feel dizzy. I didn't dare hold her for fear of being rejected. Finishing the kiss she remained silent, so I kissed her again. I was completely lost in this new experience, feeling our noses brush as we changed sides felt so intimate, as if we had kissed for years.

After what felt like a long silence, but was only seconds, I spoke softly. 'I'm sorry Andrea I was out of order.'

'No Mike, I was.' She turned and started walking back towards the Spinney, leaving me hollow and wanting more. I caught up with her, stuck for something to say, not daring to talk. As we reached the cottage I stood back, not wanting to pressure her. She opened the door then turned and smiled. Her smile faded to a sad nervous stare and then I was left stood like a helpless idiot as the door closed.

I walked away, head down in a confused state. Spot jumped up at me. I stopped and crouched down to her. 'What's happening to me, Spot?' While I stroked her she seemed to smile as if understanding me. I paused in thought. Hell, I've never felt so intense about someone like this before. I've got to get my shit together, I said under my breath as I walked down the track, occasionally glancing back at the Spinney. Inside I felt empty.

The official voice quizzed me. I said 'I was given this number by Commander Lewis to call him back.'

After a few minutes and a lot of clicks and crackles I heard his distinct voice.

'Mike, how are you keeping?'

'Can we talk?'

'Yes, all your calls are monitored and will be until we're happy.'

'Aren't you happy with things?'

'Almost, we put out the red herring. I think it's worked. You being away and not blabbing around has helped. On the whole things have gone better than I expected. They were outcasts and not members of any active unit. They were working alone. There are no strong connections to worry about. Yes, the situation is good; the press have not messed things up. What about you?'

'I don't know, no one has been around here. My dad expected someone, but no calls. Nothing.'

'Good, the longer the better. You haven't answered my question Mike. How do you feel?'

'To be honest like shit, and I'm getting jealous… I never have before. When I'm home I get so angry about the daftest things. Well, my girlfriend hasn't been home since the trouble, I suppose I'm feeling sorry for myself.'

'It will pass Mike, time will heal. You will forget the bad experience as more day-to-day things occupy you. We could arrange a meeting if you wish?'

'Do you mean counselling?'

'Sort of.'

'No thank you. We have loads to do, I can't afford the time.'

'Mike, your colleagues can deal with your business.'

'No. If I feel really low I'll call. We have to take advantage of the summer while the water is clear. No, I'll just keep busy, thanks.'

I stood looking out the window. I could just make out figures moving around in the wheelhouse. I picked up my jacket and walked into the yard, stood for a while, then walked down the lane towards the village. The Ship looked empty so I entered.

'Jonno's not in,' Sue the barmaid said presumptuously.

'Yeah I know, give us a pint of Scrumpy please.' I sat at a table staring out the window. A couple sat studying the menu I noticed they had arrived in two separate cars and

Silver Bubbles

were in a secluded corner. I looked at the man who appeared uncomfortable and shied away at my; 'I know what you're up to' smile.

I finished my pint and decided to take a stroll down the lane. The smell of the summer brought memories flooding back - my carefree growing-up years. Bike rides, finding birds' nests. I had been daydreaming for about an hour when a large car pulled up behind me. I turned with surprise, trying to see who was inside, then quickly looked for possible escape routes. Then the door opened. A woman stepped out.

'Andrea,' I said, through a smile. The other door opened and a well-dressed man walked towards me with his hand outstretched.

'Gerald, you must be Mike. Andrea has talked a lot about you.'

We shook hands. I stood totally confused; looking at Andrea, 'Yeah, she's been good to Kris, my lad.'

He was about forty-eight, on the hefty side, confident and sure of himself. He replied, 'All that business was awful. I saw it all on the television. You were outstanding.'

'I'm sure you would have done the same.'

He laughed and put his hand on my shoulder. 'You must have a meal with us I didn't know we had a hero living locally. I worked over the water for a while and have witnessed the ruthlessness of those sub-humans.' Gerald certainly liked his own voice. I looked at Andrea. She just smiled sweetly. Time froze again and even with Gerald next to me I still had a compelling desire to hold her.

'Mike.' Gerald broke the moment. 'Tonight is the only free time I have, then I'm back in the city for a while. Is that too short notice?'

'No that would be a nice change. I'll try and get myself a chaperone.'

The car purred away disappearing in "dead man's oatmeal" growing on the lane side.

A chaperone, who the hell can I take? I stopped at the sound of a yellowhammer singing its heart out. Again it reminded me of my childhood, the long balmy summer holiday bike rides, the tarmac melting from the heat of the sun, mates laughing and joking, pellet guns, getting thirsty and knocking on strangers' doors for a drink of water. I walked slowly as the sounds of the countryside mingled with nostalgic thoughts, which relaxed me almost to a state of meditation. It was so peaceful. Then a sharp tapping noise broke my trance. A grinning face through the pub window beckoned me with waving hands.

'How are you Mike?' The orange-haired woman gave me a strong hug.

'What do you look like?' I laughed. She was wearing tight white shorts, doc martins and a sleeveless top, exposing several tattoos and a large cleavage.

'It's cool,' she replied, chewing gum while grinning.

Josephine, locally known as Jo, was home. She was the daughter of a top surgeon and from a wealthy family who lived in the old vicarage house. We had been friends for years, as far back as kids. She was an activist in about everything; she ran marathons and was well educated.

'God, what does your old man think?'

'He's used to me now.' She put her arm in mine while we walked to the table. 'This is Bobby.'

'How do you do,' I held her hand. The young girl smiled.

'Pleased to meet you,' she said in a well-spoken southern accent.

'Where have you been lately, dare I ask?'

'I've been home for a while. We did the London Marathon. The New York's next. We're in training.'

'Great, you look fit as a butcher's dog. Sorry, I didn't mean you look like a dog.' She put her hands on her hips. 'You look great, that's what I mean. Anyway, you know how I feel about my sexy mate. Remember that Christmas party?'

Silver Bubbles

She grinned. 'And the bale dens.'

'Yeah, those as well.'

'With a body like mine, if I didn't run I would be a barrel.'

We sat down to a lot of stares from non-locals. Clinking glasses, she said, 'I'm dead chuffed to see you. I heard all about...' She paused. 'You know.'

'You're a breath of fresh air just when I need it.' I bent towards her and whispered in her ear. 'Are you still batting for the other side?'

'When I feel like it.' She gave a devilish grin and moved her eyes at young Bobby. I nodded discreetly and smiled at her.

She laughed. Tearing a V out of a beer mat, she stuck it on her nose. 'Who threw that?' she shouted. 'Miserable bastards aren't they!'

'You're still a nutter.' Then an idea sparked in my mind. I thought for a while, looking at her. 'Hey, would you do me a big favour? There again, I don't know whether I could trust you.'

'Trust me, my dad's a doctor.' She faced me, cross-eyed. 'What is it then?' She flashed her eyes at my crutch.

'Not that, you nutter. I want you to accompany me to a meal invitation I just received, but you...' I paused. 'How can I put this?'

She burst out laughing. 'I know and I can.' Her laugh turned into a wild smile as she drew air through her nose 'Another pint?' she shouted, 'Serving wench, more ale!'

Grumpy Sue stood her ground. I returned with the drinks.

'She's the pub's version of a crane driver. They don't try to please and they're miserable bell loving bastards as well.'

'Cheers, where is it then?' I looked at her. 'The meal, where is it?'

'Oh, you know where Mr Ryan lived? We called it the Spinney when we were kids.'

'Oh yeah, that little cottage... I thought Cooks' owned it.'

'They still do, they rent it out.'

'What's the score then, friends or family?'

'Friends, new ones, I only met her husband half an hour ago.'

Jo eyed me. 'Sounds a bit dodgy. Are you...'

I interrupted her. 'No, no it's not like that. She helped me when I was a bit low. Stop looking at me like that, it makes me feel guilty.'

'You look guilty.'

'Do I?' Young Bobby started laughing. 'You sods, you're winding me up.'

'I know you, remember. I know what you're like. Remember the Bale Dens?'

'We were just kids.'

'Yeah, a kid with a man's todger. All the girls talked about you.'

I looked at Bobby. 'Don't worry about her, she's as bad as me.'

'You can still remember the Bale Dens and all that?' I laughed.

'Yeah, me and lots of other girls, I bet.'

'Yeah, carefree days. You were missed when you went away to boarding school. You were one of the lads all right. Now look at you, you still are. Anyway, how did you know about that trouble in the river?'

'Your mate Phil, he's been trying to get in my pants for ages. He's a good laugh, but what a rake! When he mentioned that he was your partner I got interested and quizzed him to find out how you were. He told me that you had been through a rough time. I was watching the telly at home when it came on. I thought it was you, but they said it was an undercover geezer so I didn't think any more till I saw your scar.'

Silver Bubbles

'You are smart, you always were.'

'I had good mates, along with a good childhood. Do you remember we climbed every tree around here during the summer holidays?'

'Yeah it was good. Hey, don't mess around tonight ...please.'

'No, course I won't.' She looked away then back at me with a cheeky smile.

I returned home to find Phil crashed out in the living room. Len had left a note. Sue was going to drop him off at a friend's for the night. Spot had come home and been fed. The boat was locked up. Every thing was sorted. I looked at the clock then at the answer phone. There was no flashing red light.

The bath was warm and cosy and I fell into a relaxed mood. My mind was cruising with insignificant thoughts then suddenly there was a loud bang! The door swung open, causing a rush of cold air to enter the warm room.

'Bloody hell, have you been in there all day?' Phil loomed over me while struggling with the buttons on his new 501's. He leaned over the bowl with one hand on the wall to trying to stop his swaying.

'No you silly sod, I was busy.'

'You missed a good piss up. Jonno was swimming in the river. So when are the girls due?'

I remembered Lucy's call. 'Shit.' I said out loud then sat up. 'I'm sorry mate, they cancelled.'

Poor Phil looked gutted. 'You're kidding me.' His smile vanished. 'You aren't?'

He paused, looking at me then he stared back at the basin. 'Shit.' He jolted and re-aimed. 'What a bummer. I missed, did she ring?'

'No mate, it was the next message on the machine. They must have thought we were at sea. I can understand but I'm getting bad vibes, I know we've been away a lot but she doesn't even know about the shoot out. I've had fuck all support from her.'

'Yeah.' He wiped the floor with some toilet paper, threw it into the bog, dropped the lid with a loud bang and then sat on it. 'Two birds like them can pull at the wink of an eye. Maybe they've binned us. We're probably just shag gossip by now.'

'Shag gossip?'

'Yeah, notches on their food trolleys.'

'I don't think so, hell I hope not but it would have been nice to see them again.'

'You can say that again,' he sighed, resting his chin in his hands. 'Oh, Billy's made the airlift. We're going for the hose tomorrow and the scrap lorry is due about ten-thirty.'

'Great, the bank's been whinging again. It will be good to shut them up. Anyway we can have a share out. Don't forget to give them a sample of that strip lead or whatever it is, so they can get it analysed.'

'Yeah, I forgot about that. I'm a bit skint now.'

'As I said, you won't be tomorrow.'

'Are you coming to the Ship later or is it a bit dodgy still?'

'Bloody right I am. Sod them. I am doing what I want now. Hey, I've been asked out for lunch.'

'Where too?'

'Gerald and Andrea's.'

'Who the fuck are they?'

'It's that girl who rides a horse around here. They rent that little cottage down the track.'

'That black haired chick with the edible arse?'

'Edible arse? Shit, you miss nothing in knickers, do you? Yeah she's the one.'

'You're sniffing. I know you.'

'No, it's not like that. Why does everyone think that if I talk to a bird I have ulterior motives?'

Silver Bubbles

'How do you know her then?'

'I met her a few times. I tripped and twisted my ankle and she helped.'

'With a shit story like that I'm not surprised no one believes you. It's crap.'

'No, she really did.'

'You're defending yourself,' he waved his finger. 'We always catch you out when you go on the defence. Anyway her husband is always away, so I've heard and he's ancient. You *are* sniffing.'

I changed the subject. 'That reminds me. You told Jo about that shit didn't you?'

'No, that's a load of crap. She asked if it was you. All I said was you had been through a rough time. Sumo Sue behind the bar must be gobbing off again.'

'Yeah I'll get Jonno to have a word.'

'Are you coming then?'

'Yeah, for a while, then it's the meal later.'

'Do you mind if I get a shower?'

'You know you don't have to ask.'

'Cheers" He opened the door and turned on the water. 'Do you know I can't go in there without getting a hard on, just thinking about that weekend?'

'Well I'm out of here. The last thing I want to watch is you beating your sausage senseless.'

I opened the wardrobe to the smell of Lucy's clothes, well the ones that she had left here. I pulled out a short black dress, put my face into it and drew a deep breath. 'What's going on, babe?' I whispered.

Phil banged the glasses on the table. 'Guess who's just walked in?'

I shrugged my shoulders.

'Jo, she's all dolled up and looks raunchy, do you know, and I bet she shags like a rabbit on speed.' I pointed with my eyes. She was standing right behind him. 'Shit,' he muttered then turned to her and smiled.

She looked him up and down. 'No, I don't think this Bunny would last thirty seconds before making a mess in his crutch.'

I laughed as Phil hid behind his pint glass, while I moved to make space for Jo to sit with us. Her presence made me feel excited as I recalled our friendly, sometimes intimate past.

'Thanks for the invitation.' She kissed me on my cheek.

'I've been trying to pull her for bloody ages. How come you...'

She interrupted, 'We're old friends, anyway don't give up, you never know... Bugs.'

I smirked. He had no chance against such a clever girl. 'Jo likes her own gender so you might have a chance, Phyllis.'

'Yeah, yeah, you could have fooled me.'

Jonno strode up and whispered to me. 'I've had a strong word with Sue. It shouldn't happen again.'

'Cheers mate.'

Jonno looked at us. 'What's this? Are you two an item?'

'Josephine is kindly chaperoning me to a meal invitation. With my wit and her intellect we could comfortably dine with royalty.'

'Her wit and your shit more like,' Phil ragged in his usual harmless way.

'Shush, little boy,' Jonno interrupted. 'Would madam and sir like a wet on the house, Champagne maybe?'

Jo walked wobbling in her shoes down the unlit track. Outside the door I paused. 'You look lovely. No, you look stunning. I can't believe you're that bovver girl I met a few hours ago.'

'I can be full of surprises,' she said with mischief in her eyes and then stretched on her toes and gave me another peck on the cheek.

Silver Bubbles

After introductions we sat around the walnut table and quietly devoured the smoked salmon starters. Afterwards we sat chatting and drinking while the hired chef rushed around the table and prepared the next course.

'That's a great idea, hiring a chef.'

'Yes, there's nothing worse than jumping up and down amid conversation,' Gerald said in his posh drawl.

Jo was amazing. Her intelligence surprised me and I'm sure it impressed our hosts. Any subject that cropped up she handled with such charisma I was glad she was there. I struggling really hard not to stare at Andrea but I was hopelessly losing the battle. Each time I saw her she looked more beautiful than the last. She was growing on me inside and out.

As the night progressed the shoot-out eventually cropped up and there was total silence as I told them a brief version, omitting my past.

'Sorry. I'm going on a bit.'

'No, no,' Gerald said, giving me praise as if he was really interested.

Andrea stood up. 'It's not really good for Mike to discuss what happened. Please, let's drop the subject.'

Gerald shocked me with his reply. 'Well it's your bloody lot that's to blame.'

There was an uncomfortable silence then Jo replied, 'The British have a lot to answer for, Gerald. Or are you deliberately forgetting the shameful past events of our ruthless and selfish leaders?'

He squirmed in his seat like a faltering politician and hid his face in a brandy glass and then looked at me.

'Andrea told me you have a fine son.'

'Yes he's a good lad, a bit cocky at times but a boy needs a bit of spirit, a bit of go in him.'

'Apparently he often calls round and offers a hand in the garden.'

I laughed. 'You must have something I haven't got. Gardening? That's a first.'

'Maybe it's Andrea,' he replied. 'The Irish are good with soil.'

I glared at him with fire in my eyes. There was no need for this cruelty. Andrea left the room.

When she returned Jo was engaged in conversation with Gerald. I had calmed down and looked at her and winked.

She gave a discreet smile. She was mesmerising me as she walked around in her pretty red dress. Jo was taking everything in. Gerald harped on about his job. He liked his brandy and got quite loud as the night progressed. His shape indicated the wining and dining that was part of his life was catching up with him. He hardly spoke about Andrea. It was mostly 'I' this and 'I' that. He was engrossed in a technical conversation with Jo and their voices droned like traffic on a distant road. Without turning my head I looked at Andrea who was sitting opposite me. She looked such a picture, so attractive I couldn't turn my eyes from her. She caught my stare then looked away, only to look back immediately.

What was she doing with me? I maintained my eye contact and gave a careful smile then on impulse I pursed my lips and mimicked a kiss. She looked at Gerald then back at me. Lowering her head with her dark eyes uplifted, she did the same but her kiss lasted longer, which caused a wave of excitement to surge through me. I could feel my pulse increasing. I was totally bewitched by the seductive smile she gave me.

Gerald talked a lot about money, how much he could make in a deal. He was full of praise for himself.

I sat almost falling asleep in the tranquil atmosphere, when Gerald's voice made me jump and I straightened up like an army recruit.

'You look tired young man.'

'Sorry. The brandy is so good it's made me sleepy,' I turned to Andrea and my smile faded for a second, aware of being watched I regained it and looked back at them. 'Jo runs marathons you know.'

'Yes,' Gerald replied. 'She told us earlier.' I sat quiet, feeling a bit embarrassed.

Jo broke the silence. 'I think Mike was admiring your fine decanter collection at the time we discussed my running. Is that large one in the centre French?' She rescued me a few times and as the evening turned into morning, I visited the bathroom. As I came out, to my surprise and delight Andrea was there. She put both hands softly on my cheeks and kissed me quite hard. Her lips slightly stuck to mine and as she floated away from me our mutual gaze once again froze time. The look of desire on her face filled me with a nagging hunger as she picked up our coats. We thanked them for a lovely evening, swapped pleasantries and then left.

It was quite cool so I put my arm round Jo. 'Cat got your tongue?' she asked slyly.

'Sorry, I was miles away.'

'Not that far away.' She turned her head, nodding at the cottage.

'Thanks a million. You were brilliant. I knew you were bright but Christ, you made posh Gerald look really stupid at times.'

She turned and grinned.

'Do you want to come back for a night-cap?'

She smiled, 'Why not.'

I swilled the brandy around the glass. 'What do you think of them?'

'Well, in between watching your tongue licking the carpet whenever Andrea spoke...' She knelt next to me on the floor. 'I think they are a normal mismatched couple. He's so full of himself and poor Andrea didn't get a word in. She's trapped like lots of women but she wants to savour the moment. It's the beginning of the end for them. It may take decades or just months. Slowly everything they feel towards each other will

Peter Fergus

ebb away and they will be the bystanders at the death of their own relationship.'

'That's a bit heavy.'

'It's true.'

'Sad.'

'I saw you drooling. You fancy her like mad, don't you?'

'Hell, you miss nothing.'

'You should have wiped her lipstick off.'

'Shit.' I wiped my mouth. 'Was it that obvious?'

Smiling triumphantly while shaking her head, she saved me. 'You haven't got lipstick on your mouth. I was just kidding.'

'You sneaky....' Jo grinned, making me feel slightly inferior.

'Well, she is attractive, sleek and sexy. I could...' She grinned again. 'Anyway he's awful to her I reckon he's going down the pan.'

'What do you mean?'

'Money is all he talked about and he made several snipes at Andrea, about her not having any business acumen. I feel sorry for her. It's like she's an embarrassment to him. He never spoke to her once. The rotten bugger even said her accent limits them socially.'

She took a big gulp of brandy and looked at the glass then stood up and held my hands. 'Once we were like brother and sister. Now, well, now we are still great friends. Do what you feel is right.'

'What would you do?' She smiled and held her head to one side.

'You know the answer to that and your present situation. People like us go for it.' She gave me a puckish look and started unbuttoning her dress.

'What are you doing?'

'What you secretly want me to.' She slid her dress off. 'Andrea, she's after you, she's hungry for loving and he's such

Silver Bubbles

a tosser. Lucy is totally neglecting you. The way I see it, you're easy meat and as always… hot for it.'

I watched as she peeled off her pants. Her firm curvy thighs and large breasts made my heart pump fast. Then she started undoing my pants. 'I'm going to screw your ears off you, Mike Morgan. If Andrea can, so can I. Wow!' she gasped. 'This has grown a lot since the Bale Dens, a lovely living dildo.'

I stood with the look of a naughty schoolboy as she jumped on to the settee and provocatively opened and closed her legs. 'Come on Mike, come here and give the bovver girl a hug and a length of that cosh.'

'That's one challenge I can't refuse.'

Her nails dug into my buttocks, making me squirm with pleasure as her athletic firm body went rigid. Picking her up I forced her back against the wall with each of her legs over my arms.

'Oh God, come on, Mike, harder. Give it to me faster.'

I gritted my teeth and sheer rampant sex took total control of us. We exchanged smiles for a second then the lust melted them.

Hastily throwing her onto the chair I lowered my head towards her groin.

'No, not when that truncheon is waving around.' She smirked. I moved slowly.

'Don't tease me! Just screw me as hard as you can! Come on, give it to me.' I continued teasing her. 'No, come on,' she pleaded, pushing and waving her sexy body at me. 'Don't mess around, just do it hard, you fucking tease.' I obliged and soon she was screaming abuse, as she became possessed by an awe-inspiring orgasm, which launched me deep into pleasure land as my legs buckled from under me.

The door burst open and Phil stood bearing a look of shock. 'Sorry,' he blurted out. 'I thought someone was being murdered.'

We collapsed in a heap, covered in sweat and sniggering like children. 'Make us a wet, you bloody voyeur.'

Phil rushed out leaving us in fits of laughter.

I woke to the sound of the carpet cleaner. Phil was cleaning up.

'You jammy bastard,' he shouted as I passed in my boxers, scratching my head.

'Correction,' I replied. 'It's jammy bastard with a sore willy.'

'You told me she wasn't interested in men, I could have give you a hand.'

'Only men of certain qualities pal.' I stopped. 'You get on with the dusting and I'll do the thrusting.'

Phil gave a broad smile. 'Glad to have you back on board, skipper.'

As I entered the shower I thought, 'Yes, I am back on board. I feel great, thanks to Jo. What a girl, a real mate.'

'Cheers everybody, the bank is paid in full, we each have a wedge, the boat is ours, we have an airlift thanks to Billy and the tides will be perfect in two days. The long-range forecast is good; we're fuelled up and ready to go. Cheers.' We all stood up. I asked loudly, 'Quiet a minute please.' I paused. 'Thanks for everything. No, seriously, thanks for your support.' There was silence. 'We're going to sea for at least ten days, so we have to sort out all our bits and pieces. I suggest we get wrecked today and do it all tomorrow.'

When I got to the bar, Jonno looked at me. 'I wish I was going with you,' he said solemnly.

'You're welcome, you know that.'

'Yeah, but it's this place.'

'You're good at giving advice mate. Now take some. Just say "fuck it" and come with us.'

'It's not as simple as that.'

'Bullshit, you could do it! You could even have Phil's cabin.' Phil looked round.

'What was that?'

'I just told Jonno you have a nice cabin.'

'Yeah,' Phil screwed his face up.

'Think about it and remember, that "you only live once" shit is true.'

An hour and two bottle tops later, Jonno finally came off the phone.

'Well?' I looked at him.

'Yeah,' Jonno grinned. 'Sign me on, skip.'

The music on the jukebox assisted the atmosphere. Len started telling sea tales. Jonno discreetly disappeared behind the bar. Suddenly the lampshade, above where Len always sits, started swinging as if at sea, to the amusement of everybody in the cosy pub.

'What are you laughing at?' he asked looking around, then twigged on as he saw a thin length of fishing line leading towards the bar, which Jonno was pulling. 'You cheeky monkeys,' he shouted. Swinging the lamp, eh?'

CHAPTER EIGHT

Her bows threw plumes of white spray high into the air. Some crashed against the glass as if someone outside was throwing dustbins of water. She nodded up and down, making everyone stagger and hold on as they went about their chores.

'It's a bit rough isn't it?' Jonno said, as she dipped and scooped up a wave, throwing it high into the air.

'Yeah, it's the swell mainly. It will die off as we clear the headland and find deeper water.' Thirty minutes later the sea became flatter and friendlier.

'You were right, it's a lot nicer now,' Jonno said looking less concerned. I just smiled.

'Yeah, it will be fine, no problem. If that high comes through we could be sunbathing tomorrow,' Phil said with enthusiasm.

'I hope so. I've brought my cozzi.' Jonno replied.

Billy appeared in his boiler suit. 'Everything's fine and running like a sewing machine down there.'

'Great, is the shot ready?'

Billy gave me a dirty look and went to clean up. 'I take that for a yes,' I said, looking at Jonno laughing.

'He's a rock isn't he?'

'Yeah, he certainly is, in more ways than one.'

Silver Bubbles

As we got closer to the site Billy, Len and Phil prepared everything without a word and when I blew the horn the shot disappeared, followed by the two buoys. I turned her and slowly passed parallel with the two markers. Phil gave a wave then jumped in with the mooring line. I held position with perfect precision. She steered so well.

Phil surfaced soon after and put his thumbs up. Billy quickly made the rope fast to the bollard. Disengaging the drive as soon as Phil signalled caused the rope to come tight. Then *Sea Gem* swung with the tide, and settled, riding sedately up and down in the remnants of the swell.

'That was bloody amazing.' Jonno shook his head. 'You all worked so well together.'

'That's what we do mate. I couldn't keep a cellar as well as you.' I glanced at my watch then down at Phil. 'Do you want to get a few lobbies before the tide starts running?' Phil nodded and Billy started kitting him up.

The strange familiar sounds greeted him as he descended the thick line, which buzzed and vibrated in his hands each time *Sea Gem* snubbed on a swell. Approaching the bottom he cleared his ears and displaced the water that had seeped into his mask with small puffs from his nose. The visibility was only about ten feet because the marauding clouds had engulfed the sun. The shoals of pouting were still there and moving like synchronised swimmers, all the time keeping a safe distance from this noisy intruder from the world above. For some unknown reason there weren't as many lobsters patrolling the wreckage on this dive. As he scanned the twisted shapes something moved. It was eel like, and had a big black head. It scanned him through large piercing eyes while its long body rippled, snakelike. It looked menacing as it exposed its uneven jagged teeth like a monster from an old-fashioned horror movie.

Peter Fergus

He backed off, keeping an eye on it and as he moved away it slowly slid back into its lair. *'What the hell was that?'* He shivered disapproval.

He continued his search and after finding a few crabs and lobsters he started along what was left of the ship's side. Big steel plates lay twisted and misshapen, only the regimented lines of rivet holes betrayed human involvement in what looked like a natural reef. The rivets were long gone, dissolved by the sea decades ago.

Back at the bow section, as if by magic the rope to *Sea Gem* appeared in the misty water. As he looked down to take hold of it, he noticed the outline of a big flatfish buried in the sand. A bonus, he thought. Putting the bag down he pulled out his knife and drove it hard in-between its eyes. Suddenly the seabed exploded in silt. He couldn't hold his knife and almost messed himself when out of the silt stained water a big Angler fish of at least forty pounds came for him, its massive mouth was snapping like a T-Rex.

He shot up the line; breathing out of control. 'Shit, I'll have to go back and get the lobbies, they will bloody keelhaul me if I leave them'

He slowly descended. The visibility was even worse now, as his rapid fin strokes had stirred up the bottom. He didn't see the bottom until he was a few feet off it. He quickly grabbed the bag, but at the same time the big black head with its eel-shaped body shot into view and sank its teeth into it. Totally spooked, he swam up the line in rapid fashion. Still holding on to the string pull, he banged into something.

Billy grabbed the bag and thumped the large catfish on the head. Its long muscular body snaked away. Phil looked at Billy, his mask was leaking, and he was laughing out of control.

Phil's eyes said it all as they surfaced. Billy pushed him up the ladder. I offered my hand to help. Billy kept quiet as they removed the gear. He was finding it hard not to laugh.

Silver Bubbles

I cracked open the large claw and scooped out the succulent meat.

'So let's go over it again,' Billy said then took a slurp of wine, mixing it with a mouthful of lobster. 'You were harassed by a monster catfish then attacked by an eight foot angler fish and then the catfish came back to finish you off!' There wasn't a dry eye in the galley. The laughter was infectious. We were all aching and had shiny red faces.

'Oh for fuck's sake leave it out,' Phil shouted. 'I feel like that bastard, Andy. Your spoiling the scran.'

As the laughter turned to giggles then sniffs, Jonno spoke. 'Well, I can see the funny side, but I'm mega impressed at the way you understand each other. Tell me, how did you know? You scrambled Billy for what? I couldn't see anything wrong.'

'When you've spent your life with divers and diving as we all have, you can imagine what's happening down there. When he was on the shot line where it's tied to the wreck, we knew he would be coming up, but his bubbles alerted us that something was wrong. We all know what pace each of us breathes at and if the breathing pattern changes we're on alert. When Phil's did, Billy got ready and was standing by, but when Phil went down again we knew something was amiss, so Billy went immediately to assist.'

Jonno nodded. 'So even though you seem to be messing around and joking you're watching for everything.'

'Yeah, that's why we're here doing this. Most of the non-commercial diving fraternity spend time bumping into each other and waving. They miss just about everything that they go to look at. There are some bloody good divers around, but these new back-to-back training methods in warm climates are producing lots of divers with qualifications and little experience. That's why fatalities are occurring more frequently. It's purely a money thing with certain organisations. They really should be policed more strictly and not allow the blind to lead the blind.'

'Hear, hear,' Billy said. 'Spot on. You know they can't even tie knots so they tie lots. They don't train in the sea, no boat experience, divers, no way.'

'They have lots of badges though,' Phil grinned.

The seafood was tasty, being so fresh. We ate our fill and washed it down with wine. Not too much as diving and too much drink don't go hand in hand. Len drew up a watch roster, which included Jonno, so we only had a two-hour watch to do each. I was sitting at the wheel. The forecast was good. *Sea Gem* rose gently in the dark, and her deck gave a slight hum from the generator. All was well; I felt good. Then my thoughts drifted to Andrea. What is love, I asked myself? I must love her, even though I'm not allowed, she can't be mine. I think about her all the time. Lucy is fun, but Andrea makes me feel passionate, romantic and sad, all in one. I feel unsettled when I think of her. A similar feeling to when I think about Vicki and that sad bastard dribbling all over her. I thought about Kris. He was gutted having to go to school. Still, he will be on his summer holidays soon. Six weeks at sea will do him a world of good.

'Mike,' Jonno whispered. 'It's my shift. You'll have to tell me what to do though!'

'It's called a watch at sea, there's nothing to it, mate. Just sit here and look at the radar, hence 'watch'. Do you get it? You don't have to stare into it all the time; you can watch telly or read. There's an alarm on it. It will beep if a target enters within two miles of us. Then you just have to track it to make sure it doesn't hit us. We're not in the shipping lanes, but fishing boats are always around. We're displaying the correct lights, so relax. If you have any doubts give me a knock.'

'OK,' he whispered.

'You don't have to whisper. Good night, mate.'

Silver Bubbles

The airlift disappeared quickly; leaving a trail of bubbles as Billy dragged it down like Tarzan wrestling with a big snake. I received two tugs on the hose then nodded to Phil who then opened the valve causing the machine to roar and dominate the silence.

We decided to use scuba so the umbilical hose wouldn't twist around the airlift hose as the diver moved around. A few minutes later the sea above him erupted into a large mushroom of bubbles, and looked like it was boiling. Shells and stones appeared with the escaping foam and turned the area into a minestrone soup of shells and sand. Below and oblivious to all the noise, Billy stabbed the airlift, sucking up everything it contacted, making the tube rattle and bang as volumes of shells, sand and stones were liberated from years of isolation below the seabed.

'Wow,' Jonno looked on excited. 'That's clever. Does it shift much?'

'Yeah, hell of a lot. We should release lots of coils and get to the buried crates. This is real treasure hunting, don't you think?'

'Not half,' Jonno replied, staring at the bubbles.

I looked at the dive log, then at Phil and drew my hand across my neck. The compressor slowed to a fast tick over as the bubbles faded to the few coming from Billy.

Phil was kitting up as Billy spat into the sea. 'It's working a treat,' he said, breathing heavily while squeezing his nose. Jonno passed him a tissue. 'Cheers. We're well down already. A day of this and we should be into our biggest haul so far.'

Phil shouted. 'A pulling machine, that's what I'm going to get.'

'Get some bloody work done first, you're missing the tide,' Billy shouted.

He was gone. Moments later the compressor began revving again. Billy looked at Len and put his thumb up. Len nodded, he looked pleased, but his expression quickly changed. 'What's up, Dad?'

'Oh, it's nothing. I just wish I was younger and having a go down there with you. I feel I should be doing more.'

'Don't be bloody daft, you do all the rigging. Hell, dive ships need riggers and no one comes with better credentials than you. Anyway, we're the divers you're the rigger. Got it?'

'Aye aye skipper.'

Billy slapped him on the back, 'Silly sod.'

Phil dragged himself up the ladder. 'I'm well shagged.' He threw his hood on the deck. His suit was covered in silt and smelling awful.

Len got the deck hose and washed him down. He was stinking like a sewer!

I turned to Phil. 'How did it go?'

'Magic, we're right among it all now.'

'Great, see you later.'

I held my mask and disappeared into the splash. It was hard to recognise the area. Everything was covered with small shells and stones like a blanket of snow, fallout from the airlift. I smiled; it looked like a bomb crater. The many neatly stacked coils came into view. There was a wall of crates next to them.

I picked up the airlift, grabbed the feed hose, and gave it two hard pulls. Seconds later the hose stiffened and small bubbles leaked out of the Chicago coupling. I made myself comfortable then turned the stainless quarter-turn valve. It hissed into life like a giant snake, as rivers of sand and silt ran towards the shiny prongs fitted to its end. Looking up I could see millions of small shells falling like snow against the bright surface. Moving the pipe was physical. It had a lead sleeve on the end to give it ballast, which made it heavy. Like Phil, I was soon feeling the strain, but it was working well. The crater was expanding and more and more coils appeared. I could now see clearly how the ship had been loaded all those years ago. The crates were neatly stacked, butting up against the coils.

Silver Bubbles

The larger ones were on the bottom with hardly any gaps, to avoid movement at sea. Now they were going to be explored. The manifest listed lots of items, but several references to special cargo intrigued me. After all those years searching for information I was now in the ships hold and getting results. The air fizzled out. It was time to surface. The tide had changed and was running at about one knot, improving the visibility. I looked down, surprised at the size of the crater, but more so at the amount of coils now exposed. I kept looking down until the bottom dissolved into the water.

'We'll do some recovering on the next dive and get everything that's exposed. Billy, you use the drag hook like before and we will strop up.' We all agreed then sat around killing the six hours between tides. The sun was shining; only the hum of the generator and Len filling bottles down in the hold disturbed the peace.

'All the bottles are filled and the pulling rope is all cheesed down, skipper.'

'Cheers, Mr Rigger.'

'What did he say?' Jonno asked.

'Cheesed down. It means coiled flat and ready for use.'

'It's another language.'

'Yeah, I suppose it is. You see that drum, the one we use to pull the coils in?'

'Yes, this one?' He put his hand on it.

'Yeah, it's got more names than Lord Lucan. Handy Billy, Whipping drum, Slave hauler'. In the West Country they call it a 'Nigger Head.' Derived from slave hauler I suppose. We call it a whipping drum.'

'How do you know that?'

'When I came out of the army I went walkabout. I crewed on charter boats all along the South West Coast. You know, fishing and diving trips.'

'So, that's where you learned about fishing?'

'Yeah, conger eels over one hundred pounds, Blue sharks, twenty-pound pollock. We fished for all of them. Then I crewed on trawlers all around the U.K. That's how I got my skippers' ticket.'

'So, what will you do when you've cleaned up here?'

'We're awaiting conformation from the Salvage Association. We have a contract for this one. We pay them ten percent of what we recover, well, what we tell them, but it pays to be fair and it keeps robbers away.'

'What! People take stuff when you're not here?'

'Not yet, but if the word gets out everybody with a boat will be bringing divers out to rape what we have uncovered. With a contract we just call the police and they are waiting wherever they land the stuff and confiscate it. Then we collect it from them. Well, that's if we know where they're landing it. Anyway, small boats couldn't work heavy stuff like this.'

'Have you got more sites nearby?'

'Yeah, there are loads. The next one is called the 'Juno'. I think I know where it is, but identifying it might be difficult.'

'What was that carrying?'

'The manifest lists a general cargo and some printing machinery.'

'Printing machinery, Is that worth recovering?'

'No. You see that's where the research comes in. The old printing techniques used typesetting. The typeset was made out of tin, and they used to export tin in ingot form, up to twenty tons at a time. And at nine thousand pounds a ton, well, think about it!'

'Hell that would be worth-'

'One hundred and eighty grand,' I interrupted with a smile.

'Doesn't anybody else know about it then?'

'A few, but the big companies couldn't operate as cost effectively as us. Yes, we are fortunate to be in the right place

Silver Bubbles

at the right time with the right crew and equipment. It's a unique set-up, which we're going to exploit fully. I've planned this for years and it's coming together now. I've been involved with so many tossers, who sit with their hands out, without inputting any ideas or help. If you do get a decent lad, they eventually meet a young girl and get brain-screwed, losing all sense of adventure and drive. The girlfriend gets jealous and then it all turns to rat shit. So many sheep out there, no wonder the politicians enjoy shafting the sad, apathetic bastards. Sorry, I'm going off again.' I stood up and stretched. 'Anyway I think you should have a go at diving. There's a British Sub Aqua Club manual in the galley. Start reading it and I'll ask you some questions, we've got plenty of time.'

As Jonno left Phil came and sat down.

'Do you reckon the girls will be home when we get back?'

'Well, I left a note for Lucy and I changed the message on the machine. There's no excuse this time.' I paused looking into the sun squinting. 'It's shit or bust this time,'

Phil nodded. 'Hey, I might get a small house when we get some dosh. My mum isn't good on her pins. I think the social services will put her into a care home soon then the council will take back the house.'

'You know you can stay at Wood End as long as you want.'

'Thanks, I will until I find the right place. In the mean time I'll just have to sneak in and out while you shag the whole village!'

'Hey, bollocks it's not like that.'

Billy came out with a tray of teas. 'What's a load of bollocks?'

'Mike's trying to shag the whole village. He started last week with Jo.'

I looked at him. 'Shut up you twat, that was a secret between us.'

'Not now,' Billy grinned. 'What was she like?'

Before I could answer Phil butted in. 'You should have heard them howling like rabid animals! Grunting and swearing. Banging around the room knocking things over. I thought he was killing her!'

Billy was laughing. Winding me up through Phil was fair game to him.

'How come you know so much when you allegedly 'just walked in on us?' I asked, staring at him. 'You must have been behind the door fiddling with your string.'

'I was walking down the track. You'd left the curtains open again. There was a big silhouette of you both on the wall. It was like being at the fucking pictures. Anyone would have bogged it.'

Billy was now doubled over in stitches at his cheek and no doubt at the disbelief on my face.

'Pervert,' I grunted as I slunk away from the piss taking.

On the bridge I could still hear them repeating the story to Jonno and Len. Their joint laughter made me grin and then I looked at a picture of Lucy and at a family picture of myself with Kris and Vicki, but in my mind I saw Andrea moving towards me, just before she held my chin and kissed me.

The wooden case banged on to the deck, followed by Billy.

'Leave it for now!' he barked. 'Get the coils first.'

Phil and I hit the water and disappeared. Fifteen coils stropped per dive was becoming the workable target, and easier without all the silt. As we moved around, the hessian sacks containing the thin bars were placed into a neat mound, which was growing bigger all the time. The third and last dive of the day produced another fifteen coils.

We sat around the table. I asked Jonno questions about the physics of diving. Everyone was impressed at how quickly he was learning.

The next day was perfect. A light south-westerly breeze and the flat, blue sea without a horizon made everyone happy. Len was catching plump mackerel with cod feathers for the evening barbecue, which he and Phil were organising. The shellfish were boiling and thirty more coils were in the hold. The last fifteen were being pulled on to the deck, when out of nowhere, came a potting boat. It slowed just astern of us.

'What's he doing?' Jonno asked. We all stood at the stern glaring at the intruder.

'He's marking the wreck with his sounder and taking its position, the poaching bastard,' Billy said. Then his loud voice boomed out. 'Don't be potting this. We have a salvage contract on it, and will be working here for several weeks.'

The figure looking out of the wheelhouse window ignored Billy. The boat slowly moved away. 'He'll be back. Let's just hope it's only with pots.'

'We can just tow them off the wreck. Bloody divers finding it would be a nightmare.'

The last fifteen coils were stored below. 'That's seventy-five,' Billy said, as he dropped the hatch cover and pulled the dogs into their slots. 'And the bank doesn't get anything this time, only us. Our Sue will be pleased. We're going for that shop. At least we will be flush over winter.'

'Don't forget the commercial work, there's still some around but our bloody day-rates are going up a fair bit,' I said, while filleting a fat mackerel. Phil hovered around, wrapping each fillet in foil and adding a knob of butter and a pinch of crushed garlic. The salad was still crispy fresh and the wine was chilled.

The next five days passed without incident. A few snags caused a couple of tides to be missed. We were all knackered and fast losing concentration.

'That's the last one,' I signalled to Phil, as I turned with both hands spread flat, looking at the large empty crater we had made. He gave the thumbs up and we surfaced together.

'That's the lot, the last ten.'

After sorting the deck out, Billy's box was opened. The axe head widened the gap. As the sledgehammer came down hard the lid came off. Five heads peered into the box.

'What are they?' asked Jonno.

Billy looked at the small silver objects in his hand. 'They're pen nibs, thousands of them.'

I picked one out and rinsed it in a bucket. '777 M IRIDINOID' I read off the small shiny nib. 'Hell, all that time in seawater and no rust. Give them a wash Phil, dry out the box and put them back in it.' I looked at my watch, 'One more dive today. Shall we get the lead or more crates? That is the question.' I looked at Phil.

'Crates,'

'Billy?'

'Lead's not worth a lot, so crates it is.'

'OK, crates it is. Two of us can break them out. Phil can strop and recover.'

The dive was physical; so bottom time was reduced by one third. We still managed to cover the space the coils left with intact boxes of various sizes. Phil stropped as many as his allowed bottom time permitted.

Back on the surface he complained that his ears were getting tighter and harder to clear on the descent. And he was close to getting reversed ear on the ascent.

'Well, we've been at sea for seven days and recovered the remaining copper coils. Two hundred and five in all,' I said smiling. 'I don't think we could fit any more in the hold.'

Sea Gem was full with about fifty ton in her hold. She felt stiff in the water, so after pulling five crates onboard, the main engine was started.

Silver Bubbles

We decided to steam the mooring line due East and sink the end with two fifty-six pound weights. On our return, a grapple would snag the line and we would then be able to moor up without a diver burning up bottom time re-connecting it.

Billy looked at me then at Jonno. I winked at him. 'There's just one more thing we have to do on the way back in.' I said as Billy appeared from the dive store with a dry suit over his arm.

'Here.' He looked at Jonno then threw the suit at him. 'Put it on, lad.'

'We'll stop off and dive that small uncharted mark we found. It's in about fifty-five foot, a perfect depth for a first dip.'

The inflatable snubbed up and down on the line that led to the unknown mark as we helped Jonno kit up. Being fit and strong due to his active life Jonno was remarkably calm and collected. I waited, holding onto the line as Jonno joined me with a splash. A few minutes later we were slowly descending feet first, regularly changing OK signals. Jonno repeatedly cleared his ears and adjusted himself. Then the light gradually faded as we approached the seabed. On the bottom I let him relax and gather himself, exchanging signals we slowly followed the long galvanised chain towards the grapnel anchor.

The visibility was about fifteen feet and we were soon at the anchor, which was hooked into a tubular piece of steel that looked like the remains of a mast. Jonno gave an excited OK signal as he grabbed hold of it to steady himself.

We moved slowly along the mast arriving at a small pile of chain. I pointed out an old Admiralty type anchor, which was part buried in the coarse sand. I made a bow shape with my hands, which Jonno acknowledged.

Moving aft we came upon a small boiler. Jonno stopped, making me turn to him. He pulled with both hands and engulfed in a cloud of silt he dragged a porthole complete with brass deadeye into view. I pushed both thumbs at his find.

The engine was almost completely buried, and a few feet further astern, we found only sand. I checked my dive computer then pointed back towards the boilers. Passing the boiler, Jonno stopped and pointed to a large lobster.

On reaching the bow section we swam around investigating. I let Jonno swim freely as he was showing so much confidence and we split up to cover both sides of the bowsprit, which still displayed its elegant scrolling. Rubbing the iron plate to see if a name could be found I received a sudden jolt as Jonno banged hurriedly into me. He looked wide-eyed and pulled at my arm. I gave him the OK signal, which he quickly returned, then continued pulling at my arm. I followed him, bemused as he sped along the seabed. Suddenly stopping, he settled on to his knees and cleared his flooded mask like a seasoned professional.

He scanned the seabed before turning to me both with hands spread, gesticulating he had lost something. I pointed back to the bow and started finning, while watching him.

Back at the bow Jonno again pulled at me then again he shot off with me in pursuit. This time he stopped and made a gurgled shout, as he frantically dug into the sand. I moved closer and saw what all the fuss was about. Barely visible but becoming more exposed, was the rim of what could only be a ship's bell. I checked at my computer then joined in the desperate dig against time. A few minutes later the bell became loose, then free.

With it safely tied to the anchor line, we surfaced slowly, while constantly clearing our masks in between exchanging broad smiles.

Back on *Sea Gem* we hastily got changed while discussing the dive.

I turned the wheel sharply, while Billy hooked the orange buoy. It was attached to the winch and was retrieved slowly, watched intently by Jonno who was pacing the deck like a hungry animal. Slowly the bell broke surface and was passed it to him. All gathered in a circle, and we watched with interest as Jonno rubbed away the years of concretion and marine growth and as if by magic the engraved words spoke out the name, '*Caroline* 1878'.

'Bloody fantastic,' Jonno said with disbelief as he paraded the bell around.

'Well done lad.' Billy pulled the ring pull on the can and passed it to him. 'Problem is, mate, you'll have to find a bird called Caroline now.'

'You wouldn't believe it,' he replied grinning. 'I have.'

Anchored safely, awaiting the early morning flood tide, we turned in. The crates could wait until we were back home. Opening them in front of Sue and the kids would be fun.

I opened the door and walked in. The house felt warm. It had been a sunny day. I placed the pile of mail on the table and went over to the dreaded answer machine. There were several job inquiries and a few non-important messages, but nothing from Lucy. 'Ten days!' I said out loud. I couldn't believe she hadn't called in almost ten days. I went into the bedroom. A smell of expensive perfume was lingering in the air. She must be home, I thought. Looking at the pillow my heart sank. As I sat down on the bed the ring on the pillow fell to the floor, leaving the envelope taunting me.

Phil walked in and shouted, 'Are they coming then?' He paused as he saw the letter on the pillow.

'Oh shit, mate. Is that what I think it is?'

I shrugged my shoulders. 'Do us the honours, pal.'

He moved with a look of awkwardness towards the letter, squashing the ring deep into the carpet pile with his last step. Opening it he looked at me. 'It's a "Dear Mike".'

'A "Dear John" you mean?'

'Sorry, I mean a "Dear John".'

'I fucking knew it!' My outburst failed to distract his attention from the letter. 'Yeah, well go on then,' I snapped.

He continued, 'Dear Mike, I am so sorry to end things like this. I hoped to see you, but you are always at sea these days.'

I interrupted. 'Always at sea! For fuck's sake, she was always away, now she's blaming me!'

Phil continued, 'I rang you lots of times, but you never returned my calls.' He paused awaiting the pending outburst.

'That's bloody rich, the bitch! She didn't leave any bloody numbers. How the hell could I get back to her? That's just an excuse; she's set this up. It's all a bloody set up.'

Phil continued, 'And I didn't want to drive all that way to find you not there. I've met someone. He's one of the flight crew, he's a pilot.' Phil looked at me as I cursed slagging off pilots.

As I came back to earth he continued. 'Thanks for all the good times. I still, and will always have you in my heart.'

'Bullshit! Bloody bullshit,' I stood up and grabbed the letter. 'I know where this sorry excuse for a "Dear John" is going.' I marched to the cork notice board near the back door and pinned it in the middle. Standing back I shouted, 'There! That can stay there for all to see, everyone can read the crap themselves.' I stood looking out of the window. I could feel that my eyes had glistened slightly. I sniffed and wiped my nose.

Phil looked embarrassed and helpless. He said, 'It's not a very good one is it? Some of the ones in the mob were a scream. The excuses and bull was so amusing. Must admit though, it is a good way of taking the piss.'

'It's the only way mate,' I said, while reaching for four glasses. 'A "Dear John" is a one-way slap in the face. It's like the writer isn't interested in any pleas for mercy, or excuses. It's final and harsh, especially if you're away and can't do anything about it. As your loved one is being shagged senseless, all you can do is stew in torment. At least I can get on with knobbing the village. Some poor sod locked in a sub or on a six month

Silver Bubbles

posting would go half mad by the time he got home to try and sort things out.'

Billy and Len walked noisily in. 'Aha, just in time,' Len said, then stood watching me pour the drinks.

Billy cast a glance at the notice board. 'Is that all she had to say?'

'That's it, that's the lot,' I sighed. 'Three fucking years and she wrote a quarter of a page.'

Len noticed it, shaking his head as he read it. 'It was bound to happen, son. A good-looking girl working away in that sort of job, every Brillcream boy around would be....' He paused trying to find a discreet word.

'Shagging is the word you're looking for, Len,' said Phil.

'A pilot, as well,' Len said innocently. Phil looked at me.

'Yeah, I bet she's been through the whole fucking crew and half the passengers,' I sneered. 'I don't feel so bad about Jo now, it's a good job I didn't turn her down.'

'You turn a shag down?' Billy chuckled and then looked straight faced for a moment before cracking up in fits of laughter.

'All right, go on. Have a good laugh. I would do the same to you bastards.'

Phil turned to Billy. 'Did you know she was a parrot enthusiast?'

Billy shook his head. Phil grinned, 'Yeah she liked a Cockatoo.'

I grinned at his guile and at the absurdity of the situation then downed my drink in one. 'I'm going to get wrecked tonight,' I said, as I walked over to the rum bottles. 'Do you want another?' I said pouring myself one. They looked at each other shaking their heads, 'No.' There was a pause, and then all three said together, 'Oh, go on then.'

The morning came too soon. The distant banging stopped and suddenly the curtains swung in a gush of air as the back door opened.

Kris jumped on to the bed. 'Hi Dad.' His small, strong arms gripped my neck. 'I missed you.'

'I've missed you too, son.' I got up and donned my dressing gown. Holding my fuzzy head and taking a deep breath, I walked to the kettle. Vicki turned, surprised, she had been reading the "Dear John".

'Sorry, I didn't mean-'

I interrupted. 'That's why it's there. Feel free.'

She turned and looked at it. 'Mike, I'm so sorry.'

Inside she must have felt confused. I was alone now, but for how long? We were earning good money and I owned this place. Every gold digger in the area will be available to me. I reckon that's what she would be thinking.

'Lost your voice? Still no sugar, is it?'

'Yes, I mean no.' She looked at the floor then around. I stood holding the spoon. 'No sugar, thanks.'

After another pause she sighed. 'I see you've been celebrating. I saw Len down the lane, he looked rough.'

'We were chilling out after a successful week. We filled *Sea Gem* with copper. At last the lads can take home some real money, and without all the shit that comes with cheques.' I gasped after swallowing a mouthful of hot coffee. 'So what brings you round?'

Vicki shook her head. 'Mike, you called last night and said we could go over the decor of the loft conversion. Can't you remember? We were going to come the last time you were home.'

'Yeah, course I can.' I stood quiet. I couldn't remember a thing.

'You were slurring a lot and you tried baiting Nigel again.'

'That figures.'

'Sorry?'

'Ah nothing. We don't drink on the boat. It hit me a bit hard, what with Lucy, and that other shit still haunts me. I'll get a shower.'

Silver Bubbles

As I came out of the bathroom, the smell of bacon filled my nostrils. Kris slid down the new banister and ran past. I entered into in a strange melancholy trance. For a few seconds I felt the same as I had when I was happily living with my family.

'Where did you get the bacon from?'

'You've been away. I can't imagine you all rushing to the shops, unless it's for more rum!'

I looked at the dead men on the table. 'Christ! There were four of us and it does evaporate, you know.'

Vicki just smiled.

The morning was a fresh change for both of us. Kris chose his paper and colours. I stole glances at Vicki's figure, as she crouched and bent over while measuring up.

At the back door she gave Kris his orders, then a hug. He ran out with Spot towards *Sea Gem*.

'Well, thanks for coming over. I'll get all the stuff. It should look good. Phil and Len did well, don't you think?'

'They did a smashing job. It's better than I thought it would be.'

We stood like two kids staring around, I said to myself, 'Bollocks to this!' I held her. 'Thanks, this is for old times.' Her soft familiar lips fitted perfectly with mine and felt good. Holding her with one arm around her waist, the other at the back of her head, I pulled her tightly to me. The loving kiss took her by surprise. She pushed away. I felt hurt at her coldness.

She walked, head held high, to her car. Clicking in her seat belt, she turned and gave me a long stare, before driving away.

CHAPTER NINE

Billy smiled at us as the large lorry left, leaving a trail of dust. 'That's the last load. Let's get the shit out of the hold, it smells rotten.'

As Billy continued with his orders I walked to the stern. Billy's voice droned in the background as my mind cartwheeled with so many thoughts. All the money we had to share out and Vicki's kiss. I rested against the gunwale staring at the willow bushes swaying in the warm breeze, and at the blue damselflies that rode the gusting wind so effortlessly. Looking down at the path I noticed hoof marks. Like many times before the butterflies stirred in my stomach as I saw Andrea in my mind's eye.

The boat's intercom made me jump. 'Will the lazy daydreaming bastard slumped at the stern get a grip and join in cleaning the shit up?' I put my hands in the air while walking towards them.

The next day the three of us went to meet the scrap man. We were sitting in his office, which looked like a set from Steptoe and Son. The old man shuffled with piles of notes he produced from the large old-fashioned safe behind his desk.

'I will have to give you a cheque for part of it, lad,' he said staring at us. 'It's too much for cash.'

Silver Bubbles

'So what's the gross?' I asked.

'Forty-six tons in all.'

'I thought there was at least fifty.'

He produced the weigh tickets. 'It's all there, lad. You have to trust us. As I said, it's not in our interest to lie to you.'

I looked at Billy. 'There were a few part coils,' I said, nodding, then turned to Sid.

'So how much have we grossed then?' I had worked out the amount in my head and was waiting for the answer.

'Sixty-nine thousand less ten percent, that's sixty thousand, nine hundred. That leaves sixty-two thousand, one hundred.'

'How much cash can you give us?'

Sid rubbed his chin pondering. 'Twenty?' he said, looking for a reaction.

'Are you taking the piss, mate? OK, so that reduces your share by ten percent of the cheque, which is-'

Before I could finish Sid said, 'How about forty in cash then?'

I looked at him. 'With all respect Sid, you're making a good amount even if you pay us by cheque. We had a deal. If you can't pay cash then you lose an extra ten per cent. That was your offer, we're only sticking to it.'

'Forty is all I can do in cash at the moment.'

'That suits us.'

'So you want a cheque for...'

'Twenty-two thousand,' I interrupted.

'Twenty two thousand one hundred, plus ten percent. That makes it twenty four thousand, three hundred and ten pounds altogether.' Sid shook his head and paid up.

'You tight old sod, you're making your share and doing nowt for it,' Billy said.

Ignoring Billy, he picked up one of the lead rods. 'Can you get more of this?' he waved the rod.

'Yes we can. Why?'

Sid started rubbing his chin again.

'You got it analysed, I take it. We can do the same, you know.'

He spoke reluctantly. 'It's not lead, well a small content is, but the rest is pure tin. It's tin solder bar.'

I looked at Billy and Phil, grinning. 'Come on, Sid, I know what it says on the Teletext. Tin is worth nine grand on the metal exchange.'

'Ah yes, but that's for new tin,' Sid replied with a glint in his eye.

'We'll get a price from someone else then.' I picked up the bar from his desk.

'No, no! I'll get you a good price.' He looked agitated.

'You have my number, Sid,' I said, as we left the crowded, untidy room.

'Just think, there might be tons down there.'

'Sixty-four bloody grand, sixty-four thousand pounds.' Phil grinned from ear to ear as Billy smiled. 'One hundred and twenty-eight thousand, fifty pence pieces,' he shouted and pulled out the wads of twenty-pound notes and pressed them against his crutch, gyrating.

As we drove down the road Phil boasted, 'I could buy that and that,' pointing at cars in a showroom.

'Slow down mate, let's get home first and sort our shares out,' I said, grinning.

The crack was flowing as we counted the money into four piles. We insisted that Len got his savings back so we had ten thousand in cash each. The cheque would be banked to pay us a small weekly wage and cover the boat's running costs. Billy left in the van for home. Len ordered the full Monty Sky package and was hovering down the lane waiting for the installer.

'Hey, there's a message on the machine,' Phil shouted. I came through and pressed the button.

Silver Bubbles

'Mike, it's Kim.' Phil's head spun round. He looked intently at the machine.

'I would like to see Phil and you. I'm really sorry about Lucy. Mike, you can reach me on...'

Phil wrote the number down. 'Yes!' He punched the air then looked at me, 'Is it-'

'Course it is, you knob. Ring her now.' I walked into the kitchen, leaving Phil dialling with impatient fingers.

I was stirring the coffees when Phil entered his face was beaming. 'She's on her way. Oh, bloody hell, I don't believe this is happening to me.' He turned and paced up and down like an expectant father, much to my amusement. I put my arm round his shoulder. 'Phil, this is the summer of your life. Savour every minute, enjoy it to the full.'

'Thanks mate. You're like a brother to me.'

I walked into the room as Phil began spreading cookery books on the table.

Enjoying the view from the window I turned and saw a picture of Lucy smiling like a Vogue model. It just jumped out at me. I turned the photo on its face as Doris Day sang "Qué Sera" in my mind.

'How's it going?' Phil asked. I had been pressed into cooking the meal for them. Phil had been out for hours shopping and had brought back enough food for a week. He wanted surf and turf, so I prepared the medallions of monkfish with a thick juicy fillet steak.

The small hire car pulled up. Phil ran out and greeted the ever-gorgeous Kim.

After freshening up, Kim sat down at the table and Phil poured champagne while I cooked the steaks. The meal was good and it wasn't long before Lucy was the topic.

'She seemed to change,' Kim said softly. 'She started flirting with the senior officers and became selfish.' Kim bowed her head and her eyes uplifted to mine. 'She stayed out with someone. When I voiced my disapproval she just laughed and called me "Miss Prim". She tried to get me involved with them, you know.'

'Yeah…let's forget all that now. It's great to see you again. You look prettier than I remember.'

Phil was spellbound with her presence.

'I'm popping out, the place is yours.'

Phil stood up, 'No, stay. Don't go out for us.'

I smiled. 'Kim's come to see you mate. We had our fun.' I winked at Kim. 'That's in the past now, you have a good night.'

Kim kissed me on the cheek. 'Thank you, Mike.' She turned to Phil and smiled.

'Go easy on him,' I shouted as I walked down the path. Phil gave me a thumb; his other arm was tightly around his dream girl, who was smiling delightfully.

I spent the next few days relaxing, popping to the boat to study the files on shipwrecks I had acquired over the years. Phil and Kim were having the time of their lives, and that pleased me. Billy had taken his family to London for the weekend. Kris was helping me on the boat, and trying his hardest to persuade me to buy him a small moto cross bike to ride around the fields.

I had agreed a contract with the Salvage Association (S.A.) to look for the tin on the *Juno*. The name *City of Birmingham* kept cropping up, three hundred and ninety-six tons of blister copper. Copper ingots, ninety-nine percent pure, about six to a ton, were left lost or not found by the salvage company who had worked the wreck in the sixties. There was plenty to go for and lots more besides.

Phil had driven Kim back to London after, in his words, "the best days of my life." Kris was at the local skateboard park and having a sleepover at his mate's. Len had Sky TV, and was fully battened down. It was seven p.m. The cloud had spread from the east, making it cool and damp, so I lit

Silver Bubbles

the fire. Picking up the remote control, I flicked through the TV channels. '"The Life of the Dormouse". 'God, has it come to this?' I moaned.

I glanced at the phone book and dialled a number. 'Is Jo around? I see. OK then. No thanks. Bye.' The dormouse was looking around nervously clinging on to its small round nest as the big combine harvester approached. 'You've shit it, pal,' I said aloud just as the phone rang.

'Hello.'

'Hello, Mike.'

'Who's that?'

'It's Andrea.' I sat up and changed the phone to my other ear.

'Andrea, how are you doing?'

'My horse is...' She paused, 'Oh Mike I'm so upset.'

'Where's Gerald?'

'He's in London, as usual. There was silence... 'Anyway, how are you?'

'Better for you ringing, I'm just sat here by myself in front of a log fire.'

'Do you want to come round, Mike? I have a fire burning.'

'I'm on my way.' I glanced at the telly and as I turned it off the dormouse disappeared into the thrashing combine.

I had a quick shower. Five minutes later I was biking down the track with a bottle of wine.

Andrea opened the door, wearing a big, baggy jumper and tight riding pants.

'It's bloody freezing out there. It's supposed to be summer. Where's the fire then?' She stood staring, then half smiled.

'Have you been drinking?' A half-full bottle of whiskey on the table answered my question.

'He leaves me alone, and when he's here he's always horrid to me, Mike. I need loving. I've held out long enough. Hold me, please hold me.' She looked so sad, standing crying with her hands by her side.

Her hair caressed my face as she nestled into my neck, holding me tight. I held her, not knowing what to do. Feeling her tears on my neck, I pulled her gently away and looked into her full eyes.

'What is it Andrea? What's made you so sad?'

She again cuddled into me and said softly, 'They put my horse to sleep this afternoon.' She sobbed, 'Oh Mike, I loved him so much. He was all I had.'

I held her, consoling her, hugging her. What could I say? I just cuddled her as she sobbed. Tears rolled down my own cheeks. She looked at me putting her forehead on mine. 'I'm sorry,' she said, between sniffles.

'Don't be,' I whispered, wiping her tears with my thumbs. 'You need to cry. I've needed too for a long time. Things will get better and I want you to remember, you're not alone. You've got me as a friend, and I make a good friend, especially with someone as lovely as you.' I kissed her tasting her tears.

Our embrace turned into a passionate kiss. My hands moved inside her jumper, my fingers danced over her skin.

'Oh Mike, I want you.' She pressed herself against me. I ran my hands over her shapely bottom and hips. She felt irresistible. I could not hide my excitement. As I pulled her tightly to me, she moaned, submissively pushing herself against me. She led me to the bedroom and onto a beautiful brass four-poster bed. We sank into the deep mattress. I was in her private place. Her smell radiated from the pillow as my head settled onto it. I pulled off her jumper. She straddled me, hastily undoing my belt and unbuttoning my jeans. Her cleavage looked sexy as her arms pressed her breasts together. I grabbed her and kissed her hard while sliding her trousers down. Running my hands over her firm silken buttocks made her moan softly. Her shape and firmness felt so good. She squirmed on top of me, pouring herself over me while pulling off my jeans together with my pants. The sight of my nakedness made her gasp. I turned her on to her back, kissing her while removing the remainder of her clothes. Lying alongside her, I visually soaked her up, kissing her neck lightly. Biting her, moving to her breasts I gently passed my lips over her erect nipples then caressed her below and she surrendered herself to me. I rolled onto her, whilst kissing her hungrily, making her body quiver in spasms of pleasure as her strong legs wrapped tightly around my body, pulling me into her, joining us as one in an exhilarating embrace. Looking into her brown sleepy eyes, her face radiated pure desire. I couldn't hold back much longer, the pleasure was so extreme. I floated on her rippling naked body and when our eyes met again I felt I was going to explode. She gave out a long, soft moan, gripping me tighter than any woman had before. Her whole body throbbed and trembled. I was entwined so deeply within her, I didn't want it to end but her muscular movements broke me. Totally disarmed, I was captured by the mind and body-shattering pleasure that pulsated through us.

I had never experienced such a feeling of contentment, as I lay weak and drained. Andrea nuzzled into my neck and kissed me, we were moulded into each other completely, and her hot breath fell on me like a spell and sent me into a blissful sleep.

Phil removed the paintbrush and spread the grey paint, covering the scrapes on the hatch combing, making it look tidy and clean.

'What's up with him?' Billy shouted across the deck.

'I've no idea. He's too happy for my liking. He'll probably break down into a babbling idiot any minute.'

'I heard that, you knob,' I shouted from the wheelhouse then hung my head out of the window. 'You do the menial tasks, I'll do the research. Anyway, you plonkers can't even string a sentence together properly.'

'I hope she finds something worth while after all this gobbing off,' Billy said to Phil with a wink.

A couple of hours later the deck looked a lot better; painted in battleship grey. Len neatly cut the gunwale tops in with black gloss. In the galley, having a brew, I told them a tale my mate had told me.

Dave was in the Police Underwater Search Unit and was full of stories. They received a call. A man was seen throwing a bin liner into a reservoir. The witness took the man's car registration number. They got called out to search for the bin liner, which had been thrown in where the reservoir was over thirty metres deep. They found the bag, and as suspected, it contained six little kittens. Annoyed by their find, they acquired the man's address and late that night sneaked into his garden and placed the kittens in a row on his doorstep, looking at the back door. They never saw what happened, but I bet that bloke got a shock when he opened his door!'

'I would like to have seen his face,' said Phil. 'He must have shit himself. I would have pushed them through the cat flap.'

'Yeah, if they had one,' Billy said, looking out of the window. 'Hey up! It's Sid the Scrappy.'

The once elegant Merc stopped at the boat.

'Come aboard,' Billy shouted.

'I've got you a price on the bars,' he said, still breathing heavily after walking up the gangway.

'Well, how much?' I asked, still smiling, to Phil and Billy's amusement.

'Well, the lead contaminate reduces the quality and obviously the price.'

'Come on Sid, stop stalling.' Billy grumbled.

'I can offer four thousand five hundred pounds a ton less ten for cash, which is four thousand and fifty. Good, eh?' he said, looking round at us.

I smiled and said, 'That's fine with me. What about you three?' All three mumbled in agreement.

'It's OK with us,' I said still smiling. After a brew Sid left.

'How much do you reckon there is?' Phil asked.

'Got to be at least a couple of ton and we've got it piled up waiting. It's a piece of piss to retrieve. And don't forget the remaining crates. They can't all be full of tins of rotting apricots and sludge like those we brought back last time.'

'That box full of brass tubes was worth nearly five hundred. At least we know what to pick and what not to,' Billy added.

'We'll sail in two days, weather permitting,' I said while clapping my hands and rubbing them together.

'Can I come, Dad?' Kris pleaded.

'Hands up if Kris can sign on.' Nobody moved or said a word. Kris looked down at the deck dejected. Then the laughter told him we were only kidding.

'Where have you been lately?' Phil asked me. 'You stayed out the other night. Whose turn was it? Jo's again?' I smiled and shook my head.

'Come on man, we're sperm brothers don't forget. Who was it?'

'I bet it's that bird on the horse.' Billy looked at me. 'I've seen him drool and bump into things like a zombie when she's ridden past here. You just can't resist a small arse, can you?' He kept his stare on me, but I wouldn't make eye contact with him. Instead I replied,

'Look you're wasting your time!'

Billy and Phil started laughing and shouting. 'He's bitten! It's her! It's got to be her.'

I could feel myself going red.

'That's confirmed it,' Billy shouted. 'Get the bread out, we'll have some toast.' He put his hands next to my red face, as if warming them.

'You silly sod, trying to keep secrets like a little schoolgirl.'

'That's why he's been grinning like a queen in a Boy Scout's camp,' jeered Phil.

'All right, all right,' I stood up. 'You're worse than pub barmaids. You have to know everything. Anyway, you're just jealous and frustrated.'

'I'm not,' Phil said with a glint in his eye, looking at the friendship ring Kim had given him.

'No way,' Billy shouted. 'Our Girt rapes me on request.'

Trying to change the subject, I looked at Phil. 'You can't wear rings in our job, you navy wuss.'

'I can take it off when I work. Anyway, what has Irish Andrea given you then?'

I smiled and looked at them. 'I couldn't begin to explain.'

'What a load of bollocks,' Billy shouted, followed by abuse from Phil.

Turning my back on them I said, 'I'm off for a pint. You may come if your wife will allow you, Mr Wells.'

Sitting at our favourite table near the ladies toilet entrance, we planned our next trip. I was meandering, talking about four wrecks at once, confusing Billy and Phil, when a shout from behind the bar interrupted us.

Len was on the phone. 'There's a screw job on the oil terminal; they have to sail on tonight's tide. They're desperate and are willing to pay good money.'

The drinks were left. An hour and a half later, we were on the jetty and kitting up.

'You do it, big fella.' I passed the band mask to Billy. 'Phil, you're standby, I'll do the coms. and second standby.'

'I'm just going on the bridge to make sure she's all shut down.' A few minutes later I returned. 'Yeah, everybody knows

Silver Bubbles

we're diving. It's all shut down. It's another mooring rope. Billy, take two kitchen devils with you.'

'Nah, one will do.'

'Take two, they bust easy. It will save us time.'

Billy climbed down the ladder then seemed to dissolve into the brown water. Phil stood on the edge of the jetty, paying out the umbilical, as Billy pulled hard with his arms in a breaststroke motion towards the rudder, like a small spider hanging from a tread.

'On the job,' he panted, in between gulps of air.

'Roger that.'

After twenty minutes Billy announced that he was nearly finished. Just a hard melted piece of rope was left and as usual, fighting to the bitter end.

'Tides racing through,' Phil remarked. 'He's got loads of slack out.'

'He's tucked in the Kort nozzle. He'll be fine, just remember to pull him quickly to the ladder when he leaves the job.'

Phil nodded, while watching the hose vibrate in the tide.

A few minutes later Phil shouted, 'Mike, the hose has gone dead slack.'

To my horror, the ship astern of us had its propeller turning. 'Shit!' I cursed loudly.

'Leaving the job, take my slack.' Billy's voice echoed loudly through the coms speaker.

'Please, not now Billy!' I said out loud while rushing to the edge.

Phil screamed, 'The hose! It's in the prop. It's in the prop!'

I dashed to the coms 'Ditch your gear and swim away. Your hose is in a ship's prop.' I ran to the edge to see Billy on the surface, his mask off. He was desperately trying to unscrew the carabiner connected to his weight vest, as the hose dragged him closer to the slow turning propeller. For a second he looked up at us. His face sent a cold chill through me as he helplessly wrestled with the tight clip, legs flailing in the water, kicking desperately.

Pulling out my knife, I quickly took a few paces backwards, then ran and jumped off the jetty. As I hit the water I stretched out my arms. Grabbing the hose with lightning speed, I reached Billy and snatched at the carabiner, then began cutting the thick, doubled webbing that held the D ring. The small knife made a pinging sound as the blade snapped and flew into the air. I reached into Billy's leg pocket. No knife!

'Where's the knife?' I screamed at him.

'This one,' Billy's voice turned to gurgles as a wave hit him in the face, and he turned to expose his other pocket. I pushed my hand into it and produced the spare knife, then began cutting desperately. This was the last chance to save my friend.

The propeller was now only feet away. Its massive tips were pounding the water making it shake around us. The hose pulled away as I severed the webbing, but Billy spun around. The bailout hose was pulling him now. One slash with the knife and he was free, as the main hose disappeared with the band mask. We now had to swim for our lives. Although the wash from the prop was pushing us off, the strong tide was pushing us in a circular eddy, which was feeding the propeller. If the ship went astern we would die in seconds.

With no fins, just protective wellies fixed to our suits, swimming was almost impossible. I hadn't zipped my dry suit up in the rush, and was struggling to keep my head above the brown water. I was swallowing it, coughing, half- drowning as my suit filled more every second, pulling me down in the swirling current.

Billy was holding me the best he could, but even his strength wasn't enough. I felt like a child in the deep end, desperately holding my face up while pushing out my lips to stop the water from choking me. I was gasping for the life-giving air, but was losing the battle.

A sudden splash submerged our heads. Then out of the water Phil surfaced holding a rope.

'Grab it! Grab it!' He screamed.

They both pulled on the rope while helping me stay afloat. Phil had tied the rope to the jetty. On reaching the jetty, which had ladders at ten-metre intervals, we rested, getting our breath back. Suddenly the airline pulled tight above us, and the van door appeared. 'Fucking hell, the van's being pulled in.' We all span on the ladder so we were protected by the jetty and then all of a sudden the umbilical gave a loud crack as it snapped. The van thankfully had stopped up against a bollard.

Back on the jetty Billy put his arms round both of us. 'Thanks. I thought that was it.'

'Christ you did,' I gasped. We looked at Phil then at each other. There was no need for words.

All the umbilical was lost, having been hooked on the van's bumper. The coms and air panel weren't dragged in but more than two thousand pounds worth of gear was gone.

'I don't see how it happened,' said Phil, blaming himself.

'Don't you take the blame!' I snapped.

Billy interrupted, 'I pulled too much hose from you. It must have drifted down tide.'

'Pack what's left,' I said. 'I want a word with the real bastard who's to blame!'

'Why didn't you tell them we were diving?' I shouted at the berthing master. 'You nearly killed us, I can't believe it. You must have given them clearance to sail. I contacted you on the bloody VHF twenty minutes before. It was you that gave us permission to dive.' The uniformed man sat silent, not knowing what to say.

'Well, if you can't admit to a cock up, at least give me your insurance details so we can claim for our lost equipment.'

'You will have to apply in writing,' he said nervously, looking at the large pool of brown water that had drained from my sodden under suit all over thick piled carpet. 'I'm sorry, but that's procedure.'

'Procedure, where was the bloody procedure when we were diving? Procedure! That's just bullshit. Procedure when it suits.'

Billy looked at me, nodding his head sideways, beckoning us to leave before I went too far. As we walked out the door I was still chuntering.

'Procedure it is "more than my sodding job's worth" crap. It's a cop out! All bloody bullshit!'

Grinning, Phil looked at Billy and said, 'He's back to normal!'

The horn of the red sports car beeped repeatedly. I walked out the door. Phil was sitting behind the wheel beaming. 'What do you think?'

'It's brilliant, how many seats?'

'Oh, it's got two. With the top down you can get three in.' He tapped his hand between the seats. 'One can sit on here.'

'You can't sit there, its illegal.' Phil ignored the comment and sat grinning. I stood savouring the moment of Phil's first new car. Although it was totally impractical, I made an effort to share his excitement.

'Give us a cabby then?' I asked. Phil eagerly got out.

The wheels spun as we pulled out of the track, towards the Ship.

'Take that bloody wheel down Jonno, its old hat now,' I shouted as we walked in.

'No chance,' Jonno replied. 'It's a tribute to one of your funnier cock-ups. It stays.'

I walked to the bar and rested my elbows on it. 'Where can I get a good horse from?' I asked.

'You on a horse? Fuck off!'

'No, it's not for me.'

'Who's it for then?' Phil butted in.

Silver Bubbles

I gave a long sigh, 'You can't have any secrets round here, can you?'

'Where are you going to hide something as big as a horse?' replied Phil.

'I wouldn't be hiding it!' I was becoming irritated.

'Well, how can it be a secret then?' Jonno asked.

'Oh forget it!' I looked around exasperated then asked again. 'Well, where can I get one from, then?'

'It's not like buying a washing machine you know. You don't go to a shop and get one from over the counter. You can't stand them in a corner, they need constant attention.'

'I know that, for Gods sake.'

'No, you couldn't do that, it would piss and shit all over the kitchen,' Phil said.

'Will you be serious?' I snapped.

'Phil's right. You couldn't keep it in you kitchen,' Jonno grinned, looking at Phil and winking.

I walked over to the pretty barmaid. 'You ride don't you?' Hysterical laughter broke out from behind me. Phil shouted, 'I've never heard that chat up line before.'

The girl gave me a condescending look. 'Don't listen to them. I'm trying to get hold of a horse.' I screwed my face up. 'No, I mean, buy one for a friend.'

Sarah smiled. 'Is it really for you?'

'No, it isn't. It's for a friend.'

'How big is he?'

I looked at her. 'It's a girl,' I said loudly. 'I'm sorry, she's, err....' I leaned over the bar and looked her up and down. 'She's about your size, maybe a bit smaller.'

'Is she a good rider?'

Phil shouted, 'She must be. He's been smiling for sodding weeks.'

'Ignore him, he's got a problem. A fractured childhood, he was abused with a hot poker.'

She looked confused. I pretended to whisper something into her ear. She looked at Phil and laughed. I had asked her to. Phil took the bait and started countering abuse at me.

'You want a gelding with a good nature. Where does she ride?'

'All over the fields and on the roads, you know, everywhere really.'

'My friend's mum is selling a nice horse, not too young, but fit and in good condition.'

'What colour is it?'

'He's a bay with a black mane and tail a lovely horse in every way.'

'What's its, sorry, his name?'

'Misty.'

'That's a great name. Can you take me to see him?' I paused, giving her deep eye contact. 'Please.'

She blushed. 'I'm working.' She shrugged her shoulders, while picking glasses from the washer.

I turned to Jonno. 'Can I borrow this young lady for half an hour?'

'What on earth for?' Phil was about to start. I got in first.

'Her friend's mum has a horse for sale, a good one.'

'Go on then, but bring her back in one piece. I know her parents.' As we left I pulled my tongue out at Phil. 'See you later mate.' I grinned, 'Give us your keys.'

Phil followed us to the car. Sarah's skirt rode up, showing her legs as she squeezed into the small bucket seat. She pulled it down and gave a coy smile.

I smiled back. 'It was OK as it was.'

'I've heard all about you lot.'

'Good things I hope.'

'I don't know about that!' She jolted back as I dropped the clutch, causing the wheels to spin and gush out blue smoke as we sped off, snaking sideways. I saw Phil in the rear mirror,

Silver Bubbles

shaking his arms, obviously shouting obscenities as two hundred miles were taken off his tyres.

We drove slowly up the drive leading to the well-kept smallholding. Its L-shaped stable blocks were painted white and black, making it look almost clinical. Sarah was right. The horse was in excellent condition, fifteen-three hands, and three-quarter breed. He was calm and friendly.

After lots of questions I inquired, 'How much are you asking?'

The well-spoken woman said firmly, 'Two thousand three hundred guineas. Is he for you?'

'Hell no, I wouldn't know which end to get on.'

Sarah giggled.

'I want him for a friend. She's kind and would definitely fall in love with him. She's had horses before. You could check on Misty for your own peace of mind if you wanted.'

After more questions we struck a deal. I asked her if she could leave a halter on him, as I want to surprise her.

It was six-thirty a.m. the next morning. A heavy mist hung over the fields. The green Range Rover towing a smart horsebox was on time. It pulled into the yard. After the money and papers were exchanged Misty was taken out of the box. He remained calm and relaxed much to my relief. After handshakes they left.

I stood holding Misty, talking to him. Suddenly Len appeared in his dressing gown. 'What the hell? Where the devil did that come from?'

'Do you always sneak about at this time in the morning looking like a member of the Klu Klux Clan?' I said, whispering so loud that I was almost hissing.

'I heard a car,' Len replied looking at me. 'Whose is that then?'

'It's not mine. It was just delivered here. Hold him a minute please.' I ran into the house and removed the receipt from the papers, folding them into a card on which I had written a short poem. I sealed the envelope. I hadn't been this excited for ages. 'Cheers Dad.'

Len watched me lead Misty down the track, until we were out of sight.

He scratched his head, 'What's he up to now?' he sighed as he walked amid the bird song that echoed all around the private retreat.

I opened the gate to the paddock and led Misty to another gate at Andrea's back garden. I tied him there, placing a red ribbon around his neck on which I attached the card.

'Good boy.' I patted Misty. 'You'll get loved to death, fella. I'm jealous of you.' Running back to Wood End I felt great. When I got my breath back I phoned her. My hand shook with excitement as I pressed the keys. It was ringing. A sleepy voice spoke. 'Hello.'

'Good morning, Andrea.' There was a silence. 'Hello,' I said again.

'Is that you Mike?'

'Yeah,' I replied. 'I'm sorry it's so early.'

'That's all right, are you going away to sea today?'

'No not today, but soon. Tomorrow, weather permitting. That's not why I called.' I paused nervously twisting the cord round my fingers. 'I've got you a little present, to cheer you up.'

'Mike, you don't have to.' Her voice sounded soft and sleepy.

'I've left it near your back gate. You'd better go straight away. It might get cold.'

'For sure you haven't cooked me a breakfast, have you?' she replied, sounding so Irish.

'Go and look for yourself.'

'You're mad so you are,' she giggled. 'See you later then.'

'Yeah, see you soon,' I said almost whispering, then placed the receiver down gently.

I was pacing up and down and didn't see Phil and he made me jump.

'What are you up too; have you shit the bed or something? You must have got up at dawn.'

'I got that horse,'

'What for?' he paused with his finger on his chin, staring at me. 'Oh no, you haven't got it for that married bird?'

I put my hands in the air. 'I know, I know. It's a crazy thing to do. I acted on impulse.'

'You did more than that. What will she tell her husband? "Oh, Mike bought it for me." A "thank you" for the shag we had! For Christ's sake mate, what can the poor girl say? She's in a black hole and it's you who's pushed her in it.'

I was stuck for words and thought desperately for a solution. 'I'll just tell him I felt sorry for her, you know, after she lost Amber. Ah, fuck him anyway; I'll smack him if he starts.'

'You amaze me, you're a responsible bloke, a businessman. All the things you've done. You know - that shooting thing. Then you smack some poor bloke 'cause you want his wife. You're just as bad as bloody Nigel!'

I gave him a cold stare.

'Don't start on me,' he said. 'And you call me a nutter? Wait till Billy hears about this. Does Len know?' Looking at me he said, 'Obviously not. Jesus, I don't believe this.'

I walked to the kettle. 'It's not all that bad. As I said, it's only a gift. He won't suspect anything. I'll just say someone was giving it away and I mentioned Andrea's horse had broken its leg. You know, just a neighbourly thing to do.'

'You might get away with that.'

I looked up expecting support.

'If he's had his brain replaced with a wet sponge. The odds of that happening aren't in your favour mate. Even the most easygoing guy would be well pissed and angry and soon suss you out.'

'I...' The van pulled into the yard.

'Billy's here.' Phil looked through the window then back at me.

'Fill your sad boots. I'm getting a shower,' I sighed.

Even in the shower with the water running, I could hear them slagging me off. To make matters worse, Len was there as well, so I sneaked into the bedroom, shutting the door behind me and locking it. Sitting on the bed rubbing my hair with a towel, although they were only in the kitchen, I felt comfortably remote locked in here and unreachable. Then a movement through the window caught my eye. It was Andrea on Misty, her hair was blowing in the light morning breeze she was smiling and laughing. She looked so happy. I opened the window and jumped out, waving my towel. She rode towards me, pulling Misty up like a western cowboy on a quarter horse. She jumped off, despite her mount being over fifteen hands, and gave me a mighty hug. With tears in her eyes, she kissed me hard on my lips, then all over my face. She stopped and wiped her eyes.

'Oh Mike he's wonderful, he's so good...'

I interrupted, 'I'm really sorry, I acted on impulse. I've put you in an awkward situation.'

'How?' she looked surprised.

'What the hell are you going to tell Gerald? He's no fool.'

'Mike.' She put both hands on my face. 'He doesn't even know about Amber. We don't talk much. He doesn't call me. There's so much you don't know Mike,' she said, shaking her head. 'He won't even notice the change. There's not much difference between them anyway, not that he would notice. Oh Mike, Misty's the best surprise I've ever had. I thought you had left a breakfast, so I ran out looking down at the ground! He gave a snort. I couldn't believe it.' She paused, breathing heavily. 'And the little note was special. You're so kind, so you are. Can you come around tonight?' She turned and mounted

Silver Bubbles

Misty without any assistance then gave me a coy look. 'I'll have a surprise for you.'

Misty turned, chewing his bit then looked me straight in the eyes as if he was smiling at me and showing his approval of his new companion. Then he sprung up leaving big divots in the soil as they burst into an energetic gallop. I stood watching until they rode out of sight. Her ability and confidence made me even more interested in her. Then I turned and walked to face the mob.

'I still think you're pushing your luck,' said Billy.

I threw the parallel rule on to the chart. 'Look, as I told you earlier, no harm has been done. No one has been compromised. Only one thing has changed, and that is that someone who's kind and nice is a lot happier, OK? End of subject.'

'If you say so, pal.' Billy put his hand on my shoulder. 'I don't want to see you get hurt, that's all.' His big hand squeezed me before pushing me.

'Cheers mate, I know.'

All the checks were completed. Phil had replenished the stores and the fuel tanker had topped *Sea Gem's* tanks up. We were to sail on the morning tide.

'We'll get the solder bars first dive and then check out the remaining crates, but I don't think we're going to find anything special there. And we can't air-lift the whole bloody wreck looking for the mysterious special cargo, when we don't even know what we're looking for,' I said, looking at them both. 'So we can have a go at the Juno. The City of Birmingham will be in bad Vis until the end of August, and we will have to do it on the small tides.'

'Great. If we find the tin we'll be laughing all the way to the bank,' said Phil. 'Are we off for a pint tonight then?'

'I bloody am.' Billy turned to me. 'Are you coming?'

I hesitated a little too long. I should have known better.

'You can't be bloody serious man, you instigate all this bonding and team spirit and then one bird screws your brain.'

'Not just his brain.' Phil added.

'I'm coming,' I protested. 'Keep your bloody skirts on!'

I arrived at the Ship dressed smart and smelling of several aftershaves. Billy shook his head. 'I know you didn't say for how long, you hopeless knob-hound. You're worse than sniffing Phil.'

'What?' I said, grinning.

'I hope all this is worth it,' Phil said.

'That's fucking rich coming from you, I smell jealousy. It's as thick as the bullshit you're both full of. I'll get them in then.'

'Misty's great. I owe you one, Sarah.' She looked me up and down.

'You look nice tonight.'

'Thanks, so do you.' Phil came to the bar.

'You never stop do you? I thought I had a problem.'

'You've either got it or you haven't mate, and I'm full of it at the moment!'

Sitting at the table, I broke the silence. 'It's strange, when you pull, you must emit some sixth sense or something afterwards, because women seem attracted to you. It must go back to the cavemen days.'

'Its confidence, that's all,' Phil joined in. 'Even if you look like a cross between Blackbeard and Al Capone you can still pull if you flow with wit and humour.'

'I think he's calling you an ugly bastard,' Billy said to me.

'OK, watch this.' I got up and walked to the bar. 'Sarah, here a second please.' She walked over to me. I whispered into her ear. She smiled and kissed me on the lips passionately.

Silver Bubbles

'Hey, put her down,' Jonno shouted. I returned to the table, beaming.

'You see? It's easy.'

'What did you say?' Phil asked seriously.

'I'm not telling you the secret. You would only abuse it.'

Billy interrupted, 'Hey did you hear about the two nuns?'

I looked at Phil. Was this going to be a "Billy joke"?

'Well, these two nuns were driving along fully kitted up in their gear, you know.'

'Habitats,' Phil said.

I started laughing 'Habits, you pleb. How many fucking nuns have you seen in welding habitat?'

'Billy gave an impatient stare, 'Have you two quite finished?'

He continued. 'They're driving along and they pull right in front of a bloody great big lorry, making the driver brake hard. The enraged driver blows his horn and one of the nuns waves. This makes him even angrier, so when they stop at a set of traffic lights he gets out of his truck and walks towards the nuns. The nuns are terrified. As he storms towards them, the nun in the passenger seat says, 'Show him your cross quickly show him your cross!' So the nun who's driving winds her window down and shouts loudly, 'You stupid fat bastard, you were bloody speeding anyway.'

'Nice one,' I said, as we all laughed at Billy's "rare" joke.

I escaped drunken oblivion when two girls started talking to Phil. I slipped away. Only Billy noticed and I received the familiar disapproving shake of his head.

I knocked on the door and could feel my heart beating faster as a nervous sort of boyish feeling gripped me. The door slowly opened. Andrea was wearing a short, black backless dress. Her jet-black hair curled into her neck and shone against her pearl white skin. Starting at her chin it tapered down to her shoulders.

She greeted me with an evocative smile.

'You look...' I paused, eyeing her up and down. 'I'm lost for words.'

'Hungry?' she smiled, moving aside to let me enter. The smell of her perfume filled my head, as I fumbled with the bottle of champagne, not sure where to put it.

'Here, let me.' She walked into the dining room, swinging the bottle, her short dress showing her curvy figure.

'Lobster, champagne and the most beautiful host I've ever seen.' I stared at her. 'Heaven can't be as good as this. Thanks.'

We ate and drank, exchanging flirting glances. Our minds were full of anticipation knowing the real meal was yet to come.

I wiped my mouth and folded the napkin. 'That was beautiful, the sauce was yummy. You're a good cook. I love all seafood; it's my favourite. Thanks again.'

'It's me who should be thanking you.' She picked up the small, red card. 'This is so sweet it makes me cry.' She read the note softly in her haunting accent.

You felt so soft
A fallen bird
No more flying
Trapped and crying
I fixed your wing
To watch you fly
To hear you sing

'You made me happy when I was alone and heart-broken. You mended my heart and now....' She stopped and looked down, fumbling with her napkin. She looked up, 'Now you've stolen my heart.'

I felt a wave of excitement run through me. I always thought there may be a possibility of real romance, but this

Silver Bubbles

was more, this was now serious. It felt strange, like my life was about to change and I couldn't resist. I didn't want to resist the feeling; I felt my selfishness was justified. It was like my first encounter all over again.

I got up and crouched down, putting my arm around her. 'Andrea I.... I don't know what to say or do. You're inside me, tangled in my thoughts. Life is so short we're like two snowflakes falling to the ground we touch for only a short time then melt into oblivion. I... We shouldn't be doing this, but it's all I want to do. You're even in my dreams.' I whispered close to her ear, 'My snowflake.'

She stood up and held me tight. 'Oh Mike, I feel the same, so let's not talk. Tonight is my "thank you". We have to cast everything out of our minds. Hold me tight, love me, Mike.'

Her embrace, her smells made me lose all inhibitions. I lowered my hands, feeling her, pulling her against me. She felt so good, like she was all mine. 'Oh, I could eat you up!' I kissed her neck, breathing her in. She pressed her soft lips to my ear. Her breath felt warm like rays of sunlight. She whispered, 'Then devour me!'

CHAPTER TEN

My kit bag hit the deck at their feet. They were lined up, with arms folded like washerwomen.

'Glad you could make it, skipper,' Phil said, looking at his watch. Kris was standing at the stern watching almost sneakily to see how his dad was going to get out of this one.

'Well, get the bloody plank up. We've still got enough water, so stop your bitching! And when you've done that, get a brew and a bacon banjo on. I'll get on with the serious work, OK?'

'The bastard's full of it,' Phil said to Len.

Billy butted in. 'He's the skipper and don't you forget it. That goes for both of you.' He looked at Kris. 'All of you,' he snapped.

Phil looked at Len for some response but Len agreed. 'He's right, he *is* the skipper.'

'Yeah but if I came this late he would give me shit. The river will be like a bloody chicane. That's if we don't go aground.'

Len shook his head. 'If you came this late we would have been long gone.'

After a pause Phil said, 'Yeah understood, subject closed.' He turned and walked to the galley.

I was unforgivably late and we had a scary trip down the river. The tide had ebbed and the river was dangerously low.

Some of the stretches were just wide enough for *Sea Gem*. If we had gone aground it would be my fault and they would have been harsh and cutting with justification.

'You lucky bastard,' Billy said with a cold stare, as we left the river and found the deeper water of the estuary.

'The luck of the Irish, eh?' I replied tapping the side of my nose while grinning.

The rope shivered with tension as the large grapnel dragged along the seabed. I studied the sounder and plotter intensely, not taking my eyes off the screens.

'Got you,' I said out loud. As a long string shape appeared on the sounder, I slowly went astern to stop her.

'Haul it up now,' I shouted through the tannoy.

Billy put the rope round the winch's whipping drum, and started retrieving the line. They all smiled and looked up at me as the two rusty weights clanked on to the steel deck. As she settled in the tide, I turned off the main engine then clipped on the day-marks, winding them to the top of the mast to warn shipping that we were involved in underwater operations and could not manoeuvre.

'That saved a dive all right,' Billy said to Phil.

Phil replied, 'You have to hand it to him. That was shit hot wasn't it?'

'Not bad,' he smiled. 'Bloody chancer.'

The familiar sounds, the salty taste. Millions of silver bubbles enveloped us, as the excitement of exploring pumped through our veins. I tugged at Phil's arm, pointing at the mooring line, which was leading under a large, eroded piece of steel. Its sharp edge was cutting through the rope.

'Phil,' I babbled through my mouthpiece. Pointing to the surface I signalled to him. He understood what to do. Billy had to slacken the rope off so I could pull it out from under the steel. Phil disappeared.

As I waited for the line to go slack, I glanced around the seabed. I smiled to myself at the sight of Phil's knife stuck in the 'almost eaten to a skeleton' monkfish. It wasn't as big as he told us, the exaggerating sod. Suddenly the rope became slack. I pulled at it, moving along it. Pulling it was hard as it was partly buried in sand. At the end where it was almost clear, it started to become tight again. I had to let go as the thick rope tensioned against the edge of the steel plate. The steel gave a loud grating sound, moved sideways and then lifted as the full weight of *Sea Gem* bore upon it. There was another crunch as the rope snatched making the steel fold and lift like a big piece of cardboard throwing up silt like the whole thing had exploded. The stout rope snatched again, causing the steel to cartwheel and settle somewhere in the cloud of silt. As the silt began to disperse down tide I couldn't believe my eyes. Packed in a row were large tubes. I scratched one with my knife. The light, gold-coloured metal confirmed my every hope. It was non-ferrous, possibly gunmetal, which was worth more than copper. There was no marine fouling. A rub along the length with my hand revealed a broad arrow mark of the Navy. That's strange; this must be the unspecified cargo. What the hell can they be?

I was looking them over when Phil returned. I showed them to him. He swam to the end of one of them and started digging with his hand. The sand and black silt was light and hung in the water reducing the visibility to a cloudy mist. After several minutes he bumped into me and grabbed my thumb, giving me the OK signal.

We swam together to the solder bars. The metal cage Phil had brought down with him was hanging on the mooring line, waiting to be filled. This took twenty minutes. Then I had to surface. Phil still had five minutes left on his computer and could finish topping up the cage. I held on to the line with one hand then gave a couple of kicks with my fins. As I left the bottom, my buoyancy increased as the air in my suit expanded.

Gripping the rope to slow my ascent, I floated up effortlessly. The valve in my suit attached to my left arm released a constant stream of little bubbles as it dumped the expanding air. I looked down and could still see Phil's bubbles rising up towards me, expanding like mushrooms as they forced themselves to the surface. I felt so invigorated.

'OK, cock?' Billy helped me up the ladder, with my demand valve swinging from the bottle on my back. 'How's it going down there?'

'Don't go down yet. We've got a basket full already.'

'I'll do the winch.' Billy grinned and slapped me on the back.

Phil's bubbles started fizzing like a massive bottle of pop had been opened as his head broke the surface.

'Yes!' he shouted. 'Do you know what they are?' He paused, passing his gear to Kris, whose job was to wash and store the equipment and get it ready for the next dive. He continued, 'You don't know, do you? You don't know!'

Billy shouted, 'Stand clear!'

As the rope to the basket tightened and dripped water we moved to the side.

'Well, go on then, tell me,' I urged. Phil beamed.

'They're gunmetal all right.' He paused. 'Torpedo tubes. Bloody torpedo tubes, about a ton and a half each!'

The basket banged on the deck. Billy attached the hook to the bottom and tipped it up. Kris and Len started neatly packing the rods into fish boxes, washing them with the deck wash. Phil and I clipped the basket to the mooring line then pushed it over, watching as it slid out of sight.

'OK Billy, go get 'em!' I shouted. 'If you get time take a look south-east from where the line is tied. We've found some goodies.'

He nodded then jumped in, leaving a foamy circle of bubbles.

'Well, how do you know they're torpedo tubes?' I asked Phil.

'I was on subs, don't forget. The door gave it away. There are two, the loading door and the inner door. There's nothing else they could be. Eighteen feet long by twenty-one inches round, with a broad arrow stamp. This must be the unspecified cargo you were on about. There's at least ten, maybe more beneath them. Anyway, its extra dosh we never bargained for.'

I shook my head. 'God knows what lies beneath us. We'll never know. The manifests only list legitimate cargo. There must have been a black market, all the moneymen. War or no war, it was big business. And in true British tradition, the chosen ones would have exploited it to the hilt. Now it's our turn!'

Billy grumbled and gasped as he swung his leg onto the deck. 'Nice one,' he said then spat into the sea. 'Gunny all right.' He pulled off his hood. 'What are they?'

'Matelot Phil knows,' I said grinning.

'Eh?' Billy looked at us. I left Phil to tell him while I lifted the basket.

Eight hours and two dives later we had all the solder bars on board and stored it away. We sat round the table picking at the fresh mackerel Kris and Len had caught.

'This tastes great, not like that mackerel you see in the supermarkets. Dry and that soggy you can push your finger through it, like it's been there for days. Hell, you can't beat it, this fresh.'

'It's the bones that spoil it for me,' Len cut in.

'There aren't any bones in this. I filleted it. You discard the pin and rib bones by cutting it in little strips. It wastes a bit, but only the bony bits. There's plenty more where these came from.'

'Mm, the sauce is nice. How did you do it?' Phil asked.

Silver Bubbles

'Just a little white wine, some black pepper and French mustard. Oh and lemon juice and a sprinkle of parsley. Dead basic in culinary terms, but tasty. Kris, you get us some more tomorrow, mate. It's full of good oils as well.' I sat back looking proud at the empty plate.

'What's a blow job, Dad?' A deathly silence ensued. All eyes fell on me.

'What?' I snapped in disbelief.

'What's a blow job?' Kris asked again while slowly lowering his head.

'Well...' I went bright red, looking around. Well it's, err... like. Well, when a woman loves a man a lot, she sometimes kisses his... willy. It's an affection sort of thing, yeah, like blowing a whistle. I suppose because a man's willy looks a bit like a whistle having a hole at its end.' I squirmed on my seat, annoyed at my feeble answer.

'Oh yeah, you mean the Jap's eye, don't you Dad?'

'Wait a minute! How come you know about things like Jap's eyes and not about blow jobs?' I said looking suspiciously around.

Kris jumped up giggling as he ran, disappearing into in Phil's cabin. Then I noticed Phil. He was slumped over the sink holding his stomach and close to crying.

'You bastard, that's it now. You, you... I'll get you back, you sick prat.'

Billy and Len were grinning at each other. Then Len said. 'Not a bad way of putting it, I thought.'

I retreated to the wheelhouse to the sound of wholesome laughter. They had their ways of getting to me and this one had worked well.

I had a restless night. The wind had freshened and it concerned me. It hadn't been forecast. The dawn came grey and damp, with a chill in the air.

Peter Fergus

'Bloody British summers,' I muttered out loud, walking towards the stern for a leak. As I turned to walk back, I noticed a small brown bird huddled on the deck. I pushed it with my finger. It moved slightly. So I picked it up and took it to the galley where I found an empty butter tub. I popped it in the tub with some paper towels. I got the eyedropper from the first-aid box then gently forced its tiny beak apart and pressed several small drops of water down its throat. 'There you go, little fella. You're a lucky one, hang in there.'

Black water gushed out of the long tube as it swung and banged aggressively into the stern frame.

'Lower it down,' I shouted as Phil struggled. The roll of the boat made the tube swing dangerously, banging into everything near it. Every time he lowered it, it started sliding back over the stern.

'We need another rope to seize it,' he shouted.

I grabbed a rope, made a lasso knot then moved towards the tube. 'Hold it there,' I shouted. 'Hold it!' The boat gave a snub on the mooring and I slipped on some mud that had spewed on to the deck and I fell on to the tube. It lurched upwards, hitting me hard in the chest, knocking me into the water.

'Dad, Dad!' Kris jumped in after me.

Phil looked at Len. 'Here, lower it into the water and make it fast.' He ran to the stern and threw a life ring then dived into the water.

Dazed, cold and spinning in a twilight dream, I coughed and swallowed seawater. I could feel small tugs. Something was stopping me from moving my arm. I looked around. The water distorted my vision. 'Kris! Kris what's happened, where am I?'

As I regained my senses, I pulled for the surface. Then a stronger hand gripped my arm. The waves hit us and I gasped

Silver Bubbles

for air. I was helped to the ladder. Len pulled me on to the deck.

'Mike don't move, stay still.' I could feel Kris still gripping my arm tightly; he was shivering from the cold.

'Go and get a warm shower. I'm all right, son.' I gave him a smile, 'Thanks to you.'

Billy surfaced looking confused at the scene. 'What's up? What's going on?' I was sitting, getting my breath back.

'An accident, he was knocked overboard.' Len said.

'Shit.' Billy rushed over to me dragging his umbilical like an astronaut on a space walk. 'Is he all right? I thought something was wrong when the line didn't arrive.'

'I'm fine,' I interrupted. 'Just had the wind knocked out of me and got a few gobs full.'

'Where's the force three to four? It's a good five at least. Bloody Met Office, bloody weather,' Billy said, looking around.

Sea Gem rose steadily up and down in the swell. We sat around reading, eating and doing what anyone who's been to sea does to pass time away.

'Are you feeling better now, Dad?'

'Yeah, yeah I'm fine. It takes more than a bang in the chest to put a Morgan down.'

'I thought you were dead.' He hung his head.

'Hey, come here.' I gave him a hug. 'I won't go that easy. That was unlucky, but no big deal.' Kris smiled.

'How are things at home?' I quizzed him. Kris shrugged his shoulders.

'OK I suppose.'

'You suppose. What kind of answer is that?'

'It doesn't matter, Dad.'

'Yes it does. Tell me.'

'Leave it, Dad.'

'No, you tell me what's wrong.'

Kris looked down. 'It's Mum.'

'What do you mean? Is that dickhead Nigel to blame?'
'No Dad. You don't get it do you?'
'How can I get something I don't know about?'
'She cries.'
'What do you mean, son?' I asked softly.
'She cries at pictures of you.' Billy looked up then back at the book he was reading.
'She sits with the photo book. She does it when she's alone, but I see her.'

I looked away then back at Kris. 'What about him, does he comfort her?'

'Dad, he's always at the squash club, or golf. They hardly talk and Mum sleeps in the spare room a lot. She misses you, Dad.'

It was such a shock. I stood up looking out at the horizon; my mind was suddenly cast into turmoil. I went on the defence.

'Look son, I can't do anything now. We're here to work. I can't let my mind drift it's too dangerous. I'll talk with her when we get home, OK.'

Kris smiled. 'You won't forget will you? Promise me.'

'All right, I promise.' Billy looked at me over the top of his reading glasses. 'Yeah,' I said. 'What?'

'Nothing, nothing,' Billy replied.

I felt crap inside.

Suddenly Phil burst into the galley. 'Something landed on my face. It scared me shitless. It's got claws! It dug them into my face when I was having a kip. It's a big rat I think. It attacked me.'

We opened the cabin door. Phil stood back as Billy slowly went inside. 'I don't believe this, you big Nancy,' Billy shouted as he appeared with the little brown Jenny Wren cupped in his hands.

'So, Lucky has introduced herself to you then. Say hello.' The little head popped out, looking around.

'Can I hold her?' Kris asked.

'Yeah,' Billy said, looking at Phil. 'Go put her back in that box over there. And find some spiders to feed her with. We'll let her go in the wood.' He looked at Phil again. 'Attacked by a huge killer rat, what next? Oh by the way Mike, found your knife. It was still stuck in that small monkfish. He's left it near the winch.'

'I didn't know it was a bird. You would have shit yourself just the same. And it was a big monkfish.'

'Bollocks.' I grinned, 'You're getting a reputation for extreme exaggeration.' We all laughed, but my smile soon faded as I thought of Vicki.

I hit the water. It was six a.m. We would get this dive in early, so if the wind came later we would at least find out if there were more tubes below the first layer. It was a dull day, making the wreck dark and eerie. The visibility was about ten feet. Using the four-foot bar I lifted one end while Phil pushed a stone in, creating a gap big enough to pass a strop through. With a strop at both ends the lift aboard would be easier and safer. As the tube disappeared into the mist I felt down where it had rested for fifty years. It was smooth. That indicated there was more below.

Phil was bouncing up and down, bringing the line and strop back to the job after each lift, so he had to ascend slowly to avoid decompression sickness. I swam around keeping sight of the tubes, collecting shellfish. By the time Phil arrived I had four lobsters in one bag and six large cock crabs in another.

We finished the dive after raising five tubes. Billy went down to get as many as he could. He preferred working alone. No one got in his way and he could throw his weight about freely. He managed a respectable three tubes and was on the ladder when I shouted to him. 'Billy, I forgot the shellfish. They're tied to the long pipe just east of the tubes. Have you got enough time to get them?' He looked at his contents gauge, then at his computer.

'Yeah, won't be long.' Two minutes later he had found the bags, as he turned to pull himself to the line a strange feeling came over him, like he was being watched. A shudder ran down his spine as a large shadow just too far away to distinguish, circled him. He froze as it passed again. He kept his eyes on it then jumped as his computer alarm rang out indicating that he was entering decompression penalty in one minute. He slowly moved towards the line. Hand-over-hand he made his ascent, looking anxiously around.

Back safely on the boat drinking a cup of tea he told us of his scary experience.

'What do you think it was, seriously?'

Billy shook his head. 'I've no idea.'

'How did it move?'

'It just glided past. I couldn't see it, just a dark shadow. It knew I was there 'cause it circled me a few times.'

'We haven't got a spear gun, have we?' Phil looked at me. I shook my head.

'I can't think what it could be. Not a basking shark, they stay on the surface.'

'What about a normal shark?' Kris asked.

'Well, they catch them in nets off here, but that's a long way out. How big was it, Billy?'

'As I said, just a shadow, hard to tell but I would say bigger than me, a lot bigger.'

'That's all we need. What's the forecast?' Len asked.

'I hope it blows a hooly. I don't want to be eaten alive! I've just got my new car, and Kim's coming soon,' Phil said.

'Hell man. If you shit yourself when a Jenny Wren lands on you, I don't want to think of the heap you would loosen if a shark popped up in front of you.' There was little response to my remark.

Silver Bubbles

'In low Vis you can imagine silly things, but to see a shadow circling you, not knowing what it is, would break anybody's concentration. You wouldn't get any work done,' added Phil.

'Yeah, if only we had some bang, (explosives) we could scare it away,' remarked Billy.

Phil said, 'Let's go do the Juno till it goes away.'

'Oh bollocks, it's only a bloody fish and we're salvage divers. We can't do a runner 'cause of a fish, or a shark come to that. If Billy hadn't seen it, we'd be none the wiser. I bet it's gone now. Anyway, I'll do the next dive,' I said, looking for a response.

Billy agreed. 'I'll crush it if it tries anything.' Phil kept silent, looking anxious; knowing that he couldn't back out of this one.

Five hours later Billy shouted to get everyone's attention

'Come on, let's get it on.' Poor Phil was scared, but I was sure he felt happy that I was diving alone and he would dive with Billy. To save time the wire would be slid down the mooring line weighted by a heavy shackle after every recovery.

I stood up; it was time to dive. Phil passed me his big divers' knife. 'Take it, you never know.'

I couldn't help grinning. 'Get the fuck out of here. I've got my kitchen devil. I'll shred the son of a bitch.' I disappeared below the surface.

'Macho sod, he's doing this for kicks.'

Billy smiled. 'You're probably right, he's a nutter.'

Len sighed. Kris looked at the water, his mouth open in disbelief, as my white cylinder faded out of sight.

'Monsters,' I reassured myself. 'I'll kill it if it starts.' Wielding the heavy wrecking bar around making lots of noise, I fitted the strop to both ends then pulled once on the wire. One pull was returned so I gave four pulls. Four pulls were returned. As I moved away the tension came on and lifted the tube, releasing clouds of silt. Waiting at the bottom of the line I scanned all around then I felt the line vibrate as the heavy shackle dragged the wire and strop towards me.

I equalled Billy's last dive; three tubes and then surfaced with a smug look.

'Did you see anything?' Phil asked poker-faced.

'No, to be honest I never looked. There could have been a dozen monsters surrounding me!' I shrugged. 'I just got on with the job, you know like you do.'

Phil looked at me, 'Nothing at all then?'

'Well yeah! I saw a few big, well massive shadows. Something did brush past me. The Vis is poor, hand in face.'

Billy was near to cracking up and had to get in the water so he didn't give the game away.

About to splash in, Phil looked around, then back at me. I patted his knife. 'You'll be fine. You've got your big knife, you can use it like a club.' I felt a little sorry for him; he had controlled his fear and was now facing it.

As Phil approached the bottom, the wreck appeared from the gloom. The visibility was at least twenty feet. It was a high-water dive and the water was sharp and clear. The lying bastard, he said to himself, feeling relieved.

Billy had moved the first tube and was waiting for him to fit the strop. The dive went well. Fitting the strop to the last and fifth tube, Phil suddenly looked up as a baby seal pup circled in front of him doing acrobats in the water like a clown. It was only small. He laughed to himself. Maybe this is what scared Billy. He turned to see if Billy was watching. The shock made him near jump out his skin. It banged through his body like a massive throb. Two feet from his face was the biggest bull seal he had ever seen. Its head was enormous; its big yellow canine teeth snapped the water causing bubbles and swirls. He flailed his arms around and it was gone. He turned to the left. It was there, moving slowly towards him. Its big head lowered, exposing its teeth in an aggressive manner. He thrust out the bar. The seal flipped around with such speed he lost sight of it. Then suddenly he was being dragged backwards. His mask filled then he felt a sharp pain in his leg. He was being shaken violently.

A familiar noise made him turn as he cleared his mask of water. He saw Billy with a crow bar, jabbing at the big seal while shouting through his mouthpiece distorted, but audible. 'Get out. Get out!'

They slowly pulled themselves up the rope, followed by the snapping seal, and then hastily climbed the ladder.

'Jesus Christ, the bastard bit me,' said Phil with a disbelieving stare. 'Look!' He lifted his leg. Traces of blood ran from the teeth marks in his dry suit. 'The bastard's bit right through my dry bag. It savaged me.'

Before anyone could say anything Billy shouted, 'That's the biggest seal I've ever seen. It's got a pup and it thinks we're a threat.'

'We are now. The bastard thinks it owns the wreck,' I shouted. 'We'll have to scare it away. It could cause serious damage. There's no way we can work with that thing taking chunks out of us whenever it feels like it!'

Phil's leg was only grazed, but he was limping around like it had been broken. After drying his suit it was glued and stitched and was as good as new.

'So what do we do now?' Billy asked.

'I can't believe a seal has run us off the job,' I said, 'It's not ethical. I could go down with a sharp steel rod and kill it. What do you reckon?'

There was a silence then Kris said, 'That's cruel, Dad. He lives in the sea, you don't. He's got the right to be there.'

'Yeah, Kris is right,' Phil, said. 'We can't kill it, it's got a kid.'

'It's a pup, you knob,' I grumbled. 'Let's have a vote on it. Hands up we kill it.' My hand shamefully was the only one up. 'Bastards,' I muttered. 'This is tantamount to mutiny!

I'm surprised at you, Billy. We could and eat it with garlic, complemented with a nice Chardonnay.'

'Let's do the *Juno*, you crazy bastard,' Billy said shaking his head.

'Oh,' I said. 'Phil, go down and undo the mooring.'

He turned, 'Who, me?'

'I don't see any other Phils around,' I said with a wry smile.

'Why can't we stream it out like.... like the last time?' he stammered. 'And my suit hasn't dried yet. I can't do the dip.'

Billy was holding the imaginary fishing rod behind him.

'Because we need it to moor to the *Juno*!'

'But, but,' he shook his head, 'but we have to come back and there's plenty of mooring lines in the rope locker.'

'But, but, but; you sound like a misfiring moped.' I joked.

He turned and saw Billy. Kris had joined in with the invisible fishing rod. Phil put his hand to his forehead. 'You lot! I don't know... you rotten sods, oh, bollocks to you.' He stormed into the galley and shouted, 'I'm gonna poison you all.'

With the last tube secured the mooring was streamed out and its position marked on the plotter. The *Juno* was only eight miles away. By the time Phil had prepared the lobsters, we were throwing in the first marker as a datum for the search.

I turned *Sea Gem* to the west to start the search then suddenly a mark appeared on the screen. I shouted, 'It's here. We're right on top of it! Get a buoy in!'

Billy had the marker over the side almost instantly.

'I can't believe that, straight on top of it. This GPS is shit hot.' I was well pleased with myself after the long soul-destroying search for the *Benmachdui*. I felt more confident now.

It was approaching low water slack. Five-thirty p.m., the sun was out and the wind was a steady force three to four south-westerly, perfect conditions.

Silver Bubbles

I took a deep breath. 'This is the tin wreck, or it might not be! We must try to ID it. A maker's plate, lettered porthole or the bell would make life easy. According to the records and the manifest, the printing parts were stored in the number one hold, so what are you looking for?'

Phil put his hand up. 'Have you got a pen and paper?'

'You don't know, do you?' I said. 'What do you want a pen and paper for?'

'We thought we were having a test.'

Billy laughed. 'He got you.'

'No he didn't,'

'You gave him that lecture last time, remember. Engine then the boiler and then the bow and number one hold is aft of bow. Leave the lad alone and get back to your cross-stitch.'

I disappeared to the wheel. The engine vibrated through the deck as she listed in the tight turn. I popped my head out of the window. 'I'll blow the horn, OK.'

Phil, who was holding the mooring line, put his thumb up, as did Billy, he was doing the dive. I spun the wheel to the port then starboard, positioning *Sea Gem* alongside the marker like a parked car. The loud horn blew and Billy jumped, disappearing into the deep indigo blue.

Hand over hand he pulled deeper and deeper, the pressure started squeezing his mask. A little blow through his nose equalised the pressure removing the discomfort. His ears were next. Holding his nose, he blew. There was a crackling sound then everything became louder. Noisy bubbles ran passed his ears and a little water seeped into his mask impairing his vision. He held his head back and pressed the top of his mask, while blowing through his nose to force the water out at the bottom. The salt water in his eyes was a regular discomfort and would be forgotten.

A piece of steel about eight inches in diameter came into view, pointing up like small flagpole. Old netting, instead of a flag, waved gently in the slight undercurrent. As he descended, two large round shapes appeared through the misty water. The shot line had passed between the boilers.

Not a bad shot, he thought to himself. The smart arse!

Billy looked to the end of the boilers, which he noticed were out of line. He hovered above the engine like a kestrel in the wind, enjoying the excitement of being the first person to see all this. Remembering he was there to fix the mooring line, he swam off over the boilers towards the bow.

The deck had collapsed and everything had a list to starboard. Lots to explore here, what a wreck, he contemplated. On reaching the bow, which was large and also listing to starboard, he made the rope fast to the still sound twin bollard. The bow seemed to glow a ghostly white from the heavy growth of plumose and dead men's fingers anemones that covered every inch of it.

'Fifteen minutes left, time to check out the engine,' he said to himself. On reaching it, he noted three cylinders. It was a triple expansion engine. In the silt beside the front cylinder that was half-buried, he saw a round edge, just poking out. He reached down and pulled at the object. It came free with a spew of black silt. A distinct line, where it had been buried up to, ran across what looked like a brass plaque and it had raised letters on it. He grinned with triumph then swam quickly back to the shot line and pulled the weight clear. He then continued to the mooring line, to make his ascent. The tide was running hard now. Billy held on to the line with both hands, still gripping his find. The tide forced his body horizontal like a flag in a gale.

Four hands helped him up the ladder. Mask off, hood off, a large spit, then he held up the plate.

'Get your book out! This is off the engine!' I took it from him, walked to a bucket and started brushing the plate in fresh water. I looked at it. I couldn't hide my smile.

'Well done Billy! It's the *Juno* all right.'

'How do you know for sure?' Phil asked, looking over my shoulder at the builder's plate.

'*Lormont* 1920 Hawthorns & Co. Leith,' he read out, aloud. 'It says *Lormont* though!'

'It was built as the *Lormont* and then it was sold and renamed the *Juno*. It's documented that it was sold in 1934. Down below is the *Juno* and a small fortune in tin ingots,' I said with a look of satisfaction.

'I hope there are no more bloody seals,' Phil said.

'If there is, and it starts getting cocky, it'll get no reprieve. There's too much at stake this time.' I stood up. 'Right, get the airlift ready, we dive at seven in the morning. Phil, serve the grub up in half an hour, we're going to find that tin tomorrow.'

Sitting while I picked at the remains of the crab and lobster, I flicked through the file on my knee. 'Listen to this! Carbon paper, millinery, bronze tube, sandpaper, cork disks, tinfoil, pens, paper, felt, synthetic resin, tin, printing equipment, hides, and general cargo. An Aladdin's cave,' I grinned.

'What are we going to do with cork disks?' Phil asked.

'Stick them in your gob!'

'There would have to be a lot to fill that void,' said Billy, glaring at Phil as he carried plates to the sink.

'You're just bloody comforts,' Phil said. 'Come for t' day, Come for t' holiday, Come for t' fish and chips.'

I smiled, 'You're pushing your luck.'

'He's pushed it. Sleep with a weapon, lad. I might attack at night,' Billy said.

The reception was good. We watched the TV till ten and then turned in. I did the first watch as usual. Sitting in silence, looking over the shimmering moonlit sea, my thoughts wandered. Is it possible to love two women at once? I miss Lucy. Christ, I miss all of them. I envy those guys who have several wives. I smiled at the thought of Andrea riding towards me. Her face was lodged in my mind. I remembered the seriously sexy look Lucy had given me from over Kim's shoulders while they caressed each other. Vicky's kiss was familiar, loving and secure.

Billy's voice made me jump. 'Penny for them. No, let me guess. It's either women or tin,' he said in a low deep voice.

'Hell, is it twelve already?' I slid off the comfy seat and stretched. 'Women mate. I don't know what to do with them all.'

'I couldn't help hearing Kris. Why don't you ask her back?'

I shook my head. 'She wouldn't come back. She's too stubborn and proud. Do you know it's bloody amazing? When you live with a woman they stop flirting with you, but if you split up they regain their flirting ability automatically, without even knowing it. That's what kills lots of marriages. Men love their women flirting and crave for it so much that if another bird flirts with them, they're off, I reckon that's why a lot of marriages fail.'

'That's true, but they still flirt with strangers at work and when they're out with their mates.' Billy added

'If a bloke flirts they just get accused of sniffing. I just don't know. I like the freedom, but the house without a woman feels hollow. I'm really falling for Andrea, but things are so bloody complicated. If I went all out for her, I could lose Kris and Vicky. Yet she intrigues me. I might even love both of them. It's doing my head in.'

'Well, you'd better forget them. Men have died here!' He pointed down. 'We don't want to add to the list. Get your head sorted. Think tin,' Billy said with a steadfast look.

'Yeah, think tin, that's good. Cheers mate, see you later. Have a good watch.'

The shrill cries of the feeding terns filled the air and the still air told me the weather was fine. I snoozed on peacefully as the homely smell of bacon drifted into the cabin.

Silver Bubbles

The silver bubbles turned to big mushrooms bursting to the surface. As the airlift sprang to life the sand, stones and shells ran like water towards the sucking pipe. I dragged it from side to side, cupping my hand, helping the seabed to disappear before my eyes. Only two feet down I began uncovering something brown and smooth. As I continued, the shape of a roll presented itself. Pulling at it, I realised I was uncovering a pile of leather hides. Brilliant, I thought, relieved that my measurements were spot on for the number one hold. I pulled a roll free. It measured about three feet long and ten inches in diameter. I started to make a neat pile of them, but soon found that lifting them and swimming was hard work, especially using scuba.

The hose relaxed as the air was turned off. Time to surface. I pulled myself to the line, looking back at the crater as I floated effortlessly towards the sparkling surface.

'Any good?' Phil shouted, while pulling his hood on.

'Yeah, we're into the leather already.'

'Already,' Phil said with disbelief.

'Yeah, it was only a couple of feet down. Once it's buried I suppose there is no more scouring and the seabed levels out, but I think you should go on surface supply mate. It's getting physical and if we don't clear stuff well away, we'll be chasing up our own arses.'

Billy nodded and went below to get out the gear.

'On the job,' Phil's voice crackled from the coms making me feel easier. Now that I could hear my mates it all felt a lot safer.

'This is better,' Phil, shouted between breaths, 'We should have done this on the Ben boat.'

'Yeah, roger that. We will in the future.'

Billy came and stood with me. 'How long do you think it will take?'

'God knows. The drawings I have of a similar ship show the holds to be nearly twenty-five feet deep. And there are the tween decks. My fear is if they put the tin on the bottom because of its weight, we might have to empty the whole hold to get to it.'

'Yeah, but there's always the chance that the sides have collapsed and the cargo spread around and then got buried over time.'

'I hope so. That's what normally happens.'

Phil interrupted us through the coms. 'There's something big down here. Can you pull it out of the way?' Over.'

'OK, we're sending the wire down, stand by.'

Len and Billy had snaked the wire on the deck. Within a few minutes it made bottom, being attached to the mooring line with a heavy shackle.

'OK.' Phil said, having attached the wire to the object, 'Nice and easy.'

On the surface the wire crackled onto the big winch drum as it turned slowly. Phil watched with excitement as the wire came tight, then jerked as the shackle twisted. Out of the black stained gravel, a machine appeared, as if growing magically from the seabed.

'Bloody hell, it's a big.... Yeah it's a big printing machine, bloody massive. Keep pulling until it swings out of the way, over.'

'Roger that,' I answered, then looked at the rest of them standing on deck. 'There's no way we could have done that without this baby.' I patted the winch. 'This, and surface supply is going to make us some dosh.' I rubbed Kris on the head. 'Maybe a YZ 80 Motocross bike to ride in the field, eh?'

As the machine lifted off the seabed, *Sea Gem* settled down tide again on to her mooring line, taking the machine with it.

'OK, lower it down now!' There was metallic banging through the coms as Phil pulled at the cable.

Silver Bubbles

'Give me slack on the cable,' Phil shouted. 'OK. I'll keep it here. I'm going back to the air lift.'

'Roger that,' Billy replied. The loose sand and stones shot up the airlift, making the excavation hole three times larger, and all the time exposing unrecognisable shapes from the past. Phil was giving an entertaining commentary over the coms.

'I've found a sodding tandem!' echoed across the calm sea. 'Ask Billy if thee can ride tandem, lad,' he shouted.

Creased with laughter, I looked at Billy.

'He's definitely dead,' Billy said, but couldn't keep his face straight either as Phil continued.

'E by gum, it's broken up. That's knackered it! Billy lad will have to walk to the bakery now to get his Hovis! Hey up, get ready for this.' He made several straining grunts, then with a squeal of laughter he shouted, 'Going up.'

On the deck we watched in anticipation as hundreds of cork discs, about six inches round, burst to the surface. They drifted in a line down tide, like a pack of liberated animals bobbing up and down in the small waves.

'He's having fun down there,' I said to Billy, who was looking at his watch.

'Not any more.' He turned off the airlift. 'It's my turn now.'

Billy was well impressed at Phil's efforts. The hole was about twenty feet wide now and five foot deep at least. He had a quick look at the printing machine. It was about fifteen foot long, some of its chrome parts still shining like new. He grinned as he pulled away a piece of wood, releasing more cork discs that danced in a sideways movement towards the surface.

'Feels like another print machine,' he grunted, 'Standby. OK, winch it up slowly.'

Again a large machine appeared as if by magic and then swung with a heavy thud into the other one. 'This is a piece of piss,' Billy shouted. 'We're going to get to the bottom sooner than we thought.'

Ten minutes later Billy grunted. 'We've got the bottom I think.' He paused, 'Yeah! It is. I've found the wooden planks. Yeah, it's the bottom all right,' he said with a ring of disappointment in his voice. I stood staring at the deck, shaking my head.

'There's no way we've gone down over twenty feet. It must be spread on the seabed and silted up.'

Billy made the surface and Kris washed him down with the deck wash. He walked to us while pushing his hand into his leg pocket.

'What do you think this is?' He had a small shiny crest in his hand. I looked at it. It was about one and a half inches round and had a picture of a lamb and a flag pressed into it.

'I don't know,' I said with interest. 'But I'll find out when we get ashore. Interesting,' I said, looking at it again.

'Dad, Dad,' Kris shouted. 'Someone's calling us on the radio.' I ran up the steps.

'It's Bacton radio. Apparently we have traffic.'

'What's that?' Phil asked.

'Someone is calling us,' I answered as I picked up the hand piece.

'Bacton radio, this is *Sea Gem*, over.'

'*Sea Gem*, Bacton. You have traffic. Channel fourteen, over.'

'Bacton radio *Sea Gem* going down.' I turned the radio to channel fourteen.

'Bacton radio, *Sea Gem*, over.'

'Sea Gem, Bacton connecting your call. Go ahead.' There were a few crackles then a woman's voice silenced us.

'Hello Mike, it's Kim here.' I looked at Phil, who looked on in amazement. 'Hello Kim, do you want Phil?'

'Yes please, how are you?'

'Fine thanks. I'll put him on.'

Phil fumbled with both hands on the handset. 'Hi Kim, how did you do this?'

I had to remind him that every man and his dog could hear them.

'I just called. It's a service. How are you keeping?'

'I'm great, even better for hearing your voice.'

'When are you home?'

Phil looked at me. I shrugged my shoulders and told him, 'Weekend, I suppose.'

'For the weekend, we should be home then.'

'OK Phil. I'll come up to see you on Friday. I have a weekend off. Can you ask Mike if I can stay?'

I nodded. I couldn't hide my smile. 'Yes of course she can.'

'Yeah that's fine.'

'See you on Friday then, Phil. Bye.'

Phil looked at me. 'She's fucking amazing. Yes. Yes!' He pulled his fists into his waist. Billy looked on bemused, shaking his head. 'Fancy doing that, she's just so smart. She's a doll.'

I walked to the window, looking out over the calm sea. Thinking about Lucy, I felt sad. She could have done that at any time. She must have been cheating me for ages. She was probably receiving a portion from the cabin crew while those gunrunning bastards were trying to shoot me.

Phil's shouting soon cheered me up. He was beaming and dashing around with a new found energy and giving off good vibes.

Midday came quickly and it was dive time again. I surveyed the work and was shocked to see how well we had done in just one dive. The big airlift came to life and I wrestled with it. The surface supply was great. After I adjusted the free-flow to release a light stream of air across my face, breathing was so much easier. Scuba was great for dashing around, but this was the kit for hard work, and hard work it was. I was straining and sweating, pushing the pipe along the wooden slats, which was the bottom of the once proud ship.

I uncovered two smaller print machines and several crates of old style inkbottles, minus the ink. They were shaped ones, made to stand on their sides so a pen could be dipped in. The name 'Waterman's' and some numbers could be read on the bottom, but being of no value, I placed them with the machines. The pile was getting bigger, but there was still no sign of any tin ingots. The next few dives were similar, although Billy uncovered what was listed on the manifest as fatty acid. This was like lard in appearance and it irritated our hands on contact. The stuff was spreading everywhere and becoming a real pain.

Three days and still no sign of the ingots and the remnants of the bulkheads were appearing.

'Well that's it.' I shook my head. 'It just isn't there. I can't believe it. We've moved tons of stuff.' I was agitated and snapped, 'For sweet fuck all!'

'No!' Billy stood up. 'You won't find anything if you don't look. You can't score every time. Hell, we've had some bloody good luck so far. We found the tubes for instance. We never bargained for them.'

'Yeah, I suppose you're right, but I was sure we would find the tin. What do you reckon we should do then?'

Phil said, 'We can't get the rest of the tubes with psycho seal attacking us, and its Thursday now, tomorrow's Kim day.'

'What do you reckon, Billy?'

'I'm well tired. The weather is going to get crap, so let's go in and re-charge. The wreck's going nowhere and we need a bit of bang to scare the seal off. We're still well in profit with seventeen tubes and about two ton of solder bar. That's good money. Yeah, let's bugger off.'

The light blue trawler listed heavily as waves slapped into its side, forcing spray to leap up into the air.

Silver Bubbles

'He's got his trawl gear stuck,' I said, while staring for its name.

'It's called *Crystal Star*, Dad,' Kris said, smiling like he had achieved something.

I picked up the handset and offered assistance, which was hastily accepted. I knew the two brothers through a mutual friend. He called them the 'Chisets'. It was derived from them always asking 'Chiset (how mu-ch is it) I had shared a few pints with them, but didn't know them that well.

Billy and Phil dived to free the net, which had its bottom chain fast around a boiler of another uncharted wreck. I marked the position on the plotter. The brothers were grateful. We liberated the trawl, complete with its full cod end of fish, within ten minutes and were safely on board Sea Gem drifting astern.

Kris and I jumped into the inflatable and went across to collect a box of plaice the brothers had offered us in return for our help. We enjoyed watching the cod end untied, spilling a mixture of species into the pound boards along with a long rusty object, which banged onto the steel deck. I pulled it out of the pile of weed and fish.

'It's a gun! Like those fitted to aircraft. I'm sure it is.'

'Take it if you want it. We get all sorts of rubbish from round here. It's a dodgy tow, there being so many fasteners, but it produces some good plaice,' One of the brothers remarked.

'Yeah I'll try and find out what it came off. There might be a name or something stamped into it. Could you give me a copy of your tow sometime?'

'Yeah sure, give us a bell and we'll meet you for a pint.'

They thanked us again and then passed a full box of big plaice into the inflatable.

Back on board *Sea Gem*, I stored the gun in wet sacking, took five big fish out of the box, which had a covering of ice to keep them fresh and passed them to Phil.

'Plain, grilled in butter please, Chef. And break out the Chardonnay.' Phil didn't like being called chef so we felt tipped all his possessions with the word.

I opened the door to the smell of paint. Kris ran upstairs to the new loft conversion. The en suite bedroom was all decorated and painted. The long room the stairs led to was papered and painted and a thick-pile, dark-blue carpet ran through the rooms. It looked fantastic. There was a note and a pile of receipts. I had left some money for the work, but Vicki had done it all herself and she'd done a brilliant job.

I lent against the wall holding the note she had left. Looking up at the ceiling I sighed then said out loud. 'I wish things hadn't gone wrong.' I walked to the window and looked across the fields. In the distance from the now higher vantage point I could see the gable end of the Spinney cottage, just showing above the thick hawthorn hedge.

Staring and thinking, lost in personal confusion, my frozen gaze melted into thoughts of Andrea. How wrong she was, but how good. She felt like a forbidden fruit. Images of her filled my mind.

'Dad, this is brill!' Kris broke my thoughts. 'Dad, what's up?'

'Nothing, nothing, I'm fine,' I replied.

'Are you missing Mum?'

Looking at my son I smiled. 'I've always missed her.'

'Yeah, but you fancy Irish Andrea don't you?' he shouted, as he galloped noisily down the stairs.

I remained silent thinking to myself, who wouldn't?

I switched on the kettle then stopped at Lucy's letter. 'Bitch,' I said out loud.

'You don't mind Kim staying?' Phil was making prawn cocktails in the corner. I hadn't seen him.

'I've told you before, the place is yours.'

'I know, but you and Kim.... you know what I mean.'

'I am envious mate, but not jealous. I'm happy for you. She's a doll, but she's no mystery to me. I have the memories of the good time as well. This is different. It's you two now, though she probably still yearns after me!' I grinned.

Phil looked confused then realised I was only having fun. 'Are you having some scran with us?'

'Thanks, but I think I'll go to the Ship, and leave you to abuse each other. Kris is at his mate's, so you can have a game of monopoly or play cards or even bounce on the beds, but be aware, very aware of the barbecue phantom.'

'What, what do you mean?'

If I come home merry and you're humping and making rude noises, I'll be up there making a spit roast.'

Phil grinned as he put the starters in the fridge then removed two big plaice in preparation.

'Is that the last two…Chef?'

He tutted, 'Yeah, I took some to the farmer and Jonno.'

'Jonno, he'll just flog em on they'll be on his specials board by now.'

'No, he said he would eat them.'

'They'll get eaten all right. Did Len get any?'

'Two. He said he would take them to a friend.'

'Yeah, he's still at it!'

Looking tanned and feeling healthy I sat at the bar. My stubble didn't cover the scar, but there was nothing I could do about it. Jonno talked to me between rushing around, as only good landlords do. The pub was busy. Some familiar faces nodded, some whispered behind my back. We had a reputation as divers, lots of money and the good life. All that shit. A group of men walked in laughing and shouting loudly. I had my back to them and took no notice, until one voice caught my attention.

'I wupped him three, love. I had him all over the court, dropping, driving and lobbing him. He never got into the

Peter Fergus

game, I wouldn't let him.' It was Nigel, spouting to his squash club friends. I was bemused at the way he was bragging. Half an hour later he was still giving it loads. It sounded like he had never lost a game in his life. Someone mentioned a golfing week in Portugal and asked Nigel if he was interested in going.

With the drink having taken effect, he was getting loud and he shouted. 'Yeah, I suppose I could. Her indoors is still sulking and his brat can stay in that cowshed with the other misfits.'

They all laughed. Then one of them asked him, 'Have you sorted her 'ex' out yet?'

'I've warned him for the last time the other day,' he bragged. 'The next time he starts, I'll sort him out.'

'We could help you if you want,' a small, fat one said. Jonno had by now tuned in on the conversation and looked involved. His eyes dashing from one speaker to another then he looked at me with concern. I smiled, stood up and walked round the small partition. Nigel's pint slipped through his limp hand and broke like a big light bulb exploding onto the floor. His eyes nearly popped out of their sockets.

'Why don't you introduce me to your friends, Nigel?'

'That's him!' One of them whispered.

I continued, 'There are six of you. Shall we do this all together, or one at a time? I'm easy.' There was a deadly silence. I was hyped up and felt fearless. I made eye contact with each one then pushed my way to Nigel.

'So you warned me for the last time, Nigel? Well, I'm sorry you feel you have to sort me out.' I turned, looking at them. 'That's all of you I understand.' There was silence, which I broke.

'Look, can we start again and let bygones be bygones?' I put my hand out to him. Nigel gave a sneering grin. Wiping his mouth, he held my hand. His grin soon turned to anguish as my hand, which was almost twice as big as his, tightened. He stepped off his stool, crouching in agony as I intensified the crushing grip. I turned to the others, smiling. 'Hang around. You'll get your turns soon.'

Turning back to Nigel I moved my face close to his. 'Brat, cowshed and misfits?' I squeezed as hard as I could, causing Nigel to drop to his knees. The crack made him scream in agony, as I twisted his wrist, which must have dislocated several joints. Then, taking hold of a pint from the bar I poured it on the stool cushion. I pulled him up and sat him on the soaking stool. I turned to the rest of them, offering my hand. 'What's the matter?' I asked. They all avoided eye contact. 'Lost your tongues?'

Shaking my head with disgust I returned to my seat. I looked at Jonno. 'Sorry about the cushion, mate.'

Jonno came over. 'Well done. I thought things were going to kick off but you scared them shitless. He won't be playing squash for a while. Just watch your back going home.'

'Cheers mate, but I don't think they're up for it. It's a shame. I would enjoy slapping them around the car park. The hardest thing those pappy bastards ever do is struggle past their fat guts to pull on their socks.' I turned to them. They looked away and then filtered out, helping Nigel who was holding his hand as if it was suffering from frostbite.

The conversation returned to normal. I asked Jonno to put some music on then sat in the corner looking around the room at the different faces, particularly the women's. Andrea sailed straight into my thoughts. I wonder what she's doing right now. She will have seen *Sea Gem* in her mooring.

'Mike, telephone,' Jonno shouted. 'Take it in the back.' He let me through the bar.

'Hello.'

'It's Phil. I thought you would like to know that Irish bird has left a message on the phone. We were upstairs. I didn't hear it ring.'

'Well, what did she say?'

'She just said, 'Hi. It's Andrea, and the time.'

'Cheers Phil. Are you having a good night?'
'Oh, it's bliss.'
'Good. I might see you later. Thanks mate.'
'Not bad news?' Jonno asked.
'No, no. Good news really. Give us a bottle of your best champagne.'
'It's on the house, mate. You go careful. You have to take me out again, don't forget.'
'Next trip bellboy, next week. You're coming, OK? See you later and thanks.'

I stood looking where the road split. To the left was the Spinney, to the right Wood End. Pondering what to do, thinking she might have rung to warn me that Gerald was home, I looked up at the stars.

It was a still clear night and they were shining like diamonds. A small red light occasionally flashed, catching my eye. A jet way above plied its way through the dark void. I wonder if you're up there? I remembered her face, her cheeky smile. 'Mmm,' I pondered, then said out loud with a melancholy grin, 'Lucy in the sky with diamonds.' I turned left for the Spinney.

The tubes weighed nearly one-point-one ton each, with the dissimilar metals in the doors and the shit trapped inside. We agreed on one ton a-piece. There was just over two tonne of solder bar, which fetched four grand a ton, because of its high tin content.

'Can you imagine? Twenty tonnes of pure tin, we have to find it. Still, seventeen ton of gunmetal at nearly eighteen hundred a tonne and the eight grand from the bar, comes to thirty-eight bloody grand, less ten percent.' I looked up from my book. 'The old fella wasn't going to lose out and he had the cash this time. We grossed, in total, thirty four thousand and two hundred pounds. That's a quarter for the boat, eight

Silver Bubbles

thousand five hundred and fifty, leaving twenty thousand five hundred and fifty divided by four.'

'No! No!' Len stood up. 'You paid me back. I don't want a share. You're younger and need it. I won't accept anything, I mean it!'

I looked around, 'OK then, we'll tip you.'

'No.' Len said again, 'I'm fine. The matter is closed.'

'So, that's eight thousand five hundred and fifty each then.' We counted the money out and shared it out.

Phil sat smiling, holding his cash. 'This is the best time of my life. A new car, a dishy bird, shares in a boat.' He paused. 'But above all, I've got real mates.'

'Well its Tuesday, we've had a good weekend and we're all flush. Let's have the rest of the day off. Get *Sea Gem* turned around, then get that tin.'

'We need some bang first,' Billy reminded us. 'I can't get it till Wednesday.'

'We sail Thursday then, weather permitting.'

'Phone,' Phil went into the room. 'It's a job.'

I held the mouthpiece and pulled a face of disapproval. When I arrived back in the kitchen I grumbled, 'We don't need this shit any more.'

Billy stood up, 'Well, what is it?'

'It's a lock gate. It's stuck. They need us now, before the tide ebbs and they lose all the water in the dock!'

'Bollocks! Phil, come on, lets load the van.'

The white hats were dashing around the lock like ants. They directed the van near the big eighty-ton gates, which had a three-foot gap between the seals. The water was keeping its level for the moment, but would soon to change when the tide turned. Billy and Phil were kitted up, Phil acting as standby.

'What do you think it is?' I asked the engineer.

'Could be a steel drum. The gates open, but when we try to close them, one stops moving and grinds to a halt before it seals. If we lose the water all the boats in the dock will go aground. It would be a catastrophe!'

'If we sort it out, will you forget that bloody forklift cock-up?' I said with a smile.

'If you sort it, we will owe you one.'

'Well, as soon as the tide ebbs it's going to be difficult to keep on the job.'

'I know Mike, I know. Just do your best.' He looked desperate. He was responsible for the outer storm gates being out of commission, due to a badly timed service. He had taken a risk, and it had turned pear-shaped.

Billy hit the water with a loud slap, having jumped from about fifteen feet. He disappeared in a brown circle of froth.

'On the bottom,' echoed around the buildings.

'Roger that,' I replied, as trail of bubbles lead to the parted seals.

'Oh shit!' Billy sighed, 'Standby.'

'Roger.' I looked at the engineer and shrugged my shoulders.

'I don't... Shit, it's a mangy bullock! It's stuck under the gate and squashed against the clapping sill. It's bloody well under.' He gave a few grunts and strains. 'It won't budge an inch and it's got bloody big horns.'

'Roger that. Billy, come up and get a rope.'

'Take my slack, Leaving bottom.'

'Tie it round the back of its head.'

He replied sarcastically. 'Do you think I would tie it round its nuts?' I deserved the reply. I should have known better.

Phil lowered the rope with a loop spliced into it. 'Jesus Christ! It smells disgusting.' Phil ran back to the wall holding the end of the rope and his nose.

'OK. I've put a slip loop round its head, pull it now.'

About eight men pulled on the stout rope. After a little resistance it came free. As the slack came in everyone peered over the lock wall as the stinking, eyeless head and horns appeared from the water.

'Bollocks!' I cursed loudly. 'It's almost bloody jellied.'

'Give us a sit-rep, Billy.'

'Yeah,' he gasped, 'you've got the head, and I've got its arse the gate is right on top of its back. God, I can taste it. It's putrid.'

'We should have worn the Seventeen,' Phil said quietly. (A totally enclosed diving helmet)

'How the fuck was I to know there was a festering bullock trapped under the gate. It's usually an oil drum,' I snapped with frustration.

'The water's flowing down here. I'm getting pushed off the job, over.'

'That's great! That's about right!' I was ranting. 'We're failing again. It's turning to rat shit. These fucking docks are cursed.' I looked at Phil who stood silent, then said sheepishly. 'Bullshit, it's turned to bullshit, not rat shit.'

'It's not funny you...' I paused looking beyond him. 'That will do it.' I climbed into the van and came out with a bow saw.

'Pass him this. Billy, I'm passing you a bow saw, it's our only choice.'

'Thanks a lot,' was his solemn reply. Poor Billy hacked, cut and sawed through the decomposed beast. I don't think anyone else could have done what Billy did that day. Men at the surface were throwing up at the stench. Billy retched on numerous occasions, coughing and cursing while he dismembered the carcass causing pieces of rotting flesh to mix with his bubbles.

'OK, take my slack I'm leaving bottom.'

On the surface Billy held his breathing hose as Phil pulled him towards the ladder. He was covered in stinking, slimy, rotten fat from the decayed creature. The smell of death hung thick in the air. A fire hose was trained on him, but the fat clung like glue.

Dejected, Billy was carefully removed from his suit and rushed to a shower. The entire gear, mask and weight vest was placed in bin liners for steam cleaning and disinfecting.

The gates were opened slightly then closed fully, to the relief of the engineer.

'Charge us for any equipment you replace, Mike,' said the engineer. 'I'm sorry for all this. Your diver was excellent, working in all that flow and in such vile conditions. You have really pulled us out of-'

'The shit, Billy interrupted, while drying his hair, wearing only a towel. His big arms flexing their muscles as he rubbed the towel around. The engineer personally thanked Billy then went away.

'Well that was different,' said Billy, looking at me for a response.

'Sorry mate, I should have put the chef in.' I looked across at Phil, who looked almost delirious having got away with not diving. It was obvious he was itching to start taking the piss, but was carefully biding his time.

When the van was all packed up Phil came over to us. 'OK, number one.' He nodded at me then looked at Billy and said, while still nodding, 'Number eight.' I looked at Billy, confused and then sniggered uncontrollably.

'What's the joke?' Billy snapped, 'Am I missing something?' I looked at Billy. On his neck there was a scar made by the barrel of the shotgun that the poacher poked at him. The barrels, being over under and coated in carbon, had left a perfect number eight tattooed on his neck.

I pointed to the scar. Billy frowned, looked at me then grinned.

'What?' I shouted.

Billy ran his finger down my scar and said while grinning, 'Number one.'

'He's as good as dead,' I said, as we both looked at him.

'Yeah... deader than dead,' Billy repeated.

Silver Bubbles

Back in the yard I unwrapped the sacking to have a look at the gun we had found.

'It must be off a bomber,' Phil said. 'I've seen them on films, Flying Fortress or the like.'

'Yeah,' I rubbed the metal block. 'There's some writing here and numbers. Get a pencil and paper. U.S.A.A.F. 864839/1944. Hell, it's American.'

'They must have had a crap navigator,' Phil said, looking at me.

'You daft sod. The Yanks were everywhere during the war and stationed all over Britain.'

'We had better notify the American Embassy. It might have been lost with all hands; there could be family still alive. I'll do it now before stinky gets back and drags us to the Ship.'

I sent a brief letter, but omitted any positions. I just said that it had been found off the Coast.

Sitting in our little office I rubbed the silver disc, which bore the 'Lamb and Flag' logo. 'I wonder what it came off? Phil, do you fancy a trip to the library in the morning?'

'I can't. I said I'd take Billy to get some bang.'

'OK. I'll go anyway.... Well, how was the weekend, then?'

'I told you. It was fantastic.'

'That's not enough. Did she give you a massage, then?'

He stared into space, in a daze. 'A massage, an amazing blow job and then she gripped me with her sweet pussy so hard that I could barely move in and out. It was making a noise like those whistles we had as kids. You know, you slide a thing up and down.'

'Great,' I smiled. 'You're a lot more relaxed these days. Having a full load all the time does a man's head in.'

'Tell me about it.' He gazed lost in thought. 'Anyway, where did you get to on Friday night?'

'You know where I went.'

'So how was your night? Come on, I told you.'

'She opened the door wearing just a shirt. She knew I would come round, so I reckon she made herself look as sexy as she could. Her nipples pointed through the thin material. The slit at the side of the shirt ran up her thighs. When she turned I saw the top of her legs, where her bum started, she had no pants on. She overwhelmed me, I felt like an uncontrollably excited kid. She's the only woman who's ever made me feel really nervous. When I held her we just melted into one, she's so smooth, so much rhythm, I feel I'm floating on air when we make love.'

'Wow! You said the word, mate.'

'What word?'

'Love.'

There was a long silence.

'Come on you turds,' Billy bellowed out, 'You owe me a wet.' Len was walking down the path in white pants and a tropical shirt. 'I'm ready.'

Sitting in the Ship, Billy smiled, looking at the four pints of bitter in front of him. The pretty barmaid came over. 'Jonno said to give you this.' She handed him two flowery wrapped parcels.

'What? Err... thanks,' he said looking surprised.

'Well, open them,' Phil urged him.

Billy tore them open. 'Bastard,' he cursed, as the lilac smelling talc spilled out of the booby-trapped box, all over him and into his beer. He picked up the Old Spice can. As he pulled off the top to spray them, the can started spraying on its own. Jonno had rigged it. Jonno's head peered over the bar, as Billy shouted 'grenade,' and threw the hissing can behind the bar. He turned, laughing as the talc fell off him like snow.

'OK, number one. Yep, number eight.' We stood up, grabbed Phil and dragged him struggling and screaming to the bar. Jonno quickly put tie wraps round his wrists and ankles. The barmaid held the ice bucket and as we pulled slack from his trouser waist, she poured its contents down his pants then re-tightened his belt, leaving him rolling around the floor as the ice found his more delicate parts. With pockets and hearts full we were on course for a mega session.

The distant droning noise became louder. I woke with a start as the vacuum cleaner passed my face. I couldn't move my legs. Billy was laying on them. Above me, Phil's face stared at me. He was slumped on the seat, head hanging over the edge, dribbling on Jonno, who was under the seat snoring loudly, wearing only girl's pants. Phil had a bra on. Billy was topless and covered in lipstick graffiti. I sat up, wearing only boxers, as I pulled a crisp off my face. A bright blue flash made me see spots, as Jonno's cleaner took several photos.

The lady in the reference library reeled back, as she smelled my breath. Giving me a look of disgust she pointed to a row of books. I started with the shipping lines, then the history of the tramp steamers. Nothing matched the disc. Two hours later and feeling decidedly hung over, I made my way to the exit. I stopped at the index. In the local industry section I found several references to foundries and tin smelting. Capper Pass was one, I turned the page and it hit me immediately. There it was. The *Lamb and Flag,* Howell and Co., Manchester.

'Got you,' I shouted loudly, receiving several strange stares.

Back in the office I called Directory Enquiries. I couldn't believe my luck when I was given a number. So I called them. A voice answered, 'Howell and Co.'

'Is that the smelters?' There was a silence.

'The smelters...no, who is calling?'

I briefly explained. 'Oh, no, no,' The man said. 'That was years ago. This is a haulage and storage company now. All the smelting works went a long time ago.'

'I see.'

'What did you want to know?'

'I just wanted to ask about tin production. It was a long shot. Thanks anyway.'

'Just a minute, we have an old fella who worked here years ago. Perhaps he can remember a few things. Hold on I'll get him for you.'

A few minutes later the voice of an old man came on.

'Hello.'

'Yeah hello,' I replied. 'I rang for information about tin shipments from the old smelting works. We've found a shipwreck and recovered a shiny disc, with a lamb and a flag on it. I believe it's the old company logo.'

The old man laughed and then coughed. 'I remember them. It is made of tin. Is it about one and a half inches round?'

'Yeah, that's it.'

'It's off a two-ton pallet, we used to wire the ingots onto a wooden pallet and every one was fitted with the company crest. That's what you have found.'

'How big are the ingots?'

'Twenty-eight pound each, flat at the bottom. The top has a raised bit in the middle, about one third of its length and about half an inch higher, oblong in shape, about a foot long; two and a half inches deep at the thickest point. The top has the lamb and flag stamped into it.'

'That's great information. If they exported it how much would normally go?'

'Ten pallets every time, that's twenty tons, yes always ten. I fitted the company emblems. I probably fitted the one you found. They're also made of tin.'

'How many shipments went out?'

'Literally hundreds of consignments over the years.'

'Thank you very much for your time.'

'Not at all, I hope you find it.'

Silver Bubbles

'Well thank you for everything. Bye.' I smiled as I rubbed the disc. 'If you are there, so is the tin.'

The red sports car pulled up. Billy's greying white curly hair looked funny against his brown tan. Phil had pulled the top down, embarrassing him on purpose.

'I felt like fucking Noddy.'

'Did you get some?'

'Does a bird fly? Does a fish swim? Course I did. They use it all the time in the mines. Our kid has a key to explosives magazine.'

'I've been busy too, look at this.' I had typed out all the information about the tin and stapled a photocopy of the page from the library with it. Billy read eagerly, with Phil peering over his shoulder.

'This is great news. You were right all along then.'

'Why? Did you sods doubt me?' There was a silence. 'You did, didn't you?'

'No, of course not, but you can't be right every time.'

'I can,' I said, sounding childlike. I grabbed the paper. 'This proves it. Research is what matters, even monkeys can dive.'

Billy spread the explosives on the bench. Six sticks of black high explosive, twenty electric detonators, ten plain detonators and a one hundred-meter roll of Super flex detonating cord, also half a roll of safety fuse.

'Bloody hell,' Phil quipped, 'All this for one seal?'

'No, you moron. This will come in handy, you wait and see.'

'How much was that lot then?' I asked.

Billy smiled. 'Family, mate. I promised them a day out cod bashing on the wrecks.'

'No problem. October's the best month. Tell them we'll have a competition, the biggest fish and the most species. Should be fun, don't you reckon?'

'I'll give our kid a ring tonight,' said Billy, with a look of excitement in his eyes.

'So why have these dets got numbers on them?' asked Phil,

'Delays in seconds. When you blow a rock face, you set up slight delays to take advantage of the shock wave, like splitting a stone with a chisel.'

'Oh right,' said Phil, looking more confounded.

Billy wrapped the detonators in a cloth and placed them well away from the explosives. He joined me. I was watching the weather forecast.

'Hell, it's late August and look at the shit weather.' The isobars looked like a dartboard tightly packed, indicating gales.

'What do you reckon?'

'Shitty!' I looked at him. 'No really, we would be mad to go out in that. Anyway we couldn't dive safely.'

'What shall we do then?' I looked at Phil and shrugged. 'Beat your meat, I suppose.'

'Hey, all this doom and gloom. We just earned more in the last trip than we have for months of Muddy River Bank work. Cheer up, for God's sake.'

I looked in the tide book. 'Well, we will miss these neaps. If we work until the Vis starts getting crap, we still have about twelve weeks left this season. And if we find the tin we can survive till the spring easily, and still be financially secure.'

'Yeah, it's the hanging around,' said Billy. 'It does my head in.'

'Tell you what. Why don't we get that big pump running? We could use a small hose to test it and get a long one if it works well enough,' I suggested.

'Maybe, but can you imagine the drag from the tide, on thirty meters of eight inch pipe? You wouldn't hold it,' replied Billy.

'We'll stick to the airlift then. At least it works well.'

Silver Bubbles

After two days of boat maintenance, we met the Chisets who had found the gun. They were also grounded because of the bad weather, and keen for a few drinks. I got a copy of the trawl plots for the area where the net got fast and we had a good night telling tales of the sea.

The next morning, Billy was working at Sue's shop and Phil was still in bed after trying to keep up with everybody at the bar.

I got up early and went for a run. I had left some wild flowers poking out of Andrea's letterbox and was excited about her answering the little message.

Later I was sitting in the small office, studying the roll from the Decca twenty-one plotter and carefully transferring the marks on to an Admiralty chart and converting the positions to latitude and longitude. I couldn't help repeatedly looking out of the window at the trees bending in the strong westerly wind.

Spot started barking. Shortly after, a black car pulled into the yard. I walked out and stood in the workshop. Two men got out. One of them was wearing an American Air Force uniform; the other was dressed in a smart, black suit. I walked towards them.

'Can I help you?'

The man in the black suit replied, 'Mike Morgan?'

'Yeah, that's me.'

'It's a pleasure,' he said, in a strong American accent, while shaking my hand. The uniformed man introduced himself. 'Colonel Walter Parks, United States Army Air Force.'

'You don't waste any time,' I said to the one in the black suit. 'I didn't catch your name.'

He just smiled at me. 'You found one of our aircraft. Is there somewhere we can talk?'

Peter Fergus

He had a cocky attitude, which I instantly disliked. 'Yeah, sure,' I looked at him, only to be greeted with the same phoney smile.

We sat in the kitchen and I made a brew. 'How can I help?'

'We will take the gun with us, and we need a statement from you stating the wreck's location and depth, the condition of the aircraft, all the relevant details. Have you taken anything else from the site?'

I was annoyed by his attitude and looked at Walter. 'So, you're not interested in the poor crew and if there were any remains?' Before he could answer the other man interrupted him.

'If you have removed anything you will be in serious trouble. Do you understand?' He looked smug and intimidating.

'Look Uncle Sam, or whatever your name is.' I stood up. 'We haven't found a plane, just the gun. You're acting a bit strange considering I came to you offering information free of charge. So are you going to tell me anything or not?'

'The plane was lost during a mission off the Dutch coast. We need to establish the position so we can recover any remains and ship them home for burial.'

'Thank you,' I said. 'There's no need to treat me like the enemy. I'm interested in salvage, that's what we do.'

'Quite a hero, too,' quipped the one in the suit.

'You work for the Government, I take it?'

The man just smiled again. 'May I?' He pulled a packet of cigarettes from his pocket.

'No!' I said smiling.

'Can you give us the position where you found the gun?'

'I can do better. I can find the plane if you want.' I looked at the man in the suit.

He put his hands on the table. 'You see it's rather delicate. We have to maintain discretion here. Just give us the position and we will do the rest. It's a military task. It's our aircraft; we can make you give us the position through the courts. In

Silver Bubbles

fact, we could make things difficult for your salvage company and yourself.'

'So, you're threatening me now. OK, we found it where you said, off the Dutch coast, about ninety miles offshore. I don't have the position. We just dived a mark. There was nothing but sand waves so we drifted for a while. That's when we found it. It was in an old trawl net. It could have come from anywhere.' I changed my tone and leaned forward. 'I only sent you the info for the families.'

There was a silence then the one in the suit said, 'If it could be anywhere, how could you find it for us?'

'Search for it,' I said, feeling hemmed in and annoyed at my poor answer.

After taking the gun, they stood by the car. I said nothing as the one in the suit spoke on the phone. Then he walked over to me. 'We can find out, we can watch you from the sky... You cannot do anything. Is this the way you want it?'

'You level with me and I will with you. What was its name?'

'Sorry, that's classified information. We will give you a few days to think about what I said and then call you. You cannot withhold this information from us.'

'I've already told you.'

'We have your departure and arrival times of your last trip. You didn't go off the Dutch coast, you weren't away long enough.'

'We didn't find it on the last trip,' I said, looking for a reaction.

'Three days.' He stared in a sinister way, looked annoyed then slammed the door. The wheels from the big limo left two black lines on the gravel.

'Spooky bastard,' I said to myself. Then I went to phone Billy.

After a long discussion I decided to call John Steed, Commander Lewis. I told him all about the incident and the meeting. Commander Lewis was one of the good guys and still one of the lads. He said he would look into it and call as soon as he had any information.

It was three o'clock in the afternoon. There had been no phone calls. I left Phil at Len's, watching cricket on Sky and called Spot for a walk down the lane. As I reached the Spinney my heart sank. The flowers were still in the letterbox, all limp and dead. I went up to the window, putting my hand on the glass to see inside. A voice made me jump.

'There's no one home.' The burly woman spoke loudly; her hand was holding a grooming brush. 'Who are you?'

'I'm from Wood End.'

'Ah, you're that...' She looked at my scar. 'I know who you are.' She smiled politely.

'I'm a friend. Do you know when they're home?'

'They?' she shook her head and tutted loudly. 'Mrs Wilson, you mean. He's never here. The poor girl's left alone most of the time. It's a wonder she stays with him, as pretty as she is. Still, young 'uns nowadays, I don't know what the world is coming to.'

'Is Misty all right?'

'What a fine horse. I don't think she will be away long. She lives for that horse.'

I walked away feeling hollow. I kept going over what the woman had said. She did need saving and what if she met someone and I lost her. I would forever regret not making a proper commitment.

I got back home to find the red light on the phone flashing.

Silver Bubbles

'Mike, it's Andrea. Sorry I didn't have time to tell you. I popped round but there was no one there. My aunt is sick, so I am helping on her smallholding for a few days. I have got someone to look after Misty. I will call you when I get back. Bye...' There was a pause then she said softly in almost a whisper, 'I'm missing you.' I stood up, smiling. A warm feeling ran through me. I flicked on the weather. 'At last.' The forecast was looking better so I rang Billy.

CHAPTER ELEVEN

The familiar headland faded behind us as *Sea Gem* moved steadily in a north-easterly direction, effortlessly pushing aside the small white horses that sprang up from the choppy water. Behind her she left a bubbling wake, hissing and boiling in confusion.

I was sitting at the helm watching the miles slowly count down. The tubes were to be first; once they were recovered we would be in profit and earning a wage. But the tin was on all our minds, each of us having spent part of it already. I was going to put mains electricity in Wood End. Phil was going to buy a house and fit it out like a penthouse. Billy was going to pay off his mortgage and buy the shop, leaving him solvent and in his words, "owing nowt!" I smiled to myself. It's never that easy though; the sea doesn't suffer fools and gives nothing up without a fight. Len joined me.

'Looks fine, the grading hook is ready, skip.'

'Cheers, I hope it's clear this time and not wrapped around anything.'

Once on site I crossed the track we had left on the plotter, towing the heavy grading hook. One pass, two passes then three: still no rope. I shouted to Billy to put a shot in the next pass. In went the weight, pulling the line after it.

Silver Bubbles

The next pass, Billy disappeared into the deep, blue water. We drifted close by, watching his bubbles move across the surface. Twenty minutes later, a yellow lifting bag broke the surface. Attached to it was our heavy mooring line, which was quickly tied to *Sea Gem's* rear bollard. The marker was close enough to reach and was pulled aboard, shortly after Billy surfaced.

'What a pile of knitting that was. Some crabber must have shot his gear and fouled the mooring. It was in a heap. There's no way the tide could have done it.'

'Did you see the seal?' Phil asked with concern.

'No I bloody didn't,' snapped Billy. 'Get your arse down there.'

Phil's voice came clearly from the coms. 'On the job, standby,'

He worked well, recovering three tubes. I followed him, and after rushing around like a man possessed I recovered four.

Later we were sitting around the mess table. Phil looked at me. 'I cleared the way for you,' he commented as he crunched a piece of celery. 'That's why you got four.'

'That's a load of bollocks. I'm the first to get four single-handed. I might demand a bigger share if I'm doing most of the graft.'

'Many left?' Billy grunted without looking up from his plate.

'I was rushing to get the fourth, and the Vis was all stirred up so I err, didn't really see.'

Billy looked at Phil, raising his eyebrow. 'Not so perfect this time, if he doesn't even look down to where he's working, eh?'

I didn't bite. I just opened my book and quietly said, 'First dip is yours, Billy. Hey, what does a golfer shout when his ball is hit towards someone?'

Phil said, 'Fore.'

I smiled at Billy, and returned to my book.

Dawn came and with it a chill in the air. Late August and the summer, which hadn't really arrived, seemed to be leaving us already. We stood at the stern, relieving ourselves.

Phil joined us. As Billy and I headed towards the shower, Phil shouted, 'Oh shit! It's just surfaced, over there to the south. Its bloody head's bigger than Billy's.'

'The seal?' I asked.

'Yeah the same one, it's fucking huge.'

Billy lit a length of safety fuse that was connected to a plain detonator, which was taped to a small piece of the high explosive.

'Phil, where did it surface?'

'About thirty yards south,' he pointed.

Billy threw the small charge to the area. Small bubbles of smoke broke the calm surface. Then a sharp thud followed by a twenty-foot circular mushroom of bubbles pushed itself a few inches above the surface.

'That should have done the trick,' said Billy. 'Kit me up, chef. I've got five tubes to recover.' I gave him the single finger.

'No, five,' he said, as he pulled the mask to his face, holding it while Phil zipped up the hood.

The seabed was littered with dead sand eels about three inches long. Small crabs were already at work, harvesting their unexpected windfall and were all scuttling along, each claw tightly gripping a small eel. 'Nothing is wasted here,' thought Billy. As he moved towards the remaining tubes he touched each one, counting.

'There's six left over.'

'Roger that. Billy, try and get all six,' Phil replied. There was no reply, just a grunt.

'He will leave one on badness, so you had best get kitted up, anyway. I'll do the coms.'

Silver Bubbles

Much to my pleasure and annoyance, Billy recovered five tubes and was rubbing it in big style, while doing a five-minute stop on the line. I told him the fifth one didn't count because he had gone into deco to get it.

Phil was disappointed that he hadn't got all six, saving him from diving with the seal, but it was his turn now and he only had to get one tube.

As he made bottom Billy shouted, 'Oh shit, look,' he pointed to Phil's bubbles. In the centre was the bull seal. Its head looked around and pointed upwards and then its nostrils opened wide as it prepared to dive. Billy put on the scuba set and picked up a long steel rod that Phil had made on the last trip.

One of its ends was sharpened like a spear. I looked at him and said, 'Don't hang about. You won't have much bottom time banked.' We stood watching, slightly amused, but concerned.

'Do you think he will be all right?' asked Len.

'We'll soon know,' I replied, unable to hide my laughter. 'When his bubbles change to the size of dustbin lids, that's when he's seen it.'

We stood engrossed then as predicted, his bubbles increased in size.

'It's here,' Phil shouted through the coms. 'Pull me up, it's having a go.'

'Roger that,' I replied unable to hide my smile.

'I can't put the lad through this. We need the chef,' Billy said then he jumped in and sped down the line. He could see Phil's bubbles on the way down. He was up against a steel plate, waving a crow bar at the seal. It had its mouth open, snapping its big, green teeth like an angry dog.

As Billy approached it moved away and then swam around them at great speed. It darted towards them turning away just inches away. It came straight for Billy. He spun around to maintain contact with it, but it turned too quickly, grabbing his ankle. It shook him viciously.

He tried to poke it with the rod, but as he did the rod fell from his hand to the seabed. Phil grabbed the rod and thrust it into the side of the attacking seal. Blue blood stained the water as the seal contorted its body while biting the steel rod. As it pulled and twisted the rod came out. More blood stained the water. Suddenly it was gone.

Billy gave Phil the thumbs up. Phil cleared his mask and started beating his chest, while making a pathetic Tarzan-like sound. Billy surfaced leaving Phil to strop the last tube. His suit was ripped, but he wasn't badly hurt. He had bites similar to a dog's. They were painful, but we kept up to date with all the jabs, so iodine and a good dressing did the trick.

Phil was getting to us though. In his words he was "a monster fighter" and had saved Billy from being dragged away into the open sea to be eaten alive.

With all the tubes recovered, thirteen in all, it was decision time.

'Shall we look for some more of those small spools of copper that Phil found, or look for the tin?' I asked, as Billy shovelled the last pile of crud overboard.

'We're in the black already, we've nowt to lose.'

'What about you, Tarzan?'

Phil replied, 'I'm easy, I'll go with the flow.'

I stood deliberating for a while.

'How about looking at that wreck the "Chisets" got their gear fast into first? It's not far away.'

'Good idea,' Billy said. 'I might get something brass for our lass to polish.'

The sounder showed a slight scour in the seabed then the shape of something large started appearing. It peaked at about twenty feet then dropped back to a flat line. I turned *Sea Gem* and did another pass. This time, Billy dropped the weight as

Silver Bubbles

the target peaked. The rope showed up on the sounder, like an invisible finger was drawing a thin line on the screen, which ended at the wreck.

'Right down the funnel,' I joked. 'Now, who's going to be first?' I paused. 'Technically I should, because you two were the last to dive.'

Billy and Phil looked at each other. Phil said, 'It doesn't make that much difference, considering the interval time of the last dive.'

'OK then, we'll toss for it. Get your knobs out then,' I said, grinning at Phil as our thoughts turned to that special night.

Phil smiled lost in a trance then said, 'Ménage-à-trois.'

Billy, all ears said, 'What's that then chef, lemon meringue? I like that.'

Phil shook his head and looked at me, 'Toss yours then.'

'I win,' I shouted at them, both showing heads, me winning with tails being the odd man out.

'There be treasure down there,' I grinned, 'and I'm the first man down to it. Ha, ha,' I carried on taking the piss till I jumped over the side.

'Thank fuck for that. He was doing my head in,' Billy said. Phil just grinned, staring at the bubbles leading towards the unknown shipwreck.

The visibility was good: about twenty feet. Dark shadows turned to unfamiliar shapes as I neared the remains of the forgotten hulk.

The seabed consisted of millions of broken shells and stones. The white shells in contrast with the stones made it look like a patterned carpet. As I swam around the edge of the wreckage, I saw deep scours where the hull rested on the clay seabed, leaving dark, forbidding holes. Swimming upwards I held on to the rails. Everything was intact towards the bow, although very decayed and fragile.

The forward mast had collapsed and was lying on the seabed; the anchor winch still was sitting where it belonged.

Peter Fergus

'Wow,' I said to myself, as I saw the ship's bell lying near the anchor winch.

I held it in both hands. Then I closed my eyes and for a few seconds. I thought, Who last rang this? I imagined men running around the deck carrying out their tasks. This was what it's all about, true adventure. I experienced a feeling of personal achievement.

I pulled at the bell, which gave a puff of black smoke, like silt. As the thin crust of concretion was broken, a rub with my hand brought a smile my face. *Albania*. I've read about you, you were carrying a general cargo. You could have some good stuff aboard, we've got you now!'

Then I thought of Billy, who always wanted to find a ship's bell, I thought of the look of disappointment he couldn't hide when Phil ran around the deck holding his new found bell aloft.

I had to have the last laugh though, so I put a sea urchin on the deck then placed the bell back over it.

Finning down the starboard side I noticed the hatch combings were intact at the first hold. The second hold had dropped ten feet into the seabed. Where does everything disappear? It must all dissolve into the sea, eaten by the living water. Two large boilers appeared out of the gloom. The ship's side had collapsed years ago, probably when I was in infant school. The large cylinders of the engine were next, three in line. Brass steam gauges, still attached to their copper pipes, looked like sunflowers growing from the confusion of wreckage. Portholes were everywhere. The condenser pump, made of gunmetal, was in place. I estimated about one-and-a-half ton of scrap in this small area alone.

Moving aft, the seabed was winning, having buried most of the aft deck. Then it appeared to grow out of the sand again. About ten feet proud of the seabed was the steering counter, a big fan shaped piece of steel, which was attached to the strong rudderpost. Lobsters were everywhere and large shoals

Silver Bubbles

of whiting moved like a wall of silver. A brass emergency steering head, still on its binnacle and attached to the deck would make a fine trophy. Sadly, the wooden wheel had long gone. Just the brass rings remained, hanging like discarded toy hoops.

A shrill beeping from my dive computer told me it was time to start my ascent. Swimming back along the port side I saw a round shape, another porthole in perfect condition. I grabbed at it, pulling it from where it had been for over fifty years. Silt rose up reducing the visibility as I half-walked half-swam, pulling myself along the shot line with the heavy find.

It was now slack water and the line was quite long. I had travelled along it for a while still on the seabed, until all the slack was taken up. There it hung vertical from the big orange buoy on the surface.

As I pulled myself up, a glint from something shiny caught my eye. Wrapping the rope around the porthole, I dropped back down to have a look. Rows of sand waves about three feet apart, like the ones on a beach, but much bigger, made the seabed look like a ploughed field. In between one of the furrows was a shiny piece of metal. I picked it up then hastily grabbed the line and continued my ascent. I reached *Sea Gem* after finishing a five-minute decompression stop, and was slagged off for hogging the slack water. When they saw the porthole I got even more stick for selfish tatting.

Phil was in the water within seconds. As Billy pulled on his hood, I put my fingertips together and made the gesture for him to head for the bow. Billy gave a discreet nod, and then splashed in, swimming quickly to the buoy, pushing Phil out of the way.

'What's his rush? Silly old sod,' Phil said, as he put in his mouthpiece then followed the tunnel of dancing bubbles

Billy was leaving behind him. He wasted no time on reaching the bottom. Engine, boiler, bow, he thought to himself. As he pulled hard towards the big winch, he stopped.

Water filled his mask as he smiled and said to himself, 'Bell.' He dropped down to it, lying on his chest. Looking closely he could see a thin, black line where I had broken it from the concretion. He slowly pushed it on its side, revealing the sea urchin. A grunting noise made him look to his side. Phil was watching everything and gave him a thumb's up of approval before he disappeared into the haze.

On the surface Len and I were inspecting the piece of steel. 'It's not steel, it's too light, and look at all those rivets on the joint.' He paused, 'Do you know, this is off a plane? It's alloy. See, this is part of a strengthening frame.'

'Bloody hell, it must be near here.' I walked to the stern. I wonder why they want it so badly? My thoughts were interrupted by loud shouts.

'Ding, Ding. Just call me 'Billy the Bell'!' Billy shouted across to Phil. As they bobbed on the surface, Billy threw his mask to me and winked. 'It's better than your bastard,' he shouted at Phil, who was shaking his head and insisting there was a conspiracy against him. After removing their gear Phil started.

'It's all a bloody set up. I'm not biting; you're just two, sad, old men, gleaning kicks from a younger more modern and sophisticated person. You're both old and sad.' He walked to the shower. 'Sad! Sad!' he shouted.

'Got him big style,' I smiled at Billy.

'Yep, we got him.'

The piece of alloy glinted in the sun. Having been polished in the ever-swirling sand, there were no markings, but any expert would be able to tell what it had come off. 'This is an important find,' I said, as I turned it around, looking at it. 'The rest is down there all right. We will have to keep quiet about this. I wonder what Uncle Sam will do next.'

'Three days, what bollocks!' Billy said. 'Who do they think they are?'

Silver Bubbles

'Government and civil service, that's who they are; they are the most dangerous, deceitful, murdering, venal, cheating humans on this planet. There's more honour in a rat than in one of them. They have taken the Great out of Britain. They make me want to chuck up.'

'Here, here,' Phil said. 'There's deceit everywhere,' he looked at us, then at the bell that Billy was slowly cleaning. 'Everywhere!' he repeated, as he disappeared into the galley.

I swung *Sea Gem* around and edged our way towards the orange buoy. As Len hooked the end, Billy pulled the rope on to the open block that was hanging from the strong lifting gantry then wrapped it around the whipping drum on the winch. I was overseeing the operation from the wheelhouse, while Phil sat peeling spuds.

There was a slight clank. We all looked at the rope as a beautiful compass binnacle swung above the deck. Three dolphin heads served as the feet. Twisting bodies made up the upright, and claws gripped the brass bowl where the compass card was held. It appeared in excellent condition for something that had been below for so long. Unable to restrain himself Phil pushed past.

'I've got a bell already; this is the type of piece I was hoping for.' He untied it, pulled it out of the way and covered it with a wet sack. Looking at Billy then at up at me he smiled. It will go nicely in my trophy room when I get my house. You both hang around the bows of a wreck like frustrated old men standing around the ladies bog in a night club, when all the talent is at the bar.' He walked through the door and shouted, 'with me!'

'He's fucking had it,' I shouted down at Billy. 'He's getting far too cocky.'

Len grinned as he pulled back the sack. 'You've got to give the kid credit. It's the best goodie by far.'

Billy looked at me. 'You started this, now he's stuffing us.'

'I heard that, Billy. You get on with cleaning your urchin-hungry bell,' Phil's voice shouted from the galley.

I smiled, shaking my head, enjoying the crack and then looked at Billy who was also shaking his head, then I shouted, 'Under way, course set for the wreck of the steam treasure ship *Juno*.'

The big hole hadn't filled in much at all. Empty boxes lay scattered on the seabed, their contents having rotted away decades ago. I estimated where the second hold was, then marked the area with rope. I used the remainder of my bottom time surveying the rest of the wreck. I was looking for clues or anything that might lead to the tin. Twenty minutes later, I surfaced.

'Any good?' Billy asked.

'No,' I replied, pinching my nose then running my fingers through my hair. 'I've got our tea though.' I tipped three big lobsters from the bag.

'They won't pay for your electric.' Phil said. 'You didn't see anything then?'

'Nothing, just scrap. I've marked the airlift area so we might as well start there. It's bloody hard going, especially when you find sweet knack all.'

'You don't find anything without looking,' Len said. 'So stop dripping, and get to it.'

Billy looked at him. 'I'll get you a suit if you want.'

'If I was your age lad, I wouldn't have needed one,' he said, to the sound of 'woos' from everyone.

It was seven p.m. We had been airlifting now for two days and had found only brass tubes. About three quarters of a ton to show for it and we had reached the bottom of the hold again.

'I don't get it at all.' I paced up and down. 'We're doing it all right, and we haven't missed a button. We've uncovered enough leather to start a tannery, all that wasn't on the manifest.'

'What if there isn't any tin at all?' Phil said.

'Well, we won't bloody know until we look. Christ! How long is a piece of string?' I snapped.

'Where next?' Billy asked with a sigh.

'The weather is holding, so we continue here,' I said with authority in my voice. 'We start at first light. We splash at first light OK?' I looked at them.

'Yeah, loud and clear,' Billy replied, 'Loud and clear.'

A chill ran through me as I hit the dark, uninviting water. The sunrise with its billowing clouds was now just a memory. Phosphorescence flashed past my eyes like stars in a science fiction film, making me slightly dizzy as dropped deeper into the black void. I had got up early and kitted up first to motivate the team. Now I was slightly regretting it.

I made the bottom with a thump. Dull shapes appeared to be growing out of the seabed, which looked dark and scary despite it being covered in a blanket of white shells. I slid into the large hole to get the airlift.

As I struggled with it in the twilight gloom, I accidentally knocked the air valve fully on. The discharge pipe had sunk to the seabed and I hadn't noticed it so the airlift shot upward and out of control as the discharge pipe filled with air. I clung to it, grabbing around for the valve, while cursing in a cloud of swirling bubbles, legs and arms waving as I tried to keep upright. When I closed the valve I shot back down, landing on my back with a heavy thud like an upturned beetle. Immediately I felt a rush of cold water invade my back and stomach.

'Shit!' I cursed.

'Madam in a tis-was?' came over the coms.

'Bollocks!' I shouted, while reaching behind me. I felt an inch long gash in my suit. 'Where the hell have I landed?' I cursed to myself. It was getting a bit lighter, but still too dark one hundred foot below the waves to see clearly where I was.

My street cred is at risk here. I'm lost. I can't believe this. I walked the best I could, dragging the heavy airlift with me.

'Are you going to do any airlifting, over, or are you knocking one out? You're panting like a dog. Are you all right, over?' Billy sensed something was wrong and was trying to pry it from me.

'Get stuffed and standby, out.'

'Out… the cheeky sod, he's cocked it up.' Phil's white teeth shone in the dim light.

Billy looked at him, raising his eyebrows. 'It does sound like he's having fun.'

I was shivering now with my suit full of water. Then at last I recognised where I was. I cursed myself again as I made out the shape of the engine cylinder. 'How the hell did I end up here? Bollocks! I looked around; a feeling of despair enveloped me. 'What the hell am I doing here?' I was shivering and felt so cold. It was all going wrong. I felt like a child doing a man's job and making a mess of it. I strained to look at two big shapes. What I could barely make out were the boilers. I faced them square on and moved back several steps; I grabbed the airlift with both hands. As I turned the valve a little, the discharge pipe slowly filled and rose vertically. The small buoy, which normally keeps the discharge pipe vertical, had come off, which had caused my earlier problem. I turned it fully on. It juddered and then began sucking the seabed away like a giant vacuum cleaner.

Billy looked surprised. The bubbles were a long way from the mooring line.

Phil said, 'Where the hell? Is he on another wreck?' They both looked at each other, shrugging their shoulders.

'Sit rep?' Billy asked over the coms.

'I hope the bloody water is hot,' I replied. Operating the airlift was a cold job at the best of times, with all the water

Silver Bubbles

rushing past. I was so cold now. Then as if by magic the corner of a large steel object appeared.

I jabbed the sucking pipe against it, uncovering more all the time. Another corner appeared. The box was about six feet long, lying at a forty degrees slant. Three feet down its side I hit wood.

It's the bottom! Hell, the whole hold is listing to port and slightly forward. I moved the pipe to the top of the box. Black silt ran up the pipe like ink. A small grey object with a sharp edge came into sight, then another and another. As the shapes became visible, a surge of excitement hit my stomach like a punch. Then the airlift fizzled to a halt, so I pushed my hand into the black silt and grabbed something. I pulled it clear and looked at it. Just like the old guy had said. I held the ingot tightly to my chest and started my ascent.

'Pull me up, I'm flooded,' I gasped, as I sank back down to the seabed.

'Understood,' Billy said with concern. My umbilical became tight as they pulled me to the surface. In all the excitement I had ignored my dive computer. Although Billy had timed me, I had moved to slightly deeper water and had to do a decompression stop at ten feet for five minutes. I hung one hand on the compressor air hose. My other clutched the small ingot tightly to my chest. It was one of the longest, coldest five minutes of my life and I would never forget it in hurry, but the ingot I held tightly made all the suffering worthwhile.

Six eager hands grabbed at me, pulling me on to the deck like a bag full of water. I lay there while many hands unclipped and unzipped me.

'Put your arms out, you knob,' Billy shouted at me, 'I can't get your harness off.'

As I pulled my arms from my chest the ingot banged onto the deck. There was a deadly silence. We all exchanged glances then I was patted like a dog, and pushed as if I had scored a winning goal. Questions invaded me, but I was shaking uncontrollably.

'Get him into the shower. Come on, get a move on, we can talk later.'

Billy took charge of the situation, rushing me towards the shower. I caught a glimpse of Len looking at me. He was nodding and beaming with pride.

On the next dive, Billy and Phil recovered one hundred and sixty tin ingots. We stood on deck grinning at each other. I felt so proud, but omitted to tell them what had really happened. It was my secret. The team had faith in me and I had found the ingots against all odds.

'Nothing can stop us now!' Phil shouted up at me.

I appeared at the window, 'What were you saying?'

'I said, nothing can stop us now,' he repeated.

'How about a north-easterly gale eight?' I nodded, 'Yeah, they just gave it.' I looked around, 'Look how clear it is. That's the sign the wind is going round to the north. Get the airlift and undo the mooring. We're out of here. It's imminent. We will be back.' I slid the window up, rubbed my hands and said out loud to *Sea Gem,* 'Lets see what you can do.'

We all stood in the wheelhouse looking at the rows of large swells that ran before us. They looked like the backs of sea monsters. Big and wide, with waves curling on their tops like flames, rolling and spitting.

I held course as each swell picked *Sea Gem* up like a toy, hurling her down the slope, trying to swallow her up in a wall of water. Again and again she was forced down the water slide, to crash into the back of another large wave-topped swell.

'It's a bit crap,' Billy said. 'I'm glad we're going with it.'

'Yeah,' I agreed. 'It would be like being in a washing machine.'

Len gave a wry smile, as did Phil. 'You pussies, you don't know the meaning of the word rough,' Phil said.

Silver Bubbles

'Yeah, but that's in a bloody destroyer. This is a toy compared to one of those.'

'Cape Horn,' Len said. 'In a steam ship for two weeks and we went backwards for a week, until we were among the ice. Many never got out of that trap, a small engine at the mercy of the southern ocean. It was far too rough to cook. I was fifteen and thought for sure I wouldn't see sixteen. We carried coal outbound. It rubbed so much on the hull the friction made it catch fire. The hull got red hot. We nearly lost her. Still, the master cracked on. If you want to swing the lamp, I'll tell you some tales. Call this rough?' He shook his head, 'Anyone for a brew?'

'Billy sighed. That told us,'

'Yeah,' I paused. 'It certainly did.'

Sitting on deck safely in our mooring and looking across the fields, we talked about the trip and the prospects of more tin being found. Len broke out the rum and passed pint glasses around.

'What's this?' Billy asked, 'Bloody pints?'

'The sun's well gone. You lads deserve a wet. These save running about filling your glasses.' He smiled as he covered the ice cubes with the dark nectar, making them crack loudly.

I interrupted, 'Well...' I looked at the piece of paper. 'Do you want to know what we've earned?'

'Yeah, yeah,' Phil sat with his wrists hanging while panting, as if mimicking a dog.

'Bloody suits you,' Billy quipped.

'*Albania* the urchin bell, eh?' Phil said with a smirk.

'Well,' I continued, 'We should have grossed forty thousand, one hundred and forty pounds. Not bad eh? With Fagin's ten percent off...' I looked at Len.

He said, 'No, no. It's settled. You didn't have to give me that tip last time. I've got enough.'

'Cheers Dad. So that will be nine thousand, three hundred and fifteen for the boat fund, and the same for each of us.'

'Yes!' Phil stood up and punched the air. 'Ten grand towards my pad.' He paused, looking at us, 'Cheers lads.'

Jonno arrived with his new girlfriend, whom Phil and I couldn't keep our eyes off.

'Let me show her around,' Phil said to Jonno, who just smiled and ignored him.

'You should know better, bringing a beautiful creature on board when we've been at sea for days,' I said, making Caroline blush.

Jonno produced a bottle of rum. 'I've brought a ticket.' He swung the bottle at head height.

'OK, we'll let you off this time.'

'There are a few blokes talking in a pub. One of them said, 'I got shit last night when I got in. Do you know, I turned off the engine and coasted without lights into the drive, sneaked upstairs naked and without a sound, got into bed, she elbowed me really hard right in the eye, cursed me, then turned over.'

That's all wrong mate, said another one, totally wrong. I speed up and down with my radio full on. I squeal down the drive, bang the door a few times, barge through the front door, put all the lights on, then burst into the bedroom and say 'Come on darling how about it then?' That's what I say.'

The man who got elbowed asked, 'What did she do?'

'She just laid there snoring, pretending to be asleep.' '

I smiled, but my attention was elsewhere. I could just make out a speck in a distant field. Someone was out riding. The now familiar wave ran through my stomach. 'Andrea,' I said out loud.

'No, I'm Caroline,' she said, looking at me.

'Sorry, I was miles away.'

All-eyes Billy saw it all and shook his head.

'What's up with you?' I stared at him.

'I ain't got the problem pal,' he replied, with a cocky smile.

'You have a problem?' Jonno asked.

'No, it's just Billy Bones over there, or should I say, Mrs Wells?'

'How did you do then?'

'Phil, show Jonno the tat.'

They went below. Caroline stood with an empty glass. 'Can I get you another?' I gave her a smile. She blushed, swapping the glass in her hands.

'Err, yes, yes please.'

As I poured the wine a strong hand gripped my arm. Billy then whispered to me, 'Leave it out, he's a mate.'

'I know, I know,' I said.

'Well, you're like a dog on heat. It's embarrassing us all.'

I looked at my friend. 'Really, am I?'

Billy nodded. 'Save it for Irish if you must.'

I nodded to him, passed Caroline the glass, and then returned to Billy.

'I don't know I'm doing it.'

'Well you were.'

'OK, understood.'

'Wow! You've done well this trip. I wish I could have made it.' Jonno said. He called Caroline over.

Phil began telling them about his "near death" fight with the Sperm whale size man-eating seal.

'Hell, if that seal gets any bigger, it will be a bloody shipping hazard!' Billy said, laughing.

'Was that a Billy joke?' Phil asked me.

'I think so, it's hard to say. They're so rare.'

Caroline looked confused. 'Don't take any notice,' said Jonno. 'They always do this.' She smiled; entertained at the constant ragging we were dealing each other.

'Anyway, I forgot to ask,' Phil shouted to me, now half pissed. 'How did you get the air lift past the bloody boilers and engine so quickly and why?'

Billy looked at me. He was interested to hear what sort of answer I was going to give. 'Yeah,' Billy joined in. 'We couldn't work out what you was doing in all those bubbles.'

'Maybe he sat on the air lift and rode it like a rocket,' Phil said to Billy, while swaying from the effect of the rum.

I couldn't stop myself going red-faced, so I tried to change the subject. 'I thought I'd try hold three.'

'Got him,' Billy said to Phil. 'Got the bastard, hold three... bollocks.'

Caroline and Jonno were confused, but amused as Billy and Phil waded into me, firing questions like barristers. Then I made the vital mistake they were digging for.

'If you had tied the bloody buoy on the discharge pipe properly...' I paused. 'Shit, shit.' I shook my head. They had me. Billy and Phil were ecstatic.

'Yes! We've got him. He did ride the airlift just like you said,' Phil shouted at Billy. 'That's how he ended up there.'

'Don't forget the suit,' Billy grinned. 'How do you do that to yourself unless you're falling backwards?'

'Exactly!' Phil almost screamed with excitement. 'A major cock up, and the jammy bastard came out a fucking hero.'

'Err, language, mate.' Billy smiled at Caroline, who was shocked at our behaviour, but still laughing with us.

'It wasn't like that at all.' I tried to wriggle out of the trap they had set, but was failing miserably, much to their pleasure.

'The six P's,' Billy said in a posh voice, making Phil spit his drink on to the deck. He continued, '**P**erfect **P**lanning **P**revents **P**iss **P**oor **P**erformance. How many times have we had that rammed up arses?' he said in hysterics. 'Well, if all fails, just fuck up and come out smelling of roses, the jammy sod!'

Phil was crying with laughter. I looked at Len for support. Len wiped his tears away with his handkerchief, then stuck it

Silver Bubbles

on the brush handle and passed it to me, while jerking with laughter.

'Not you as well,' I stood, holding the brush. Jonno placed his baseball cap on my head back to front, and took a photo of me. The laughter could be heard a long way away.

Over the fields and in the garden of the 'Spinney', a pair of beautiful dark eyes turned and looked towards the boat. The eyes turned to a smile.

I opened the door and placed my bag on the worktop. Phil followed me in. I stopped, looking around. Phil stood behind me.

'What's up?'

'I don't know. I'm sure I can smell smoke.' Phil pressed the smoke alarm. It beeped loudly.

'No,' I looked puzzled, 'Cigarette smoke. I'm sure that's what it is.'

'Nobody smokes though,' Phil said, as he squeezed past me towards his room. 'It must be on your clothes.'

The answer machine was flashing. 'Lewis. Call me when you receive this.' Pressing the button again, I smiled as he heard the voice of Kim, while writing down a number she could be contacted on. There were three more messages. Two were job inquiries. The last was short but the best one of all. It just said, 'I'm alone and lonely for you.'

'Yes!' I said loudly.

'Yes, you're heading for deep shit.' Phil surprised me.

'You're getting as bad as Billy.'

'Just don't want to see you get hurt, pal. That's all,' he said, as he picked up the phone and twisted the pad round to read the number.

'I'll leave you to dribble down the mouthpiece in private. Oh, and give her my love and a kiss and tell her...'

'Get out of it, you rake,' Phil interrupted, throwing a cushion at me.

I was in my bedroom undressing for a shower. I stopped, staring on the floor near my built-in dresser.

'I don't believe this.' I bent down for a closer look. On the carpet was a piece of cigarette ash, only small, but there was no doubt in my mind where it had come from.

'The bastards,' I shouted. 'I'll kill him.' Everything was in place, but they had been here searching.

I showered, cursing constantly and then I told Phil.

'Did you leave any charts or notes here?'

'No. I take them all with me when we go on a trip so they won't have found anything.'

'What about your cash stash?'

'I take it with me as well.'

'Yeah, so do I. What if they've planted something or bugged the rooms?'

'No. Why would they do that?'

'Those bastards will do anything. You should know that.'

I looked out of the window. 'Yeah, you're right they must want that position badly.' I picked up the phone and pulled a piece of paper from the book. Five minutes later I rejoined Phil in the kitchen.

'What did he say?'

'Well, that guy in the black suit is CIA. He has so many names even Commander Lewis doesn't know his real one, but listen to this. The plane was lost just as the war ended and it was coming from Germany via Holland.'

'It must have been carrying something interesting,'

'Yeah, I reckon so. Bloody hell, this could be big. I don't think they would break in here just for some dead airman's bones.'

Phil stood up. 'They could be listening to us right now.'

'If they are,' I raised my voice, 'Tell that smoking bastard I'm going to give him a good kicking! Bollocks to them. How's Kim?'

'She's got a couple of days off. I would like to go and see her. What do you reckon?'

'This northerly is set in for a while and it will leave a big swell for days. We did well, this trip. There's two job inquiries in, but they only want a price so, yeah, no problem.'

'Shit hot! I'll pack now. Oh, what about unloading?'

'Get gone, you knob. We can manage that. Have a good time, but don't blow loads of dosh, mate. Go steady, stay in your room, and practise sex!'

'Good idea, but I always do that anyway,' he said grinning from cheek to cheek.

I played Andrea's message back a few times, and the music in the background sounded vaguely familiar. 'I wonder, was it her who had been ringing anonymously?' Phil rushed passed with his bag, leaving me pondering with my thoughts.

Sitting in a posh restaurant in London Phil was watching Kim. She was eating with chopsticks. The bowl hid her face as she scooped up pieces of food. He smiled at her every time she lowered the bowl. She even ate stylishly, he thought. He watched her, revelling in excitement and anticipation.

Later after their top class meal they walked back to the hotel. He put his arm around her waist. She felt so good. He pulled her closer, making her stagger slightly as she walked. They laughed then Phil suddenly stopped, looking into a restaurant window. He stared in disbelief.

'Fucking hell!' Kim put her small hand over his mouth.

'What is it?'

Phil was moving his head around, like an owl about to pounce on a mouse. 'Sorry love.' He turned to her. 'It's Andrea's old man, I'm sure of it,' he said with a look of disbelief. 'And he's with two birds, the dirty old sod.'

'I'm sorry, I don't understand.'

'No need, babe. I'll explain later. Do you fancy another coffee?'

They sat down at a table close by. Andrea's husband was well inebriated and rather loud. He had two young working girls with him.

'The condescending prat,' Phil whispered to Kim. 'And I've given my mate shit.'

She looked confused, 'Sorry.'

He lowered his head and continued, 'He's married to that Irish bird that Mike has been seeing. I've been slagging him off about it, but just look at him.'

Gerald was kissing and cosseting like a pervert, almost dribbling on to the young girls, in between noisily guzzling brandy. He had the look and manner of the classic army Rupert: an officer fresh from Sandhurst, arrogant and stupid.

'He's a really loud man,' Kim said softly.

'I'm so chuffed. What goes around certainly comes around,' Phil said, while trying not to look.

The waiter came to Gerald's table and whispered into his ear.

'What?' Gerald shouted. 'This is preposterous.' He knocked a drink over as he clumsily stood up. The waiter gestured innocence with his hands, while walking backwards.

'Here, take this.' He struggled to remove his watch and pushed it in his face. The waiter, embarrassed, passed the watch to his partner who looked at it and nodded.

'I should think so too!' Gerald glared at them, then stormed out cursing, tailed by the bewildered girls.

'Well, well,' Phil said. 'He must be going down the pan. His credit card was refused.'

Kim gave a sweet look of concern, 'Will Mike be all right?'

'Yeah, even more so when he hears about this.'

'Be careful,' she said in a serious tone, while putting her hand on his. 'Please think carefully about this before you say anything.'

He held her hand and kissed it. 'Thank you.'

'For what,'

'For being concerned, for being Kim.'

She smiled and looked down. 'Lucy asks about Mike every time we meet. She cheated on him for a long time and I feel so bad about it.'

'Hey, it was nothing to do with you.'

She stood up, 'Lets go now, we have a lot of catching up to do.' As they walked out, Phil put his arm around her and gave her several squeezes, making her smile wonderfully.

A thrush sang in the garden. The clear, crisp notes drifted into my mind. I felt totally relaxed. A slight draft of fresh air refreshed the room as I took a deep breath. For a second I didn't know where I was, then I felt her warmth. I opened my eyes. She was sleeping so blissfully. With her black hair lying across her face, she looked so beautiful. I stared for what seemed ages, then kissed her cheek. Her smell made me grin. I held her and rested my face into her hair, slowly drifting back to sleep. Half awake, she felt my presence. Moving her hand she held my naked waist. We melted into an intimate embrace.

I opened my back door and a familiar voice made me jump. 'I don't have to be Sherlock Homes to guess whose bed you were sleeping in last night.'

'You may not be Sherlock, but you do sound like daddy bear. God, I can't fart around here without everybody knowing about it.'

Billy shrugged, sensing that he was going too far. 'I suppose we only live once.'

'At last,' I said as I flicked the kettle on.

Billy sat down. 'I wonder how the boy's doing in London,'

'Kim won't scank him, she has class. Anyway, we work hard so why not chill out. At least he'll come back fitter.' Billy smiled.

'You always see the funny side of things.'

'Look at that.' Billy raised his voice. 'The bastards are putting more tax on fuel.' Billy pointed to the television.

I looked at the screen. 'I can't believe this country. The banks, insurance and pension companies make billions. They produce nothing and all the money goes out of the country. So the stupid thick politicians add more and more tax on fuel, increasing the cost of everything to the public. Wankers, all of them. They won't windfall tax the banks, the corrupt bastards.'

'Yeah,' Billy said, agreeing. 'They're all fingering each other. We had better get a move on. The wagon is coming in half an hour. I'll give Len a shout.'

'Don't bother, he's on his way,' I said, looking at Len, who was marching down the path.

Then someone tapped at the door. Vicki peered inside. Billy stood up and placed his cup in the sink. 'I'll be outside with Len,' he said, quickly disappearing.

'Hi, come in.' Vicki walked in, looking around. I pulled out a chair, 'Tea or coffee?'

'Tea please.' She followed me with her eyes as I moved around her.

'How are things?' I asked while pouring the tea.

'OK.'

'OK, that sounds ominous.'

'Why do you say that?'

I looked at her. 'Look, I'm not going to bullshit. Kris told me you were really down and depressed. Is Nigel making your life miserable?'

'No, not at all. Why?' she replied, shaking her head.

'Come on Vicki. Kris told me about... you know.'

'I don't know,' she said, standing up.

'I know you're not getting on.' I leaned against the worktop. 'Not sleeping together and all that.'

Silver Bubbles

'Did Kris tell you that?' I stood silent. 'It's a ploy Mike. He's just trying to get us back together.'

'Do you mean you don't sleep in separate beds?'

'No, of course we don't. We have our differences, but we get on well together.'

I stood feeling stupid, strangely hurt and jealous. 'Oh I...' I remained silent.

'Kris is starting his senior school next week and we think you should get more involved.'

'We?' I snapped. She looked away.

I checked my temper. 'Yeah, if I can, no problem.'

'Nigel has been off work with a hand injury. He got it trapped in a safe door.'

'Yeah that figures,' I said. 'So you're still sleeping with him then?'

'He will be off work for a couple of weeks.'

'You didn't even hear what I just asked you!' She looked at me.

'Are you still... you know, sleeping together?'

'That's none of your business.' She looked angry. I felt coldness from her I had never felt before. She avoided my eyes; she seemed so distant, like I didn't know her.

'What is it, Vicki? What's bothering you?'

'If you don't know then I feel sorry for you.'

'Hey, don't start on me. You left and succumbed to that sad bastard. You started all this. You left me don't forget!'

'Here we go again, the... "It's not my fault" speech.' She looked coldly at me. 'It's old hat, Mike. It's the past,' She opened the door and turned to me. 'Enjoy your leprechaun before she deserts you like all the rest have!' She slammed the door.

I couldn't believe what she had just said. I stood hurt and angry, then snatched open the door. 'That shit's giving you one, so what's wrong with me doing it, eh? It's all right for you!'

Vicki looked at me, then at Len and Billy. Saying nothing, she climbed into the car and slammed the door. She turned and gave me another frigid stare, which ended in an angry shiver, before driving away.

'Bollocks to you too!' I almost screamed. 'That's it! Don't come back here, bitch.'

A few minutes later Billy appeared at the open door. I was still wound up, sitting and breathing heavily, hands clenched on the table. I looked up, and my eyes couldn't conceal the hurt I was feeling. I said quietly, while looking at the shapely lipstick print on her unfinished teacup. 'I've fucked it this time.'

'We have work to do, kid. Put that shit behind you,' Billy said bluntly. 'I told you that you couldn't have two loves. It's time you started listening to the truth. She's made it more than clear this time. Come on.' His big arm pulled me to my feet and then went around my shoulder. 'It was bound to happen, pal, sooner or later. Come on, let's sort the boat out.'

As we left, the phone started ringing.

Phil put the receiver down then turned over to Kim. 'They must be on the boat.'

'If they are working, Phil, it's only fair that you should too.' She rolled on top of him, sliding up and down. Rubbing her nose on his she giggled, 'I want one hundred percent effort now.'

'I'll do my best, me lady.' He grabbed her small buttocks and pulled her tightly to him, making her squeak with pleasure.

We were washing down the deck. The lorry had left with all the scrap. Sid had promised to bring the cash the next day. Billy nodded his head as the black limo pulled up.

'I want a word with this bastard,' I said, throwing the brush down.

Silver Bubbles

'Wait a while,' Billy held me back. 'Play him at his own game.'

I looked at Billy, 'But if he gobs off I'll snot him one. I'm in the mood to give someone a good slapping.' Billy nodded.

The same two men got out of the car. The plain-clothed one looked all over *Sea Gem*. His stare ended on me.

'So... this is the poachers' tool.'

I leaned on the gunwale and coldly replied, 'So who made you the fucking game keeper then?'

'Have you got an import license for the stolen stuff you bring into the country?'

'Have you got a death wish?' I snapped.

'Touchy isn't he?' He looked at Billy who said slowly, 'There's nothing for you here.'

'It's all legitimate, authorised by the Salvage Association and within British territorial waters. We do it by the book, not like you lot,' I said calmly.

'We know where you went.'

'Look pal.' I raised my voice. 'Stop playing games, tell us what you are looking for and we'll help you.'

'We want the position and assurance you will stay away from the area.'

'And what do we get in return?' asked Billy.

'We leave you alone.'

'Guys, guys, this is our property. It belongs to the United States,' the man in the uniform interrupted.

'The plane is,' I said, getting the reaction I wanted. The suit pointed his finger at me.

'I'm warning you, sonny. You're getting yourselves into something you will most certainly regret!'

'It would be embarrassing should the press hear about what you got up to during the war. Not to mention the rush of treasure hunters that would cock it all up for you,' I replied, fishing for a response.

'Treasure hunters?' He paused. 'You said you hadn't found anything but the weapon.'

I looked at Billy and nodded. There was a stand off as the suit sat in the car talking on a phone.

'This is a delicate situation,' the Air Force man said. 'We need to deal with it.'

The man in black walked back towards us. 'I have someone on my telephone who wants to talk with you, Mike.'

I walked to the car and glared into his face. 'Who is it? I asked without emotion.

'Here.' He passed me the handset, wearing a smug grin, which tempted me to punch him, but I acknowledged it with a mean stare back.

'Mike, its Commander Lewis.'

'Bloody hell, you're not involved in this are you?'

'No, but I want you to tell them all you know, Mike. Assist them.'

'The bastards broke into my house. They broke the rules.' I looked at them. They nonchalantly looked away.

'They make the rules up, Mike. They have diplomatic immunity.'

'We only want to be treated professionally, not like bloody morons,' I said in a raised voice, again looking at them.

'You can't beat these guys. Tell them all you know and they will be gone.'

'OK,' I agreed reluctantly. 'I suppose we really have no option. Yeah, we'll do that.'

'Come aboard,' I said, shrugging my shoulders as I said to Billy, 'Commander Lewis has advised us to help.'

'Yeah, that figures.'

In the wheelhouse I opened my chart. Looking at the men I said, 'This is what you were looking for, I take it?'

The suit just smiled, having the satisfaction of getting what he wanted.

Silver Bubbles

'We haven't found a plane, just the gun and this.' I fetched the piece of alloy from my cabin. The airman looked at it and nodded to the suit.

'What else did you find?' asked the man in black.

'Do you mean the gold bars you lot stole from the Germans?' I said.

He turned to me. 'Good try. I like you, Mike. We pulled your file. You should have stayed in the army. Who knows what you would be doing now.'

'Not with my temper. I don't exactly wrap myself in the Union Jack. I didn't attend the right school and I'm not a member of *the* club.'

'We gathered that.' After taking all the positions their attitude changed to almost friendly.

I looked at the airman. 'Are you a jet jockey then?'

'NASA.'

'Hell, an astronaut?'

'Six missions completed.'

'Anyway, this loot you're after, who will get it, then?'

'You don't give up, do you?' said the suit.

'I understand now why you want it back. If the likes of us were to get our hands on it, not to mention the press, it would look bad, eh?'

'Look guys, you can't tell anyone,' said the Air Force man.

'We know, but just out of a matter of interest, what could you have done to stop us?'

The suit looked at me. 'There's a thousand ways available to us. We can pull any strings that are necessary, tax, corruption, sleaze, entrapment. We have all the modern weapons and will use them to effect. You could have had this little boat confiscated if you had obstructed us,' he said with a sinister smile. 'You're lucky, you have gained influential allies since your little skirmish.' He stood upright and sighed. 'Thank you for the position gentlemen.' He waved his notepad. 'You will no doubt hear a few press releases regarding the area. Just smile to yourselves and say nothing to anyone.'

'Will you let us know when you're finished, so we can work the *Albania*?'

'Sorry?'

'The shipwreck that is close to the plane.'

'Oh yes, we will do that. Have a nice day.'

As they drove off Billy said, 'It's a good job we told them.'

'Yeah I reckon so. I suppose taking on the biggest power in the world is a bit out of our league.' I looked at Billy, 'Hell, I nearly gobbed him.'

Len came out the galley and brought three sundowners. 'Loose lips sink ships.' He raised his glass. 'Cheers, shipmates.'

'What are you grinning for?' I asked.

'Gold,' Len said. 'I bet there's something interesting down there.'

'Yeah. Still, they haven't found it yet. Who knows? Cheers.' We raised glasses.

The next day, I sat with Billy; counting and sharing out the wads of twenty-pound notes that almost covered the table. Sid had called first thing and as promised, had paid us in cash.

'What's the postman come down here for?' Billy said as he rushed out the door to avoid him seeing the money laid out. He returned with his back to the half-open door as if defending the room from attack.

'Mike, you have to sign for a letter.'

I returned with the official looking brown envelope: placed it on the table and peeled it open. It contained a fancy embossed letter. 'Bla, bla. Fucking hell!' I sat down shocked.

'What's up mate?'

I shook my head. 'I don't believe this.' I passed the letter to Billy.

Silver Bubbles

'Hell!' He stood up making the chair scrape over the paved floor as it fell backwards. 'This is mega. I've got to show Len.' He dashed out and ran down the path, leaving me sitting in a daze.

'Len, Len, look at this.' Billy rushed in, making the big, static caravan rock slightly. Len was watching Sky as usual, and eating a pilchard and onion sandwich. He held the letter and squinted at it then put his specs on. As he read it his face turned into a big smile.

'Well, well.' He stood up, brushing crumbs into the fire hearth. 'This is the proudest day of my life. My son awarded the George Medal for bravery.' He reached for his hanky as his eyes filled with tears.

They walked in. I looked at Len. 'I suppose it's something of a thank you.' He was quite overcome and gave me a slap on the back.

'Come on, Dad. All you guys from the war deserved a lot more than this.'

Len smiled as he read it again.

Phil pulled into the yard followed by a cloud of dust, then climbed out of his car. He grabbed his bag and walked with a swagger towards the door. The rum was out. 'What's this?' He looked at the clock. 'A bit bloody early, isn't it?'

Len passed him the letter. Phil put his bag down, 'Bloody hell.' He looked at me. 'What is it?'

Billy shouted, 'Read it properly you pleb.'

Phil read it again. 'Hell, does this mean we have to call you sir?'

'No, you knob. It's a bravery medal not a knighthood.'

'Well done pal.' He smiled. 'We'll have to get a bigger hood. His head won't fit into the old one after this.'

I passed him the fat brown envelope. 'There you go, just short of ten grand.' Phil kissed it then nodded his thanks.

'Good weekend?'

'I'm knackered. My knob's in shock!'

'We don't want to know,' snapped Billy. 'Anyone would think sex is all you two think about.'

'And wrecking,' I added. 'I think of that between the 'S' word,' I sniggered at Phil who grinned approval at me.

He stopped grinning and his face took on an unusually serious look. 'I want a word,' he said to me, while Len and Billy were talking.

'Go ahead, 'I replied. Phil looked at the other two and shook his head, then nodded towards the door.

We walked into the yard. 'What?' I asked.

'You wouldn't believe what happened this weekend.'

'Try me.'

'Kim and I were walking back to the hotel, and guess who we saw?'

I looked impatiently around then changed my stare to Phil. 'Elvis,'

'No, you daft sod. Fucking thingy. You know, her husband.' He pointed towards the Spinney.

My mood changed to serious. Frowning I said, 'You mean Andrea's husband?'

'Yeah.'

'Gerald?'

'Yeah him. I've only seen him a few times in the Ship, but I recognised him all right.'

'Well, he does go to London a lot.'

'No,' Phil said. 'He was with two hookers.'

'What!'

'Yeah, two birds. Eighteen or nineteen, that's all they could have been. You know, dressed in short skirts and all that.'

I felt angry, 'The dirty old bastard! Then he comes home and struts his moral stuff.' I walked a few paces. 'Jesus Christ!'

'That's not all.'

Silver Bubbles

'What! There's more?'

'He had his credit refused. He paid the bill with his watch. He was out of his skull. He's a right posh twat, isn't he?' He paused and said quietly, 'Sorry pal, I had to tell you.'

'I'm glad you did.' I shook my head slowly. 'What the hell do I do now? Andrea is so sweet and innocent and he obviously doesn't give a shit about her. He's strung her out for years, the bastard. From what I can read between the lines, she's an embarrassment to him. That's why he's dumped her here. What a prat, I can't believe such a fat lump could pull such a good looker then have the blind arrogance to dump her.'

'Those birds weren't posh, bloody right little slappers. What are you going to do?'

I put my hand up to Phil. 'I'm thinking,' I said, again shaking my head.

'I know what I would do Mike, but that has its complications.'

'What's that then?'

'She could move in here but I don't think Vicki would approve.'

'Yeah, well, Vicki and I had a bust up while you were away. The last of the bridges have been burned. We're history now.'

Phil stared into space. 'It's all gone to rat shit, hasn't it?'

'Not really, she's getting dicked by Nigel but expects me to smile about it and live the life of a sodding monk! She must have somehow heard about Andrea. She called her a fucking leprechaun. Bollocks, you're right. She can come and stay here if she wants.'

'I still haven't met her to talk to. I've only seen her from a distance.'

'All that could change soon mate, very soon.'

'Your drinks are getting warm,' Billy's deep voice bellowed.

'What have the two pervs been discussing then?' Billy asked.

'Men's talk mate,' Phil said candidly.

'Oh, men's talk, woo, don't you mean pointless girly gossip?' I jerked slightly, amused at Billy's harsh down to earth words.

'Cat got yer tongue?'

'OK, OK. Andrea's old man is cheating on her. Shit.' I cursed myself, wishing I had rephrased that.

Billy looked at Len. 'Did you hear that Len? Mr Adultery has chucked his dummy out, 'cause somebody else is cheating as well. I told you it would be girly talk.' Len looked at Phil, shaking his head.

'It'll end in tears, it always does.'

'I'm not listening to this crap. You two are like bloody "Hinge and Bracket". Don't give me all that monogamy bull. You were always at sea, a girl in every port. That's what they say isn't it?' I looked at Billy. 'She left me, so you can lose that adultery shit.'

Len ignored me, nervously spinning his glass around on its base. Billy lowered his head.

'Come on, don't let this turn into a fall-out,' Phil said, 'There's enough of them at the moment. This is what we're here for.' He picked up the parcel of money. 'Together we're invincible, divided we're knackered. Here's a toast. He picked up his glass. 'To us, and Mike's medal.' We all drank Phil's toast. Then conversation turned to the medal.

My mind was turning over. How was I going to break the news to Andrea? Billy made me jump.

'Phone. It's Dave from the Police Dive Unit.'

'I wonder what they want? The last time they rang it was a "can you just".' I disappeared into the room.

CHAPTER TWELVE

I was diving and Phil was standby. The man who maintained the reservoir had seen the tyre marks leading into the water when he arrived for work. Dave's teams were busy preparing for a royal visit to the docks and everything had to be searched, all their divers were involved.

'I bet it's a bloody dumped MOT failure,' I shouted as I slid into the water. First it appeared slightly orange, then as black as black could get. The peat, being washed from the moors had stained the water. It was ginger and dark. I lay horizontally, waving my hand from side to side in front of me.

'Twenty more feet,' Billy told me over the coms, as he guided my bubbles towards the oil that was leaking from the vehicle.

'Roger that.' I felt the bumper of the vehicle and pulled myself upright.

'It feels like a Transit van, over.'

'Roger that. Connect the winch wire to the axle then have a feel inside.'

'Understood.' A few clunks later I reported, 'I'm going to the driver door.'

'Roger that.'

I felt for the handle and pressed the button. 'It's locked. I'm going back round to the other side. Take my slack.'

'Roger that. Got your slack.'

I found the other door locked as well. 'They're all locked, pull me in.'

I sat half in half out of the water, holding the band mask while Billy trudged off to phone Dave.

'Why not just pull it out?' asked Phil.

'It's all we can do, but best we check with Dave first.'

Billy came back. 'Pull it out,' he shouted. Phil gave me a childish smile.

I moved to the side as the recovery van started pulling with its winch. As the tension came on, the vehicle started sliding on the grass towards the water. Try as he might, it wasn't working.

'You'll have to disconnect my wire.' the driver complained. 'We'll need the big truck. They told me it was a car.'

'Go and ring Dave again,' I asked Billy.

Billy headed for the office, glancing at Phil who was sat in van with his suit rolled down to his waist. 'Double,' Phil shouted. Billy ignored him.

Billy returned. 'Dave said have a look inside. We might have to come back tomorrow to connect another wire.'

'Whatever,' I shrugged.

'I'll do it,' Phil said, holding a lump hammer. 'I like breaking windows.'

'All right,' I said standing up.

As he walked, hammer in hand, towards the water; Billy spoke into the coms box. 'Did they teach you how to use a hammer in the Navy?'

'You would be seal shit if it wasn't for me!'

Billy laughed, 'I was about to rip it apart when you scared it away.'

'Yeah, yeah, Yawn, yawn,' Phil voiced over the coms, while gradually disappearing with each step.

'On the job, wire disconnected.' A few gurgles and gasps then he said loudly, 'Here goes.' A few dull thuds could be

Silver Bubbles

heard. 'Doors open. Can't feel anything, the hand brake is still on.'

'Yeah, roger that. Can you have a feel around in the back?'

'Yeah, there's no bulkhead, standby. Oh shit! There's fucking arms and legs everywhere.'

'Roger that. Calm down! Stay calm.'

Breathing heavily Phil spoke, 'I... I think there are two of them.'

'OK, stay calm.'

Billy screamed out, 'the hose!' Billy was holding onto the hose and was being pulled like he was losing a tug of war.

'Give me slack. Give me slack,' Phil screamed. Billy looked at me.

I nodded. 'Yeah, give it!'

'The van's moving,' crackled loudly from the coms box.

'Get out, Phil. Get out!'

'I... I think it's rolled over!' The fear in his voice worried me and my mind started spinning.

'OK, OK, stay calm, stay calm. Can you get out?'

'There's stiffs bumping into me. How the fuck can I stay calm?'

'You're all right, you've plenty of air, we'll have you out in a minute.' I looked at the depth gauge. To my horror it read eighty feet.

'The hose is trapped in the door. The van's on its right hand side.'

'OK Phil, no sweat. Can you reach the back door?'

'Negative.'

'Can you reach any means of exit?'

'Negative. My hose is trapped. I can only reach the door I came in and it's in the silt. It's on its side.'

'OK, I'm sending Billy in. He will break the windscreen. If he can't free your hose you will have to ditch your gear and share with Billy. OK, have you got that?'

'Tell him to use the heavy end of the hammer and brush his teeth.'

I smiled. 'That's good that's more like it. We'll have you out in a minute.' I nodded to Billy. Within seconds he was gone. My heart was pounding heavily. I was shaking.

'God, we've got to stop doing this shit,' I said to myself. I took a deep breath to calm down. Phil was special. There was only one Phil.

'I can hear him, he's on the job.'

'Roger that mate. We'll have a few tonight, eh?'

If Billy disturbs the van it could move further down the slope. I glanced at the air hose. Why didn't we use the hundred metres instead of this short one? I'm not switched on. This woman shit is frying my head.

'I'm ditching my gear. Billy is with me, see you in a minute.'

It was the longest few minutes in my life. The coms gave out loud bubbling noises as the band mask free-flowed air. The hollow, helpless feeling brought memories flooding back. All I wanted to do was see them surface. The bubbles on the surface became larger then two heads appeared.

I gave a loud sigh. Then said quietly, 'Thanks Billy and thank you... "Lady Luck".'

We left the air hose pegged to the bank. The Police team would do the rest. I called Jonno and asked him to get some steaks out and uncork some good red wine. We needed to chill, but this had scared me. Were we becoming too laid back? If they weren't good divers it would have been fatal. I blamed myself. There was no excuse. I found it hard to smile that night.

Back at home I sat staring into space. Phil pushed a glass in front of me. 'I wonder who those poor sods are down there.'

'Yeah, well Dave will give us a ring. They'll probably be there now.'

'What are you going to tell Andrea?' He sat down. 'I don't envy you.'

I remained silent. I had forgotten about it. 'What can I say? I don't want to get shot as the messenger.'

Silver Bubbles

'Shot,' Phil repeated, looking at me. 'What was it really like? You know, when you shot those terrorists? I often think about it and wonder what I would have done. I don't think I could have kill... shot them as easily as you did.'

'To tell you the truth, it happened so fast. It was instinctive, I suppose.'

'But you looked so professional, like it was your job.'

'It was, in a way, once, but I wasn't in control then. I've never been so scared. You feel incredibly sad and sorry for yourself when you're trapped under water, but that was different. It was harsh. They were so cruel and vicious.'

'How did you know how to use the gun?'

'You never forget. When it's burnt into your mind, with such intensity as it was in those Belfast days, you simply never forget.'

'Yeah well, I think you deserve that medal and more. It must have been fucking scary.'

'It was more annoying being forced into it. Still, they got theirs. One of the bastards hit me in the head with a big deck brush. He used it like a polo stick. No, those types have no regard for life. That's what makes it easier to live with. Anyway what the hell am I going to tell her?'

'Tell the truth. You care for her and you don't want that slob anywhere near her again, especially now he's a strong candidate for a list of STD's, HIV and all that manky stuff.

'Shit. Yeah there's that. No, you're spot on. I have to tell her. He's out of the picture now. I'll make sure of that.'

'Andrea's done nothing but she needs your protection now. Why don't you get your head down? Things might seem clearer tomorrow.'

'Sleep is the last thing on my mind at the moment.'

'Well I'm turning in. That scary shit knackers you out.'

'Tell me about it,' I sighed, staring into space. 'Good night mate.'

'Wake up you lazy bastard, we're going for a six miler.'

I looked at the clock: it read seven-thirty. 'Hell, I've just climbed in. I crashed on the settee.'

'Tough titty, get your gear on. Fit body fit mind. Your words pal, your words.'

Into the third mile we stopped, coughing and spitting. We were sweating like pigs.

'This is killing me,' Phil spluttered.

I wiped the sweat from my forehead. 'We'll have to do this more often. Dive fit is one thing, properly fit is another level.' We stopped at the three-mile mark and stood bending, with hands on knees.

'Well, have you thought what you're going to tell her then?'

'Not yet,' I said shaking my head, causing sweat to fall like raindrops.

'Well you better think on, mate.' He nodded, pointing with his stare. Andrea was galloping towards us across the stubble field.

'See ya pal.' Phil ran off.

'Hey, wait a minute.'

'No way, I'm out of here. Sorry, she's not seeing me like this.'

The heavy hoofs replaced Phil's voice as they pounded the ground. She looked incredibly pretty with her hair tied back under the riding hat. It emphasised her high cheekbones. A real beauty, I thought. I can't let her slip through my hands. Vicki told me in no uncertain terms that Nigel was for her. There's nothing to stop me now.

'Morning Mike,' she smiled, pursing her lips.

'Good morning, gorgeous.'

She pulled Misty up to a halt. He made her jolt forward as his head dropped to eat some grass. She dismounted. Her tight pants made me smile.

'Have you heard from Gerald?' She looked puzzled at the question.

'No.' She shook her head.

'When is he due home?'

'For sure I don't know Mike.' She hunched her shoulders, 'Why all the questions?'

Here goes. I felt nervy. 'Come and sit down.' I sat down, patting the grass next to me. She sat sideways to me, her left arm supporting her. Pulling a piece of grass, she smiled innocently then started tickling my arm with it.

'I don't know where to start.' I looked into her sparkling eyes. Her smile faded as she noted the seriousness in my voice.

'You know my partner Phil went to London over the weekend? Well, he saw Gerald in a restaurant.'

'He's working….'

I interrupted her. 'Please let me finish. He was with two girls.'

She didn't look too surprised. 'I know he's been cheating, Mike. A woman senses it. He's always away. I'm not stupid. You know we don't… we don't sleep together, we haven't for a long time now.'

Good, I thought. 'He had his credit card refused. He had to pay for a meal with his watch.'

She looked down. 'Was he drunk again?'

'Apparently,' I said softly.

She turned, wrapping her arms round her knees. Her face turned to despair as she looked away, squinting at the sun. 'We got a letter from the bank and the people who own the 'Spinney' called about the rent. We owe six months. He's drinking and gambling our lives away.' She lowered her head as tears trickled down her cheeks.

'Hey, hey,' I put my arm around her.

'I don't want to leave here. I'll lose Misty.' She looked at me with doleful eyes. 'I'll lose you.'

I held her tight. My mind was a fluster of thoughts. 'You're not going to lose anything Andrea. You can live with me if it comes to that.'

'I have nothing, Mike. He's spent all my savings. I can't be a burden.'

'You wouldn't be a burden. You would be my lover, my partner, my friend.'

She buried her head into my shoulder, crying. 'Don't do this. You're just making us sad.' We kissed; and I felt her tears on my face.

'What do you want to do?'

'I want this, I want you, but I can't just jump into your life. You're still married and I have nothing to contribute. Only debt. I'm so trapped.'

'My marriage is dead now. It's finished. So don't worry about that, but what are you going to do about *him?*'

'He's more or less left me. There's nothing but debt for him here. He even made me send the decanter collection to him. No doubt he's sold them by now.'

'Let me pay for the "Spinney". You can stay there until you decide what to do. Don't go out of my life Andrea, please. I'm doing well at the moment and my life would be lonely and hollow without you. I feel so good when I think about you.' I paused. 'I think I'm falling in love with you.'

She looked at me, her lips slightly parted. 'Oh Mike.' She held me tight. 'If I hadn't met you I don't what I would do. I'm so in love with you. Meeting you made me realise how rotten he had become. You removed the loneliness in my life and gave me hope the first day I saw you.' She looked into my eyes and gave a sad smile, while biting the corner of her lip.

I held her shoulders. 'Go and see the Cooks this afternoon and pay the rent. I'll give you some money. Also, change the agreement so it's in your name. Have you any other debts?'

She suddenly looked angry. 'When I met him I had seven thousand pounds saved. He's spent it all. I've been so naive. All the big ideas, all the broken promises, I feel so stupid.' She sat rubbing her hands, shaking her head. I moved close to her.

'Listen,' I turned her face, holding her chin. 'You have me as a friend.' I smiled, 'And a lover. As I told you once before, I make a good friend. As your lover I would die for you. Don't worry, we can sort this out. It has to be done.'

'I owe the vet's fee for Amber' She stared in thought. 'Poor Amber was a good horse, a few small bills.' She raised her voice, 'But, Mike, *he* owes thousands and thousands.'

'That's his problem. He'll go bust and start all over again. That's what people like him do, they don't care.' I looked stern-faced. 'He won't bother you anymore. I can guarantee you that, for sure. We'll change the locks as well. Are you... are you certain it's what you want? You do have a choice. You could go back to Ireland if you think I'm moving too fast, or you want some time.'

'Ireland?' The way she said the word made me feel good. 'I couldn't, my folks are old and poor. My entire family struggle to make ends meet. I was the wealthy one who made good, the one who always treated them. Now look at me.'

'I am looking at you and I like what I see. Are you ready for a roller-coaster ride of fun, excitement and good loving? All you have to do is say yes.' I pulled her to me and kissed her softly. 'Well?'

She gave one of her sleepy smiles and then pressed her silken lips to my ear. 'Yes,' she breathed softly.

Phil was sitting reading a paper when I got back.

'Do I need a new suit, or are you going to collapse in a depressing fit of gloom?'

I smiled at him. 'Neither,' I said, as I headed for the shower.

'What! What did...?'

I closed the door, laughing. 'Get a brew on, you nosy bastard.'

'I would do the same mate,' Phil said holding the mug in both hands. He smiled as he thought of Kim. 'I'm glad for you. At least you can still sneak down there without Billy and Len knowing all your business. No, it's a great idea. I won't tell anybody.'

'Cheers,' I said, feeling happy with Phil's support.

'Oh yeah,' he lowered his voice. 'Dave rang earlier there were two young kids in that van.'

'Oh God, not kids.' I looked round at him.

'Yeah,' he said quietly. 'They had run away from an arranged marriage and were in sleeping bags, kipping in the back of the van. The brake didn't hold, or failed. The poor sods didn't have a chance.'

'How old were they?'

'Just kids, teenagers.'

'The bloody leveller, I call it. Every time you seem to be riding high, something brings you down to the ground, how sad. Damn religion, it's a killer. They're idiots, all of them, in their glistening dresses. Brainwashing people, forcing them to do things they don't want to do. Give another dollar to the man with the diamond ring and he'll pray for you. It's utter bollocks.'

Phil agreed with a nod. 'Yeah, and if you contribute enough money and faith, you shoot straight to heaven and live forever in paradise along with trillions of innocent animals. It's that fucking simple.'

'Anyway, Dave's serviced the band mask. They'll drop it off when they're passing. What are you going to do about this?' Phil held the official letter informing that my name was on the Honours list. 'You receive it in April.' Phil browsed through the letter. 'Top hat and tails, that's a grin, guest vetting, might be the Prince, depending on her engagements. You can have the whole thing videoed for a fee. Oh, bowing and shaking of hands, photos, and a one-minute chat. You get fully briefed so you don't mess up. Should be fun, can I come?'

I gave him a stare. 'Don't know. You'd probably fart or something.'

Silver Bubbles

Phil looked over his shoulder. 'Telephone,'

I came back after twenty minutes.
'Was it her then?'
'No, no, it's a job, well, an old mate. He's got a small dispersal company. There's a job off here, about eighty miles out. A Spanish coaster sank in a storm, the cargo of grain shifted. He's got the job from Trinity House and wants to hire the boat and us to do it with him.'
'Explosives is spooky stuff. I hate it.'
'Not if you know what you're doing.'
'Yeah, but I've seen all the pictures and more. We don't want atomising, not while everything is just coming together. Can't you tell him we're busy, we can earn more doing the salvage… It's just too fucking risky.'

Phil's comments made me think for a while. 'It's just one big bang then back home. It's got a bronze prop on it.'

I looked for a favourable response. 'I was on a job once after a fuck up, a guy I knew.' He shook his head as the door burst open. 'It's just not worth the risk!'
'What risk?' Billy inquired as he closed the door.
'We'll have to change your name to "Billy big lugs"!'
'Well, you like risks.' He coughed. 'There's one in everything you screw, I mean do!'
'Ha bloody ha.' I shook my head. 'That ten grand has given Billy a sense of humour.'
'Let's give him our dosh as well. He might tell more jokes,' Phil added.
'Fancy a bit of sparring lads? We've got gloves in the workshop,' Billy replied.

There was silence. Billy looked at us, smiling. 'Did you hear that?' He looked around the room. 'A tiny fly just farted!'
'Nowt to it, it will be a change and good demolition practice.'

Peter Fergus

'It isn't a bloody rehearsal, once it goes bang you're dead,' said Phil.

'Billy's right. John has lots of experience and Billy and I blasted rocks for the South Uist ferry terminal. That was every day for months. Let's take a vote. Who says yes?' Billy and I put our hands up.

'It's on then. I'll ring him.'

Billy looked at Phil, 'Kilick diver, huh just a lad.'

Later that morning, I left Phil and Billy on the boat and went to see Andrea. I gave her the amount she owed for the rent, three thousand one hundred pounds altogether.

'I don't want this mentioned ever again,' I told her, as I gave her a further two thousand pounds.

'Put the rest somewhere safe, hide it really well. I'm going away in a couple of days for about four nights. Here's my key just in case he comes here when I'm away. Take some of the money and treat yourself to some new riding gear.' I looked her up and down, 'Or a nice new outfit.'

'I feel so–'

I interrupted her. 'Hey, we have a deal. You promised me, remember?' I put my finger on her lips and repeated in a whisper, 'Remember?'

Kissing me, in a passionate embrace she whispered, 'I love you, take care.'

Sea Gem approached the lock-head slowly. On the quayside several police vehicles were parked either side of a white armoured van. A small man waved.

'That's John,' I said, while spinning the wheel quickly as *Sea Gem* went astern. I pulled her parallel with the wall. Billy deployed the mooring ropes and had her secure within seconds. After brief introductions, a human chain was formed, and about twenty cardboard boxes were placed on the deck. The boxes contained mostly high explosives, along with some priming charges and detonators. We had to leave for sea immediately. The harbour master was not happy and almost refused us permission to load here, until he thought up an extortionate fee.

'This is a fine bit of kit,' John said, walking around the wheelhouse. 'How did you afford this?'

I smiled, 'Hard graft, luck and good mates.'

'Some tool. Do you owe much on her?'

'No, all paid for,' I answered, smiling, realising how lucky we were.

'The forecast looks good,' I said as Phil walked in. He looked at John with indifference.

'I'll get the scran on then. Is there anything you don't like?' John shook his head, as he said, 'No.'

'Right then,' Phil said bluntly, then disappeared into the galley.

'I don't think your cook likes me,' John said looking over at me.

'For fuck's sake, don't call him a cook. He's an ex CD, a good one. He'll come round. He didn't want to get involved with large amounts of bang.'

'It is dodgy stuff I agree, but treat the job with military precision and it's as safe as houses.'

'Never a truer work spoken,' Billy remarked as he joined our company. 'What's the plan of action then?'

'The bow is the high part. It's just a case of blowing the shit out of it. We'll place most of the stuff in the forepeak and around there and then knock down any remaining high bits with what's left. It shouldn't take long. Two, maybe three dives each. And you might get the prop as a bonus.'

'That will do for me,' said Billy looking my way, 'Is chef still sulking?' He glanced towards the galley.

I gasped. 'Yeah, he's got a right shitty on.'

Len took the watch, while we sat in the galley watching the TV picture flicker from good to snowy.

'How many have you lost then?' Billy asked John.

'Five, well six if you count the horse.'

'A horse,' Billy looked at him.

'Yeah, someone galloped too near a trenching charge. Poor bastard flew fifty feet into the air, still sitting on his bloody horse!'

Phil looked at him with disbelief. 'You blew a horse and rider up?' Billy made a noise through his lips. He couldn't restrain himself any longer and burst into laughter.

Phil stood up. 'Up yours too,' he snapped then went to his cabin.

There was silence. Billy sniffed loudly then picked up a video. Pushing it into the machine he said, 'Don't know what's got into the lad.'

I walked out, as the telly sprang to life with another of Billy's classic boxing videos. I tapped on the door then opened it. Phil was lying on his bed reading a letter. I sat down, 'One of Kim's?'

'Yeah, it came this morning.'

'What's up mate? This isn't like you.'

'That stuff out there, and "Ye-ha John",' he said without looking up.

'He's done it for years, he's good.'

'You never know if you're bad at it, just a flash, then blackness.'

'There's something else, isn't there?' I asked with concern.

Phil looked up. 'A guy with twenty-two years of service thought he was good as well. He only had a few weeks left to serve. He had three kids and a lovely wife. He and two others were completely fucking atomised by that stuff. It could have been a radio signal, or a rusty knife. There weren't enough of them left to fill half a body bag. And I know. I helped find the pieces. The young kids' faces at the funeral crippled my mind. And the look of despair on their mother's face summed it all up. It's just not worth it. One cock up, that's all it takes. It's

Silver Bubbles

a stupid risk: so many things can go shit-faced. We shouldn't be doing this. My life is too good to waste helping some idiot make a few quid.'

I looked down, stuck for words. 'You're right pal. I'm sorry, I shouldn't have agreed to it but we're committed now, so what we have to do is get everything right, and keep an eye on those two. We'll check everything meticulously ourselves, together OK?'

I noticed Phil's slow nod turn into a shake as I left his cabin. I passed the television. Billy was on the edge of the seat, ducking and weaving, fists clenched. John was asleep, with his head back and mouth wide open.

'How's it going, Dad?'

Len looked at me, then back at the compass. 'About sixty miles to go,' he replied, in a reassuring tone.

'We should arrive about first light,' I said, looking at the GPS. 'We'll get the job done as quickly as we can. I've got an uneasy feeling about this one.' Len nodded.

Sea Gem's engine changed its tone as Billy eased her speed to a crawl then disengaged the drive. 'There it is.' He pointed. A green buoy rolled gently in the small swell. The words 'WRECK' painted in white lettering looked strangely menacing.

Thirty minutes later *Sea Gem* pulled alongside the marker we had placed into the wreck. Billy was the first to dive. He disappeared, pulling arm over arm into the green blue water, followed by the heavy mooring rope. Ten minutes later he surfaced. Holding on to the buoy, he gave the thumbs up.

'There's our cue.' I steered slowly towards Billy, who was holding on to the rope with one hand. The other held his mouthpiece while he breathed in between the small waves that splashed into his face. With Billy back on board, *Sea Gem* settled in the tide, rising and falling gently.

'It's a fine day for it,' I said, as Phil tied the big inflatable buoy to the mooring line.

John opened each box of high explosives in which he put a primer. Each one had a three-metre length of detonating cord attached to it.

'We'll place the boxes all around the forepeak like we agreed and tape the ends together then tape two detonators to the det cord.'

Billy and I used our dive to place the boxes in position. Phil had the unfortunate job of taking the dets that were attached by wire to the surface and taping them to the detonating cord. Before he dived, he checked that the wires on the surface were twisted together I double-checked them as well. This was to prevent the possibility of a static charge setting off the detonators.

Phil looked at the boxes as he taped the dets onto the cord. A scary shiver ran through him, as the gravity of the risk became reality. As soon as he finished he quickly fled the area for the surface.

'What are you doing?' I asked, as John placed the dynamo on the deck next to the wires.

'She's steel. The bang won't bother her.'

Phil stepped forward and picked up the dynamo, 'No way pal. You sit in the inflatable and we will stand off, half a mile away.'

I agreed with Phil. Billy sided with John, but backed down when he saw our stern faces.

We steamed half a mile and then turned *Sea Gem*, so her bow faced the inflatable. I blew two long blasts on *Sea Gem's* deep horn.

A few seconds later, a sharp powerful thud shook through the hull. Back on the mooring we hastily got kitted up to survey the effect. Phil took the inflatable to pick up a few codling that were floating on the surface.

Silver Bubbles

The visibility was good and from well above the wreck the seabed glistened with dead sand eels. Various types of fish lay on their sides with sad eyes staring. I looked at the bow. It was split in half, like someone had cut it with a grinder. One side laid on the seabed shattered with sharp twisted splits, a grim reminder of the immense power of explosives.

I swam to the highest part remaining and looked at my computer to get a depth reading. As I held on to the steel, I could feel it moving slowly, swaying in the tide like a tree in a gentle breeze. John joined me and surveyed the scene, then gave me the thumbs up.

'We'll have to knock that high bit of the bow down.' He pulled off his hood. 'Trinity House won't pass it like that. We'll cut the remaining tubes of bang in half and place them like a dotted line along the base to form a shaped charge. That should do the trick.'

Phil stood looking at John as he cut the orange plastic tubes that contained the explosive. It looked and smelt like marzipan.

'If you touch this you can end up with a bad head,' he said looking up at Phil.

'I know that,' Phil snapped. He turned and walked away.

I was monitoring John's every move and was glad to see all but one of the orange tubes slide down the line into the deep blue. Thirty minutes later Billy and John surfaced.

They climbed into the inflatable. Moments later Len steered *Sea Gem* to a safe distance. We waited as another crack, softer this time, shook the hull.

'Mike, Mike, come here,' Len shouted. I arrived in the wheelhouse.

'Look at that. What is it?'

I grinned while looking at the sounder. 'It's a wreck. Well done, take her back over.' As Len followed the track on the plotter the big mark filled the screen. I pressed the GPS and a number appeared on the screen, marking its exact position.

Peter Fergus

'We'll have time to check it out today before we bugger off. Well spotted, Dad.'

Len smiled, feeling proud to have contributed.

After breakfast we had a two-hour interval to fizz out then Billy and John dived to check their work.

'Good job but we left a little bit,' Billy said. 'One small bang should do the trick.'

Billy and John were preparing the last charge. A jagged piece of hull remained standing. It was probably low enough but they wanted to make sure.

'They're like kids playing with fireworks,' Phil hissed with contempt.

'I've never seen you so wound up, mate. Chill out, we'll be steaming home soon. Oh, by the way, Len found a new uncharted wreck when we moved away. We'll have time to dive it later.' I smiled. 'Those two will burned out and have no bottom time left.'

'Ideal,' Phil replied.

'That's more like it.' I put my hand on his shoulder.

John and Billy returned. 'There's no need to move her off this time. This last one is only small and it's the last of the stuff,' said Billy. Phil walked up. 'What are you doing? Billy looked up at him. 'This is only a small one. You won't even feel it.'

'What about the bang on board?'

'There isn't any,' Billy replied.

'Yes there is! That stuff you got from your kid.'

Billy thought for a moment. 'Oh, that won't be a problem.'

'It bloody won't be without this.' Phil grabbed the dynamo again.

'For fuck's sake,' Billy protested putting his hands on his hips.

'Put it into the inflatable and cast it off for now. We can pick it up later,' Phil said. 'Or this goes for a swim.' He held the dynamo over the gunwale.

Silver Bubbles

I stood with Phil and nodded, 'It won't do any harm.'

They put the small bag, which contained five sticks, into the inflatable. Billy cast it off, looked at John and tutted disapproval.

'Now can we end this farce?' Billy looked at Phil then at me.

'Give it a bit longer,' I said.

Billy got off his knees and sat on the deck, impatiently nodding his head. He wound the little handle and with a sarcastic look at Phil shouted, 'Fire in the hole.' As he pressed the red button his head sank into his neck. We all dropped to the deck, covering our ears, as the heavy thudding bang pounded us like a mighty kick all the way through our bodies.

The charge had set off Billy's explosive. The stuff John was using was far stronger and the shock wave from it caused what is termed "a sympathetic detonation". This unforgiving phenomenon has in the past claimed the lives of lots of unwary souls. The inflatable, complete with the new, forty horsepower out-board was reduced to tiny little pieces.

'Are you fuckers pleased with yourselves now?' Phil shouted, as shreds of red hypalon from the destroyed boat, fell from the sky.

Billy looked at me, embarrassed and lost for words.

Len put his arm around Phil then shouted at John and Billy. 'Well at least thank the kid for your lives. He was right all along, he's ex Royal Navy you know!'

'Dissimilar explosives different blisteen values, that's what did it,' John said, still shocked at the near miss.

Billy looked at us, 'Look I'm…sorry, I…'

I stared. 'It's done now, but you can replace the boat and engine.' I gave Phil a wink, held my hand to my mouth and coughed. 'Tossers!' This was our way of taking the piss without harping on and on.

After a few hours of silence, conversation started up again. Billy was avoiding Phil like the plague, avoiding eye contact.

Phil being Phil was starting to enjoy his new and rare hold over Billy.

I was watching, smiling while thinking of the inevitable piss taking that would occur over the next few weeks. Len was still annoyed with Billy's near fatal mistake and was blanking him.

The shot line splashed in again, followed by Phil. Billy looked on like a boy who was being punished and missing out on the fun.

The visibility was magic. The depth was one hundred and ten feet. Fifty feet down we could make out a dark shape. She was sitting on an even keel, a good twenty feet proud of the seabed. The bridge was still there; the whole wreck stood intact. Not being on the chart and in a safe depth, it had never been dispersed. Madonna's "Like a Virgin" played in my mind.

Phil finned towards the bridge while I hovered above amidships, savouring our find. I swam over the number two hold and over the port side where I found a large hole in the hull. Stone or granite blocks had spilled out from the hole and lay all over the seabed. On making the bottom I looked at my computer. I was deeper here, being in the scour and I felt light-headed. Nitrogen narcosis was taking effect. Looking down among the blocks I spotted a big, brass steam whistle in perfect condition. Unclipping a lifting bag, I tied the whistle to it and inflated it with the air gun, which was attached to my spare take-off. The rope tightened and then slowly the bag rose upwards and disappeared, leaving a trail of silt.

The stone blocks were everywhere. The whole port side of the ship had split and poured out its cargo.

I continued swimming towards the bow picking up large lobsters on the way; each one thrust their claws upwards defiantly. Grabbing them behind their claws avoided a crushed finger. I attached each one to a small plastic lifting bag.

Billy was kept busy retrieving the bags, while Len shouted instructions as and when they appeared on the surface.

Silver Bubbles

As I approached the bow and passed the number one hold, which was full of blocks I recognised the anchor winch. In front of this was a steel crook-shaped pole where the bell would have hung.

I glanced quickly around the deck. Bingo! I grinned; thinking this is getting easy as I pulled the barnacle-encrusted bell from where it had laid for decades. I dragged it to the shot weight, securing it to the chain. Phil swam to me, sticking both thumbs up obviously pleased with himself. Then we made a slow ascent to the shimmering surface together.

I dropped my weight belt on to the deck, then swung my cylinder to my left arm and lowered it down gently. I was pulling off my fins when Phil shouted with excitement.

'Did you see the bridge? It's intact, look.' He pointed at the steering and compass binnacle, a pair of binoculars, a sighting compass and several brass wheels that Billy had retrieved from his lift bags.

'Not a bad dive eh!'

I was showing him the whistle as Billy was pulling in the shot line.

'Ding fucking Dong,' he said in a deliberate boring tone. Then he passed the bell to me. 'Is that all?'

'I don't think we did badly,' I replied, looking at Phil. Billy slithered into the galley to make a brew. The deck vibrated under our feet as Len increased speed. Phil and I, still in our suits, looked over our finds, as *Sea Gem* steamed homeward leaving a straight broad trail of foam and bubbles.

It was two a.m. when we opened the kitchen door.

'I'm turning in,' Phil said, sniffing the air. 'I don't think we are alone here.'

I gently opened the bedroom door and moved towards the bed. Her shiny black hair had spread on to my pillow. It slightly glistened in the moonlight that flooded the room. I slid into the sweet smelling flannel sheets. Her back was to me so I snuggled into her and placed my hand over her. She pulled it into her warm breasts.

Phil peeped around the door
'Where is she then?' he whispered.
'She's gone to feed and groom Misty.'
'I haven't even met her yet. I've only seen her on a horse in the distance.'
'How about going go to the Ship for lunch?'
'Yeah, I've got to meet her. I don't just want to bump into her. Is she staying here then?'
'No not yet, she slept here, well because, she's scared he'll come back.'
'The fat useless sod. After what you told me surely he wouldn't have the cheek?'
'Those thick-skinned twats are all the same. Just like politicians. They get voted in then dictate to us. Condescending bastards, they don't care.'

Midday and Phil reappeared.
'Where are you going all dressed up?'
'I'm not meeting Andrea looking like a hippie in jeans.' He looked at me.
'All right, I'm going.' As I changed, Phil made a couple of Captains.
'Did you take the fish and lobsters to the farmer?' I shouted from my bedroom.
'Yeah, they were dead chuffed. He said we're safe with the moorings as long as we want them.'
'Ideal. What's this for then?' I inquired as he passed me the drink.
'Dutch courage. I'm nervous.'
'I don't need courage, but I'll have it. Cheers mate.' We chinked glasses.
We drove slowly to the Spinney. 'I told you to get a bigger car,' I complained.

Silver Bubbles

'We can walk, it's a nice enough day,' Phil said looking into the mirror while adjusting his hair.

'I'll take her there if you want, you could walk behind us.'

'Cheeky git. It's my bloody date, not yours, pal.'

'Old habits,' Phil grinned. His good looks unnerved me slightly.

'How's the scar looking?' I asked as I pulled down the vanity mirror.

'Fucking terrible, I don't know what she can see in a bust up old sod like you.'

As the car doors slammed, Andrea opened her front door. She stood on one toe, placed her hands on my shoulders, kissed me then turned and smiled sweetly at Phil. She looked stunning in a red leather dress and high heel shoes that laced up her ankle. Phil stood speechless, with his mouth open.

'Hi, so you must be Phil.' Her voice, in combination with her warm sleepy smile and dark eyes, made him grin openly.

'Pleased to meet you,' he said formally, while blushing slightly.

'Stand at ease lad,' I laughed. 'Chill out man, you're not meeting the Queen.'

Andrea smiled then looked me. 'Don't be horrid to him,' she said with a grin, then put her arm in mine.

'Horrid!' I laughed. 'I think I'm going to have to introduce you gradually to my mates if you think that was horrid.' We laughed and joked as we walked down the sun-baked track.

Local gossips stared as we ate lunch. Phil got on great with Andrea, telling her tales about our humorous encounters on diving jobs. She was enjoying every minute.

'You're like two girls,' I said. 'You've never stopped gabbing.' Andrea sipped her drink while smiling at me. I stared at her, enjoying the moment. Then she stood up and walked to the ladies room.

'Fucking hell man,' Phil looked at me. 'No wonder you stuck your knob out for her. She's drop dead gorgeous, those eyes and her body. Wow! She's so well ...so!'

'Sexy?' I interrupted.

'She's more than sexy, she's Kimish, you lucky bastard. You watch all the eyes on her when she walks back to us.' Phil's prediction was right.

As Andrea turned to sit down, she put her hand to her mouth. With wide eyes she laughed uncontrollably at the collage on the wall. 'My God these are awful,' she laughed each time she looked at the funny, embarrassing shots of the team. 'Who took them?' She looked at me.

'Him over there, well most of them,' I raised my voice and nodded towards the bar. 'That frustrated landlord.' Jonno's head turned with a look of concern then he smiled when he saw it was us.

We had a few more drinks then left. As we walked back down the track, I noticed tyre marks on the cinder track. As we rounded the bend, Phil said in a raised voice, 'It's our van.'

Billy had pulled the van behind a horse trailer, which was attached to a white Range Rover. He was talking to four men.

'What's going on, Billy?' I asked.

'They're trying to take the horse.'

Andrea unlaced her shoes and dropped them and then ran passed us towards the single stable. She looked inside, then turned and stood facing us with her back to the door spreading her small hands tightly against it.

'I've got the right of ownership,' one of the men shouted, as he pushed a Bill of Sale into my face. I grabbed the paper and looked at the signature; the signature at the bottom was by Gerald Wilson.

'That's not the same horse, pal,' I shouted. 'His horse had to be put down. This horse is mine. I paid for it, you've wasted a journey.'

Silver Bubbles

'We're not leaving here without that horse.' He rudely pushed his way past. 'You'd better move this now,' he shouted, slapping his hand loudly on the bonnet of the van.

I composed myself. 'Calm down,' I said. 'I'll go and get my receipt to prove ownership.'

'Look, we've been paid to recover a fifteen-hand chestnut from this address, so let us take the horse. I'm warning you now! My men recover goods for a living.'

'The horse is mine, well Andrea's. It's fifteen-three hands and a bloody bay! Can't you tell the difference, you fathead?' I shouted loudly. I was losing my temper fast.

Andrea stood looking on. I could see she was scared, holding both hands to her mouth. Her face said it all, which annoyed me even more. Billy saw this and walked over. 'Don't worry, pet.' He leaned down to her, 'They'll take nowt from here.' He gave her a reassuring smile then turned and walked into the middle of the track. His loud voice caught everyone's attention. 'You won't listen to reason, so let's have it over with.' Unbuttoning his cuffs, he rolled up his sleeves then stood in a boxer's stance.

'Flatten that daft bastard,' the man with the receipt shouted nonchalantly to one of his goons. His red pappy face gave me an urge to hit it.

The biggest of the heavies strolled over to Billy, swaying from side to side as he walked like "Odd Job". He stared at him, then his fist snapped out like lightning at Billy's head. Billy pulled back, making him miss. He threw another punch, but again Billy dodged it. He looked shocked. Realising he had a problem, he turned his head and called one of his colleagues. 'Come and hold this daft old bugger for me.'

He made the mistake Billy was waiting for, for he had taken his eyes off him. A combination of bone crushing blows left him twitching on the ground, as egg-sized lumps instantly grew on his face. Billy looked at him with a triumphant sneer then shouted, 'Next!'

The other two men approached Billy hesitantly.

I saw my opportunity and grabbed Fatface. I spun him around and got him in a neck-breaking stranglehold then applied a lot of pressure.

'I won't snap your neck until you've seen your pals pulverised, you fat bastard.' I gripped harder, making him splutter.

'Phil, go and get the receipt. Make a copy and bring it back here.' Phil sprinted off. Billy stood his ground. They looked at each other then one of the men threw a punch. Billy ducked, at the same time he dropped on to his side, kicking the man's legs from under him, making him fall to the ground. The other man landed a hard blow into the side of Billy's face. Almost before he could draw back his arm Billy countered with a flurry of savage jabs and crosses. The man's head jerked back at the hammer-like blows, until he collapsed, limp and unconscious.

Phil re-appeared and kicked the other man, who was getting up, in the stomach, lifting him off the ground. He quickly threw several short hard jabs into his face resulting in distasteful slapping sounds, then stood with his foot on him like a hunter. Billy nodded approval to him.

'Where's the Bill of Sale?' I shouted to Phil.

'I came back to help,' he said then ran off to get it. I held the man until he calmed down and apologised and then I gave him a copy of the proof of ownership. They helped each other into the vehicle without taking their eyes off Billy and left.

Andrea ran and put her small arms tightly around Billy's neck. 'Thank you, thank you.' She looked at him and kissed him, holding her hand on his cheek where a purple lump had appeared. She smiled and said softly, 'You're a special man, Billy Wells, so you are.' Billy's face melted from a stern look into a beaming smile.

He turned, looking at me, as if giving visual approval then walked past and in a low voice he said, 'She's a fine-looking lass. I like her.'

Silver Bubbles

I was sure he had enjoyed every second of the encounter. He invited Phil to go with him to Len's for a well-deserved wet.

As the van drove off, I turned to Andrea. She was crying openly. 'Hey, what's this rainy face?'

'What if they come back and you're not here. What could I do?' I held her close to me. She was shaking. She felt so small without her shoes on and vulnerable. She had been sad and lonely for so long and now this. I felt sorry for her. She shouldn't be going through this; I felt I should be looking after her better.

'Don't worry, they won't be back, no way. I've still got his receipt; I'll send a legal warning. Hey, it's all right now. It's all right.' I held her for a few minutes.

'Why don't you get changed and go for a ride. It will relax you and cheer you up. Bring Misty to Wood End; the lads are having a few drinks. Billy and Phil are talking again.' Still upset, she gave a hapless smile.

I folded the letter and placed it with the others.

'What's that then? I know it's from Scotland, I saw the postmark,' said Phil.

'It's from Jamie. It's just a thank you and a short note. They want me to go for a few days. You two could come if you want.'

'Wouldn't mind,' said Billy, but our lass wouldn't leave the shop, it's just picking up.'

'We could plan it for when Kim's here and I could take Andrea,' I said, looking at them for approval.

'Shit hot!' Phil said.

'I'll keep an eye on things around here,' Len said, looking at Billy as if he had avoided doom.

'Shit!' Phil jumped up. 'The acid bath, I left the tap on.' He ran outside to the newly acquired tin bath he was filling up with hydrochloric acid and water. Any salvaged article that was covered in marine growth would come out clean after a soak and be ready for buffing and polishing. Wearing a safety mask and gloves, Phil carefully lowered the binnacle into the mix. It immediately fizzed as the calcium started to dissolve. Next he gently put the heavily encrusted bell in then stood back, looking proud.

'It's working great, fizzing away.' Phil grinned to himself as he picked up his drink. 'Did you see the news about the UFO that was spotted?'

Billy, having always claimed to have seen one, looked up with interest. 'What did they say?'

'They scrambled two jet fighters to intercept it.'

'What! They admitted to doing that?' Billy sat upright, tapping the table with his finger. 'They must have seen it on the radar to do that.' Phil walked to the cupboard and took out a bag of crisps. 'What was it then, what did they say?'

Phil looked at him, straight-faced. 'It turned out to be a Mercury forty horsepower outboard motor,'

'A what?' Billy screwed his face up.

'It turned out to be an outboard motor apparently flying at thirteen thousand feet, still attached to a wooden transom.'

'Bastard,' Billy rubbed his brow looking down at the floor. 'You bastard,'

I bounced up and down, grinning. 'You had better get used to it mate. We'll get a few miles out of this one.' Phil chinked my glass and we shouted like football supporters, 'She... fucked up!'

The laughing faded to the sound of hoofs as Andrea arrived outside. She tied up Misty and then popped her head round the door. 'Have you room for a wee one?' We all stood up, making lots of noise as the chairs scraped on the floor. Billy moved Phil's chair out, 'Come and sit here, lass.'

'Did I miss a good joke? I heard you all laughing as I rode up.'

'No, Phil was caught out being childish again,' Billy said looking at us with a warning stare.

Silver Bubbles

Andrea fitted in like one of the lads and was instantly accepted, much to my pleasure. 'Who could dislike such a beauty?' I thought, as she laughed and joked with my best friends.

We spent a cosy night by the fire. Shared a bottle of wine and listened to music, before melting together, intimately entwined between the soft cosy sheets.

Phil was up at first light like an excited child. He felt into the frothy water and carefully removed the bell. He placed it into a tub of fresh water and rubbed away the film of brown slime. 'Here we go,' he said out loud, as the name engraved into the bell became discernible. '*LYRA* 1917, that's a strange name, it must be Italian.' He pulled the compass binnacle on to its end. 'A bit longer for you, fella,' he lowered it back into the acid.

The polisher slowed down as he removed the mask. 'What a good job,' he praised himself and then carried the shiny bell to the house.

I slowly awoke. I felt suddenly alone. Was she just a dream? I turned and felt for her. She was still there, warm and cosy. I drifted back into paradise.

Ten minutes later I turned and stretched. The smell of bacon had seeped into the room! Then tapping on the door made me look.

It opened slightly and Phil whispered, 'Breakfast in twenty minutes. I've got a surprise waiting.'

Oh no, I thought. What the hell is he up to now?

While showering, I felt the air chill as someone entered the room. I opened the door. Andrea slid off her slip. Naked she moved towards me. 'Morning,' she teased, pressing her body close to mine.

'I, I'm out of here,' I stammered. 'We haven't got time, Phil's done the breakfast.' I looked her up and down. 'Wow! I'll deal with you later.' She lowered her head and uplifted her eyes giving me a tantalising stare, then closed the door. I walked out, experiencing a pleasant twinge.

'Bloody hell, it looks brilliant. When did you do this?' I picked the bell up.

'It's Italian isn't it?' Phil said looking smug.

'Wait a minute, this is all wrong! If this is....' I paused and went to my book cabinet. 'Yeah SS *Lyra* built 1917. But it shouldn't be there, it's supposed to be further inshore. Bloody hell, what a knob.'

'What on earth are you on about, what's wrong?' Phil asked looking a little annoyed.

'I was a little narked up and didn't even check. What a pillock. Bloody ingots, big alloy ingots and I thought they were grey stone blocks. Who would carry stone blocks as perfectly shaped as them? And there's tons spilling out of her port side. Look.' I passed Phil the open book then poured three coffees.

'So this must be the same wreck?'

'Definitely,' I said, 'Without a doubt.'

'How much was it carrying then?'

'It doesn't say, but I saw them as clear as day... there's loads, Tons and tons, hundreds. Why did you think she was Italian?'

Andrea walked in. 'What Italian girl is this?'

'No, it's daft lad. He thought Lira was spelt Lyra.' She smiled out of politeness, shrugging her shoulders. We tucked into our well-cooked breakfast.

It was now October and the weather was becoming less clement. Ambiguous weather forecasts forced us to cancel several sailings. We had done well so far, but wanted another attempt on the *Juno* and the high value tin ingots. I was really

Silver Bubbles

fired up about the *Lyra* and kept talking about the ingots that I'd seen. Another week passed and as the weekend approached the forecast said strong southerly winds. It would be too strong for us to work the deck. Kim was coming for the week, so we decided to drive up to see Jamie for a couple of days. Billy had been roped along with the promise of some scallop diving.

It was a long drive, so we stayed in a motel on the way and wined and dined. Kim took a shine to Andrea. They were similar ages and had a common interest, which was great.

The sea mist hung like a still blanket as we drove the last few miles.

'There's *Stormdrift*,' I pointed. As the car rounded the shore every one looked. The little village appeared, surrounding the harbour, which had moorings outside in the sheltered loch. *Stormdrift* and other fishing vessels lay in the smooth water. It looked idyllic, just like an oil painting.

'Got to find the pub to check in first,' I said. Billy sighed.

'I'm glad you don't navigate at sea like this! Look, it's right in front of us.'

'I know. I was just checking to see if you were paying attention.'

Andrea put her hand over her mouth and smirked. Kim smiled at her. 'Wait until they're on form, they never stop.'

We checked into our room, which was overlooking the harbour. It was perfect. After freshening up we met in the bar.

'Are you open yet?' Phil asked, putting his hand in his pocket.

The landlord chuckled, 'We never close laddie. What will it be?'

I passed a piece of paper to Andrea. She read out the number as I dialled Jamie on the old-style telephone. The landlord watched. He was listening to the conversation then he suddenly rushed from behind the bar and stared at me.

'Are you the man who saved my young nephew, Jamie Ferguson?' I looked down then up at him.

'It was a joint effort.' The man hugged me like a bear. He had tears in his eyes. I looked at Andrea, embarrassed. Her eyes were glistening, too. He changed his grip and held my hands. 'Thank you from the bottom of my heart. I near brought that lad up, he's like a son to a lot of folk round here.'

'Anyone would have done the same,' I said, feeling humble.

'Be off with you man. There's a lot of close family in this area.' He lowered his head and said quietly, 'They all have a copy of the *Stormdrift* video.' He nodded, as though he was sharing a secret, while discreetly looking at the scar on my cheek.

Then he looked round at Phil. 'Put it away. You're not paying for a thing in this village,' he said with authority. Phil hastily put his money back in his pocket, as if it had offended the strong character who was now swaying with excitement, standing behind the bar.

'He said you were coming.' Then he excitedly made several calls. Before we finished our drinks people started pouring into the pub. All of us were greeted like long lost family. Everyone acknowledged us. Some nodded, some shook hands and I got lots of embraces from the women. Everyone showed genuine emotion. A partition was moved revealing a dance area and a stage.

Billy lowered his head, 'Prepare for take-off, my friends. This one will make history.'

The barman came with another tray of drinks. 'They've closed the village lads, everybody is coming,' he grinned.

A cheer rose up as Jamie rushed through the now full bar, to find us. We shook hands and patted each other, finding it hard to control our emotions. There wasn't a dry eye in the pub. A small girl tugged at my arm, as Katrina put her arms around me, holding me tight. She cried, speechless, as I picked up their little girl and smiled.

Silver Bubbles

Jamie's mum held me tight. She was shaking. His dad, overcome with emotion, put his arm round us. It was overwhelming. I looked at Kim and Andrea. They both had hankies out. Then someone started singing, "For He's a Jolly Good Fellow". I looked at Billy then at Phil. They raised their glasses to me. I put my arm around Andrea and Kim, totally lost for words.

Strangely I felt a hidden tension lift from inside me. This was the final piece, the final part of the whole experience. It was closing, as if every one around me was taking a little piece of the stored tension with their close embraces.

Andrea held me tight and whispered, 'I love you Mike Morgan, for sure I do. I'll never let you go.'

As the music started everyone clapped while beckoning us to the floor. We held each other and were joined by a sea of smiling faces.

A few drinks later Jamie took me outside.

'What can I say?'

'We've said it all mate, it's all gone now. I feel so much better. This is like the ending for me.'

'I really mean the money, Mike.'

'What about it?'

'Twenty-four thousand pounds, Mike. It's a hell of a lot.'

Surprised, I said, 'Wow, that much?'

'Yes, most of it was in fifties. It's too much, Mike. We have to give you some back.'

'Jamie, all the money in the world couldn't buy what you have given me tonight. We're doing fine. Use it to help this big family of yours through the winter.'

'But Mike, I got four thousand for the charter. It's only fair we split the rest. In fact, I insist. Don't insult me Mike. Don't spoil things.'

'It's only payback, Jamie. Think of it as payback.'

Jamie gave me a thick envelope. 'You need payback too, after what they did to you. I wouldn't be here but for you.' His face was stern and honest.

'You're just as I remember you, Jamie. Don't ever change mate.'

As the night matured it was obvious that Billy had an admirer. A bubbly woman, about forty kept asking for dances and was smothering him with kisses. Phil was hysterical, elbowing me every time she compromised Billy.

'He's pulled, the bloody big cretin. All those lectures about monogamy he's given us.' He slid down his seat then wriggled back up, laughing. Kim and Andrea looked on, amused at our behaviour.

'I'm, I'm sorry. What are we supposed to do, walk out?' I slurred, making the girls laugh more. 'We have to stay and, and accept their hospi... their... hos... you know what I mean.'

Billy came and sat down and looked at me. I shook my head. 'What can I say fella? You've scored big style.'

Phil stared Billy in the eyes. 'Well, Wellsie, seal got your tongue? Ha!' He slid down the seat again, grinning wildly at Billy as Kim pulled him back up.

'Andrea, what can I do?' Billy looked at her.

'Tell her the truth Billy Wells,' she smiled. 'Tell her that you're happily married, but tell her for sure that you've enjoyed her company as well.'

I looked at Andrea. I had noticed over the weeks her accent was returning and I loved it. 'Well said, babe.' Billy stood up swaying and then looked at me.

'She's a doll that one, a real doll.'

'Go on then big man, spoil her night,' Phil shouted.

Billy looked lost in front of the girls. He had to behave, but deep down inside I'm sure he fancied a bit of mischief. The group started to play the last song, so everyone left standing staggered to the dance floor. After a few minutes of slow dancing, the group broke into a lively Scottish jig. As the tune reached its crescendo, Billy picked his admirer up and flung her over his shoulder. He danced, spinning around like a madman. Then there was a stomach-churning thud as the poor girl's head hit the bar post. Billy slid her down his body, looking distraught. A bald man who was a doctor dashed to them, examining her. 'She's out cold!' he exclaimed while looking at Billy.

'Sorry.' Billy looked gutted then she opened her eyes and gave him a drowsy smile.

Billy sat down, looking dazed.

'Well pal, that's a fucking good way of getting out of a squeeze. If you can't knob 'em, clobber 'em,' Phil teased.

Billy looked at him and nodded. His eyes read like a book. 'Language,' he snapped back.

Everyone had left, but for a hard core of drinkers circled around the bar. We bid goodnight and staggered up the old wood panelled stairway, which creaked loudly. Minutes later I lay in the cosy bed, with a gentle breeze filling the room. I recognised my two favourite smells, Andrea and the sea.

The next day was spent on *Stormdrift*. I felt strange as I stepped on board. The deck had been painted with grey non-slip paint, but the winch still bore the scars made by the bullets. Everyone looked discreetly at the bullet marks, which brought back the reality of how serious and desperate things were back then. *Stormdrift* moved out slowly, as Billy donned his suit. The day was easy. Barbecued lobster and huge king scallops cooked in white wine. The southerly winds made it feel warm, despite the northern latitude. It was a perfect day with perfect friends.

Len and Spot greeted us after our long drive home. Billy went back to Len's place, no doubt to tell him all that had occurred. Phil and I planned the remaining week. Kim had a few days left and she had promised to cook a Chinese meal for us. Phil had taken her to the shops while Andrea and I went for a walk along the riverbank. It was a breezy day, with the sun bright and low in the sky.

'I can feel the change already.' I looked around. 'It's been a rush, but still a hell of a year.'

'It's not over yet, Mike.'

'No, we'll get a couple of trips in I'm sure.' We walked along in silence for a while.

'I, well, we know so little about each other. Where do you actually come from? Your accent is more Southern than Northern Irish.'

'How do you know the difference?' she asked, smiling.

'The telly, I suppose.' I, like many who had served in Northern Ireland, wouldn't tell anyone unnecessarily, especially Andrea. She could come from a Republican background and it could make things awkward for her, for both of us.

'You never watch the telly.'

'So where actually do you come from then?'

'A small place, you wouldn't have a clue where it is.'

'Try me, I was good at geography.'

She laughed. 'Where's Keady then?' I stopped in my tracks. It was a long time ago, but the name brought back memories. It was what they called "bandit country". I had to be careful. There was a lot of hate around there for the army.

'Give me a clue?'

She thought. 'Have you heard of a place called Armagh?' Before I could answer she said, 'Newry then?'

'Yeah, those places were always on the news,' I felt guilty because I was cheating her and lying. I asked, digging myself in deeper. 'Did you see all the troubles?'

'We were fourteen-year-old schoolgirls. We had great fun with the soldiers. My parents didn't get involved with the troubles. There was, and still is, a lot of divided opinion. Most folk ignore the troubles and get on with their lives.'

'So, it never bothered you directly?' I thought, 'please say no'.

She smiled deep in thought. The smile meant something. 'No, just a young girl's past.'

We stopped at a stile and sat down. 'Are you going to tell me your secret, then?'

'No, for sure you'll only laugh at me.'

'I promise I won't.'

'Well, we were about or fourteen or fifteen. Our school was in Armagh. At the time, the Paratroopers were stationed there. Most of the girls loved them. Marry one and they would take you to England, away from all the troubles.' She held her head back, looking up smiling. 'It was our little dream. They used to stop the school bus on purpose and we used to flirt, you know, like young girls do.'

My pulse increased as I drifted into the past, vaguely remembering doing similar things to what Andrea was describing.

'Are you listening?' she said, with a look of embarrassment.

'Yeah sorry, I was trying to imagine it in my mind. Go on.'

'They were there for about four months. We had a crush on one of the youngest. He was so cute. You reminded me of him when I first saw you. Those blue eyes of yours, he had a blue square on his jacket sleeve, which matched his eyes. He didn't look old enough to be there, he had such a bonny face.' She smiled, looking down.

'Yeah,' I said softly.

'We had to get out of the bus so they could carry out a search. It was good fun for us girls. One day, Jeez, I've never forgot it... No, you'll think it's corny for sure.' She laughed.

'No go on, finish what you started,' I said now with a serious look.

'As the door opened and before we could get out, an old ticket fell on to the ground. And the one we all fancied picked it up. He tore it in half, and looked at us crowded in the doorway. We froze, all of us, then he gave one half to me, he chose me, he then put the other half in his beret and said, 'Bring this back when you're eighteen,' then he winked at me. We giggled like mad. I blushed so much my cheeks were burning up. All the other girls were so jealous. I kept the ticket for ages, but he never came for me. He was on my mind for years.' She stared into space, 'Just a teenage crush.'

I had feelings running through me like I had never had felt before. A blast from the past, how could it be? I vaguely remembered doing something similar, but my life was in constant turmoil back then and my memories were vague and all fragmented.

'I got a job in Belfast. All my friends left to find work. I trained as a nurse; you were given accommodation. I had just qualified when I met Gerald. He brought me to England. It was all rosy at first, then he got promotion and we had to entertain clients. He would go mad at me when my accent slipped. He would shout at me and call me a common Mick. He became so hurtful and I eventually stopped loving him. The rest you know.'

She smiled and squeezed my hand tight. 'I'm so glad I found you, I was so lonely.'

As we walked slowly back home, I hardly spoke. I was trying to think of a way of telling her about my past without her feeling that I had lied and deceived her, by keeping it all from her.

'You've been deep in thought, Mike. I haven't upset you, have I?'

'No. I know what you're going to say and the answer is, no. I love the Irish Andrea as she is. Not as he tried making you.'

'It's my birthday on Saturday.'

'If we have to sail, will you let me off? We can have your birthday when we get back.'

'Just come back safe to me.' The look in her eyes was so sincere; it reached deep into my soul.

Billy and Phil sat at the table. Len joined us. 'You know that money I snaffled from those terrorists? Well, there was

Silver Bubbles

more than we thought, and Jamie insisted I had some of it, ten grand actually. What I want to do is get mains electricity in here, and put a small stable block, but I can't pay cash. So if I give you two grand each and get the mains through the business, it will solve the cash problem and you get something out of it too. What do you say?' They all agreed.

I spent the next few days organising things. Phil got the stores for *Sea Gem*, while Billy serviced and fuelled her up. I hadn't seen Kris for a while, so I rang Vicki. She seemed fine, although a little distant. Kris had a few words with me. He said that the senior school was great and he had made lots of new mates and had more homework to do, so he hadn't had time to stop over. This made me feel sad inside; my little boy was growing apart from me.

Too soon it was time to set off. Andrea gave me a big hug and a wet snog. I walked across the field looking back at Len and Andrea, who were instructing the builders where to put things. I had asked Len to stay with Andrea after the horse trouble. I didn't wipe her kiss. I just licked my lips.

I sat at the helm telling Phil about the twist of fate in my life and the problem that I had created myself by not telling her of my past. Phil couldn't believe it either. The subject kept popping up as we thought a little more about the chance encounter. All I had from those vague memories was a tin containing bits and pieces that my mother had kept. Later that day, when we were all together, I flicked off the television.

'The forecast is better, everything is ready and ship-shape, let's go and get that tin!'

The diving was uneventful. There was thirty minutes of airlifting, moving unrecognisable machines and objects that had corroded beyond recognition. I hoped that the corrosion of the buried objects was a result of them being near the tin, which would have, over the years, caused the iron and steel to corrode quicker.

'We'll find it tomorrow, its Andrea's birthday. She's thirty-three,' I said aloud while drying my hair with the damp communal towel.

'You'll have to ask her to say it without talking,' said Phil, grinning.

'Oh yeah, tirty tree... you cheeky bastard she's not that bad.'

'Leave her alone you couldn't get a cuter girl than her,' Billy shouted from the galley.

It was now Monday morning. We had worked three tides a day for four days and were feeling the pace. Our ears were becoming hard to clear. A blocked-up feeling in everyone's sinuses, due to the constant changes in pressure, was taking effect. We called it soggy ear. This type of diving was the most dangerous and physically demanding of all. We reduced the bottom time to twenty minutes for safety, but it seemed we were hardly getting into the dive and then had another six hours to wait for another, mad twenty minutes. Relationships took the strain - no arguing, but a miserable atmosphere filled the whole vessel. A sick feeling of failure we hadn't experienced before infested all our thoughts.

On the evening dive, Phil had stayed on the bottom a little too long for our liking, and we made him do some decompression stops. He was humming through the coms.

'What's made him so bloody happy?' sneered Billy, 'He can't be playing with himself.'

'Beats me,' I said indifferently, looking at the sky. 'Sodding winter, I hate it. Even the sea temperature will drop soon.' I looked at my watch and reached over to the coms box, 'OK you knob, you can surface now.'

A loud 'Ye-ha' came over the coms. Phil surfaced and threw a tin ingot onto the deck. He pulled his mask off and punched the air shouting, 'Yes.'

Silver Bubbles

'Where were they?' I asked, grinning excitedly.

'That flat piece of steel we assumed was a side plate from the hull was the side of one of those boxes. There's at least two ton in it, just like the last one.'

'Well done, Kilick diver.' Billy patted him hard on the back. 'You've just about earned the title.'

All that evening I kept reminding them two ton was a possibility, but four ton made it more likely to be a twenty-ton shipping consignment. The first slack of the day was prior to dawn, so Phil took the winch wire, to try and pull the box out.

'OK, OK, take it in slowly. Whoa, Whoa! It's slipping, give some slack, standby.'

'Understood.'

'Ok, nice and slow now. Steady. She's coming, steady.' Suddenly, without warning, the hook slipped along the edge of the steel box.

Phil screamed in agony, 'Shit! Shit, my hand!'

Billy instantly stopped the winch. 'Come back Phil.' Billy looked at me, while throwing a bottle on his back like it was made of polystyrene. I held my hand up to Billy.

'Pull me up, I've bust me hand,' Phil whimpered.

I cut the work glove off and examined his hand. 'These two are broken, and this one looks badly bruised, perhaps fractured,' I told him as I carefully held his fingers.

Phil shaking with cold and pain was helped to the warm galley where we gave him painkillers and a hot sweet tea while we dressed his hand.

'That's fucking great! I won't be able to drive or knock one out for weeks.'

'What are we going to do?' Billy asked, totally ignoring Phil's last comment

'What do you reckon Phil, how do you feel?'

'Well I don't need a fiddle just now.' I grinned. Billy shook his head with disapproval.

'Get your arses down there. The ingots have spilled out waiting for us. I can do the winch with my left hand.'

Billy made bottom, dragging the stout metal basket with him. He unclipped the offending hook and secured it on to the lifting eye on the basket. Then he started throwing ingots into it, like a crazed person in a supermarket challenge. We worked hard for two tides, collecting all the exposed ingots. Sitting on the deck, physically exhausted, Billy rolled his suit down and scratched his side and stomach.

'Let me have a look.' I pulled Billy's sweatshirt up, which revealed a big red rash. 'Shit, you've got a skin bend.' I ran into the dive store and came back with a small green mask. 'Put this on.'

Billy donned the oxygen mask and started breathing in the pure oxygen. 'Feels great,' he said.

I sat him down in the galley. 'You'll be all right pal. I'm just making sure. After you've breathed this, get a hot shower and I bet you any money the rash will have gone.'

I steamed the mooring line out and sank it. 'Navigation lights, radar, set track back.' I shivered as I settled into the big soft seat. We had sailed a little too close to danger and had casualties. All the time we had spent here had felt good. Now the place felt cold and hostile like the sea had put up with us but now wanted rid of us. It was time to leave while we were ahead.

'Three hundred and nineteen,' Billy shouted up the steps. Phil looked at me.

'That's confirmed it!' I shouted. 'There must be twenty ton down there. We missed one, though. There's eighty to a ton, remember.'

'It can't be that far away.'

Phil shook his head. 'It's on the galley table, you big daft prat. It's the one I brought up!'

I laughed as Billy looked sheepishly at Phil.

'Christ, Phil the other fourteen ton can't be far away!'

Silver Bubbles

'Yeah I know.'

'We've still grossed over thirty grand in one trip. How's your hand?'

'Sore as hell. It's throbbing like a nun's pussy.'

'I wouldn't know,' I said smiling. 'It will be a plaster job I reckon, four weeks possibly.'

'Hell, four weeks without a fiddle! I'll use my left hand, I'll have to.'

Billy joined us. 'There are more of these.' He passed me a handful of the small company emblems, then looked out of the window and asked how long we had to go.

'We have the flood up our arse all the way. We should be tied up by seven or eight o'clock.'

'Right, I'll get the bridge man to phone our Girt, and have her waiting to take him to hospital.'

'No, I'll get Andrea to take him in his car. It is fully comp. isn't it?'

Phil smiled, 'Yeah, course it is. You never know. If I'm lucky, she might have one of her short skirts on.'

'In your dreams, Casanova. I'm going to tell Kim what a knob-hound she's got involved with,' Billy said as he looked in the mirror, twisting around to check the rash.

'Involved, I like that word. Anyway, listen who's talking. You swapped spit and licked the tonsils of that Scottish bird all bloody night. I wonder what "The Monogamy Kid" would have got up to, if Andrea and Kim hadn't been there to keep an eye on you.'

'It was the atmosphere that caused that,' Billy said, in defence.

'I can imagine your Sue's face if you told her, 'I'm sorry love, the atmosphere made me give her a portion.''

Billy glared at Phil. He put his damaged hand in the air, shrieking, 'Injury, injury.'

As Billy left us Phil shouted, 'Who taught you to dance anyway, Giant Haystacks?'

'He'll bide his time and get you back, you know,' I warned him.

'As long as he knows I'm joking. Christ! When he hit that guy who walked like "Odd Job", did you see the power of his punches?'

'Yeah,' I smiled, 'A really good mate in a tight corner, the best.'

As we passed the site where the pieces of the plane were found we couldn't miss the large, grey, unmarked vessel that was positioned over the site.

'I wonder if they'll find anything?' Billy said, while looking through the binoculars. That's some boat. It must be costing a bomb.'

'Yeah, they're looking for more than a plane and bones for sure. Let's hope they leave some of whatever they're after.'

'You never know,' Phil added. 'If they're as crap as I remember them, they'll leave us something for us to find. I'd put a bet on it.'

'Well, we'll just have to have a sniff around some time in the future, eh?' I smiled; remember Billy's saying, "If you don't look, you'll find nowt!"'

CHAPTER THIRTEEN

Phil returned with his hand in plaster and his arm in a sling. I was sat at the table, staring at the eleven tin logos.

'At least four weeks,' Phil moaned. 'What a bummer.'

'Smaller share for you, lad. If you can't dive you're as useful as a "eunuch in a porn movie,"' Billy joked.

'Eleven.' They stared at me. 'Eleven. We've recovered six tons. So where did these five come from?' I had separated them into two piles.

'What if they took them off the pallets and stored them in those steel boxes? They would be more stable,' Phil said, looking at us both.

'That's it!' I jumped up. 'You've got it! It's obvious. They must have broken the bands off the pallets and put the ingots in the boxes as you said. That would account for these extra logos. They must have dropped them on the floor as they broke the bands. The bands would have rotted but not the logos. This means there must be twenty ton there!'

Phil smiled proudly then looked at Billy. 'Call me Sherlock Roper.'

'More like Sherlock Poker,' Billy chuckled.

'Look Billy, you don't have to feel inferior because Mike and I are the tin kings.'

I grinned while waiting for Billy's response.

'Not tin kings, more like wankings.'

The laughter echoed into the cold evening. Then Andrea entered the room causing a sudden silence. She looked stunning. I was taking her out for her birthday. She was wearing a straight, simple black dress, finishing just above her knee. A beautiful diamond necklace that I couldn't resist buying her complemented the outfit. The silence embarrassed her, causing a bashful smile.

'God, you look wonderful,' I said, greeting her with a kiss.

'Hear, hear,' Billy and Phil said. Phil was drooling.

'Come on love.' I placed her coat over her shoulders. 'Don't take any notice of these dirty old seamen,' I said, grinning.

'Have a good night.' Billy said.

'It's pretty obvious he's going to have a good one,' Phil said, looking at me, then at Andrea's bum, while making a circle with his mouth and frowning.

'Nighty night, Phil.' She blew him a kiss. He smiled, shaking his head, while looking her up and down.

'In yer dreams, boy,' I heard Billy say as I closed the door.

A week later we were on the deck, waiting for the "Wells" clan. The weather forecast was good, but with Phil not being able to dive, it was a good time to fulfil our promise and take Billy's family out on a fishing trip. Two cars approached.

'Hell, that car's got a puncture. Look, it's leaning over.' The car stopped, and the doors opened.

'Bloody hell,' Phil looked at me. 'We're in the land of the fucking giants.'

'We need a bigger boat,' I looked at Phil.

'I hope we've got enough food,' he replied.

'Now then,' Billy's brother shouted, as Billy walked to greet them.

'There are six of them. At least a ton and a half of muscle,' I said to Phil. The men, all middle-aged, were huge. Not fat, just really big and broad. Bigger than Billy!

Silver Bubbles

'This is Mike, our skipper.' Billy introduced me with a look of pride. I shook their hands. The rough, strong grips and genuine smiles told me that they were going to have a good time, regardless of the fishing.

'And this is our cabin boy, Phil,' Billy said, grinning at him, as they all shook hands. After loading the gear, including what must have been a ton of booze, we set off. Andrea sat on Misty, waving as *Sea Gem* slipped round the corner and out of sight.

I spun the wheel for another pass over the wreck, which was lying in a deep trench called the "Silver Pit". The horn sounded, and Billy threw the marker buoy over.

I adjusted the drift then shouted to the lads, 'OK boys, down you go.' The big fishing reels paid line out in harmony as the chrome lures raced towards the large wreck, that lay over two hundred feet below us.

I watched the sounder. Phil was by my side taking everything in. 'Any minute now,' I said in a whisper.

'I'm in,' one of the lads shouted, as his rod tip jerked up and down bending almost double.

'I'm in.'

'Here we go,' Billy looked up at us. 'Come and help me with the gaffing.'

I looked down with pride as a big double-figure cod thumped onto the deck, followed by pollock, coalfish and ling. We hadn't let them down. Drift after drift, the fish slapped on to the deck, keeping Billy and Phil busy. Roars of excitement bellowed through the air each time one of them struck into a big fish, making us all grin. After the hectic session, the fish were iced down and stored below. The next day was similar. A large monkfish made Billy's brother's day, as it put him ahead on the species tally.

Later, moored in the estuary with everyone squeezed into the mess room, tired and happy we drank and told tales late into the night. "Play hard, drink hard and fight hard," was their motto. It was a brilliant two-day break for all involved. Billy was especially proud, and had a permanent grin on his face.

In Phil's words, 'He must be on extra strong happy pills.'

Four weeks had passed since Phil's accident, but we had made enough money to last us well into the next season. 'Wood End' now had mains electricity. Andrea was more settled, having heard nothing from Gerald, and was spending most of her time at my place. Kim was talking of leaving her job and moving up to be with Phil. I suggested that Phil should approach the owners of the 'Spinney' to see if they would sell it to him.

I pulled back the revs and slowed the engine to a tick-over. *Sea Gem's* deck vibrated, to almost a hum. We were on maintenance, painting and servicing her for the winter lay up, but I was hoping for another trip and was watching the weather like a hawk.

We sat round the galley table, drinking tea. 'Oh yeah, Andy Chiset rang. He saw the salvage boat over the *Albania*, but guess what?'

'Go on then.' Billy looked with interest.

'Well, they tow their nets around several obstructions in the area and if they pull debris or junk up in their nets they dump it onto the *Albania*, so they don't pick it up again. All the trawler skippers do it.'

'So what are you getting at?' Phil said, leaning forward.

'Well, apparently they know of an obstruction, they call it the bomber. It's about a mile north-east from where the Yanks are searching. Someone got a net fast into it. When they eventually pulled it clear it had a radial engine complete with four blades still attached to it!'

'Who told them?' enquired Billy.

'Gary's uncle. It was him who pulled it up.'

'Bloody hell, they're on a wild goose chase,' laughed Phil.

'We'll say nowt,' said Billy. 'When they get pissed off with finding heaps of junk and give up we will have a shufty, eh?'

'Spot on mate, but we will have to keep quiet. They wouldn't take it kindly. In fact it could go tits up if they found out.'

'We work in the area. If we found something we could tell them, for a salvage fee of course. And maybe we could snaffle something for posterity.'

'Yeah like a rake of gold bars,' Phil said with a wink.

I paused. My mind was occupied with different thoughts. 'Let's give it one more trip,' I said loudly. 'Phil's hand has healed. Hell, we've had no work in for ages and there's got to be more tin where we left off. We're just sitting around here like old farts.'

'Speak for yourselves, I'm not fucking old,' Phil said in his usual coarse and carefree way.

Sea Gem rode the hidden waves as she drove on into the misty darkness.

'I'm not too sure about this. It's bloody late December,' Phil remarked, while squinting through the window. 'It's getting thicker by the mile.'

We had dived on the *Juno* only to find the underwater visibility to be nil, rendering the site unworkable, so I suggested the *Lyra* and all the alloy ingots I had seen. Being a long way from the coast, the underwater visibility was bound to be better.

'You're looking through the window. Here, this is what you look at, you tit.' I tapped the radar. 'You might as well black the windows out, we're on instruments only, now,' I said, my smile showing confidence. Then in a louder tone I continued. 'Bloody weather, who said you don't get wind with fog? What bullshit. The forecast was perfect for a late steal. Even lobsters are eight pound a pound this time of year and that entire cargo of alloy lying on the bottom is waiting for us.'

'Yeah, but we've had a cracking first season. I've never been better off,' Phil said, looking at us both.

Billy agreed. 'Why don't we turn back? I've still got some Christmas presents to get. The alloy won't be going anywhere, the wreck isn't even charted.'

I raised my voice. 'Listen to you two. If the mist lifted and the sun came out, you would be grinning like kids.'

'It's four-thirty, dark nights,' Billy said, casting a glance at Phil.

'Hell, we've steamed nearly seventy miles! This shit might be gone tomorrow and then we can get a bonus for Christmas. It's always miserable when it's like this. We're safe with *Sea Gem*. She's indifferent to all this moody stuff. We've got work to do, and out here you're going to get good Vis, let's give it until tomorrow and if it's still crap, we'll bugger off home and call it a day until the spring. OK?'

Billy and Phil agreed. They didn't really have much choice. I was in "wrecking mode" and focussed.

'Did you hear that?' I turned the radio up. 'I'm sure it was a Mayday. It must be a long way away.'

'I heard fuck all,' Phil said, listening with his head to one side.

'There it is again.' A crackly message stole our attention.

"Mayday, Mayday. Mayday, This is 'MV Basto.' We are taking in water and we have lost power, Mayday, Mayday, Mayday,"

The voice on the radio started to give a position. I quickly grabbed a pencil. 'Shit! That's got to be near. Here, hold the wheel, Phil.'

I looked at the chart and drew lines with a parallel rule. 'Hell it's about two miles away.' I called the Coast Guard, but we were nearly eighty miles offshore and only a few crackles could be heard.

Basto, Basto, Basto. This is Sea Gem, Sea Gem over.' All three of us looked at the radio. It crackled into life then a broken voice shouting for help sent shivers through all of us.

'I've got him here, look,' I pointed at a small blip on the radar. I then pushed the throttle to full speed, while spinning the big wooden wheel. 'Put your suits on and get some lifejackets and ropes out, just in case.'

Turning south towards the stricken vessel I began to realise just how rough it had become. *Sea Gem* began to roll and pitch heavily in the dark troughs. 'God, it's so thick I can't see the bow,' I said looking at my friends, who were now in their drysuits and holding on to the grab rails.

'What's the plan of action?' Billy asked calmly.

'Stand by mate, let's get a visual first,' I said, while steering *Sea Gem* on the radar. Its range was now set at one mile.

'Get outside and keep a look-out on either side.' The urgency in my voice made them disappear.

The mist was like smoke. Totally grey at times, then twenty-foot visibility and very patchy. I had the radar set to the minimum distance. Now the blip on the screen was all around us, like an encroaching green cloud. I held the wheel, not knowing which way to turn.

Then Phil gave a shrill whistle and shouted. 'There, I've got it, there.' Someone was waving. A white cloth appeared through the mist. I pulled the throttle back, not knowing where *Sea Gem* was going to drift in all the confusion and poor visibility. Phil, now joined by Billy, was pointing towards the vessel, guiding me nearer to it. Then the full picture slowly started to emerge. A life raft was hanging from the stern of the coaster. A woman and two young people were clinging to each other. A man was shouting across, beckoning us closer. His grief-stricken face showed openly the agony that he was enduring. The scene shocked us, involving us instantly in a pending disaster.

I held our position the best I could, spinning the wheel from one lock to the other, while feathering the throttle on and off. Billy threw a rope across to the coaster, which landed at the feet of the huddled family. They didn't move, until Billy screamed at them. 'Grab it! Grab it!'

The man dived on the rope and then secured it to the rail, as a huge wave ran up the deck. Much of the deck was now low in the water. Billy swung down the line like a commando, hitting a passing wave, which launched him, sideways. His strong arms held on, and within seconds he was on the vessel. Phil followed. I watched, concerned that his injured hand wouldn't be strong enough for him to hold on. Fortunately Phil had donned a safety harness and had clipped himself to the line. He made the journey across, pulling hand over hand, as the waves leaped up at him like hungry animals trying to snatch him away. He reached the boat and was pulled effortlessly over the rail by Billy.

The radio crackled into life. 'Mike, Mike.' Billy had taken a hand-held radio with him.

'I'm receiving you, loud and clear.'

'I'm going below to try to get a pump working. They've lost the engineer; he made off in another life-raft.'

'Understood Billy, take care.'

For most of the time, the only thing I could see was the rope trailing over the stern of *Sea Gem*. My eyes strained to see, while I manoeuvred blindly. Suddenly, I sighted the coaster, this time on my stern. The wind was blowing on to the bridge, making it easier to manoeuvre. A crackled message that I could hardly make out came from Billy. I realised that if he were down below, in the steel hull it would weaken his VHF signal. Then a loud crack made me jump, as the rope between the two vessels parted. I continued to hold my position the best I could.

Silver Bubbles

On board, Phil was trying to make some sense of the screaming woman. She was pointing to the life raft. She kept putting her hands to her breast, then holding them out to him, screaming hysterically, squealing in some foreign language.

I was dashing back and forth from the aft windows, to the controls. This was the only way I could hold *Sea Gem* in position and keep in contact with the stricken vessel. Suddenly, something caught my eye. It had fallen out of the life raft, which was hanging over the stern by its white painter line. I poked my head out of the window for a clearer look.

'Oh God, no' I yelled loudly. Between the waves I could make out small bodies thrashing around in the water. I jumped down the stairs, looking on helplessly, as two young children drifted ten feet away, parallel with the hull.

My hands were on the gunwale moving along with them. Despair engulfed me as the small lights on their lifejackets disappeared and reappeared in the misty wave troughs, each time a bit further away.

My mind was spinning, and then I remembered the life rafts. I rushed up on to the foredeck and released the retaining strap that secured the raft. My hands repeatedly slipped on the smooth canister as I struggled to throw it over the side. As it hit the angry sea I frantically pulled the soft white painter line. Suddenly the capsule burst open and the life raft appeared like a red and black hissing monster, as it grew larger, bucking up and down on the snatching waves. Looking through the mist I saw a small dim light. The life raft was drifting and being blown in the same direction as the kids. Slack painter line was laid all over the deck, so I led it through the rail, wrapped it around my wrist several times, gripped it tightly and dived over the side. I felt a severe jolt then a loud bang, stars burst out everywhere and then cold and pain smothered me.

The line had snagged on a chain, which was fitted on the rail, causing me to swing into the steel hull. Spitting out water,

I looked frantically around. I started to swim, but the pain in my right arm was unbearable. I kicked off my rigger boots then, swimming with one arm; the other pulled into my chest, looked desperately around. For a split second I saw a light and swam painfully in its direction. There it was again; I could hear the sound of children crying. I swam the best I could in that direction. Suddenly they appeared in front of me, two little heads dwarfed in over-sized lifejackets.

I struggled to them, grabbing them with my left arm. They cried loudly and were shivering uncontrollably. Their eyes were wide open and staring out sheer terror.

I felt for the painter line from the life raft. My right arm was completely numb. As I grabbed for the line I felt a sharp piece of bone protruding through my skin.

I pulled desperately only to find a frayed end. Taking a deep breath I despairingly looked around.

My stomach went hollow as I realised our fate. 'No, No,' I shouted. 'Not like this! For fuck's sake- not like this!'

I put my hand through the tie straps on their jackets. They were holding on to each other, crying and whimpering. 'I'm Mike. Listen,' I shouted. 'Mike is going to save you. Mummy and Daddy are waiting for us, so we have to swim. Come on, swim!'

I tugged at them, making them cry louder, while swimming in a frog-like movement. I changed my direction, frantically looking for anything that would get us back to safety. The cold was so painful and it slowed me down. I continued for a while then stopped, panting. I looked at their little faces.

'Please! No!' I said quietly through gritted teeth as I tried swimming again, but my legs were numb and I was only bobbing up and down.

Billy smiled as the Petter diesel engine kicked into life. Steam rose from it as it warmed up. The water level began to fall, revealing a column of water spraying from a corroded

Silver Bubbles

intake pipe. Billy closed the valve and the flow stopped. He felt quite proud of himself as he climbed the ladder to the deck.

Up on the deck, it was mayhem. Phil was shaking the woman, trying to get some sense out of her. Her husband was desperately attempting to pull the life raft up on to the deck. Billy pulled with him and between them they managed to get it partly over the rail. The woman rushed to it and looked inside. Frantic, she fell to her knees, wailing and banging her fists on the deck.

'What the...?' Billy looked at Phil.

'They put the two kids into it but the painter line wasn't long enough and it just touched the water. They fell out, the poor little sods,' he said, shaking his head.

'The boat's not going to sink. Where's Mike?'

'I don't know, probably standing off. Give him a call.' Billy called and called, but he got no response.

Then a strange voice came over the radio. 'Station requesting Mayday, this is the standby vessel, *Boston Prowler*. Can you give me a count, one to ten...over?'

'Roger,' Billy said, and then began slowly counting.

'We have your bearing and are proceeding to your location E.T.A. twenty minutes. What is your situation?'

Billy told them then looked at Phil. 'Where is he? He wouldn't lose us. Not Mike.' Phil stood with a blank stare as water dripped off his nose.

I was feebly moving my legs, making an effort to swim, but all I was doing was getting colder. The children were ghostly silent with shock. I spun in the water looking for anything and then something pricked my neck.

I moved again and it rubbed on me. I felt around. There it was a line. The painter - the piece of wire threaded into the line had pricked my neck. As best I could I pulled it, holding the slack in my teeth.

After several arm lengths, it became harder then a light and a shape came into view. It was the life raft.

I painfully pulled and pulled until I was with it. I grabbed one of the kids, but I was too weak to lift the small body up. Annoyed, almost crying with frustration, I gripped the rope on the raft with my teeth. With all my strength I lifted the child up. I kicked hard, bending my arm and forcing my elbow against the small body. Success, I'd done it! I succeeded in repeating the trying task.

With them both in the raft I hung on to the side, weak and desperately cold. I knew my time was running out. The cold made me strangely sleepy and I didn't want to move. Then I thought about Kris, Phil and Andrea. I had to get into the life raft if I was going to survive. Again and again my attempts ended in pain and failure. At least the kids have a chance I thought. I was holding on to the rope, while my legs dragged under the raft, banging on the hard air cylinder that hung below the water. I gasped in sharp breaths. My body felt frozen in one solid shiver.

It wasn't worth the effort any more. The cold claw that Len had spoken of was now pulling me down. Then a tiny voice interrupted my trance. 'Mr Mike, Mr Mike.' A little face looked down at me like an angel. The small girl spoke in broken English, 'You come, you come in, Mr Mike.' Small hands tugged at me. It was like a dream, but her persistence forced me to try again. I had rested a while; I knew I had to make the effort. So I leaned back and lifted one foot up, and slid it over the edge of the raft. The little hands held on while I lifted my other leg up. I bent my knees and pulled myself up, swallowing seawater as my head dipped below the surface. This is it I thought, as the cold water washed my face. I held the rope with my left hand and twisted to my left. I straightened and pulled with my knees. The children helped as best as they could.

Silver Bubbles

I gave a few frantic wriggles – and I was in! Gasping for breath I looked at their faces and gave a scared smile. Through the gloom from a dim light in the raft I made out their white teeth and eyes.

After regaining my breath I found the large box of stores. It was sealed with watertight tape. I pulled at it then chewed at it. 'How the hell, are you supposed to get into this with one bloody arm?' I muttered despairingly. I felt around the side of the tube and found a blunt-ended knife. I cut open the box. Sacks of water and biscuits spilled out, but more important, I found thermal protection gear. I tore at them with my teeth and good arm.

The raft was a twelve-man one, so we had plenty to go at. Struggling painfully, I put both children into one suit. Just two pairs of eyes could be seen peering out of the hole in the big orange bag.

I struggled half into one, then laid panting, holding my throbbing arm. My shaking had slowed down now but my whole body felt devoid of energy as I struggled to stay awake. I tried talking to the kids, but kept nodding off halfway through a sentence, only to jerk awake, which made my arm throb painfully as I woke from the deathly sleep. Trying to keep occupied I leaned over and pushed my fingers into the kid's hood. They felt warmer.

> *Children's voices joined me in a dream. I was in bed, warm and cosy. The children were at my bedside. It was dark, warm and peaceful and their voices relaxed me.*

'Mr. Mike. Mr. Mike.'

I opened my eyes and was met with discomfort, then fear. 'Yeah, yeah,' I said indifferently as I my mind wandered in and out of reality.

'Ship, a ship,' the voice said, making me wake abruptly. I shook my head and turned on the torch that I had found in the pack. The light revealed the life raft was littered with things - like a room on a Christmas morning, but a cold and wet one. With the torch in my mouth searching the floor, I picked up a rocket flare. I held it between my knees, trying to tear the thick plastic.

'Come on, you bastard,' I cursed, as my hand slipped off the wet plastic.

I dropped the torch and ripped the flare open with my teeth. Holding it against myself, I slid the plastic off, inch-by-inch.

'Right, you bastard,' I paused holding the flare, 'how the fuck are you supposed to do this one handed?' I shouted, with a forlorn grin. Grimacing with pain, I moved to the slit in the cover and lifted up the flare. Gripping the plastic loop in my teeth, I pulled the flare upward. A loud 'whoosh' then blinding pain, as it recoiled into my nose.

'Shit,' I moaned.

The sound of giggling in the darkness made me look at them, although it was dimly lit. All the action and cursing was making me feel warmer, but as I got warmer the pain in my arm became worse and the sticky feeling down my side told me I was bleeding steadily.

A strong searchlight caught their attention as the fast rescue craft appeared from the gloom and bumped alongside. A young man climbed aboard and asked if there were any casualties. Billy told him what had happened. While they spoke he relayed the information through his radio.

'There's a vessel stopped about half a mile north-west. Do you know who she is?'

'It's got be ours. It's *Sea Gem*, but the skipper's on board. What the hell is he doing?' Billy looked at Phil. 'Can you take us across to her?'

'Hell! Not in the rib. We haven't got radar, and the Vis is almost zero.'

'Can you take us to the *Prowler* then?'

The young coxswain called his skipper. 'We will stay here with the casualty. They will launch another F.R.C. to pick you up, and then the *Prowler* will take you to your boat.'

All eyes were straining as *Sea Gem* loomed up like a ghost ship. Once onboard, Billy ran up the deck, shouting for Mike. He climbed the ladder into the wheelhouse, all the electronics where still on and the engine was running.

They searched the boat, but could find no sign of him. The skipper on the Prowler suggested that he might have fallen over the side. Billy was having none of it. Poor Phil stood helpless, fearing the worst. As the *Prowler* moved off, its lights disappeared instantly, leaving them alone. Billy stood looking helpless at the radar, then at the plotter and then at Phil.

'Well, how do you work this stuff?'

'The plotter, he always marks things, its numeric.'

Billy stood back, 'Nu-what?' He looked again at Phil. 'Well, do it then.' Phil looked at the array of lights and numbers, then back at Billy.

'That's the line the boat has drifted on. We could go back down it.'

Billy put his hands on his head. 'How are we going to find him in this?' he brushed his hair back. 'We've got to be realistic. How could anybody survive in this?...Oh God,' he looked down, as tears pricked his eyes, 'I've never felt so fucking helpless in all my life.'

Phil looked at the plotter, engaged the engine and turned the wheel.

I chewed and tore at another flare

'You plastic bastard,' I cursed. Whoosh, it went off, the case hitting me again. I felt as though I had my hands tied and was being punched in the face by a handy boxer. My body shook as blood dripped from the cuts. Turning and feeling for another flare, I repeated the now exhausting task. The next flare hit the water. I slumped back and thought of Andrea. I should have told her.

> *Voices echoed around my mind. This time I was on Stormdrift, lying behind the winch. They were pulling me out on to the deck and trying to push a pistol into my mouth.*

'No Mr Mike, no do that.' I vaguely realised it was them, but found it so hard to open my mind to reality. Things were much easier with my eyes closed.

Phil turned the wheel, looking at Billy. 'Don't just stand there, get out on the bow and look for him, you big fucking lump. We're not giving up!' He gritted his teeth and sniffed loudly as tears swelled in his eyes.

Billy stared into the grey mist. Putting his foot nearer the rail he felt the wooden cradle that the life raft had once sat on.

'The raft has gone!' He bellowed. 'The port side one, it's not here!'

Phil looked up like a squirrel. 'He's launched it. He must have, so he must be in it!'

Phil called the *Prowler* and told its skipper.

'They're mounting a search. Another stand-by vessel is on the way. The chopper is useless at the moment, but if he's in the raft it has radar reflectors and we can pick it up!' Phil stared closely at the radar, not really knowing which button to press. He expanded the range to three miles, cleared his eyes and started working a search pattern out. But he had set the radar on a higher range, and it was picking up the big waves, making detection of such a small target near impossible.

Silver Bubbles

> *The very same waves lifted the life raft up and down. The motion was drawing me like an invisible hand, pulling me deeper and deeper into a painless world devoid of all feeling. No more urgency, no more people. I was alone without a care in the world and sliding down a smooth tunnel, totally relaxed, addicted to the warm painless feeling.*
>
> *A bright light appeared in my dream, then voices.*

'Mr Mike, Mr Mike.' Again I found it difficult to open my eyes. I saw inquisitive, scared face. The little girl, having reached the torch, was shining it into my eyes, waking me up.

'No, Mr Mike, you vely bad man, you wake up.' A new pulse ran through me. She was so close, and scared yet helping me, it brought me back to reality.

I held the flare. The little Filipino girl pulled the cord and smiled, despite our dire situation.

'What was that?' Billy pointed to port quarter. 'I'm sure I saw a red flash.'

Phil turned the wheel and brought *Sea Gem* to a halt. He said nothing. Billy stood on the bow, holding the rail. He strained into the dark, focusing his eyes, as the swirling grey mist taunted him with hopeful visions. Suddenly a red flame shot towards him. He ducked as it hit the side of the wheelhouse and burst into millions of sparks.

'That's the last,' I sighed. 'Thanks, you're....'

She was ignoring me, looking past me and out of the split in the life-raft canopy. She pointed, 'Ship, ship, ship.'

I looked out. Almost on top of us, *Sea Gem's* bow appeared then disappeared, like a ghost in the mist. A huge splash, then like a sea monster, Billy's head burst to the surface. With a rope in his hand he grabbed the raft. Then his head pushed into view.

'Where the hell have you been?' His smile turned to shock when he saw the kids, 'Hell! Let's get you sorted.'

The life raft jolted against the stern, causing me pain. I cried out in agony as Phil and Billy helped me out. On deck I fell to my knees, holding my arm as blood dripped onto the deck.

'Get me warm,' I mumbled in a low voice.

'What happened?'

'Not now!' Billy shouted. 'Get this gear off him, he's got hypothermia.'

As Phil pulled the thermal bag over my shoulder, I cried out again. Phil's face distorted with shock as he pulled the blood-soaked fabric down, revealing my forearm, which had bone poking through the skin.

'Billy, Billy. Get the first-aid bag, and make a ring bandage. His fucking arm's all bust up. He, he's bleeding like hell!'

'I wish Len were here.' Billy said out loud, as he pushed the kids into the base of the steps. He passed them some blankets and told them to stay there.

'Get him into the warmth first,' screamed Billy. They dragged me into the shower. Phil held my legs up of the floor, while spraying warm water over me. Billy checked the kids over. They were stripped, and wrapped in warm dry blankets. They were fine. It was me who concerned him. He and Phil had limited medical knowledge and I wasn't responding well. I kept drifting in and out of consciousness.

Phil looked up at Billy. 'There's blood all over, and his pulse is too low and rapid. We have to get to that stand-by boat. They've got paramedics.'

The fear was apparent in Phil's eyes. Billy ran up to the wheelhouse and picked up the radio. He told the skipper of the *Boston Prowler* the situation and our position. He also told them the good news that they had found the children safe and well.

After what seemed like hours, but in reality was only ten minutes a jolt then a crunch of fenders made Billy run on deck. The skipper of the stand-by vessel hadn't wasted any time. He had come alongside *Sea Gem*. The crew pulled the ropes and secured the two crunching vessels together. Two paramedics jumped on board. Billy brought them quickly to me.

'Get the stretcher,' one of the men ordered.

Within seconds, I was placed on to a stretcher and strapped in. Like an army of ants, everyone helped, as I was taken across to the stand-by vessel. They then moved away to a safe distance. While all the commotion was going on, a press photographer, who happened to be running an article on stand-by vessels and their important role, recorded the whole event.

Hours later the sun broke through as the fog cleared. The whole event felt like a bad dream. Three vessels drifted with the tide. The *Basto*, having had all the water pumped out, sat disabled and helpless, waiting for a salvage tug. The larger Boston Prowler stood off about six cables away, rolling steadily in the swell.

An F.R.C. came across to *Sea Gem* and the second mate climbed aboard.

'How is he?' Billy asked, grabbing the man's hand.

'He's stabilised. There's a chopper on its way. He needs an operation on his arm, but should be fine. We've got the *Basto's* crew and family on board. There's a tug coming for her. The two kids apparently drifted off and were lost. We can't understand how they ended up in one of your life rafts. I need the details for my report.'

'Can't Mike tell you?' Billy asked him.

'He's on morphine: totally out of it! The children said, well, what we can understand from them, is that he came out of the mist from nowhere. Swam around for a while and then hit the water shouting for the raft to come and it did. He then lifted them into it. The rest is strange. They said he was going to leave them, but they made him stay. They speak hardly any English. The mother thinks your man "Mr Mike," as they call him, is sea spirit or something. They get so carried away, and talk so bloody fast all at once. Did Mike... Oh, I need some details about him and a contact number before I'm finished. Did he say anything to you?'

'No, just that he was cold.'

'It was close, his core temperature was dangerously low and he'd lost a lot of blood. Another half an hour and he wouldn't be with us. You did well to find him in all that weather. We found their engineer. He... He paused and looked down. 'He never made it.' After taking a few more details he left.

'Well I suppose we had better get under way,'

'Yeah,' Phil replied. 'What a night!'

He pushed the throttle forward as the yellow rescue helicopter came into view.

Phil looked at Billy. 'This will slow the mad bastard down a bit!'

Billy looked down to the deck. Bloodstains covered and surrounded the life raft, which was rippling in the breeze. He turned, looking ahead, then back at Phil, 'Don't count on it.'

CHAPTER FOURTEEN

Len rushed to the cottage and banged repeatedly on the door. Andrea turned, startled as he rushed past her, pointing wildly at the television.

'Put the news on, put the news on,' he shouted. She picked up the remote control and switched on the television.

'To re-cap on today's headlines,' the newscaster said. 'A dramatic sea rescue took place last night, seventy miles offshore. A foreign-registered cargo vessel started to sink after suffering engine difficulties. The salvage vessel, *Sea Gem*, answered their distress call.' Andrea's mouth opened. 'The vessel and its crew, who were first on the scene, dispatched two men on to the stricken vessel.

The crew and passengers, mainly from the Philippines, were having difficulties boarding their life-rafts. During the rescue, two small children and the ship's engineer were lost into the sea. Miraculously the two children, a boy and girl aged eight and ten, were saved from certain death by the skipper of the *Sea Gem*, who, it is reported, abandoned his own vessel to rescue them. The engineer sadly lost his life. Thirty-eight year old Mike Morgan suffered hypothermia and arm injuries during the rescue, and has been airlifted to hospital. The stand-by vessel, *Boston Prowler*, evacuated the crew and passengers, and is standing by. A salvage tug has been dispatched to tow the stricken vessel to port. Now, the weather.'

Andrea looked at Len. The forlorn look in her face prompted him to put his arm around her. 'Don't worry love, he'll be fine. He's a strong lad. Come on, lock up and we'll go to the hospital.'

The phone rang. Len picked it up and snapped, 'Hello. Yes! No love, we're just going now. He'll be fine... no, not serious, so don't worry Kris. I will call when we've found out... yes, she's with me. All right love, I will. Bye.'

'That was Vicki,' Len said, rolling his eyes in disapproval. 'Let's go.'

I felt like I was dreaming, floating on white clouds. Faces looked at me and then merged into the cotton wool. White lights and square corners moved past me. Then I slipped back into nothingness.

Andrea and Len sat quietly in the waiting room. Andrea fiddled with her handkerchief nervously. 'He's been in there ages,' she said, staring at the floor.

The door opened and a doctor walked towards them. 'Mr Morgan?' They stood up. 'Your son will be fine. He's suffered from hypothermia and has a compound fracture of his right forearm, which we had to operate on. There are a few other cuts and bruises, they are already healing. He'll make a full recovery. He's a very brave man indeed. You can see him now, the nurse will take you.'

Andrea sat by my side, holding my left hand. Heavy bruising covered what bit of my face she could see. My arm was in plaster up to my shoulder. I gave her three little squeezes as I turned to her.

'Hi babe did you bring a wet?'

After four days in hospital, I was allowed home. The press were everywhere, coming to the house, phoning me for interviews. Chat show hosts were calling. It was chaos. I was a hero; this time a public one.

It was two days before Christmas. A new Yamaha 'Moto x' bike was hidden in the workshop, for Kris. The tree was laden with presents. Everyone sat around the roaring log fire.

Sue asked me what had made me jump off the boat instead of driving the boat and picking up the children. The conversation stopped. Billy was going to say something to her, but I had already started my answer.

'The turning circle of the boat is so large that I would have lost them in the fog.'

'You wouldn't have got me jumping in, not knowing if I would get back,' she said. 'Not for anyone.'

I smiled politely. 'I had no choice. Their little faces would have haunted me for the rest of my life. There wasn't a choice,' I repeated quietly. Andrea rested her head against me and held my hand with a squeeze. There was a long silence.

'Hey, look at this one.' Phil laughed as he held up the paper, showing a picture of us; my head was hanging down. "A Modest Hero" was the heading.

'Why did you put your head down, Mike?' Kim asked quietly.

Phil, as tactful as ever butted in. 'Hell, look at that face. He looks like he's had it chewed by a dog then punched by Billy a few times.'

I grinned and nodded, 'Cheers mate.'

We read the pile of papers and joked into the night.

I stood up, holding my plastered arm. 'You know we've only just scraped the surface. All round this Island lays sunken treasure. This year has had its ups and downs.' I smiled. 'But nothing comes easy, and as Billy always says, 'If you don't look, you will never find'.' I looked at Billy. 'Don't forget these words, mate:

'Better by far to live and die,
Under the brave black flag we fly,
Than to play a sanctimonious part
With a pirate head and a pirate heart.'

'Let's drink a toast to us and to next year, and new adventures.'

We stood up and drank our glasses dry, 'Another one?' Len shouted.

I looked up. 'No, no... ah, go on then!'

I closed the door behind them as they left. Kim helped Phil stagger to the Spinney. They were both tipsy and laughing like carefree children.

I returned to the fireside. 'Alone at last, sweet face. Give us a kiss.'

Andrea, engrossed in one of the papers, ignored me, looking up, then back at the paper.

'What's in there that's more interesting than a kiss?'

'I don't understand this,' she said, with a look of total confusion. 'Look.'

She placed the paper gently on the floor. I sat down beside her and spun the paper round to read it. Its title read, 'A Dramatic Rescue'. I read the article. 'Yeah... yeah... bla... bla... bla...' Then abruptly stopped, I was silent for a while and then I looked up at her.

'What does it mean, Mike? Why would they say that?' She knelt in front of me, pushing her hair behind her ears, resting her hands on her knees, staring at me intently.

I picked up the paper and read it out loud. 'The Skipper who made the dramatic rescue, diver and *ex-Paratrooper*, Michael Morgan, abandoned his...' I put the paper down and looked deep into her eyes. They were half-closed, almost pleading.

'I've been... I mean, I've wanted to tell you for ages, but I was scared you might...' I looked down. 'It might cause a problem, you coming from where you do. I was going to tell you on Christmas Day.' I looked around taking a few deep breaths, then at her again, eyes blinking. 'When we talked about your past, I was going to tell you there and then. I don't know why I didn't. I needed time to think. To make sure I was right. But the longer I left it, the harder it became to tell you.'

'Tell me what, Mike?'

I got up and left the room, returning moments later with a large round tin and sat back down. I passed it to her. 'My mum saved some stuff.'

She looked at me inquisitively. I nodded.

Opening the tin she removed a Red Beret. The cap had a silver Para's Wings badge attached to it. She looked at it, lost for words. Then she picked up a medal, which had 'For Campaign Service, Northern Ireland' engraved on it. My stare was locked on her as she put her hand in the tin again. The lights from the flickering fire danced all around the room as she removed a photograph, which she held in shaking hands, 'Its…it's…' Tears rolled down her cheeks. Looking at me she bit her lip and sniffed, as she fought with her emotions.

'My God. It's…it's the soldier I…told you about.'

Unable to hold back my feelings, I drew a shaky breath as she picked a small brown object from the tin, and carefully placed the torn bus ticket with the photograph. As the penny dropped, she pulled it to her breast then looked up at me through glistening eyes. 'Oh Mike,' she said, in a whisper. 'It's *you*.'

I held her tightly, nuzzling my face into her hair. 'We've found each other again, my love. This time it's forever.'

ABOUT THE AUTHOR

Peter Fergus is a charter boat operator living and working in Plymouth. He is a professional diver and worked for over twenty-five years in the industry as well as being an active sport diver. He now conducts diving and general workboat duties which include film and media work. Peter has written two other diving-related fictional thrillers entitled *Revenge* and *Deep Deceit*.

Printed in the United Kingdom
by Lightning Source UK Ltd.
122430UK00001B/7-36/A